Revised & Expanded

The Christ
Clone Trilogy
Book One
In His Image

THE CHRIST CLONE TRILOGY

In His Image
Birth of an Age
Acts of God

The Christ Clone Trilogy

Book One

In His Image

Revised & Expanded with Study Guide and
Prophecy Cross Reference

James BeauSeigneur

SelectiveHouse
Publishers

Cover design by Abigail Seigneur.

Unless otherwise noted, Scriptures are taken from the HOLY BIBLE: NEW INTERNATIONAL VERSION®. Copyright © 1973, 1978, 1984 by International Bible Society. Used by permission of Zondervan Publishing House. All rights reserved.

Scriptures noted KJV are taken from the King James Version of the Bible.

SelectiveHouse
Publishers

Gaithersburg, MD

Library of Congress Control Number: 2012906792
BeauSeigneur, James
    In his image / James BeauSeigneur. SelectiveHouse Publishers ed.
       p. cm. — (Christ clone trilogy – book one)
    ISBN 978-0-9854298-3-6
    1. Second Advent—Fiction. 2. Holy Shroud—Fiction. 3. Cloning—Fiction. 4. End of the world—fiction. I. Title.

Facebook page: http://www.facebook.com/ChristCloneTrilogy

Webpage: http://selectivehouse.com/

*For Gerilynne, Faith, and Abigail, who sacrificed so much
to allow this trilogy to become a reality.*

*But most of all for Shiloh, who sacrificed far more.
May it serve you well.*

Acknowledgments

While writing The Christ Clone Trilogy, I called upon the support of specialists in many fields of endeavor to ensure the accuracy and plausibility of my work. Others provided editorial direction, professional guidance, or moral sustenance. These include: John Jefferson, Ph.D.; Michael Haire, Ph.D.; James Russell, M.D.; Robert Seevers, Ph.D.; Peter Helt, J.D.; James Beadle, Ph.D.; Christy Beadle, M.D.; Ken Newberger, Th.M., Ph.D.; Eugene Walter, Ph.D.; Clement Walchshauser, D.Min.; Col. Arthur Winn; Elizabeth Winn, Ph.D.; Ian Wilson, Historian; Jeanne Gehret, M.A.; Linda Alexander; Scott Brown; and Mike Pinkston.

Sincere appreciation to poet Nguyen Chi Thien for his unfaltering spirit; and to the staff of the Library of Congress; the Jewish Publication Society of America; the Zondervan Corporation; Yale Southeast Asia Studies; and the hundreds of others whose work provided background for this book.

About the Author

James BeauSeigneur is a former intelligence analyst for the National Security Agency (NSA), the Defense Intelligence Agency (DIA), and the Army Intelligence and Security Command (INSCOM). As an author, he has worked with the Department of Homeland Security as a participant in Terrorism Red Cells to speculate on possible terrorist targets and tactics. He has been a newspaper publisher, taught political science at the University of Tennessee in Knoxville, and in 1980 was the Republican nominee for U.S. Congress running against Al Gore. He is a member of Mensa and the Association of Former Intelligence Officers.

Table of Contents

Prologue 1

The Right Place at the Right Time 3

The Shroud 9

Body of Christ 19

Mother of God 31

Christopher 37

Secrets of the Lost Ark 47

The Tears of Dogs 61

When in the Woods and Meeting Wild Beasts 67

Dream a Little Dream of Me 79

Disaster 97

The Master's Promise 121

Why Hast Thou Forsaken Me? 141

The Color of the Horse 159

Dark Awakening 165

Plowshares into Swords 181

The Hand of God 195

Master of the World 211

Revelation 231

The Prince of Rome 247

Through a Glass Darkly 261

When Leaders Fall 271

Simple Arithmetic 279

Offering 291

The Elect 307

Old Enemy, Old Friend 323

The Reason for It All 331

Stopping at Nothing 341

The Power Within Him — The Power Within Us All 347

Prophecy Cross Reference 357

Study Guide Notes 379

"Are these the shadows of things that will be, or are they the shadows of things that may be, only?"

— Charles Dickens, *A Christmas Carol*

Prologue

It was the worst of times.

Twice in twenty years, nuclear war had engulfed large regions of the planet. A mile-wide asteroid struck the Pacific Ocean south of Japan, fracturing the Earth's mantle, and creating massive earthquakes that killed tens of thousands. Mountain-like tsunami submerged hundreds of Pacific islands, stripped the coastal regions of four continents to bare stone and steel, and left the ocean's eco-system uninhabitable. The fractured mantle ignited eruptions throughout the "Ring of Fire," and volcanoes spewed ash and poisonous fumes into the atmosphere.

And now, a demonic homicidal madness has left one third of the world's remaining population dead — brutally murdered by their own family members.

Truly, it was the worst of times.

Never before had the world been so ready, so eager for a savior.

And all of it was premeditated 2000 years before.

Chapter 1

The Right Place at the Right Time

Knoxville, Tennessee

Decker Hawthorne — He typed out the letters of his name and his hands paused on the keys as he quickly scanned the editorial for reassurance he had made his point convincingly. It would have to do. The deadline had passed, the newspaper was waiting to be put to bed, and Decker had a plane to catch.

As he left the offices of the *Knoxville Enterprise*, he paused just long enough to straighten the hand-lettered placard that hung outside the door. It was a weekly paper, small by any standard, but it was growing. Decker had started the paper with a short supply of money and an abundance of naïveté. The upside was that with his aggressive — sometimes reckless — approach, the *Enterprise* frequently scooped the two local daily newspapers, including once with a story of national significance. It didn't always work so well, however, and he had also printed a few stories that turned out to be scoops of a different sort. He had always been a risk taker, and while he lost at least as often as he won, he liked to believe he had a knack for being in the right place at the right time. Right now though, he was supposed to be at the airport, and he wasn't.

"You're going to miss your plane," called Decker's wife, Elizabeth.

As the plane left the runway, Decker looked out over the city of Alcoa on the southern outskirts of Knoxville. Below, he could pick out his small house on the edge of one of Alcoa's many parks. The steadily receding sight recalled disquieting emotions. He had spent most of his life traveling. As a boy it was with his family, moving from one army post to another. Later he had spent a year and a half hitchhiking across the United States and Canada; then four years in the army. Partly he felt a little cheated: He had never really had a home. But partly he felt blessed. He hated leaving, but he loved going.

Decker's flight arrived late into New York and he had to run to make his connecting flight to Milan, Italy. Nearing the gate, he looked for a familiar face but saw none. In fact, at first glance, there was no one at the gate at all. He saw the plane out the window, but at that instant he heard the engines begin to whine. Thundering down the red-carpeted incline of the jetway, he almost collided with a ticket agent.

"I've got to get on that plane!" he told the woman, as he put on the sweetest "help me" look he could muster.

"You have your passport?" she asked.

"Right here," he answered, handing it to her along with his boarding pass.

"What about your luggage?"

"This is it," he replied, holding up an overstuffed and somewhat oversized carry-on bag.

The plane hadn't actually moved yet, so after notifying the pilot, it was an easy task to move the jetway back into place. After a quick but heartfelt thank you, Decker boarded the plane and headed to his seat. Now he saw a sea of friendly and familiar faces. On his right was John Jackson, the team's leader. A few seats back was Eric Jumper. Both were from the Air Force Academy in Colorado Springs. Jackson had his PhD in physics and had worked extensively on lasers and particle beams. Jumper, also a PhD, was an engineer specializing in thermodynamics, aerodynamics, and heat exchange. In fact, almost everyone around him had a PhD of one sort or another. Altogether there were more than forty scientists, technicians, and support staff. Though he knew most only by sight, many paused long enough from their conversations to offer a smile of welcome or to say they were glad he hadn't missed the flight.

Decker found his seat, stowed his luggage, and sat down. There to greet him was Professor Harry Goodman, a sloppily dressed, short man with gray hair, reading glasses half-way down his nose, and thick bushy brows that blazed helter-skelter above his eyes and up onto his forehead like a brush fire. "I was beginning to think you'd stood me up," Goodman said.

"Just wanted to make a big entrance," Decker answered.

Professor Goodman was Decker's link to the rest of the team. Goodman had taught biochemistry at the University of Tennessee, and during his junior year Decker had worked as his research assistant. They had many conversations, and though Goodman wasn't the type to get very close to anyone, Decker felt they were friends. Later that year though, Goodman had grown very depressed about something he refused to discuss. Through the rumor mill Decker discovered that Goodman was going to be denied tenure. Primarily this could be traced to his policy of "Do now, ask permission later," which had gotten him into hot water with the dean on more than one occasion. The next semester Goodman took a position at UCLA, and Decker hadn't seen him since.

Though Decker had changed his major from pre-med to journalism, he was still an avid reader of some of the better science journals. So it was that he read an article in *Science* magazine[1] about a team of American scientists going to examine the Shroud of Turin, a religious relic believed by many to be the burial shroud of Jesus Christ. He had heard of the Shroud but had always dismissed it as just another example of religious fraud designed to pick the pockets of gullible worshipers. But here was an article in one of the most widely read science journals reporting that credible American scientists were actually taking their time to examine this thing.

At first the article had aroused only amused disbelief, but among the list of the scientists involved, Decker found the name Dr. Harold Goodman. This made no sense at all. Goodman, as Decker knew from his frequent pronouncements, was an atheist. Well, not exactly an atheist. Goodman liked to talk about the uncertainty of everything. In his office at the university were two posters. The first was crudely hand-printed and stated: "*Goodman's First Law of Achievement: The shortest distance between any two points is around the rules*" (a philosophy that obviously hadn't set well with the dean). The second poster was done in 1960s-style psychedelic print and said: "*I think, therefore, I am. I think.*" Mixing the uncertainty of his own existence with his disbelief in God, Goodman had settled on referring to himself as "an atheist by inclination but an agnostic by practice." So why was a man like Goodman going off on some ridiculous expedition to study the Shroud of Turin?

Decker filed the information away and probably would have left it there had it not been for a call from an old friend and classmate, Tom Donafin. Tom was a reporter for the *Courier* in

Waltham, Massachusetts, and had called about a story he was working on about corruption in banking — something that Knoxville had plenty of at that time. After discussing the banking story, Tom asked Decker if he had seen the article in *Science*.

"Yeah, I saw it," he answered.

"I just thought you'd be interested in what 'Old Bushy Brows' was up to," Tom laughed.

"Are you sure it's him? I didn't see him in any of the pictures."

"I did a little checking, and it's him," Tom confirmed.

"You know," Decker said, thinking out loud, "there might be a story here. Religion sells — especially here in the south."

"I tried to dig into the particulars, but hit a brick wall," Tom said. "They're limiting coverage of the expedition to one reporter: a guy from *National Geographic*."[2]

"Sounds like a challenge," Decker said.

"I'm not saying it can't be done."

Decker began to toy with the question of how he might, if he wanted to, go about getting the story. He could take the direct approach of trying to reason with whoever was making the rules. After all, why should they have only one journalist? On the other hand, what possible reason could he give to convince them to take someone from a tiny unknown weekly in Knoxville, Tennessee? Clearly, his best bet was to work through Goodman.

Over the next three weeks Decker made several attempts to reach his old professor, without success. Goodman was doing research somewhere in Japan and even his wife, Martha, wasn't sure exactly where he was. With little to depend on beyond luck and determination, Decker arranged to fly to Norwich, Connecticut, and booked a room in the hotel where he had learned the Shroud team was scheduled to meet over the Labor Day weekend to plan their research. He arrived the day before to look things over.

The next morning Decker found that a private dining room in the hotel had been prepared for about fifty people and reasoned that this was a good place to start. A few minutes later the first of the team members walked in. The eyebrows were unmistakable. "Professor Goodman," Decker grinned, as he approached Goodman and extended his right hand. Goodman looked puzzled.

"It's Hawthorne," Decker offered. It was obvious that Goodman was struggling to place the face. "From the University of Tennessee," he added.

A gleam of recognition began to show in the pale green eyes beneath the massive clumps of hair. "Oh, yes, Hawthorne! How are you? What are you doing in Connecticut?"

Before Decker could answer, someone called out, "Harry Goodman!" and came over to where they were standing. "So, where were you last night?" the new arrival asked. "I called your room, hoping to have dinner with you."

Goodman didn't respond but proceeded instead to introductions. "Professor Don Stanley, allow me to introduce Decker Hawthorne, a former student and research assistant of mine from the University of Tennessee, Knoxville."

Professor Stanley gave Decker a quick once-over, then shook his hand while looking back at Goodman. "So Hawthorne here must be the research assistant that I heard you'd suckered into helping out. What a shame," Stanley added grimly, as he looked back at Decker and finally released his hand. "I'd have thought you looked too intelligent for that."

"He is," responded Goodman, "and, unfortunately, so is the young man you're referring to."

"Oh," Stanley said, quickly recalibrating his assumptions as well as his assessment of Decker's sagacity. "So he jumped ship on you, did he?"

Goodman shrugged. "It is quite a lot to expect a young man to pay his own way on a wild goose chase," he reasoned. "It hardly enhances one's curriculum vitae."

Decker was ready to pounce. The possibility of replacing the missing research assistant provided a much better chance of getting on the team than did any of the alternatives he had considered.

"If you're so sure it's a goose chase," Stanley asked, "why do you insist on going?"

"Somebody's got to keep the rest of you honest," Goodman grinned.

By now several other members of the team had filed into the dining room and were gathering in small groups for conversation. One of the men caught Professor Stanley's attention and Stanley walked over to greet him.

"What is it that your research assistant was going to do on this trip?" Decker pressed.

"Oh, everything from collection of data to general gofer work. We've got hundreds of different experiments planned and we may have as little as twelve hours to do them all. It's the kind of environment where an extra pair of trained hands can be very helpful."

"I don't suppose you'd be interested in a substitute?" Decker asked. He was counting on the fact that Goodman didn't know he had switched his major from pre-med after Goodman left Knoxville. Decker felt a twinge of guilt, but this wasn't the biggest omission of fact he had used to get a story. Besides, he could certainly qualify as a gofer.

"What?" Goodman responded. "After what I just told Stanley?"

"Really, I'd like to go," Decker persisted. "Actually, that's why I'm here. I may be a little rusty, but I read the article in *Science* and—" here he stretched the truth beyond recognition, "—I've got experience with most of the equipment you'll be using."

Goodman frowned and shook his head, then continued, "Well, I'm not going to refuse help. But you know that you have to pay your own way?"

"I know," Decker answered.

Goodman squinted as he studied his former student intently. "You haven't gone and gotten religion, have you?"

"No, nothing like that," Decker assured him. "It just sounds like an interesting project." He realized it wasn't a very convincing answer, so he quickly turned the question around. "Why are you going?" he asked. "You don't believe in any of this stuff."

"Of course not!" he said defensively. "I just want a chance to debunk the whole thing."

Decker refocused the conversation. "So, can I come along or not?"

"If you're sure," Goodman agreed at last, shaking his head.

So, just that quickly, Decker was in. "The right place at the right time," he whispered to himself.

It would be forty eight years before he understood that it had been something else entirely.

Chapter 2

The Shroud

Northern Italy

Barely more than misplaced starlight, the lights of Milan peeked dimly through the window as the jet flew over northern Italy. Decker studied the outline of this landlocked constellation as he considered the consequences of the job ahead. Like Professor Goodman, Decker was certain the team's research would prove that the Shroud was nothing more than a cheap medieval forgery. The problem was he knew that there were a lot of people who wouldn't appreciate having their bubble of faith burst by the truth, including Elizabeth's mother, a devout Catholic. So far his relationship with her had been pretty good. How would she take all of this?

The team had chartered a bus to take them the 125 kilometers from Milan to Turin. By the time they arrived at their hotel it was midnight, and though it was still early in the U.S., everyone decided to go to their rooms to try to get some sleep.

Porta Palatina, Turin

The next morning Decker, who was never very good at adjusting to different time zones, got up before the sun. Because of the time difference going east, he should have wanted to sleep in, but it made no difference; he was ready to get up. Hurrying from the hotel to enjoy some early morning sightseeing, he walked down Turin's long, straight streets, which intersect at nearly perfect ninety degree angles. On both sides were homes and small stores occupying one- and two-story buildings, none of which appeared to be less than two centuries old. Beyond the city, to the north, east, and west, the Alps pierced the atmosphere and clouds on their way to the sky. *Elizabeth would love this!* he thought. About a quarter of a mile from the hotel he came to the Porta Palatina, an immense gateway through which in 218 B.C. Hannibal, after a siege of only three days, drove his soldiers and elephants into the Roman town of Augusta Taurinorum, as ancient Turin was known. A mile or so farther and the wonderful smells of morning began to drift from the open windows along his path. The sounds of children playing soon followed. And then, suddenly, the timeless atmosphere of the old city was intruded upon by the droning of a television in someone's kitchen. It was time to head back.

After breakfast, several members of the team decided to walk the half mile from the hotel to the royal palace of the House of Savoy, which for centuries had been the residence of the kings of Italy. It was in a suite of rooms in the palace that the team would be conducting its investigation of the Shroud. When they reached the palace they were surprised to find tens of thousands of people standing several abreast in lines that stretched for more than a mile to the east and west, and converged at the Cathedral of San Giovanni Battista, adjacent to the palace. In the cathedral, in a sterling silver case sealed within a larger case of bullet proof glass filled with inert gasses, was the Shroud. Two or three times a century the Shroud is taken out and put on public display, drawing pilgrims from all over the world. The crowd that day represented only a small fraction of the three million people who had traveled from all over the world to see what they believed to be the burial cloth of Christ.

The team was escorted through a courtyard into a restricted part of the palace where heavily armed guards stood at every corner. They paused as they entered, awestruck at the size and splendor of their surroundings. There was gold everywhere: on chandeliers, on picture frames, on vases, inlaid into carvings in the doors and other woodwork. Even the wallpaper was gold-gilt. And everywhere were paintings and marble statuary.

At the end of a long, opulently decorated hall was the entrance to the princes' suite, where the team would conduct their experiments. Beyond the ten-foot doors was a fifty-by-fifty-foot ballroom, the first of seven rooms that made up the suite. Crystal chandeliers hung from the ceiling, which was painted in classical frescos of angels and swans and biblical scenes. The second room, where the Shroud would be placed for examination, was as magnificent as the first.

Somewhere in the life of ancient buildings that remain in use comes a point when time and progress can no longer be ignored and aesthetics ultimately yield to the demands of modern convenience. In the princes' suite the evidence of compromise was a bathroom and crude electrical wiring stapled to the wall. The bathroom, a strange arrangement of two toilets and five sinks, would double as the team's photographic darkroom.

"We'll need to run electric cables up here from the basement," said Rudy Dichtl, the team member with the most hands-on electrical experience. "I'm going to need to find a hardware store."

Decker told Dichtl he had noticed a hardware store while walking that morning. He wasn't entirely sure of the location, but thought he could find it again. "Great," said Dichtl. "If they have what we need, I could use some help lugging it back."

* * * * *

Delayed in customs for five days, the team's equipment finally arrived at the palace on Friday afternoon. Soon the public viewing of the Shroud would end and it would be brought to the palace for examination late Sunday evening. There were seven days of setup and preparation to be done in little more than two. Some of the tests required bright light, while others required total darkness. The first part would be easy, but the latter required sealing off the eight-by-ten-foot windows with thick sheets of black plastic. Maze-like light baffles made of more black plastic also had to be built for the doorways. In the Shroud room the team assembled its steel examination table that had been specially designed and constructed to hold the Shroud firmly in place without damaging it. The surface of the table was constructed of more than a dozen removable panels to allow inspection of both sides of the Shroud at the same time. Each of the panels was covered with one-millimeter-thick gold Mylar to prevent even the tiniest of particles from being transferred from the table to the Shroud. The adjoining rooms were established as staging areas for testing and calibrating the scientific equipment.

Finally, on Sunday night at about midnight, someone in the hall said, "Here it comes."

Shroud being laid out on the stainless steel table built for examination.

Monsignor Cottino, the representative of Turin's archbishop-cardinal, entered the Shroud testing room accompanied by seven Poor Clare nuns and followed by twelve men carrying a sheet of three-quarter inch plywood, four feet wide and sixteen feet long. Draped over the plywood, a piece of expensive red silk covered and protected the Shroud. The testing table awaited the transfer. Silence fell over the room as the men lowered the plywood sheet to waist level and the senior of the nuns began to carefully pull back the silk, revealing a sheet of off-white herringbone linen. Decker waited for a moment for this second protective covering to be removed, until he understood that it wasn't a covering at all. It was the Shroud itself. He squinted and stared at the cloth, struggling to make out anything resembling an image.

Even though he believed the Shroud to be a fraud, he discovered that from a strictly emotional point of view he really wanted to feel something — closer to God, awe, perhaps just a twinge of the strangely religious excitement he used to feel when looking at a stained glass window. Instead he had mistaken the Shroud for nothing more than a protective drapery.

Disappointed, he stepped away, and to his amazement, the image became much more distinct. Surprised and confused, he rocked back and forth, studying the strange phenomenon of the Shroud's appearing and disappearing image. Why, he wondered, would an artist have painted it so that it was so hard to see? How could he have done it at all, unless he used a paintbrush six feet long so he could see what he was painting? Few, if any, of Decker's drives were greater than his curiosity. He wanted to understand this puzzle.

He watched as Monsignor Cottino walked around the Shroud, stopping every couple of feet to remove thumbtacks that held it to the plywood. Rusty and old, their stains defaced the fabric with iron oxide that spread well beyond where the tacks had pierced the cloth. So much planning and effort had gone into keeping even the tiniest foreign particles away from the Shroud, only to find that the centuries, perhaps millennia, that preceded them had been far less careful.

* * * * *

During the 120 hours allotted, three groups of scientists worked simultaneously — one at each end of the Shroud and one in the middle. Despite the sleep they had already lost in their rush to set up and prepare, over the next five days few would sleep more than two or three hours at a time. Those who weren't involved in a particular project stayed near at hand to help those who were, or simply to watch.

Thirty-six hours into the procedures, as husband-and-wife team members Roger and Marty Gilbert performed reflectance spectroscopy — a method of using reflected light to identify chemical structure — something highly unexpected happened. Starting at the feet and moving up the image, the spectra suddenly changed.

First day of formal examination

"How can the same image give different spectra?" Eric Jumper asked. No one had an answer, so they continued. As they moved the equipment up the legs, the reading remained constant. Everything was the same except the image of the feet, and more specifically, the heels.

Jumper left the Shroud room and found team member Sam Pellicori, who was trying to sleep on a cot in another room. "Sam!

Wake up!" he said. "I need you and your macroscope in the Shroud room right away!"

Pellicori and Jumper positioned the macroscope over the Shroud and lowered it until it was just above the heel. Pellicori focused, changed lenses, focused again, and looked, without saying a word. After a long pause, he reported, "It's dirt."

"Dirt?" Jumper asked, surprised. "Let me see." He looked through the macroscope and agreed. "Okay. It *is* dirt," he said. "But why?"

It seemed to Decker a strange thing to get so excited about.

As the next shift of scientists came on, everyone met for a review and brainstorming session to determine the direction and priorities for the next set of tests. "Here's what we know," Jumper started. "The body images are straw yellow, not sepia, as all previous accounts indicated. The color is only on the crowns of the microfibers of the threads and doesn't vary significantly anywhere on the Shroud in either shade or depth. Where one fiber crosses another the underlying fiber is unaffected by the color.

"The yellow microfibers show no sign of capillarity or blotting, which indicates that no liquid was used to create the image, which rules out paint. Further, there is no adherence, meniscus effect, or matting between the threads, also ruling out any type of liquid paint. In the areas of the apparent blood stains, the fibers are clearly matted and there are signs of capillarity, as would be the case with actual blood."

"Tell 'em about the feet," Marty Gilbert prompted. For those who had just come on duty, Jumper explained what had happened with the reflectance spectroscopy test.

"Of course there's dirt," one team member said after Jumper's explanation. "What could be more natural than dirt on the bottom of the feet?" That was Decker's thought exactly.

"Yes," said Jumper, "but that hypothesis assumes this is an authentic image of a crucified man."

Decker had missed that entirely and was stunned by its implications.

Still, the obvious was becoming harder to deny, for not only was there dirt on the heel, but the amount of dirt was so minute that it wasn't visible to the naked eye. As startling as the whole question was, more startling still was that it was Professor Goodman who put it into words. "If the Shroud is a forgery," he posed, "why would a medieval forger go to the trouble to put dirt on the image that would require a modern macroscope to see it?"

Debriefing the team between shifts

It had now been three days since Decker had slept and he resolved at last to return to the hotel. Drawn to the hotel dining room by the voices of other team members, he sat with Roger Harris, Susan Chon, and Joshua Rosen, unwinding with a slowly stirred cup of decaf coffee heavily laced with Irish cream. He entertained little thought of interviewing anyone. Over the past few days, he had come to see himself much less as a reporter and much more as a member of the team. Habitually, though, he continued making mental notes.

One of his companions, Dr. Joshua Rosen, was a nuclear physicist from Lawrence Livermore National Laboratory who worked on laser and particle-beam research for the Pentagon. Rosen was one of the four Jewish members of the team, and Decker couldn't resist the opportunity to ask him about his feelings on examining a Christian relic.

"If I weren't so tired I'd lead you on a bit," Rosen smiled. "But if you really want an answer on that you'll have to ask one of the other Jewish members of the team."

"You don't have an opinion?" Decker queried.

"I have an opinion, but I'm not qualified to answer your question. I'm Messianic," he said. Decker didn't catch his meaning. "A Christian Jew," Rosen explained.

"Oh," said Decker. Then after a moment added, "This isn't something that happened in the last few days, is it?"

Rosen laughed.

Roger Harris snorted, barely managing to force down a mouthful of coffee.

Decker's remark hadn't been that funny, but the pained look on Roger's face caused Susan Chon to erupt and soon the four overtired, punch-drunk team members were laughing uncontrollably.

On the other side of the room, a woman watched intently as they talked, building up her courage to approach. Their laughter made them seem somehow more approachable and human, while its infectious nature seemed to brighten her own dark mood. Finally, she rose from her seat and walked slowly but decisively toward them.

"You are with the scientists examining the Shroud?" she asked when their laughter passed.

"Yes," Susan Chon responded.

On the woman's face Decker saw lines of worry; on her cheeks, the evidence of recently blotted tears.

"Is there something we can we do for you?" Joshua Rosen asked.

"My son — he's four — is very ill. The doctors say he may not live more than a few months. All I ask is that you allow me to bring flowers to the Shroud as a gift to Jesus."

None of them had gotten much sleep in the previous four days, and no one could speak to reply to the woman's modest request. Rosen was the first to manage more than a nod. It would be impossible for the woman to bring flowers to the Shroud herself, Rosen explained. However, if she would bring the flowers to the palace the next day, he would take them to the Shroud himself.

In his room, Decker fell quickly asleep and felt totally rested when he awoke at noon the next day. When he arrived at the palace an hour later, Rosen was talking with the woman from the hotel. The cloud of depression that had covered her the night before was replaced by a look of hope. She smiled in recognition at Decker as she started to leave.

Rosen started up the stairs with the vase of cut flowers but, spotting Decker, turned and waited.

"Pretty neat, huh?" Rosen said.

"Pretty neat," Decker responded. But to himself he wondered what would happen to the woman's faith if her son died.

Chapter 3

Body of Christ

Alcoa, Tennessee

It was cold outside. The usual warm autumn weather of East Tennessee had given way to a cold snap that sent the local residents scurrying to their wood piles for added warmth and atmosphere. Decker and Elizabeth lay a bit more than half asleep, snuggled together before a waning fire, dreaming to the sounds of the crackling hardwood embers. One-year-old Hope Hawthorne slept soundly in her crib in the bedroom.

The fire's warmth and glow offered more than enough reason for not getting up when the phone rang. But by the third ring all were awake — Decker heading toward the offending instrument in the kitchen, while Elizabeth went to comfort the baby.

"Hello," Decker half growled, half mumbled, not yet fully alert.

"Decker Hawthorne?" responded the voice on the other end.

"Speaking," Decker answered, now accomplishing the full growl he had been going for.

"This is Harry Goodman."

"Professor?" Decker asked, a little dumbfounded.

"I have something you'll want to see." Goodman said. His voice was excited but controlled. "It's a story for your newspaper. Can you come to Los Angeles right away?"

"Whoa. Wait a second. Professor. I . . . This is quite a surprise. It's been . . ." Decker paused to reorient and attempted to count the years. "How are you?"

"I'm fine," Goodman answered hastily, not at all interested in small talk. "Can you come to Los Angeles?" he asked again, insistently.

"I don't know, Professor. What is this about?"

"If I tell you over the phone you'll think I'm crazy."

"Try me."

"It's about the Shroud."

"What more is there to say about it?" Decker said. "They did Carbon 14 dating. It's not old enough to be the burial cloth of Christ. It was on the front page of *The New York Times*."

"You think I live under a rock or something? I know all about the Carbon 14 dating." Goodman was obviously not pleased at having to explain himself. "Decker, this may be the most important discovery since Columbus discovered the New World. Please, just trust me. I promise you won't be disappointed."

Decker knew that Goodman wasn't given to gross exaggeration. So obviously, whatever it was must be something pretty important. He did a quick mental check of his schedule and agreed to fly to Los Angeles two days later.

"Who was that?" Elizabeth asked when Decker joined her by Hope's crib.

"Professor Goodman," he replied, as he leaned back against the wall in thought.

Elizabeth gave Decker a puzzled look. "Henry Goodman, your old professor, the one you went with to Italy?"

"Yeah," Decker replied without much enthusiasm. "Only it's Harry, not Henry." Decker stroked Elizabeth's back and gave her the bad news. "I'm afraid I'm going to have to skip the drive up to Cade's Cove on Saturday. I have to fly out to Los Angeles to see him about a story."

Sadly resigned to Decker's axiom that work always came first — though he would never have put it quite that way — Elizabeth sighed and snuggled the baby but didn't object.

That night Decker and Elizabeth lay in bed puzzling over what Goodman had found. Decker hadn't even talked to Goodman since three years after the Shroud team had formalized the findings in a published report. In short, the report said that the image on the Shroud was clearly not the result of a painting or any other known method of image transfer. Based on thirteen different test measures and procedures, the scourge marks and blood around the nail holes and side wound were, indeed, the result of human blood. Fibrils beneath the blood showed no evidence of oxidation, indicating that the blood was on the cloth prior to whatever process caused the image. Finally, the report said that while the material of the Shroud may be old enough to be the burial cloth of Jesus of Nazareth, it is impossible to even guess at its age without Carbon 14 dating, and that could not be done without destroying a large portion of the cloth.

But that was old technology. As science advanced it became possible to perform accurate Carbon 14 dating using a sample the size of a postage stamp. And soon afterward the Catholic Church announced that it would permit the Shroud to be Carbon 14 dated by three laboratories. The labs found that, with a combined certainty of 95 percent, the Shroud was made of flax grown sometime between 1260 and 1390, and therefore, the cloth was simply not old enough to have been the burial cloth of Christ.

"What was it he said?" Elizabeth asked. "That it was the most important discovery since Columbus discovered America?"

"Yeah," Decker responded, shaking his head as it rested on the pillow.

"If the Shroud is a forgery, then what could he be talking about?"

"The only thing I can think of is that he's discovered how the image was made. But if that's what this is about, he's blowing this way out of proportion."

"Then he must have discovered some way to prove it's real," Elizabeth concluded.

"Nah, that's crazy," he concluded. "Even if the dating was wrong: proving the Shroud is a forgery is something science can do; trying to prove it's really the burial cloth of Christ would be nuts." Decker paused and then added, "Not to mention totally out of character for someone like Goodman, who's not even sure of his *own* existence, much less the existence of God."

Los Angeles, California

Harry Goodman met Decker at LAX, and once in his car, wasted no time getting to the subject at hand. "You remember, no doubt, the effect it had on me when we discovered the minute particles of dirt in the heel area of the Shroud," Goodman began. He presumed too much — ten years had passed since Turin — but Decker politely nodded assent if not recollection. "It made no sense," Goodman continued. "No medieval forger would have gone to the trouble of rubbing dirt into the image unless it could be seen by the naked eye. It was then that I began to question my assumption that the Shroud was a forgery."

Decker was confused. Could Goodman actually be suggesting he thought the Shroud was authentic?

"You, of course, recall that some of the most conclusive work on the Shroud was done by Dr. John Heller using the samples gathered on strips of Mylar tape." Decker did recall. Heller and Dr. Allan Adler had used the samples to prove that the stains were human blood and had also determined that the images were the result of oxidation.[3]

"Yeah," Decker replied. "But how can any of that matter now that we know the Shroud's not old enough?"

"I wanted to examine the samples from the heel and foot more closely," Goodman continued, ignoring Decker's question. "You'll recall that each slide was cataloged by where it came from and then hermetically sealed in a case. Unfortunately, that was like closing the gate after the horses have already gone. In Turin, I counted more than a dozen different contaminated articles that came in contact with the Shroud: the silk covering, the plywood, the rusty thumbtacks." Goodman shook his head. "I saw two team members and three priests kiss it — it seems that's been going on for centuries. Even our procedures to prevent contamination introduced some contaminants. The cotton gloves we wore surely carried American pollen.

"The point is that the tape picked up all sorts of garbage that had nothing to do with the origin of the Shroud or the creation of the image. In his report, Dr. Heller noted finding both natural and synthetic fibers, fly ash, animal hairs, insect parts, beeswax from church candles, and a couple dozen other assorted materials, not to mention spores and pollen.[4] Because of all this clutter, Heller decided that most of his examination should employ levels of magnification just powerful enough to examine substances that could have been used to create a visible image and to ignore the smaller, irrelevant materials.

"For his purposes, he did exactly what he should have done, but his procedures would have missed what I was looking for. That's why I decided to have a second look. I believe that what I found will explain the whole Shroud mystery." Goodman paused. "And there's more."

Decker waited but Goodman was silent. "Well, what is it?" he asked.

"Where's your sense of drama, Hawthorne? You'll see, soon enough."

Goodman drove to the William G. Young science building on the east side of the UCLA campus and parked in the tenured faculty parking lot. His office was on the fourth floor and looked out over a courtyard westward toward the engineering building. It was arranged very much the same as the office he'd had at UT, including the ragged but now framed *"I think, therefore, I am. I think."* poster and *Goodman's First Law of Achievement*, now engraved on a plaque.

Motioning to the plaque before sitting, Decker laughed, "I see some things never change."

"No need to change when you're right," Goodman asserted. "Now before we go any further, I need your assurance you won't release this before I'm ready."

Decker frowned. "Then why was it so important that I come out here right away?"

"Because," Goodman answered, "I need a witness now. And the way I figure it, you owe me. You could have gotten me in a lot of trouble with my colleagues when you ran your story about the Turin project. The only reporter that was supposed to be there was Weaver from *National Geographic*. We weren't even supposed to talk to anyone from the press. And then a week after we got back, the whole world reads wire reports of a story in a Knoxville paper by some jerk reporter who managed to pass himself off as a member of the team. And that jerk reporter just happened to decide to pass himself off as my jerk assistant!

"If anyone thought that I had knowingly helped you get onto the team, I'd have been blackballed forever as a security risk."

"Hey, I was just following *Goodman's First Law of Achievement*," Decker responded. "'The shortest distance between any two points is around the rules.'" But Goodman was right and Decker knew it. His conscience had always bothered him a little about the way he'd gotten onto the Shroud team. "Okay," he said at last in response to

Goodman's disapproving stare. "It was a lousy thing to do. I do owe you. I'm here. So what is it you want to show me that I can't tell anyone about?"

"Good!" the professor said in a self-congratulatory way. "In time, I'll want you to report it. Just not yet. Right now I need a witness, and you know I can't stand reporters. Truth is, you're just barely tolerable," he added, trying to lighten the mood a little. "You've covered the Shroud story from the beginning. People will believe you when you report what I'm going to show you, but if the story comes out too soon, it could doom the whole project."

"If this is about some research you've done, why don't you just publish it yourself in a scholarly journal?" Decker pressed.

"Later, of course. But . . . I'm afraid I need to break the ice with the public before I reveal the exact nature of my research to my peers."

Decker squinted apprehensively but with growing curiosity.

"It's just, well, I'm afraid I've applied a little of *Goodman's First Law* myself. And there are those in the scientific community who, because of their narrow-mindedness, might condemn my methods."

Decker frowned. His interest was now piqued.

"My hope," Goodman continued, "is that as the story evolves and once the benefits of my work are known, public opinion will be too strong in my favor for my peers to object."

There was a lot packed into that statement. "What do you mean, 'as the story evolves'?" Decker asked.

"I expect that there will be several installments along the way before you can report the overall story."

"And what 'benefits' are you talking about?"

"I'm getting to that," Goodman deferred.

Decker nodded for Goodman to continue.

"In short, if you provide me with confidentiality, I'll provide you with exclusivity."

Decker nodded again, this time indicating agreement with Goodman's terms.

"On the other hand," Goodman warned, "if you report the story before I say to, I'll deny every word of it, and you'll make a total fool of yourself. You'll never prove a thing."

"I thought you just said that people would believe me."

"Yes, if I back you up and you back me up. But by yourself, and with my denial, they'll think you've lost your mind. Look, I'm offering you the biggest exclusive of all time on the greatest discovery — scientific or otherwise — in the last five hundred years. But it's also the most bizarre."

"Okay," Decker half relented, half implored. "Let's hear it."

Goodman leaned back in his chair, his elbows on the arm rests, placing his fingertips together, and gazed off into space, apparently considering his words. "Consider the following hypothesis," he began, professorially. "The image of the man on the Shroud of Turin is the result of a sudden burst of heat and light energy from the body of a crucified man as it went through an instantaneous regeneration or 'resurrection,' if you will."

Decker didn't move. There was a long silence as Goodman awaited his response, then at last Decker began to laugh. He couldn't believe that Goodman would go to such lengths, but there was no other explanation. And he had fallen for it hook, line and sinker. "This is all payback, isn't it?"

"I assure you, I am entirely serious."

Decker still laughed, while trying to read Goodman's face for any hint that despite his denial, he was, in fact, playing a practical joke, inflicting his revenge for Turin. Decker really didn't want to be played any further, but finding in Goodman's expression only a sincere look of confusion at Decker's jocular response, he continued, "Professor, that's not a scientific hypothesis; that's a statement of faith."

"On the contrary," Goodman insisted. "It's based entirely on science and sound reasoning. As with any hypothesis, it can be tested and proven to be true or false." Decker had stopped laughing, which Goodman took as his opportunity to proceed. "By way of explanation, what do you know about Dr. Francis Crick?

Decker now had no idea where this was all leading, but decided to go along for the ride. "I know he won the Nobel Prize in medicine back in the early sixties—"

"Sixty-two," Goodman interrupted.

"—for his discovery with James Watson of the double helix structure of DNA."

"Good! And are you familiar with Crick's book, *Life Itself*"?[5] Goodman asked, rising to take a copy of the book from his shelf.

"You can't possibly take that thing seriously," Decker objected. "It's an embarrassment. It made Crick a laughingstock."

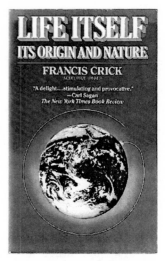

Goodman ignored Decker's protest — a practiced talent, which Decker now recalled, he had honed while teaching at the University of Tennessee. "You'll recall," Goodman continued, "that in the book, Crick examines possible origins of life on this planet. He raises the question of why, with the exception of mitochondria, the basic genetic coding mechanism in all living things on Earth is identical. Even in the case of mitochondria the differences are rather small. From what we know of Earth's evolution, there's no obvious structural reason to explain this. Crick doesn't entirely discount the possibility that life originated and evolved naturally on Earth, but he offers a second theory: that perhaps life was engrafted on this planet by a highly advanced civilization from somewhere else. If all life on Earth had a common origin, that would explain the apparent bottleneck in genetic evolution."

Decker was familiar with Crick's theory and again grew suspicious that this was an elaborate practical joke.

"Crick argues," Goodman continued, "that if these intelligent beings wanted to colonize other planets they wouldn't start by sending members of their own species. Instead, they would first prepare those planets for habitation. Without plant life, there wouldn't be sufficient oxygen for intelligent life to exist. And of course there wouldn't be food for the colonists either. To establish the needed plant life, they would only have to place some simple bacteria, such as blue-green algae, on the planet and let evolution and the eons of time do their work."

"Professor," Decker interrupted, throwing up his hands and now demanding to be heard, "I've read the book. What's the point?"

"The point is, what if Crick is right? What if life was planted on Earth by an ancient race from another planet? The obvious question is: Where are they now? Why have they never come to check on their work? "

Decker wasn't going to play, so Goodman answered his own questions, "Maybe they all died. Maybe they lost interest in space travel. Or maybe they *have* visited, but they didn't find Earth suitable for their particular needs."

Decker scooted down in his chair and looked at the ceiling. Certainly, this wasn't what he expected when he agreed to come to Los Angeles. He could have been at Cades Cove right now with Elizabeth and Hope.

"But certainly," Goodman went on, oblivious to Decker's body language, "Earth wouldn't have been the only place where they planted life. They would have seeded planets throughout the galaxy. So, what if when they finally got to this particular planet, they found that it was already populated, and not just by plants and animals. What if, through some set of parallel twists of evolution, they found that it was populated by beings not far different from themselves? Would they simply invade and colonize it anyway? Or might they instead decide to observe it and let it evolve naturally?"

"Professor," Decker interrupted again, "what has all this got to do with the Shroud of Turin?"

"Think about it, Decker. Somewhere in the galaxy there may be a civilization of beings, billions of years advanced to us, who are responsible for planting life throughout the galaxy, including Earth!" And then finally, Goodman revealed where he had been leading. "I believe that the man whose regeneration caused the image on the Shroud was a member of that parent race, sent here as an observer: a man from a race so far advanced to us that they are capable of regeneration, possibly even immortality. Not true gods — but not far from it."

Decker concluded at last that this wasn't a practical joke. Goodman simply wasn't capable of it. Which left only one other possibility: he was losing touch with reality. Closing his eyes, Decker took a long breath to gather his composure. "Professor, look, you're a scientist. You know a reasonable hypothesis from a—"

"I am *not* crazy!" Goodman shot back.

Decker stood up, ready to leave. "I'm sorry, Professor. You don't want me. You want someone from the *National Enquirer!*"

Quickly, Goodman placed himself between Decker and the door. "When you see what I've found on the Shroud, you'll understand."

Decker stopped and decided to give the professor just a little more rope.

Goodman opened a locked cabinet in his lab and pulled out a plastic case containing several dozen slides. Decker recognized it as the case of tape samples taken from the Shroud of Turin. "As I told you earlier," Goodman explained, "I borrowed the slides in order to examine further the dirt particles that were found in the left heel area of the image. I wondered if it might be possible to determine the specific makeup of the particles and perhaps see if any unusual characteristics could rule in or rule out given points of origin. In other words, was there anything about the dirt that would indicate it had originated in the Middle East or, conversely, was there anything that would instead indicate that it was from France or Italy or perhaps even somewhere else?

"If it was from the Middle East, or even from Jerusalem itself, it wouldn't necessarily prove anything, of course. A forger who went to all the trouble of putting dirt on the Shroud in such tiny amounts might just as well have thought to import the dirt from Jerusalem. It makes about as much sense, which is to say: none at all. I just wanted to get another look at it."

Goodman sat down in front of a microscope, turned on its lamp and placed a slide on the scope's stage. "In the car I told you that Dr. Heller had avoided using too much magnification because of what it was he was looking for." Goodman paused, looked through the eyepiece lens, and adjusted the scope's objectives and focus. "In my case," he continued as he looked back at Decker, "I used between a 600x and a 1000x." Goodman stood and motioned for Decker to look through the scope. "This first slide is the sample taken from directly over the left heel."

Decker moved the slide around on the stage, refocusing as necessary. "Nothing unusual," he said, still scanning the slide.

"Certainly not enough dirt particles for the kind of tests I had in mind," Goodman said. "I checked the grid, but the only other samples from the feet were from the nail wounds in the right foot."

Goodman took the slide from the microscope and carefully placed it back in its designated slot.

"You remember that the right foot actually had two exit wounds, suggesting that the feet had been nailed left over right. The right foot was nailed down first, with the nail exiting through the arch. The left was then nailed on top of the right with the nail passing through both feet, leaving an exit wound in the arch of the left foot and the heel of the right. Neither of these samples seemed very promising, though, because any dirt that had been in the wound areas would likely have been bonded to the cloth by the blood."

Goodman took a second slide from the plastic case. "This is from the blood stain of the right heel. I really didn't expect to find any dirt there, but I looked anyway." Goodman paused.

"That's when I found it."

Goodman reached around Decker, shut off the microscope's lamp, and handed him the slide. Decker placed it on the microscope's stage, adjusted the mirror to compensate for the loss of light from the lamp, and focused the lens. Goodman rotated the objective to 800X. On the slide before him, Decker could see a cluster of strangely familiar disk-shaped objects surrounded by and imbedded into crusty blackish-brown material that he assumed to be blood.

After a moment, he looked up at Goodman. His eyes had grown wide and his mind raced in disbelief and confusion. "Is that possible?" he asked finally.

Goodman flipped opened a textbook to a well-marked page and pointed to an illustration in the upper left corner. What Decker saw confirmed his suspicion. The caption below the picture read, "Human dermal skin cells."

Decker looked back through the microscope to be sure. Inexplicably, despite hundreds or even thousands of years, they appeared to be perfectly preserved. He felt Goodman reach around him again, this time to turn the lamp back on. The brighter light made the small disks appear transparent and Decker could clearly see the nucleus of each cell. Within a few seconds the lamp began to gently warm the slide. Decker looked away to rub his eyes and then looked back.

In the warmth of the artificial light, the nuclei began to move.

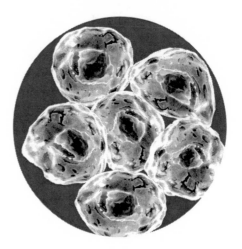

Dermal Skin Cells

Chapter 4

Mother of God

Decker's chest felt heavy and his head light. He struggled to catch his breath. Silently he watched the nuclei of the cells as they continued to undulate. For some indeterminate time, his mind seemed to float in the sea of warm cytoplasm before him, void of points of reference except for the cells. A thousand questions rose and fell, fighting for his attention, but he was incapable of enough focus on anything outside of what he saw to even realize his confusion. It was only when he ceased trying to understand that his senses began to reemerge from the ooze. Slowly his ears became aware of Goodman's voice.

"Decker ... Decker ..." Goodman touched him on the shoulder and finally he looked up. "Are you hungry?"

Decker hadn't eaten since breakfast, but right now he thought Goodman's question was insane.

"Believe me," Goodman said, "I know just how you feel. The same thing happened to me. I went looking for dirt and found live dermal skin cells! I nearly got religion!" He laughed. "That's when I made the connection to Professor Crick's theory." Goodman took the slide from the microscope and carefully placed it back in the plastic case.

"But how?" Decker pleaded.

"The cells were picked up on the Mylar tape along with some small flecks of blood. Apparently when the Shroud was laid over the crucified man, some of the exposed flesh of the wound was bonded to it by the blood. When the man was regenerated, and the Shroud was pulled away, a small amount of dermal material came with it. The same thing can happen when bandages are removed from any large wound. I suspect the weight of the heel resting on the cloth helped some, too." Goodman hid the excitement he felt at finally being able to share his discovery, and his calm, understated response simply served to accentuate Decker's confusion. "What you have just seen are cells at least six hundred years old with absolutely no sign of degeneration. In short: They're alive."

"Six hundred?" Decker asked, surprised that Professor Goodman hadn't said two thousand.

"If the Carbon 14 dating is correct, yes. On the other hand, I think it's rather unlikely that anyone would have been crucified in the thirteenth or fourteenth century. My guess is that the Shroud does date to the first century and was, in fact, the burial cloth of Jesus. The historical evidence is rather conclusive that Jesus did exist. I've never doubted that any more than I've doubted the historical evidence of Alexander the Great or Julius Caesar. Actually," he said smugly, "it all fits perfectly into my hypothesis that Jesus' reported abilities resulted from the fact that he came from an advanced race."

"Why aren't the blood cells alive?" Decker asked.

"That's an interesting question. I assume it's because the blood is from the body that died. The skin cells, on the other hand, are from the body *after* it was regenerated."

Goodman put his hand on Decker's shoulder again and gently nudged him in the direction of the door. "I don't know about you, but I'm starved and my housekeeper is expecting us. It'll be just you and me for lunch. Martha is away, visiting her mother."

* * * * *

Goodman's house was an English Tudor with brown trim and stone on a quiet dead-end street about twenty minutes from the campus. The two men were greeted at the door by Goodman's housekeeper, a young Hispanic woman. "Maria, this is my guest, Mr. Hawthorne." Goodman spoke slowly, enunciating each word. "We'll have our lunch now."

Decker looked around the house. Just about every wall had shelves full of books. A few shelves had additional books neatly stacked beside them. Decker had never met Goodman's wife, Martha, but she was obviously very tolerant of her husband's profession.

"Professor, we need to talk," Decker said as they sat down at the dining room table.

"Of course," Goodman answered.

Decker's eyes glanced to the housekeeper and then back to Goodman.

"Don't worry about her," Goodman said. "She barely speaks any English."

"We can't keep this to ourselves," Decker started.

"I have no intention of keeping it secret forever, but think about it. You remember the crowds in Turin lined up to see the Shroud. What do you think would happen if word leaked out that live cells from the body of Jesus were in a laboratory in Los Angeles? Every sick or dying person in America would be at my door hoping to be healed. A lot of desperate people would waste their time and money. And my work would come to a standstill. But if we wait until I've finished my research, we may be able to offer some *real* healing power."

Decked took a deep breath. Again Goodman had packed a lot into a brief statement. This day kept going in directions he didn't expect. His expression said it all.

"Are you blind?" Goodman asked. "You saw those cells. What do you think I've been talking about?"

"I'm not sure I know anymore," Decker said, perplexed.

"Those cells are hundreds or even thousands of years old," Goodman said, a little exasperated that an explanation was necessary. "They've survived intense heat and freezing cold. As far as we can tell, they're immortal. Yet in most respects they're human. With time, I may be able to learn their secrets: discover things that can lead to new vaccines, create powerful new life-saving drugs, extend life, perhaps even bring about our own immortality!"

Decker tried to take this all in. "I'm sorry," he said finally. "I hadn't even considered anything like that. This is much bigger than anything I had imagined. I confess, I thought you had lost it."

Goodman nodded his acceptance of Decker's apology. "Perfectly understandable," he allowed. And now that he felt he had won Decker's confidence, he was ready to tell him more. "Actually," he began, "I'm already deeply involved in research on the cells. I've been able to grow a substantial culture. My plan is to start by exposing the cells to a whole range of agents and examining their effect."

Goodman scooted forward in his chair and leaned over the table, lowering his voice despite the fact that Maria wouldn't have understood, even if she could hear them from the kitchen.

"However, there's another area of research worthy of pursuit as well." Goodman considered his words. "Decker, how much do you know about cloning?"

Decker didn't want to challenge Goodman so soon after having just apologized to him, and he really wasn't a religious person, but this rubbed him entirely the wrong way. "Hold it! You don't mean . . . You're talking about cloning Jesus?!"

Goodman apparently hadn't anticipated the intensity of Decker's response, but he quickly recovered. "Just wait a minute!" he replied. "To begin with, we can't be certain the cells are from Jesus."

"Well, it's a pretty good guess!" Decker shot back, incredulously.

"But even if they are," Goodman continued, "I still find my hypothesis about his origin far more reasonable than any silly religious notions you may have."

It was then that Decker put it all together. "That's what you were talking about before! That's how you plan to test your hypothesis that Jesus was from an advanced alien race! You're going to try to clone him!"

"That's ridiculous!" Goodman insisted. "Human cloning simply isn't possible yet. Yes, they've cloned a couple of sheep and dogs and such, but humans are much more complicated. All I meant was that you might *someday* be able to test my hypothesis of the man's origin in that manner."

"Look, Professor," Decker said, "it's one thing to do lab research or grow cells in a petri dish, but you just can't go around cloning people, especially if the guy you want to clone just might be the son of God!" It was an emotional response. Decker knew the professor was right. He didn't understand the science of it, but he had read many times that human cloning was still way too complicated.

"Decker, use your brain! If the image on the Shroud was from the son of God, then tell me this: Why would an all-knowing, all-powerful creator allow the cells to get stuck to the Shroud in the first place?"

"Who knows? Maybe as a sign or something."

"And why would he allow *me* to find the cells? If it was some kind of sign, wouldn't he at least have chosen someone who believed in him?"

Decker didn't have an answer.

"But more important," Goodman continued, "how could a mere mortal manage to clone the son of God? If there is a God, would he really allow himself to be so easily manipulated?"

Decker listened. As uncomfortable as it made him, what Goodman was saying made sense.

"I really expected you to be more open minded about this whole thing. Where's your scientific curiosity? I can't even suggest a hypothesis without you getting all religious!"

That stung.

"Surely you can see that even if I did manage to clone the man on the Shroud, it would be proof positive that he was *not* the son of God."

Decker couldn't argue with Goodman's logic. An all-knowing, all-powerful God wasn't likely to just leave a bunch of his son's cells lying around. He was irritated at himself for getting emotional about what was so obviously an academic discussion.

During their conversation the two men had taken only a few bites of their food. Goodman now focused his attention on the plate before him, and Decker did the same. After the meal, the conversation grew more amiable, though a bit forced. There was no more discussion on the Shroud, except that Goodman promised to call when the next step in his research was under way.

As they stood to leave for the airport, Maria cleared the dishes and silver, stretching across the large table to reach Professor Goodman's saucer and cup. Carrying them back to the kitchen, she tugged lightly at her apron and adjusted her maternity dress.

Chapter 5

Christopher

Los Angeles

"How much longer?" Hope Hawthorne asked her father as they drove down the exit ramp of I-605.

"Just a few miles," Decker answered.

The announcer on the radio reported the current temperature, "It's seventy-eight degrees — another beautiful day in Southern California."

"Seventy-eight degrees! Is this heaven or what? It was thirty-seven when we left DC," Decker commented as Hope tried to find some music. They had flown in that morning from Washington to visit Professor Goodman, who was about to announce a major breakthrough that could prove to be a cure for several types of cancer. The discovery was a result of research with the C-cells (as Goodman had come to call the cells from the Shroud) and, in accordance with the agreement they had made twelve years earlier, Decker was to be given an exclusive report prior to any formal announcement. To this point, the research hadn't been nearly as successful as Goodman had originally hoped.

Decker had seen Goodman only once since their initial discussions about the origin of the cells. It was in the summer four years earlier, when Goodman believed he was close to developing an AIDS vaccine. What he found instead was a dead end. Most humiliating was that Goodman had discovered the error in his research two days *after* Decker's article was published. The story had generated national attention for Goodman's work and Decker's paper, only to be followed the same week by embarrassment. This time they were sure it would be different.

Decker turned the rented car down the narrow street and stopped in front of Goodman's house. They were greeted at the front door by Martha Goodman and by the delightful smell of something baking in the kitchen. Decker politely reintroduced himself to the woman who smiled warmly at her two guests. "Oh, I remember you," she said brightly.

"Well it's been four years," Decker allowed.

"And this must be Hope," she said giving the girl a grandmotherly hug. "Harry said you were bringing your daughter with you. Such a pretty girl! How old are you, dear?"

"Thirteen," Hope answered.

"We decided to mix pleasure with business," Decker explained. "We're going to drive up to San Francisco this afternoon to visit my wife's sister for a few days. Elizabeth and our other daughter, Louisa, flew out two days ago."

"Yeah, but I had to stay in Washington and take a math test," Hope interjected.

"In the news business things are very mercurial. It seems that our vacations have never worked out as planned, so we try to take a few days whenever we can. Sometimes that means the kids have to miss a few days of school," Decker said.

Mrs. Goodman looked at Decker with disapproving puzzlement on her face. "Your daughter is in school in Washington? I thought you lived in Tennessee. Do you really think that a boarding school is appropriate for a girl Hope's age? Especially so far from—"

"Hope's not in a boarding school," Decker interrupted. "We moved to Washington two years ago after I sold the paper in Knoxville and went to work for *NewsWorld*."

"Oh, forgive me," Martha Goodman blushed. "I didn't realize. It's just that, well, my parents sent me to a boarding school and I hated it. Anyway," she said, changing the subject and turning her attention again to Hope. "I'm glad you were able to come along, dear. Harry is out in the backyard playing with Christopher. They probably didn't hear you drive up. I'm afraid the professor's hearing isn't what it used to be. I'll tell him you're here."

Decker and Hope waited as Mrs. Goodman went to call her husband. "He'll be right in, Mr. Hawthorne," she said as she returned and then excused herself to the kitchen.

A moment later Professor Goodman appeared. "How are you, Decker? How have you been?" He didn't wait for an answer. "You look like you've put on some weight and lost more hair." Decker cringed a little at Goodman's recognition of what was obvious to everyone but himself.

"And you must be Hope," the professor said, looking in her direction. "I'll bet you'd like to meet my grandnephew, Christopher." Goodman turned toward the back door where a young boy was standing with his nose pressed against the screen, looking in. "Christopher, come in here and meet Mr. Hawthorne and his daughter, Hope."

Decker had never seen Professor Goodman so animated or in such a good mood.

"I'm very pleased to meet you, Mr. Hawthorne," Christopher said as he entered and extended his right hand.

"It's very nice to meet you as well," Decker responded, "but actually we met about four years ago when you were seven. You've grown quite a bit since then."

Martha Goodman emerged from the kitchen with a plate full of chocolate chip cookies. "Oh, good. I love chocolate-chip," said Professor Goodman.

"They're not for you," teased Martha. "They're for the children. Hope, would you and Christopher like to come out in the backyard with me and have some cookies and milk?" Hope — who didn't like being placed in the general genus of "children," but who did like chocolate-chip cookies — nodded and went with Christopher and Mrs. Goodman to the backyard.

Decker and Professor Goodman settled in for a long conversation. "Professor, you look great," Decker began. "I swear, you look ten years younger than the last time I saw you."

"I feel great," Goodman answered. "I've lost twenty-four pounds. My blood pressure is down. I'm even regular most of the time," he added with a chuckle.

"That's another thing," Decker said shaking his head. "You seem . . . well, almost jolly. What's going on?"

Goodman looked toward the back door. Christopher was standing there with the screen door part way open, watching as Hope and Mrs. Goodman inspected some flowers. Certain he wouldn't be missed, Christopher ran to his granduncle, and from his shirt pocket, pulled two chocolate-chip cookies. Goodman took the cookies and accepted the hug that came along with them. Christopher put the side of his index finger to his lips to signify a pact of silence and then went over to Decker and reached back into his shirt pocket. As he did, he saw the results the hug had on the two remaining cookies. Looking at the broken remains, he offered them apologetically to Decker, who accepted graciously as Christopher gave the same code-of-silence signal and ran out the back door before he could be missed.

"What's going on?" Goodman said, repeating Decker's question. "That's what's going on." Goodman nodded toward where Christopher had made his exit. "I may look ten years younger, but I feel like I'm forty again."

Decker knew from his last visit that Christopher's parents had been killed in an auto accident. His closest surviving relative was his grandfather, Goodman's older brother, who was unable to take care of him because of failing health. So Christopher had moved in with Harry and Martha.

"Originally, I thought we were too old to take care of a child, but Martha insisted," Goodman continued. "We never had any children of our own, you know. Christopher has been the best thing to ever happen to us. But, I was right — we were too old. So we just got younger."

Decker smiled.

"Okay. Let's get down to business," said Goodman. "This time we've really got something. Let me go get my notes." Goodman left the room for a moment and returned with three overstuffed notebooks. Two hours later it was clear to Decker that the professor was right. Goodman had developed a vaccine for treating many of the viruses that can cause cancer, including Rous sarcoma and Epstein-Barr. Further testing was necessary to determine if the vaccine development process was universal, and there would have to be actual testing in humans, but all of the tests to date had been remarkable, proving as much as 93 percent effective in lab animals.

"So what you've done is to grow massive cultures of the C-cells, and then introduced the cancer virus in vitro," Decker summarized. "In that environment, the virus attacks the C-cells, which respond by producing antibodies, which have resulted in the complete arrest and ultimate elimination of the virus in animals."

"In a nutshell, that's it," Goodman agreed. "And if the vaccine development proves out, it should work with any virus, including

AIDS or even the common cold. Admittedly, those will be a little tougher because of all the mutations of the AIDS virus and all the varieties of cold viruses."

"This is amazing work," Decker agreed. "I'd be surprised if my editor doesn't put you on next week's cover. I'd like to spend some more time looking over your notes, but I promised Elizabeth we wouldn't be late."

"I've already had them scanned for you. Just make sure you keep the files under lock and key and call me if you have any questions."

Goodman gathered his papers and the conversation soon turned to small talk while they waited for Martha and the children to return from a walk. Decker told Goodman that after visiting with Elizabeth's sister for a few days, he'd be going to Israel for six weeks to relieve the *NewsWorld* reporter covering the recent unrest there. "By the way, do you remember Dr. Rosen from the Turin expedition?" Decker asked.

"Joshua Rosen?" Goodman said. "Of course. I read something about him somewhere a couple years back."

"That was my story in *NewsWorld*," Decker responded. "I sent you a link."

"Something about him leaving the U.S. and going to Israel after they cut his program from the defense budget."

"Right. I'll be staying with him for a couple days."

"Well, tell him I said hello." Goodman said.

At that moment Martha Goodman, Hope, and Christopher came in the front door from their walk. Seeing that the men were finished with their shop-talk, Martha asked, "Would you and Hope like to stay for supper? We'd love to have you."

"I'm really sorry," Decker replied. "Elizabeth and Louisa are expecting us."

* * * * *

As the miles rolled by and the highway scenery grew redundant, Hope told her father about her visit with Christopher and Mrs. Goodman. "He's a nice kid," she said. "It's a shame he'll be thirteen in a couple years."

"Why's that?" Decker asked.

"Because thirteen-year-old boys are so obnoxious," she answered.

"Obnoxious?" he laughed. "I thought you saved that term for your little sister."

Hope didn't answer but her father's comment reminded her of something. "Mrs. Goodman said that it's tough on Christopher because he doesn't have any brothers or sisters to play with, and there's no one else his age in the neighborhood. She said that she and Professor Goodman were both only children, too, and that I was really lucky to have a little sister. I told her I didn't think so. So, anyway, if it's all right with you and Mom, I told her she could have Louisa to keep Christopher company."

Decker rolled his eyes. "Real funny."

"Yeah, Mrs. Goodman didn't think you'd go for it, either."

As they continued their trip, Decker's thoughts went back and forth between his discussion with Professor Goodman and his planned trip to Israel. He looked forward to visiting with the Rosens, and he especially looked forward to spending some time with his old friend Tom Donafin, who had joined *NewsWorld* magazine a few weeks earlier. He was not, however, looking forward to being away from Elizabeth, Hope, and Louisa for so long, although they would be joining him there for Christmas.

They were now about a hundred and twenty miles from Los Angeles. The temperature was still near perfect, though the sun would be setting soon.

Suddenly Decker took his foot off the gas pedal and let the car drift to a stop on the shoulder of the road.

"What's the matter?" Hope asked.

But Decker didn't answer. For a long moment he just stared and tapped a finger on the wheel. "How could I have missed that?" he asked himself finally.

"What?" Hope asked.

"We're going back," he said without explanation. Hope tried to object, but it was fruitless. Decker forgot all about his promise to Elizabeth not to be late.

Two hours later they were back where they had started at Goodman's house, with Hope, who was still operating on Eastern time, asleep in the backseat. Decker went to the front door and knocked.

Professor Goodman and Christopher opened the door together. No one spoke for a moment. Goodman stared at Decker in confusion. Christopher stood beside him dressed in pajamas, his hair still damp and freshly combed after his bath.

"Did you forget something?" Goodman asked finally. But Decker had already stooped down to Christopher's level and was closely examining his facial features.

"Hi, Mr. Hawthorne," Christopher said. "It's nice to see you again. Can Hope come in and play some more?" The intensity in Decker's eyes began to melt away, until he looked back up at Goodman, who was staring down at him.

"What on Earth is the matter with you?" Goodman asked, uncomfortably.

Decker stood up again. "You did it. Didn't you?"

"What are you talking about?" Goodman asked, doing his best to appear unaffected.

"You know exactly what I'm talking about! The cloning!"[6]

Goodman felt like a rabbit in a snare. "Christopher," he said as calmly as he could, "Mr. Hawthorne and I need to talk. Go back in the house and tell your Aunt Martha I'm on the front porch and will be in after awhile."

Decker waited until Christopher closed the door before speaking again. "You cloned the cells from the Shroud!" he said in a whisper so loud and emphatic he may as well have been shouting. "Christopher isn't your brother's grandson! You don't even have a brother! You were an only child!"

The night was warm and the moonlight shone on Mrs. Goodman's flowers; their fragrance filled the air, but it went totally unnoticed by the two men. Goodman looked closely into Decker's eyes, examining his face for any sign of a twitch that might signal that he was bluffing. He found none.

Decker didn't flinch, but he *was* bluffing, at least a little. While he now knew that Christopher couldn't be Goodman's grandnephew, that certainly wasn't conclusive evidence he was the clone of the man on the Shroud. The story about Goodman's brother might have been created for a dozen other reasons that had nothing to do with the Shroud.

"You can't tell anyone. You can't," Goodman pleaded. "They'll make him a zoo specimen. He's just a little boy!"

Decker shook his head, stunned both that he had actually been right and that he had gotten Goodman to admit it. "That's why you named him Christopher, isn't it?"

"Yes," Goodman answered, realizing the damage was done and hoping to inspire a cooperative spirit in Decker.

"After Christ!"

For a moment Goodman honestly didn't understand what Decker meant, then it hit him. "Christ! Don't be absurd!" he said, indignantly. "Columbus! I named him after Christopher Columbus."

"Why would you name him after Columbus!?"

The question surprised Goodman, who thought the answer was obvious.

"I told you I had made the greatest discovery since Columbus discovered the New World. I wasn't just talking about finding the cells or the possible medical benefits," he admitted. "I was talking about Christopher. I had already successfully implanted the cloned embryo in the surrogate mother, and she was several months into an otherwise normal pregnancy." Goodman shrugged. "I never expected it to work!" he said, eschewing credit in order to disown blame. "It shouldn't have worked! But the C-cells proved so resilient that transfer of the genetic material to the surrogate's egg worked the first time. I was going to tell you twelve years ago, but you got so bent out of shape that I didn't dare.

"Don't you see, Decker? The man on the Shroud may have come from the same race of people who first planted life on this planet four billion years ago. I thought that if I could clone the man on the Shroud, I could learn more about them. I hoped that like Columbus, Christopher might help lead us to a new world — a better world.

"When he was born I studied him. I watched him. I tested him. And you know what I found? Not an alien; not a god. What I found was a little boy!"

"He's not just a *little boy*," Decker insisted. "He's the clone of a man who lived two thousand years ago!"

"But he has no memory of any of that!" Goodman argued. "For all he knows, he's just a normal kid."

"And you're saying there's no difference?" Decker was incredulous.

"Yes, all right, there are some differences," Goodman agreed reluctantly. "He's never been sick and he heals quickly. But that's all!"

"He seems awfully intelligent," Decker countered.

"Yes," Goodman conceded, "but not exceptionally so. Besides, both Mrs. Goodman and I have spent many hours working with him at home in addition to his schoolwork."

"Mrs. Goodman?" Decker asked. "Does she know about Christopher?"

"Of course not. After he was born I paid the surrogate and dispatched her immediately back to Mexico to prevent bonding. I hired a nurse to take care of him in her home. I know it sounds terribly irresponsible now," he confessed, "but I had absolutely no plans about what to do with him when he got older. I was so involved with the scientific aspects that I didn't think about the child as a person. When I realized what I had done, I couldn't just leave him on the doorstep of some orphanage, so I left him on my own doorstep. I put him in a basket, left a note, the whole nine yards. Martha had always wanted children, and after a few days of taking care of him while we 'considered what to do,' it wasn't very difficult to convince her that we should keep him in case the mother ever came back looking for him. Later we made up the story about my brother.

"Maybe it was a mistake, and you can say 'I told you so.' But I don't regret it. He's been like my own son."

Goodman had told all, and now he made his plea. "If you report that Christopher is a clone, you'll destroy three lives: his, mine, and Martha's. Christopher will never have another normal day in his life. You can't do that to him. You have children. Can a story in some stupid magazine really be worth that much?"

Goodman waited, but Decker didn't like the answer that came to mind. No, he didn't want to ruin Christopher's life, but he couldn't just let the story go. There had to be some way to report the story and still protect those involved. The standard promise of anonymity wouldn't work. It was too big a story. Someone would figure it out. And if he didn't use names and explain the circumstances, no one would believe him anyway. There had to be some way around it. He needed time to think.

Goodman waited so long for Decker's response that he began to worry he wasn't going to get the answer he wanted. "Look," he offered, "why don't you come back here next week and spend some time getting to know Christopher better?" His hope was that the more Decker got to know Christopher, the less willing he would be to risk hurting the boy, no matter how big the story was.

It sounded like a good suggestion to Decker as well, but for a different reason. It would give him the time he needed to think, and if he *did* figure out something, he would have a lot more information for the article.

Decker's answer was implied. "Can't do it next week. I'm going to Israel, remember?" Then a thought hit him. It was a long shot, but Decker's career had been built on long shots. "How about if I take Christopher with me to Israel? Who knows? Maybe it'll jog his memory."

Anger swept over Goodman's face. "Are you crazy!" he stormed. "Absolutely not! How would I explain that to Martha?!"

"Okay! Okay! I just thought it would be a neat idea."

"Well it's not!" Goodman shot back.

"Look," Decker said, preparing to strike a bargain, "I'll keep my mouth shut for the time being. I'll be back from Israel in January, so plan on having me around for at least a week."

Goodman swallowed hard. He was thinking more along the lines of a few hours, a day at most. He agreed anyway in hopes of arguing later for a compromise.

Chapter 6

Secrets of the Lost Ark

Six days later

Nablus, Israel

"How do you take yours, Tom?" Joshua Rosen asked as he poured coffee for himself, his wife, and his two American guests. Tom Donafin wanted his black. Decker started to answer for himself, but Joshua interrupted. "I remember," he grinned. "You like yours with *too* much cream and *too* much sugar — just like you'd serve it to a baby."

Decker made a face, but took the coffee just as Joshua had prepared it. It was a late breakfast for the Rosen household, but it was midnight in California where Decker had been the day before. The coffee provided a welcome assist in adjusting to Israeli time.

"So, Tom, tell us about yourself," Ilana Rosen urged. "How do you know our Decker?"

"We met in school," Tom replied. "Decker was one of the few people that didn't treat me like a freak." Tom was five foot ten, of medium build, bearded with thick dark hair and unremarkable in most of his features. The one exception, the source of much distress, especially in earlier years, was his forehead, which protruded grotesquely, giving him an appearance most would call Neanderthal. "My family was in a car accident when I was a kid; killed everyone but me," he continued, answering the question he self-consciously, but correctly, assumed most people had upon first encountering him. "That's where I got my good looks. I grew up in foster homes."

Tom's humor was his defense. Ilana wasn't sure how to respond. He hadn't intended to make her uncomfortable and he quickly changed the subject. "Decker told me a little about you and Joshua on the flight over," he said, "but there's still a lot I don't know."

"Well, in brief," Joshua volunteered, "Both of our parents' families escaped to England from Austria shortly before World War II. Later my father, though a very young man, was a highly regarded physicist, and was recruited to come to America. He was one of more than thirty Jewish scientists who worked in atomic research for the Manhattan Project. After the war, Ilana's family also came to America. We were both born a few years later and when we were old enough, as arranged by our parents, we were married. I went on to study nuclear physics and then became involved in laser and particle beam research."

"That's how you got involved in strategic defense," Tom said, filling the brief silence while his host took a bite of breakfast.

"Yes," Joshua confirmed. "Then a few years ago the president decided to cut back on nearly all directed energy research."

"And that's when you decided to come to Israel."

"Well, not right away, but soon after. My father helped build the first atomic bomb to end World War II. I wanted to help build a defense against atomic bombs to *prevent* World War III. When it seemed clear that the United States no longer had the resolve to build such a defense, I decided to come to Israel to continue my work here."

"Decker said something about your son turning you in to Israeli immigration authorities so that you couldn't become citizens," Tom probed.

At this Ilana responded in defense of her son. "Scott is a good boy. He was just a little confused."

"Scott and I haven't seen eye-to-eye on most things for quite some time," Joshua explained. "Our family was never very strict in our practice of Judaism: we kept the feast days, but only out of tradition. Then, just to understand our Jewish roots, Ilana and I began studying the Scriptures. After about a year and a half of study, we began talking with some Messianic friends and — to make a long story short — Ilana and I accepted Yeshua as the Jewish Messiah. Three months later my father died."

Ilana patted Joshua's hand and gave him a supportive look. "Scott took his grandfather's death very badly," she explained.

"He actually blamed us for my father's death," Joshua continued. "He thought it was punishment from God for Ilana and I accepting Yeshua and 'abandoning' our religion."

Tom nodded sympathetically, though he didn't entirely follow what Joshua was saying.

"We had some pretty heated arguments," Joshua admitted, "and then — perhaps he felt that he was punishing us — Scott cut off all communications, left the United States, and came to Israel."

Ilana continued the story. "When *we* came to Israel two years ago, we hadn't heard from Scott in more than fifteen years. But then, when we went to complete the paperwork for our Israeli citizenship — which is granted to most Jews almost automatically by right of *aliyah* — we were denied. Later we found out that Scott had told the authorities we had renounced our faith, and he insisted we be denied citizenship. We decided to fight the charge." Ilana said.

"We have never renounced our faith!" Joshua asserted, becoming a little agitated. "Many Jews are agnostics or even atheists; and Israel grants *them* citizenship! But because we believe the prophecies about the promised Jewish Messiah, they say *we're* the ones who have denied our faith! Accepting Yeshua is not denying our faith; it's completing it! Do you know that over the centuries there have been more than forty different men who have claimed to be the messiah? And no one ever accused their followers of denying their faith!"

Ilana squeezed Joshua's hand to remind him that he was among friends. It was obvious he had delivered this defense before, not always to a friendly audience. He paused and smiled to offer silent apology for any hint of unintended belligerence.

"I had already talked with a number of officials in the Defense Ministry about coming to work in Israel," Joshua began again, getting back to his story. "That's when Decker called." They looked across the table at Decker, who was sound asleep. Ilana softly brushed her fingers through his hair, and Joshua continued, speaking more quietly to keep from disturbing their guest. "He was doing a story about the decline of American strategic defense research and had heard about my decision to move to Israel. I suggested that he compare the capabilities and goals of the two countries' programs."

"So you knew him before that?" Tom asked.

"Oh, yes," Joshua answered. "We met on the Shroud of Turin project."

"No kidding. I didn't realize you were part of that."

"Please," Ilana intervened, "don't get him started."

Joshua pretended not to hear his wife's last remark, but went on with his story. "Anyway, when Decker arrived I convinced him there were really two stories. First was the US decision to scrap lasers and particle beams; and second was about Israel's policy of denying citizenship to Messianic Jews."

Ilana interjected, "Decker wrote a very thorough article about Israel's citizenship policy, but in the end the editors at your magazine cut it down to a sidebar."

"While Decker was preparing the other story," Joshua said, "he interviewed several members of the Knesset, who are staunch supporters of Israel's missile defense. When they became aware of my situation, they demanded that the bureaucrats grant us citizenship immediately. Within two weeks we were given a hearing that went so quickly we weren't even given a chance to speak. Before we knew what was going on, the judge found in our favor and soon after we became citizens. You see," Joshua explained, "without citizenship, I wouldn't have been allowed to work on Israel's defense programs. We were trying to draw attention to the law against Messianic Jews, but that became moot when we became the exception to that law."

"Scott was at the hearing," Ilana said. "Apparently, seeing us there, fifteen years older, made him think. He called us two days later and asked to see us. He's never exactly apologized, but he has learned to accept us. And it turns out that, at least in one way, he's followed in his father's footsteps."

"Yes," Joshua said proudly. "Scott has proven himself to be a first rate physicist. That's how he found out that we were in Israel and seeking citizenship: he too is involved in strategic defense research."

"Now we see him every few weeks," Ilana concluded.

"We've even worked together on a couple projects," Joshua said.

Each now paused and took another sip of coffee. "You've mentioned 'Yeshua' several times," Tom said retracing their conversation. "I'm afraid I'm not familiar—"

"*Yeshua ha Mashiach*," Joshua answered in Hebrew. "You're probably more familiar with the Anglicized pronunciation of the Greek form of his name: Jesus, the Messiah."

Tom raised an eyebrow in puzzlement. "But how can you be Jewish and Christian at the same time?"

Joshua smiled sadly. "A great many people in Israel ask the same question. But surely you know that *all* of the earliest Christians were Jewish. For most of the first century, Christians continued to live among their Jewish brothers as equals and became a rather large sect within Judaism. Even today, there are a number of practices in the Jewish Passover celebration that come directly from Christian influences. In fact, the first real disagreement among the followers of Yeshua was whether or not Gentiles had to convert to Judaism before they could become Christians."

"I guess I never really thought about it," Tom said. "So the reason that your son turned you in is because you're Christians."

"We prefer 'Messianic Jews,'" Joshua answered. "But yes."

* * * * *

Following breakfast and after waking Decker from his impromptu nap, Joshua and Ilana took their guests on a whirlwind tour of some of the standard sites. Tom was particularly interested in the Wailing Wall, which was the western wall of the ancient Jewish Temple. As they approached the site, the men were given black paper *yarmulkes*. The Israeli government allows tourists to visit the wall but requires men to wear the traditional head covering. Near the wall, dozens of darkly clad men, most standing, but many sitting in white plastic lawn chairs, formed a constantly moving mass as they rocked back and forth, in a practice called dovening, while they prayed or read from prayer books. Some of the men had cords tied around their arms and wore phylacteries, small boxes tied to their foreheads like headbands. Inside the boxes, Joshua explained, were pages from the Torah, the first five books of the Bible.

As he had at their other stops, Joshua gave a brief history of the site. "The original Temple," he began, "was built by King Solomon but was destroyed during the Babylonian captivity. It was rebuilt beginning in 521 B.C. and later went through major renovations under King Herod. In about A.D. 27, Yeshua prophesied that all of the buildings that comprised the Temple would be destroyed a second time before all of those listening to him died. And just as he predicted, the Temple was destroyed in A.D.70 when Titus invaded Jerusalem to put down a Jewish revolt against Rome.

"A curious point of disagreement exists on the extent of the destruction Yeshua prophesied," he said. "What he told his disciples was that the entire Temple and all its buildings would be destroyed before the last of them died. But, as you can see, this portion of the wall is still standing. Some say that he meant to include only the structures within the walls of the Temple. Others say that the western wall was merely part of the foundation and therefore, by their reasoning, wasn't included in Yeshua's prophecy. But according to the historian Josephus, who was present at the Roman siege, Titus ordered that the wall be left standing as a monument to his accomplishments.[7] He wanted everyone to see the kind of fortification he had to overcome to defeat the Jews."

"Does it really matter?" asked Tom.

"Well, Yeshua was very specific. He said that 'not one stone will be left standing upon another.'[8] Since the wall is still standing, there are only two other possibilities that I can think of: Either Yeshua was wrong — a hypothesis that I cannot accept — or," Joshua concluded with a strained chuckle, "at least one of his Apostles is still alive today."

"Cool," Tom mused, and then asked, "This is where the Ark of the Covenant was kept, right?"

Joshua nodded. "Near the center of the Temple, yes."

"I've seen *Raiders of the Lost Ark*[9] half a dozen times," Tom said, "and, assuming it's not lost in a government warehouse somewhere, does anyone know what really happened to it?"

Joshua smiled. "There are a number of theories. The Bible doesn't mention the whereabouts of the Ark after the Temple was destroyed in the Babylonian invasion. Some assume that the invaders took the Ark with them, but the Bible says that when Ezra returned from Babylon to rebuild the Temple, he brought back everything that had been taken.[10] Some people have speculated that the Ark was taken by Titus in A.D. 70 and that it was either stripped and melted down or perhaps locked away and is now in some secret treasury room in the Vatican. However, in Rome there's an arch dedicated to Titus in honor of his siege of Jerusalem. Carved into the arch are scenes of the destruction and looting, including a detailed carving showing the treasures taken from the Temple. Strangely, the Ark isn't among the treasures depicted, even though, as the most highly valued item, it surely would have been included, had Titus taken it.

Tom nodded.

"Some people claim the Ark is in Ethiopia," Joshua continued. "Another theory, based on one of the apocryphal books of the Bible, is that to prevent the Babylonians from finding the Ark, the Prophet Jeremiah hid it in a cave on Mount Nebo in Jordan."[11]

"So, where do you think it is?" asked Tom.

"Hoo, boy!" exclaimed Ilana's voice from the other side of the partition that divides the plaza into men's and women's sections. "If I have to listen to Joshua's theories about the ark again . . ."

"Ilana," Decker laughed. "I didn't know you were over there."

"That's why he kept you close to the partition," she explained as she stuck her fingers through a hole and wiggled them so they would see. "He knows I hate to miss out on the conversation."

"Actually," Joshua answered, ignoring Ilana's plea. "I have my own theory. I think the ark may be in France."

"Why France?" Tom asked.

"Well," Joshua began, "I never gave it much thought until a few years ago when they announced the results of the Carbon 14 dating of the Shroud of Turin."

"Hold it!" Decker interrupted. "What does all this have to do with the Shroud?" The discussion had suddenly become a lot more interesting to him.

"Please, Decker," Ilana's voice urged. "Don't encourage him."

"Sorry," Decker replied, though he really wasn't.

"From a purely scientific point of view," Joshua went on, "I thought the Shroud was just too good to be a fake. But the Carbon 14 dating seemed conclusive. Then one day I was reading some of the writings of St. Jerome who quotes from a book he called the Gospel of the Hebrews, a book which, unfortunately, either no longer exists or is lost. He doesn't quote extensively, but the small piece he *does* quote reveals a very interesting bit of information about the Shroud. Of course, there's no way of knowing how authentic this gospel really was," Joshua allowed, "but it says that after Yeshua rose from the dead, he took his burial shroud and gave it to the servant of the high priest.[12] That's the only record we have that indicates what happened to the Shroud following the resurrection."

"So who was the servant of the high priest and why would Jesus give him the Shroud?" Decker probed.

"That was my question as well," Joshua said. "There's a reference to him in each of the gospels.[13] His name was Malchus, and he was among those who went to arrest Yeshua on the night before his crucifixion. The Apostle Peter attempted to fend them off, and in the scuffle, he cut off Malchus' ear. Yeshua told Peter to put his sword away and then picked up the ear and placed it back on Malchus' head and miraculously healed it."

"That's bound to make an impression," Tom laughed.

"I would imagine so," Joshua agreed. "As servant to the High Priest, Malchus would have been in the Temple on a daily basis and would have seen the curtain — which separated the people from the Holy of Holies — inexplicably torn in two after Yeshua's crucifixion."[14]

"The Holy of Holies was where the Ark was kept," Ilana's voice interjected. "It was the most sacred place in the Temple. When Yeshua died, God himself tore the curtain from top to bottom, allowing ordinary men and women access to his presence."

"And, of course, Malchus would have been very aware of Yeshua's miracles and the evidence of his resurrection," Joshua explained. "So it seems reasonable to me to assume that Malchus, having experienced all this — especially the healing of his ear — may well have become a follower of Yeshua himself. If so, it would explain Yeshua's contact with him after the resurrection."

"But it still doesn't explain why he would give Malchus the Shroud," Decker pressed.

"That was the tough part," Joshua continued. "Then one day, something just clicked, and I realized it might have been to preserve the Shroud as evidence of the resurrection!"

Tom and Decker waited for an explanation.

"I think Yeshua told Malchus to put the Shroud in the Ark," Joshua revealed.

"Um, okay," Tom allowed. "Why would he do that?"

"It's a little complicated," Joshua advised. "As I said, we're pretty sure that the Ark wasn't in the Temple when it was plundered by Titus and the Romans. So where was it? Between the Babylonians and the Romans there were several other times when bandits tried to rob the Temple. I think the priests probably developed an evacuation plan to hide the Ark. Surely when the Romans conquered Israel, the priests realized that the Temple was once again an extremely attractive target. I believe the Ark was hidden in the tunnels beneath the Temple by the high priest. If so, very few people would have known about it, but it's likely that his servant — that is, Malchus — would have been one of those who knew."

Decker and Tom nodded tentative agreement.

Joshua continued. "Okay, so now let's jump ahead in time about eleven hundred years, during the time of the First Crusade. Not many people realize that the Crusaders, who were mostly French, were quite successful in their first attempts to take the Holy Land back from the Muslims. They even succeeded in capturing and holding Jerusalem and establishing a French-born king over the city, claiming that he was a descendant of David. Shortly after that, an order known as the Knights Templar was formed in Jerusalem."

"Oh, yeah. I've seen lots of movies about those guys," Tom said.

"They were pretty powerful," Decker offered.

"Yes, but not at first. The purpose of the Knights Templar was to protect Jerusalem and to aid European pilgrims coming to the Holy Land. This was a rather unrealistic undertaking, however, since originally there were only six or seven members in the order. And they were very poor. Ironically, poverty was one of their vows. I say ironically because somehow over the next hundred years this small group of knights not only grew in number, they grew unbelievably wealthy. In fact, the Knights Templar became the first international bankers, loaning money to kings and nobles throughout Europe. How they acquired their immense wealth has been the subject of great speculation."

"And you think you know the answer?" Tom urged.

"I think so. And if I'm right, it explains a lot more. You see, the headquarters for the Knights Templar was in the Mosque of Omar — that is, the Dome of the Rock — that sits on the site of the old Temple. It's been suggested that the knights excavated the tunnels beneath the Mosque and found the treasures of Solomon."

"So you think they found the Ark," Decker concluded. "But how does the Shroud of Turin fit into all this?"

"The Ark was a container for certain sacred objects," Joshua explained. "The stone tablets on which God wrote the ten commandments; the first five books of the Bible written by Moses; a container of manna, which God provided each morning for the Hebrews to eat while they were in the desert; and Aaron's staff, which God had miraculously caused to sprout, bud, and bear almonds.[15] Those things were placed in the Ark as a witness to later generations of God's power and of his covenant with Israel.

"But something always struck me as odd about that list," Joshua said. "Stone tablets will last forever. Protected in the Ark, the parchment that Moses used to write the Torah might last thousands of years. But the manna, under normal conditions, would turn to dust within a matter of days or weeks. And Aaron's staff — though it might survive for centuries as a simple wooden staff — without the sprouts and buds and almonds wouldn't be much of a witness of God's power. That's when it occurred to me that perhaps the power of the Ark is greater and quite different than we may have realized."

"Like in *Raiders*?" Tom suggested. "Where it made the Nazi's faces melt."

"Well, no." Joshua laughed out loud. "But think about the staff for a minute. How tall do you imagine Aaron's staff would have been?"

"Oh, gee," Tom answered, "I hate to show my ignorance, but in *The Ten Commandments*[16] it seemed like Moses' staff was about six or seven feet tall."

"I can't say much for the reliability of your sources," Joshua said, "but I think that's a fair guess. Shepherding hasn't changed much over the centuries, and all the shepherd staffs I've ever seen are about that long. So when you think about Aaron's staff, with the limbs and sprouts and almonds growing from it, it would have had quite a large diameter in addition to its length. But," said Joshua, about to make his point, "based on a standard eighteen-inch cubit, the absolute longest that staff could have been and still have fit in the Ark is four feet, nine inches,[17] and that's without any branches. The only way that a six-foot staff could fit into the Ark is if the inside dimensions are not limited by the outside dimensions."

"I get it! Sort of a *Mary Poppins*[18] effect," Tom said. "Where Mary Poppins was able to put all sorts of things in her carpetbag that were much bigger than the bag itself."

"I loved that movie," offered Ilana as she started to softly sing, "Just a spoonful of sugar . . ."

Tom and Decker laughed.

"I was thinking more along the lines of Doctor Who's TARDIS,"[19] Joshua replied, "but yes, exactly. If the container of manna and Aaron's staff were to be a witness to future generations, there must be some miraculous, preservative power to the Ark. What I'm suggesting is that perhaps inside the Ark there is a total absence of dimensions: no length, width or height, which would explain how Aaron's staff could fit; and no *time*, which explains how the manna and the staff could be preserved!"

Suddenly it all became clear to Decker what Joshua was getting at. "So you think the servant of the high priest put the Shroud into the Ark, where it remained until it was taken out, more than a thousand years later, by the Knights Templar when they discovered the Temple treasures!"

"Exactly!" Joshua said. "Of course, it's mostly just conjecture, but it does offer a unified theory that would provide a consistent explanation for a number of unanswered questions. Besides, it makes perfect sense that the Shroud — the only physical evidence of Yeshua's resurrection and the consummation of God's *new* covenant[20] with his people — would be kept in the Ark of the Covenant, together with the evidence of God's *old* covenant."

"Wait a second, wait a second," Tom said, trying to catch up.

"Don't you see?" said Decker. "That's why the Shroud flunked the Carbon 14 dating. For more than a thousand years it totally escaped deterioration and aging while it was inside the Ark!"

"Holy sh—" Tom caught himself, but his excitement showed in his raised voice, and many of the nearby tourists and worshipers turned to stare at him disapprovingly. "That's incredible!" he said in a more controlled voice. "But what about the Knights Templar? Is there any connection between them and the Shroud of Turin?"

"You're making this too easy for him, Tom," Ilana objected.

"As far back as it can be traced," Joshua answered, "the first person who we can positively prove had the Shroud was a man in France named Geoffrey de Charney. Some years later his family gave the Shroud to the House of Savoy, who later moved it to Turin, Italy."

"And is there a link between de Charney and the Knights Templar?" Decker asked.

"As a matter of fact," Joshua glowed, fully expecting the question, "there is. As we said, the Knights Templar became very powerful throughout Europe. Later, the King of France, Philip IV, began to worry they were becoming a threat to his power. He accused them of hideous sins and atrocities and they were arrested and tortured. Those who confessed to his trumped-up charges were locked away in prisons; those who refused, were burned at the stake. Two of the last to be executed were Jacques de Molay, the grand master of the Knights Templar, and Geoffrey de Charney, preceptor of Normandy. *That* Geoffrey de Charney apparently was the uncle of the later Geoffrey de Charney, who was the first person we can positively determine had possession of the Shroud."

"Incredible!" said Tom.

"Additionally," Joshua continued, "one of the accusations against the knights was that they worshiped the image of a man."

"The Shroud of Turin!" Decker concluded.

Tom and Decker took a moment to think on this, then Tom prodded, "And that's why you think the Ark is in France?"

"Yes. It's my theory that the Ark and the other Temple treasures were taken from Israel and hidden in France by the Knights Templar. If so, they may still be there, hidden away.

"What about the tunnels?" Decker asked. "Are there really tunnels under the Temple where the Ark could have been hidden before the Knights Templar found it?"

"Not just tunnels, but large vaulted rooms," Joshua said. "Most have never been excavated, but they have been identified by radar soundings."[21] Joshua pointed to a pair of low arches to the left and perpendicular to the wall. "Over there is the opening of one of the tunnels that's been excavated," he said. "There's a side tunnel that leads north in the direction of what today is the Dome of the Rock, but two thousand years ago would have been the Holy of Holies. Some rabbis were excavating that tunnel, but the government stopped them and sealed it off."

"Why?" Tom asked, obviously disappointed at such an uneventful end to the tale.

"When Israel captured Jerusalem in the Six Day War in 1967, we made a pledge to allow the Muslims to continue to control the area of the Dome of the Rock. When they found out about the digging, they immediately protested and the tunnel was sealed. Some people believe the Ark may still be buried there and that the Muslims don't want us to have it. It's also possible that they fear that Jewish zealots might get into the tunnel and blow up the Mosque in order to bring about the rebuilding of the Jewish Temple. It wouldn't be the first time that Israelis have tried to blow up the Dome. A group of zealots tried it back in 1969. They failed, and their leader, Meir Kahane, was later assassinated."

Chapter 7

The Tears of Dogs

Jerusalem

The next evening Decker and Tom went to the Jerusalem Ramada Renaissance Hotel, which was serving as the temporary Middle East headquarters of *NewsWorld* magazine. The office was nothing more than a hotel room with a southern view of the old city of Jerusalem and an adjoining room for the correspondents to sleep in. The room stank of stale cigarettes, which lay in a half dozen overfull ashtrays. It had apparently been some time since the trash had been taken out. A laptop and a small printer sat on a table, along with several crumpled sheets of paper and a day-old cup of coffee. Suitcases sat by the door, ready for the departure of the current residents to the airport.

"Nice place you've got here," Decker winced as he surveyed the condition of the room.

"It's all yours," responded lead reporter Hank Asher.

"Yeah, try not to disturb anything," photographer Bill Dean added dryly.

As soon as Decker had deposited his own luggage, Asher handed him a notebook. "You've reviewed all the briefing documents I sent?"

Decker nodded. It was a lie or at least an exaggeration; he'd get to it later. He flipped through the notebook.

"This is a list of contacts in the government and the Israeli press," Asher said. "If you need them, just tell them who you are and that you're filling in until I get back. Most of them are pretty good to work with." He flipped to a tabbed section. "These are informants. Guard these with your life. Don't contact them unless they call you first." Flipping to another tab, he continued. "I've emailed you both a bunch of useful links. Some are for government sites you're not supposed to have access to. These are the passwords. I spent a lot of time developing these, so don't do anything that'll raise suspicion."

Two weeks later

Washington, DC

Elizabeth Hawthorne worked at her desk preparing for a meeting with her boss while outside her office window, a light snow began to fall. On her wall, photos of Decker, Hope and Louisa looked down approvingly upon her efforts. Glancing at the caller ID as her phone rang, she realized it must be Decker. No one else would be calling her from Jerusalem. "Hello," she chimed, eschewing her typical business response.

"Hi, babe," Decker said.

"Hey stranger."

"Just wanted to hear your voice."

"I love you," Elizabeth said, looking up at his photo.

"Yeah, that's the one," he purred. "I love you, too."

"Are you being careful over there?"

"Of course," he assured her. "Things have been very quiet. Tom's been doing a lot of sightseeing, but I'm waiting until you and the girls get here."

"You know I want to go to Bethlehem for Christmas Eve," she reminded him unnecessarily. She had been talking about it since he got the assignment.

"Of course," he obliged.

A reminder on her computer screen told her she had just five minutes before her meeting. She sighed reluctantly. "I'm sorry, babe," she said. "Bad timing. I've got a meeting about to start. I'll call you later." Then looking at her calendar, she added, "And I'll see you in twelve days. Love you."

"Can't wait," he replied. "Love you."

Jerusalem

At about six in the evening a few days later, Tom returned from visiting one of Jerusalem's many shrines and sat down just as the phone rang. On the other end was a man whose accent suggested he was Palestinian. "I need to speak to the American, Asher."

"I'm sorry, he's not here," Tom responded. "May I help you?"

"Tell the American, 'Many dogs will weep tonight, but their tears will find nowhere to fall.'"

"What?" Tom asked. "What does that mean? What are you talking about?" But the man had hung up.

"What was that?" Decker asked, responding to Tom's excited but puzzled expression.

"Not sure," Tom said. "One of Hank Asher's informants maybe. Either that or a kook."

Decker waited a second for Tom to continue and when it seemed he might keep the mystery to himself, finally asked, "Well, what did he say?"

"He said to tell Asher 'Many dogs will weep tonight, but their tears will find nowhere to fall.'"

Decker puzzled on this for a moment and then asked, "Any idea what it means?"

Tom shook his head as he picked up the phone and began dialing. "No, but I know who might."

Hank Asher's cell phone rang as he sat watching the Redskins in a tight game against Dallas. Reluctantly he decided he should take the call. Tom explained the situation.

"Sometimes one or more of the Palestinian factions will call after a bombing or a kidnapping to take credit for it," Asher suggested. "There's quite a bit of rivalry that goes on among the different groups. Sounds like this guy is trying to establish responsibility up front. If so, you can expect a second call after the fact. I suggest you call the police."

"Okay," Tom said. "Listen, give us a call if you think of anything else."

"Sure," said Asher. "But when you call the police, don't tell them the guy asked for me. I'm trying to take a vacation over here."

Police Inspector Lt. Freij promptly arrived at the hotel to take the report. There wasn't much to go on. "Most of it's pretty simple," he said. "We call them dogs; they call us dogs." He shrugged. "'Weep' and 'tears' obviously means they intend something that will cause grief for Israel — nothing new there. He told us that whatever they've got planned is going to happen tonight. Beyond that it's guesswork." Lt. Freij also suggested that it might be a hoax and that such things weren't uncommon. "Just in case, though," he said, "I'll order all the standard precautions and

see that all the appropriate authorities are alerted to the possibility
of a terrorist attack."

Tom and Decker discussed the caller's message for a while
longer but came to no conclusions.

As the evening wore on, Tom flipped through the television
channels, landing at last on an old John Wayne and Jimmy Stewart
movie. Decker retreated to the balcony, propped his feet up, and
began pecking at the keyboard of his laptop. "The Christ Clone,"
he began. "He seems like an ordinary boy." Decker thought back
to his discussion with Professor Goodman about Christopher. In
truth, the matter was never very far from his mind. He didn't want
to destroy the kid's life, but he couldn't let the story go untold.
Frustrated, he looked out over the beauty of the old city of
Jerusalem. For the most part, it lay silent in the late evening
darkness, with only scattered points of light shining in defiance of
the moonless night. The gold-covered Dome of the Rock sparkled
in the starlight near the Wailing Wall.

Suddenly he understood. "That's it!"

"Tom!" he shouted as he burst into the room. "Quick! Get
your shoes!"

Tom shoved his feet into his running shoes, grabbed his
camera and coat, and headed for the door. "What's up?" he asked.

"The phone call! They're going to blow up the Wailing Wall!"

"Of course!" Tom exclaimed as they ran for the elevator.
"'Weeping' but 'no place for their tears to fall!'"

Tom called Lt. Freij while Decker drove the short distance
from the hotel to the Jaffa Gate and turned down David Street into
the old city. They were only a mile from the Wailing Wall, but at
their present speed Tom thought the car might shake apart on the
ancient roads before they reached it. Because it was late, the one
way street was clear, and Decker had no trouble as he made the
sharp right onto Armenian Patriarch Street, past the Zion Gate and
then onto Bateimahasse Street. They were almost there.

Decker pulled the car into the parking lot and slammed the
door as he and Tom ran toward the Wall. All was quiet and
deserted in the cold, late night. Even the tourists had gone to bed.
Slowing to a jog, they soon stopped entirely, looking around for
any signs of activity, but found none. The only sound was the wind

and the barely audible late-night sounds of the new city outside the walls. They looked at one another obtusely.

"You know," Decker said slowly, "any minute now Lt. Freij is going to show up with his sirens blaring and his lights flashing and we're going to look like total idiots."

They sighed together. That's when it hit them.

"What's wrong with this picture?" Tom whispered as he scanned the scene more closely.

"No police," Decker answered. The ever-present Israeli security were nowhere to be found.

At that moment, they were startled as six men ran from the entrance to the tunnel Joshua Rosen had shown them. The next instant an engine started and they realized they had overlooked the significance of one lone van in the otherwise empty parking lot.

Immediately Tom began taking pictures, but doubted he had a clear shot of any of their faces.

Decker ran to the tunnel entrance, followed closely by Tom once the van had sped off. The bodies of four Israeli security personnel lay in pools of blood, each of their throats cut. Decker leaned over them, vainly looking for any sign of life. Tom snapped a few shots, feeling a little ill. Then from somewhere he caught the distinctive smell of a burning fuse.

"Decker! Run!" he shouted as he grabbed Decker's arm.

The two men bolted from the tunnel and ran as fast as they could. Sixty yards away they slowed and turned, thinking they were far enough to be safe. In the distance they heard the sounds of Lt. Freij's sirens. As Decker looked toward the approaching police cars, the ground suddenly shook and the blast of a massive explosion thundered through his head. Instantly, he dropped to the ground as dirt and rock and tens of thousands of prayers written on bits of paper flew all around him. Almost at once, a second and third detonation followed, filling the air with a heavy, opaque cloud of dirt and smoke and rock dust, which obscured everything. The ground shook again and again as hundreds of immense stones tumbled from the Wall with heavy thuds, demolishing the plaza floor and breaking the stones that had fallen before them to various states of rubble.

Decker lay on the ground choking for air, his shirt pulled over his mouth and nose to filter out the dust. He couldn't see what had happened to Tom and for that moment he almost didn't care. All he knew was he needed to breathe. His death seemed almost certain — only his continued gasping and the pain in his lungs made him sure he was still alive. He could hear nothing but the ringing in his ears.

Several minutes passed before, nearly unconscious, he felt hands drag him away. Finally emerging from the edge of the settling cloud, he could see the face of Lt. Freij looking down at him.

"Are you alright?" Freij asked.

Decker tried to answer but immediately began coughing and vomiting up dirt-filled mucus. Through the dust caked in the corners of his eyes, he saw Tom lying on his side nearby. Still coughing, Decker crawled to his friend's side and managed to call his name.

Tom, like Decker, was covered from head to toe with thick gray dust. His breathing was short and labored. Hearing Decker's call, he opened his eyes, and Decker could see he was obviously in pain, and then he began to smile.

"What?" Decker asked, trying to understand Tom's unexpected cheer.

Tom forced out the words. "I got the explosion," he managed, holding his camera up like a trophy before breaking into a fit of coughing.

"You idiot," Decker laughed.

As Decker rolled to his back next to Tom, he scanned the area where the Western Wall had stood for more than two thousand years. He thought only briefly about how glad he was to be alive. And though he was sickened by the destruction of this awesome historical site, he couldn't help but envision Tom's picture on the cover of *NewsWorld*, along with his article as the lead story.

The phone caller had been right: There was much weeping that night. The Palestinians had planted far more than enough explosives to do the job. Bits and pieces of broken stone lay everywhere. The earth of the Temple Mount behind the Wall caved down upon the rubble. And of the Wall itself, not one stone was left standing upon another.

Chapter 8

When in the Woods and Meeting Wild Beasts

Jenin, Israel

The morning was clear and cold. As Decker drove slowly through the Palestinian neighborhood, Tom checked the spreadsheet on his laptop. "According to the database," he said, "the plate is registered to someone on this street, but there's no house address." While Tom's camera had not captured the faces of the men as they ran to their van, he did have a clear shot of the van's plate. And with a little help from Hank Asher's notebook, they had gotten access to the Israeli motor vehicles license data.

"There!" Decker said, pointing to the van parked on the street.

Decker drove past the house and then pulled off. For a moment they just sat there.

"Okay, so now what?" Tom asked finally. "We just waltz in there and ask to interview them?"

Everything so far had fit perfectly in Decker's model of being in the right place at the right time. He had been given the assignment in Israel, and been there for the call, and figured out the caller's riddle, and made it to the Wall just at the right time. And now they had tracked down the van. This was fate. He couldn't let this story go, any more than he could forget about the story of the Christ clone.

"Look," he reasoned. "Somebody called Asher to let him know this was going to happen. They wanted us to know. We're not their enemy. As long as they know we're from an American news magazine and we work with Asher, we should be okay."

They looked at each other and took a deep breath. Decker placed their "Press" sign in the car's front window as Tom slid his laptop under the seat. Then, hanging their *NewsWorld* IDs around their necks, they walked back to where the van was parked. Continuing down the short dirt path to the cement block house, Decker knocked on the door.

After a moment, a middle-aged woman answered. Immediately, Tom and Decker held up their press ID. "We're with

NewsWorld Magazine," Decker said. "We're Americans. We work with Hank Asher."

Without responding, the woman looked back into the house and closed the door to a crack.

"Asher?" a man's voice said, and a moment later the door opened.

A man signaled them to enter.

"Great!" Tom Donafin said.

As the door swung shut behind them, Decker heard a loud crack as his skull absorbed the impact of a club.

Somewhere in Israel

The pain in Decker's head crawled down his neck and shoulders and came to rest in the pit of his empty stomach. Ropes bound his feet and hands. Lying on his side with his face to the floor, he wondered where he was and how long he had been there. He could hear the sound of rolling dice and two men talking, but for the present decided not to let them know he was conscious. Slowly, carefully he opened the eye closest to the floor, and when it became clear no one had noticed, he strained to look around as much as he could without moving. What he saw told him very little. He was in a room with one small, boarded-up window. About five feet away Tom lay on the floor in much the same condition, facing away from him. Two men sat playing backgammon on a makeshift table, paying very little attention to their captives. Decker closed his eyes and rested from the strain.

Some hours later, Decker realized he had fallen asleep. The nausea had subsided and the pain in his head was somewhat less. What woke him was the sound of a door closing and men talking, which he took to be a changing of the guard. His eyes still closed, he could feel the men moving about the room, stopping to look down at him and then moving away. Carefully he opened one eye and saw the men gathered around Tom.

"Wake up, Jew!" said one of the men, as he landed the toe of his boot squarely in the middle of Tom's back. The force drove Tom several feet across the floor, his back arched in agony as he gasped for breath.

"Stop!"

The four men looked over at Decker, who had somehow managed to sit up. The man who had kicked Tom looked down threateningly. Decker had the feeling that he was being inspected; the man was looking for something. When he failed to find whatever it was, he shoved Decker back to the floor with his foot and went back to Tom.

Tom still struggled to catch his breath and an anguished moan issued from deep inside him. The man had hurt him badly and he was preparing to do it again.

"Stop!" Decker shouted again.

This time the man returned to Decker and kicked him in his left shoulder. The pain was unbearable, but it was obvious to Decker the man had not kicked him with nearly the enthusiasm or force he had used on Tom.

"Keep your mouth shut or you'll get the same as the Jew," the man threatened and moved back to Tom.

"Wait!" Decker wailed, sitting up again and ignoring the man's warning. The man looked over at Decker, who continued, "He's not a Jew!"

For an instant the man's eyes registered uncertainty. He paused, and then looked as though he would ignore Decker's infraction of his order and concentrate on Tom.

Decker persisted. "He's not a Jew. He's an American, just like me. Check his passport. It's in his pocket." Scenes of the bloody death of *Wall Street Journal* reporter Daniel Pearl played through Decker's memory. Pearl, who was Jewish, had been videotaped as he was forced by his Islamic kidnappers to repeat, "I am a Jew. My mother is a Jew." Then, with the tape still running, he was brutally murdered.[22]

"We've seen your passports," the man responded. Decker had at least bought Tom a little time: he had gotten the man talking. "It makes no difference to me whether he is an Israeli Jew or an American Jew."

"But he's not a Jew at all!" Decker said. Decker remembered also the 1994 abduction of three British tourists by Ahmed Omar Saeed Sheikh, the same man who engineered the Pearl kidnapping and murder. After several weeks in captivity, the Britons were released unharmed. The obvious difference between Daniel Pearl and the British tourists was Pearl's Jewish heritage. Decker knew it was imperative that he convince his captors Tom wasn't Jewish.

"He looks like a Jew to me," the man said, as though that made it so.

"I'm telling you, he's an American and a Gentile," Decker responded with the same intellectual level of argument.

Decker knew that, right or wrong, if the Palestinian was really sure, he wouldn't be taking the time to argue about it. But there was another force at work in the room, simple but powerful: peer pressure. The other men were watching their comrade to see what he would do. His judgment was being challenged and he felt he had to respond.

Tom had stopped moaning and was now lying nearly motionless on the floor, taking short, labored breaths. The Palestinian was unimpressed with Decker's response and decided at last to refocus his attention on Tom.

Decker blurted out the first thing he could think of. It was risky, but neither he nor Tom had anything to lose: Another blow from the man's boot might break Tom's back. "If you don't believe me," Decker said, once again getting his captors' attention, "pull down his pants."

The Palestinians looked at each other, not sure that they had understood, and then started to laugh as they realized what Decker meant. If Tom were a Jew, he'd be circumcised.

The one who had kicked Tom wasn't so sure about the idea. He didn't want to risk appearing foolish. But the other three laughed and went to work loosening Tom's pants. They were enjoying the contest between their leader and the American. Besides, it seemed an amusing way to settle an argument where a man's life hung in the balance.

There was just one problem, and therein lay the risk: Decker had no idea whether or not Tom was circumcised. But with his life on the line, Decker's only choice had been to set that as the defining criterion. When the three lackeys pulled down Tom's pants, they committed themselves to that criterion. Knowing that many American men, Jew and Gentile alike, are circumcised, Decker was well aware that he still might be condemning his friend to death.

The leader was disappointed with what they found. Tom's foreskin had saved his life.

The three Palestinians gave Tom's pants a tug and pulled them most of the way back up. Again they were laughing, but this time, in part at least, they were laughing at their leader. An angry glare abruptly stopped their merriment. The leader quickly changed the subject and, after shoving Decker back to the floor with his heel, signaled for the others to follow him out of the room.

* * * * *

In the morning a man brought some food, and it now appeared less likely they would be killed right away. As Decker's mind went to thoughts of Elizabeth, Hope, and Louisa, his fear of torture and death was entirely overshadowed by his distress for his family. Thoughts of Christopher Goodman completely left his conscious mind.

In the evening two of the guards blindfolded them, shoved rags into their mouths, and gagged them. Decker guessed they were about to be moved to another location. He lay in that condition for about twenty minutes, trying not to choke on the rags, before being dragged outside and made to lay flat on his stomach. A moment later a truck door slammed and an engine started. Everything was moving too fast. Exhaust filled the air, and Decker could hear the vehicle moving toward him. He wanted to move, to try to escape, but didn't know if doing so would take him clear of the oncoming wheels or cause him to be crushed beneath them. In a moment, his choice was made as the truck, backed over him and came to a halt.

Seconds later eight hands grabbed him and lifted him until his back pressed firmly against the object above him, and he was strapped tightly into this position. And then he heard the sound of a metal door sliding shut as it brushed across his face. In a minute, he heard the men straining again, lifting Tom, he assumed, as they had lifted him, and then another metal door. Now he understood. He and Tom were strapped beneath the bed of a truck in hidden compartments used to ship weapons and, on this occasion, people through check points and past border guards.

Tel Aviv

Elizabeth Hawthorne and her two daughters walked through the concourse of David Ben Gurion International Airport in Tel Aviv. A few days earlier Elizabeth had been sitting in her office thinking about how slow business was and how much she missed Decker. On the spur of the moment she decided to take some extra vacation time, get the girls out of school, and fly to Israel a week early. Surprises had always been Decker's forte, but this time Elizabeth decided she would do the surprising.

She was totally unprepared for the news that awaited her.

As she and the girls walked toward the exit with their luggage, a somber-looking man and woman in their mid-sixties approached.

"Mrs. Hawthorne?" the man asked, requesting confirmation.

"Yes," she answered, a bit surprised.

"My name is Joshua Rosen. This is my wife, Ilana. We're friends of your husband."

"Yes, I know," Elizabeth responded. "Decker has mentioned you. Did he send you? How did he find out that we were going to surprise him?" she asked, not discerning the seriousness of the situation.

"Could I speak to you for a moment in private?" Joshua asked.

Suddenly Elizabeth realized that something was wrong. She wanted to know what and she didn't want to wait. "Has something happened to Decker?" she demanded.

Joshua Rosen preferred not to talk in front of Hope and Louisa, but Elizabeth insisted. "Mrs. Hawthorne," he began, "according to the clerk at the Ramada Renaissance, Decker and Tom Donafin left their hotel in Jerusalem three days ago. Last night Hank Asher from *NewsWorld* called to ask if I had any idea where they were. He said that their editor had been trying to reach them. He tried to call you at your office, but they said you were on vacation. He couldn't reach you at home either."

Elizabeth was growing impatient with Rosen's explanation. She wanted to know the bottom line. "Please, Mr. Rosen, if something has happened to my husband, tell me!"

"Oh, Mom!" Hope cried, pointing.

On a TV screen in the concourse, the local news ran a video. Decker was on his knees in front of armed, hooded men. One held a knife to Decker's neck as he spoke in Arabic. The news banner read: "American Reporters, captive in Lebanon."

Elizabeth shook her head in denial and disbelief. "No! There must be some mistake!" she demanded, as if by sufficient insistence she could alter what she couldn't bear to face.

Hope and Louisa wept.

Elizabeth collapsed into the arms of Ilana Rosen, who held her as she watched the screen and sobbed.

Four months later

Somewhere in northern Lebanon

Decker picked a flea from his beard as he counted the lines he had scratched on the wall. As near as he could tell, he believed the date to be April 9th, Louisa's birthday. He imagined what Elizabeth and the girls might be doing to mark the day. His helplessness filled him with both self pity and rage. He longed to tell his family he loved them and that he was still alive. The need to reach out and comfort them made all his physical pains of no consequence. He knew he might never go home. He might never see his wife's face again or his children. In his anger and frustration, he pulled at the bonds that held his hands and feet. He couldhave broken the ropes even when he was in peak condition, but in his weakened, half-starved state, it was doubly futile and only added to his despair.

Leaning against the wall, Decker closed his eyes and grasped escape from his nightmare. At once he was transported to his home in Maryland.

"Happy birthday," he told Louisa, who was in the kitchen eating cereal. She showed no sign of surprise but smiled broadly at his arrival.

"Thank you, Daddy."

"Do you know what you want?"

"For you to come home," she replied.

"Besides that," he smiled sadly.

"Just some jeans and a phone."

"A phone? Who would you call?"

"I could call you."

"That would be great, but I don't have a phone here. Has your mom planned a party?"

"Just Mom and Hope. I wish you could come."

"I wish I could too, babe."

Decker had thought through again and again the events of the day he and Tom were captured and all that followed. His best guess was that he was in Lebanon, though he just as easily might have been in Jordan or even Syria. He searched for any clue to support his hunch. If just once his captors would bring his food wrapped in old newspaper or if he could catch the sight or sound of a seagull from the Mediterranean . . . But the most he had to go on was the occasional use of the word *Al-Lubnān*, Arabic for Lebanon, by his captors. He refused to believe Tom Donafin was dead, but he hadn't seen his friend since that night in Israel when they were blindfolded. For that matter, he hadn't truly seen anyone. The men who held him captive wore masks when they came into the room and they almost never spoke.

Nor had he seen anything outside the locked door of his room, but he perceived that he was in an old apartment building. The ropes on his feet were tied manacle style with about twelve inches between his ankles so he could take small steps. To prevent him from untying himself — an act that would have resulted in severe punishment — the ropes around his wrists provided almost no slack. Personal hygiene was nearly impossible, and he was provided with a bucket of water with which to bathe only once a week or so.

One of his captors had given him a copy of the Quran in English. He'd wanted to tear it to shreds, but he knew that for Muslims, to deface the Quran is not just to insult Allah, it is to *assault* him, and thus invite his wrath, the exercise of which was the responsibility and pleasure of his followers. Besides, with nothing else to do or read, it provided Decker with some distraction. He had heard the claims that Islam is a peaceful religion — that those who murder and take hostages and commit acts of terrorism in Allah's name don't represent "true Islam." But as he sat on the floor reading with his feet and hands tied, he found that hard to believe.

His captors hadn't tortured him since early in his captivity, apparently growing bored with it all. The burns had healed and the cuts had closed. Only the most serious ones left noticeable scars. Despite all they had done to him, he had found it strangely easy not to scream or weep. His surprise and curiosity at this fact was itself an extremely propitious distraction. It was as though he watched rather than participated, observing in amazement that the victim didn't cry out. He recalled a short poem by Nguyen Chi Thien, which he had read many years before. It explained his silence under torture. Nguyen, a prisoner of the Communist Vietnamese for twenty-seven years, had written a volume of poetry about his life called *Flowers From Hell.*

> I just keep silent when they torture me,
> though crazed with pain as they apply the steel.
> Tell children tales of heroic fortitude —
> I just keep silent thinking to myself:
> "When in the woods and meeting with wild beasts,
> who ever cries out begging for their grace?"[23]

Somewhere along the way, like Nguyen Chi Thien, Decker began to compose poetry, reciting each line over and over to commit it to memory. Mostly they were poems of regret to Elizabeth.

> Moments lost, I thought would last;
> Promises broken I cannot mend;
> Dreams of days from a wasted past;
> Days of dreams that never end.
> Nights and days form endless blur.
> Walls of drab and colors gray,
> Pain and loss I scarce endure,
> While dirty rags upon me lay.

> I've wasted such time that was not mine to take,
> Leaving sweet words unsaid, precious one.
> Now walk I on waves of a limitless lake
> Of unfallen tears for things left undone.

There are many things a man can think about when left alone for so long, and it seemed to Decker that he had thought about them all. Usually he thought about home and Elizabeth and his two daughters. He had missed so many things because he had always put his job first. And now, because of his job, he might never see them again.

* * * * *

Decker awoke and began to smile. Eagerly he scuttled to the wall and scratched a new day — number 903 — by which he added a tiny asterisk. He hadn't eaten in two days and had little to drink, so he was undistracted by any need to relieve himself. Instead, immediately he stood in the middle of his room, and to the extent he could, brushed the dust from his ragged clothes to make himself presentable. Taking a breath, he let his eyes drop shut.

The room was large and lit by endless rows of silver candelabras. Decker wore a black tuxedo, neatly tailored to account for his reduced form, and Elizabeth was beautiful in an amazing pink evening gown.

"Happy anniversary, my love," he whispered, looking deep into her brown eyes.

"Happy anniversary," Elizabeth answered.

"Twenty-three years. You were such a beautiful bride." She glowed. "You're still beautiful," he added, standing back to take in her full beauty, but not letting go of her hands.

Elizabeth smiled again as music played and Andy Williams began to sing *Moon River*. "My favorite," she sighed.

"I told him," Decker said, taking her in his arms to dance in the center of the large floor.

"Yes. I've heard you have a lot of pull around here."

"Well," he demurred, "Andy's very accommodating."

"How have you been?" she asked as they swept gracefully across the floor.

"Okay," he lied.

"No more torture?"

"Not in months," he assured her, and then whispered in her ear: "They think I'm nuts."

Elizabeth threw her head back and laughed, and Decker took the occasion to gracefully dip her.

"It's been two and a half years," Elizabeth noted after a moment.

"Nine hundred and three days," Decker replied. "But who's counting?

"I am!" she assured him. "And so are you, obviously."

"And I'll go on counting until I'm home. And then I'll count our days together."

"I hope you won't insist on marking the walls."

Decker laughed.

"I've written another poem for you," he whispered.

"But all your poems are so sad," she resisted. "Couldn't you write a happy poem?"

Decker shook his head. "I'm sorry, my love. I need my time with you, but I've got to hold onto my torment. It's my compromise with insanity."

"Because none of this is real?"

"No," he corrected softly. "Don't say that. This is real. It's just a different real."

"Oh," she said.

"If I let go of my pain — if I let go of my life there completely — I'll never be able to come home. And I will come home to you," he promised. "And then I'll write you happy poems."

Chapter 9

Dream a Little Dream of Me

"Mr. Hawthorne."

"Mr. Hawthorne."

"Wake up, Mr. Hawthorne, it's time to go."

Decker opened his eyes and looked around the room. As he twisted his body and shifted his weight to sit up, the ropes that bound his hands and feet slipped off like oversized gloves and shoes.

"It's time to go, Mr. Hawthorne," the voice of a young boy said again.

Decker rubbed his eyes and looked toward the voice. There in the open doorway of his room stood Christopher Goodman, now fourteen years old.

"Christopher?" Decker asked, completely confused at this turn of events.

"Yes, Mr. Hawthorne," Christopher answered.

"What are you doing here?" Decker asked in disbelief.

"It's time to go. I've come to get you," he replied, making no attempt to explain.

Christopher walked from the room and signaled for him to follow. Decker didn't understand, but quickly lifted the 115 pounds that remained of his body and followed Christopher from the room and toward the front door. Halfway there, he stopped. There was something he was trying to remember, something too important to forget, something he couldn't leave behind.

"Tom!" he said suddenly. "Where's Tom?" he asked of the friend he had not seen since they were brought to Lebanon.

Christopher hesitated and then raised his arm slowly and pointed toward another door. Silently, Decker opened it, looking for any sign of his captors. There was none. Inside, Tom lay sleeping on a mat with his face to the wall. Decker entered and quickly began untying the bonds that held his friend's feet.

"Tom, wake up. We're getting out of here," he whispered.

Tom sat up and looked at his rescuer, uncertain. For a moment they just stared at each other's faces. Decker hadn't looked in a mirror at any time during his captivity, and though he knew his body was emaciated, he had not seen his face, where the most dramatic effects of his deprivation were evident. Seeing Tom's face, he understood not only his friend's condition but his own; he was closer to death than he had known. Finally, he forced his eyes away and began untying Tom's hands.

Outside the apartment, Decker and Tom walked stealthily down the hall, desperately hoping to avoid detection. Christopher, on the other hand, went on ahead showing absolutely no sign of concern. Quickly they descended three flights of stairs, smelling of urine and cluttered with trash and broken bits of plaster and glass. Still there was no sign of their captors. As they emerged into the open air, Decker closed his eyes as the bright sunlight struck him in the face with its warmth and glow.

When he opened his eyes again, he was staring at his empty room. The morning sun shown in on his face through the cracks in the boarded-up window.

He realized he had been dreaming.

Usually Decker dreamed of his family. When he awoke from those dreams he would close his eyes again to try to hold on to the vestiges of the illusion. This dream, however, was just a curious distraction. He had not thought of the boy for as long as he could remember.

Decker flipped over onto his back, and as he twisted his body and shifted his weight to sit up, the ropes that bound his hands and feet slipped off like oversized gloves and shoes.

He shook his head; was he still dreaming? He wasted no more time thinking about it, but quickly got to his feet. The door was unlocked, and he quietly cracked it open to look into the apartment. It was abandoned, just as it was in his dream. Cautiously he approached the room, which in his dream, had held his friend. Until this moment Decker had not known where Tom was, or even if he was still alive, but just as in his dream, there was Tom.

Moments later they were walking down the hall and then down the same foul-smelling, cluttered stairway. He still didn't understand, but as they emerged from the building, Decker used his hand to shield his eyes in anticipation of the sunlight. None of this made any sense, but if he was dreaming, this time he didn't want to wake up.

The two men moved from doorway to doorway, building to building, staying out of sight as much as possible. As they continued down the street they saw no one; it was like a ghost town. They decided to try to put as much distance between themselves and their captors as they could right away and then wait until nightfall to go on. All they knew to do was to move south, which they hoped was toward Israel. They had no idea how far they were from the border, but with their eyes they silently pledged each other to die rather than be recaptured.

When they were a safe distance away, Decker related his strange dream, but omitted any reference to Christopher's unusual origins.

* * * * *

For the next three nights Decker and Tom worked their way south, staying off the roads and away from any sign of population. On this night they risked starting early, about an hour before sundown. Their time was running out. Tom had not fared as well as Decker and soon he would be too weak to travel. Their diet was limited to what they could find or catch, which meant mostly insects, snails, various weeds, and grasses.

Just before dark they came to a well-traveled road, which they would have to cross. Waiting in a field of tall grass, they planned their crossing for after dark, hoping that traffic would be lighter and they could pass unseen. But as night fell, the traffic continued nearly unabated, with only occasional gaps of perhaps a minute. A series of trucks passed, then there was a break. The nearest vehicles were coming from the east, about two miles off.

Decker and Tom moved quickly, and as they reached the small rise on which the road was built, it seemed they would have no trouble getting across in time. Inexplicably, halfway up the rise, Decker felt a stabbing pain and a tug at his leg. Looking down, he realized he had caught his pant leg on some barbed-wire fencing. He tried to pull free but the barbs dug into his leg and he fell, catching his other leg in the same tangled mass.

Tom had already stepped into the road when he heard Decker call out. He hurried back to help, but as the seconds passed, they were forced to reassess the situation. The next group of vehicles was getting too close. Their only option seemed to be to lie flat and still and hope the slight rise of the road would conceal them from the headlights of the passing vehicles.

Neither one breathing, Tom lay next to Decker on his stomach. The vehicles inched closer, moving much slower than they had first thought. Had they seen Tom on the road? As the first truck passed, Tom suddenly moved, and before Decker could stop him, he ran into the road, shouting and waving his arms. *It's over*, Decker thought.

The next truck stopped a few yards from Tom. From the back of the first truck jumped men in uniforms, carrying rifles. They surrounded Tom, their weapons pointing at him in the glow of the second truck's headlights. Another group quickly encircled Decker. Slowly he rolled to his back and looked up at the men. Each wore a light-blue helmet with large white letters and an emblem of olive leaves surrounding a globe. The same emblem, which Tom had seen on the first truck, was emblazoned on the flags that flew from the antennas and was painted on the door of each of the vehicles. Decker recognized it. They were from UNIFIL, the United Nations Interim Force in Lebanon.

* * * * *

United Nations Interim Force in Lebanon (UNIFIL)

As the convoy entered a fenced compound, one truck pulled aside and stopped in front of the mess hall, where it was met by the UN commander. "I got the call you were coming," the Swedish UN colonel told Tom and Decker as some soldiers helped them from the back of the truck. "Let's get you something to eat, then you can call home."

But before they could move, a Humvee from the convoy pulled up beside them.

"Hold up there, Colonel," said the Humvee's passenger, a British man in his mid fifties. "I'd like to meet these lads."

"Ambassador Jon Hansen, this is Decker Hawthorne and Tom Donafin of *NewsWorld*," the Colonel said. "Though I've not yet established which is which."

"I'm Hawthorne," Decker offered along with his hand as the ambassador exited the vehicle. "This is Tom Donafin." The ambassador was well built and over six feet tall with blonde hair, the kind of man others assume is a natural leader.

"A distinct pleasure," the ambassador said. Then motioning to another man who joined them, added, "This is my aide."

"Jack Redmond" the aide said in a heavy Cajun accent.

"Ambassador Hansen is here on a fact finding mission," the Swedish colonel explained. "It was his convoy you stopped. That's why the men responded as they did — they thought you might be Hezbollah."

"So how is it you came across our convoy?" Hansen asked.

"Sheer luck, sir" Decked replied. "We were just in the right place at the right time. We escaped three days ago and have been heading south ever since."

"Luck is a good thing to have on your side," Jack Redmond interjected. "From the looks of it, I'd say you were due for some."

"I'll send a detachment to take them to Israel tomorrow," the colonel volunteered.

"Nonsense," Hansen contradicted. "I'm going there myself in the morning." Then turning to Tom and Decker, he asserted, "You'll ride with me."

The ambassador's aide, understanding Hansen's intent, stepped away to make a call on a satellite phone.

"But, Sir," the Swede advised, "You're scheduled—"

"Didn't I mention, Frank?" Hansen interrupted. "There was a change of plans." Then to Tom and Decker, he concluded, "Now go get something to eat."

As Tom, Decker and the UN Colonel at last entered the mess hall, Ambassador Hansen turned to look for Jack Redmond, who was walking toward him as he talked on his phone.

"Hold on a moment," he told the person on the other end of the call.

"Jack, I want you to—" Hansen began.

"—have Jackie call the media to let them know you'll be bringing two escaped American hostages with you to Israel."

Hansen nodded to indicate that his aide had assumed correctly.

"About noon, sir?"

Hansen nodded again.

"Noon, Jackie," Redmond said.

It was just after one o'clock in the morning on the east coast of the U.S. when the phone rang. Only partially roused from sleep, Elizabeth Hawthorne picked up the phone. "Hello," she mumbled, her eyes still closed.

Decker listened to the sleepy, sweet sound of her voice. "Hi, babe. It's me," he said as tears began to roll down his cheeks.

Elizabeth quickly sat up in bed. "Decker?!"

He could barely breathe as he answered, "Yes, it's me."

"Where are you?" she pled. "Are you all right?"

"I'm in Lebanon at a United Nations post. Tom's with me. We're both okay. We escaped."

"Thank God!" she cried. "Thank God!"

"They'll be taking us to Israel to a hospital for a checkup and observation. Can you come right away?"

"Yes! Of course!" she said as she wiped her tears.

"How are Hope and Louisa?"

"They're fine, fine. They won't believe me when I tell them you called. They'll say I was dreaming. I'm not dreaming, am I?"

"No," he answered, reassuringly, "You're not dreaming."

"Do you want to talk to them?" she asked. Her voice was excited and hurried. Her mind raced. She wanted to ask everything, say everything, do everything all at once.

"No, don't wake them. I'll call once we get to the hospital. Just tell them I love them. Okay?"

"Of course," she said. And then it occurred to her that she didn't know where he was going in Israel. "Where will you be? What hospital?"

"I'm sorry, babe. I don't have any details, but I didn't want to wait to call you."

"No. No. That's okay," she said and then thought for a moment. "The girls and I will be on the next plane. If we leave before you reach the hospital, call Joshua and Ilana and let them know where you'll be. When we arrive I'll call them for the message."

"Joshua and Ilana?" Decker asked, surprised at the apparent familiarity. "You mean the Rosens?"

"Of course, Decker. They've been a great help and support while you've been gone. They're such wonderful people. Here's their number."

Decker took down the number. "I've got to go now," he said and then paused to be sure she would hear him. "I love you," he said softly but clearly.

"I love you!" she answered.

* * * * *

In the morning, Tom and Decker — dressed in UN camos — joined Ambassador Hansen and Jack Redmond for the trip to the Israeli border and from there, to the hospital in Tel Aviv. The drive provided Hansen an opportunity to question the circumstances leading up to their kidnapping, and for Tom and Decker a chance to catch up on world events. "So you're the lads who were there when the Wailing Wall was destroyed. That was a tragic but amazing photo you got just as the bombs went off."

Tom nodded appreciatively. "Thanks."

"That event triggered our current problems," Hansen said. "A week later, a group of Israelis blew up the Dome of the Rock. We almost had all-out war. After a while, it calmed down a bit and then three months ago the new prime minister announced that Israel would begin building a new Temple where the Dome had been.

The Muslims are furious. That's why I'm here now. We're doing what we can, but war could come at any time."

"Can I quote you on that?" Decker asked.

"Only if you'd like to get out and walk the rest of the way," Hansen replied with a grin.

"We're approaching the border, Sir," Jack Redmond advised.

"I hope you don't mind," Hansen said. "Jack took the liberty of sharing the good news of your escape with our friends in the press."

"Wave to the cameras, boys," Redmond directed as they passed slowly through the boarder crossing.

There were more reporters at the hospital in Tel Aviv. Hansen handled questions from the press himself in order to 'take the burden off the boys,' as Jack Redmond explained it, but agreed to allow a few pictures, curiously managing to figure prominently in each. Neither Tom nor Decker really minded. They liked Hansen. But he was a politician; getting publicity was part of his job. They were just happy to be free.

When they had checked in, Decker phoned the Rosens. Feeling a bit of his old humor, he decided to be a little playful. "Joshua," he said as though nothing unusual had happened, "this is Decker. So where have you been lately? I haven't seen you around."

"That'll do you no good, Decker Hawthorne," Joshua answered. "I know all about you and Tom. Elizabeth called us as soon as she made her plane reservations to tell us the good news. Besides, you've been on the news all day."

Decker laughed warmly. "When will she get in?"

"Just a second. Ilana!" Joshua called to his wife. "Decker's on the phone. What time did Elizabeth say her plane would be arriving?"

Ilana took advantage of her husband's poor memory for such things, and took the phone away from him. "Hello, Decker," she said. "Welcome home! We've prayed for you constantly."

"Thanks, Ilana. It's good to be home," he answered, by which he meant anywhere away from Lebanon.

"I saw you and Tom on TV," she said. "You're skin and bones."

"Yeah, well, we didn't care for the menu."

"You know, I make some of the best chicken soup."

"Tell him about Elizabeth, already," Decker heard Joshua saying in the background.

"Oh, yes. Elizabeth's plane will be here tomorrow at 3:36 P.M. Don't you worry about a thing. Joshua and I will pick up her and the children at the airport and bring them to the hospital. If you'd like," she added, "I'll bring you some of my chicken soup. I've heard the hospital food is atrocious."

Decker appreciated their kindness. "That sounds great, Ilana."

Decker next called the Washington office of *NewsWorld* and asked to speak to his editor, Fred Wattenburg. He was all ready to say, "Hi, Fred. This is Decker. Any calls for me?" when the switchboard operator said that Tom Wattenburg had retired and that his replacement was Hank Asher.

"Hank," Decker said when Asher came to the phone, "you mean they promoted you ahead of me?"

"Well, if you'd show up for work once in a while," Asher growled. "And by the way, I've got a bone to pick with you. I get up this morning and what do I see? Your ugly mug on the *Today Show*. You guys called NBC but you didn't notify your own magazine!"

"Hey, we didn't have anything to do with that," Decker said in his defense. "But no kidding? The *Today Show*?"

"Yeah; seems like everywhere else, too," Asher said, trying to sound disgusted. "But at least they mentioned you guys work here."

Actually the publicity for *NewsWorld* was great and would certainly boost sales for the edition Asher had planned for Tom and Decker's 'first-person' article on their lives as hostages.

Tel Aviv

The next morning as he shaved and brushed his teeth, Decker studied his face in the mirror. He had accepted his skeletal appearance, but now he was thinking of Elizabeth. How would she react? The important thing was that they were together; in a year or two he'd be back to normal physically. It was best to concentrate on the positive. What would never be "back to normal" was the way he felt about her. The bittersweet truth was that in his isolation he had come to love her in a way he otherwise never could have.

Because of her flight, Elizabeth probably hadn't seen him on television, so when she walked in the door of the hospital in a few hours, she would be seeing him in his emaciated condition for the first time. As he finished brushing his teeth, he noticed a box of sterile cotton balls and was struck by one of those crazy ideas that sometimes hit him. Experimenting, he stuffed a few pieces of cotton in his cheeks to see if it would make his face look fuller. It had worked for Marlon Brando in *The Godfather*. Looking in the mirror, he frowned and shook his head. He looked like he had mumps.

One thing was certain, though. He didn't want to be wearing a hospital gown when Elizabeth arrived. He tried to charm a nurse into doing some shopping for him, but to no avail, and none of the local stores he found on the Internet would guarantee delivery so quickly. Then he thought of Hansen. He called the British Embassy, and this time he was in luck. Ambassador Hansen sent over two aides and a local tailor, who measured Decker and Tom for suits. The aides did some quick shopping at Polgat's on Ramat Alenby, an outlet of fine men's clothes, and brought the suits to the hospital. On the spot, the tailor set up a sewing machine, hemmed the slacks, and put in a few temporary stitches to improve the fit.

When Elizabeth arrived with the girls and the Rosens, Decker and Tom were sitting in the hospital lobby sipping tea and reading the English edition of the *Jerusalem Post*. They looked like transplants from a fancy gentlemen's club. The act worked fine until Elizabeth's and Decker's eyes met. Then it was all tears, hugs, and kisses. Despite the suit, Elizabeth immediately realized the seriousness of Decker's condition as she put her arms around him. She could count his ribs even through the fabric.

Ilana Rosen put down her thermos of chicken soup and hugged Tom. Hope and Louisa jointly hugged their dad. Somehow the hugs merged and evolved into a mass. Even Scott Rosen, who had come along with his parents, joined in.

After a few moments they sat down to talk and Ilana poured soup for Tom and Decker. Elizabeth sat beside Decker and they held hands as they all talked about all that had happened over the last three years. On the other side of Decker, Hope and Louisa took turns sitting next to their father. Decker was amazed at how much his daughters had changed. Hope was now sixteen and Louisa eleven. He was pleased at how much they both looked like their mother. He had missed so much of their lives.

Joshua and Ilana introduced Tom and Decker to their son, Scott, a brawny, 260-pound, six-foot-three-inch Orthodox Jew with thick black curly hair and beard. The Rosen family had grown closer over the past three years.

Everyone wanted to know how Tom and Decker had escaped and what had happened during their captivity. Neither mentioned Decker's strange dream — it was silly and not worth the time to explain — and the subject soon turned to how they had become hostages in Lebanon in the first place. Until that moment no one realized they had actually been abducted in Israel and smuggled over the border. Everyone had assumed they had gone into Lebanon to pursue some story and were taken hostage while there.

"You had a lead on who destroyed the Wall?" Scott Rosen erupted. "Have you told the police?"

"That was three years ago," Tom countered.

Scott was dumbfounded and shook his head as he rose to his feet.

"Maybe you're right," Decker admitted, trying to make peace. "Tom and I will file a report later today."

But the concession wasn't enough. "I'm going to call the police myself!" Scott said as he stormed away.

Ilana Rosen, who had been getting more embarrassed by the minute, apologized for her son. "I'm really sorry," she said. "When the Palestinians destroyed the Western Wall, Scott went crazy with rage. He wanted to put every Palestinian in Israel on trial."

"He wanted to do much worse than that," Joshua interrupted, earning himself a firm pinch on the leg from Ilana. Despite the pinch — or more likely to spite it — he continued. "If he hadn't been with us at the very time it happened, I might believe he was one of those who attacked the Dome of the Rock."

"Yeah, we heard about the Dome," said Tom.

"Did *NewsWorld* have a team here to cover it?" Decker asked.

"Oh, Daddy!" Hope groaned in recognition of the triviality of his question.

"It was terrible here for many months." Ilana said. "We've been in Israel for some of the worst, but you cannot imagine all the fires and suicide bombings. Security was unbelievable. I couldn't even go from our house to the market without going through checkpoints."

"Things settled down a bit with time," Joshua said. "The Muslims demanded to rebuild the Mosque; many Jews wanted to rebuild the Temple. For two and a half years the area remained roped off. Then three months ago, after Moshe Greenberg became prime minister—"

"Prime minister?" Decker interrupted. "That radical?"

"Nowadays he's considered somewhat of a moderate," Joshua explained. "That's less because he's changed and more that the mood of the country has swung so far as a result of the continuing threats of war. But as I was saying, Greenberg announced that Israel would immediately begin rebuilding the Temple."

"I'm surprised the Muslims haven't already declared war," Tom said.

"They never cease their war with us," Joshua replied. "But since they've never been able to win an all out war with Israel, they prefer terrorist actions. I don't mean to minimize the danger of war. Even now the Syrians and Egyptians have troops amassed near our mutual borders, and there are always rumors about some huge terrorist attack being planned."

"What about the Temple?" Tom asked.

"It's a massive undertaking," Joshua replied. "They removed all the stones from the remains of the Western Wall and from the old steps that had been excavated. They'll use what they can and the rest will be put in a museum or something. They dug out the tunnels, but found only minor artifacts."

"I guess that supports your theory that the Knights Templar took everything," Tom said. "So, how long before it's finished?"

"The completion date is set for four years from now. Assuming of course, that we don't go to war—"

"Enough news and politics, already," Ilana interrupted as she gave her husband's leg another pinch. "Maybe Elizabeth would like to say something."

Joshua thought hard for a second. "Oh, um, yes, of course," Joshua agreed, as though he suddenly recalled his part in some conspiracy with Ilana and Elizabeth. "Maybe Elizabeth has . . . uh . . . something to say."

"Go ahead, dear," Ilana said, urging her on. Decker listened intently.

"Decker, while you were gone, you know that Hope and Louisa and I spent a lot of time with Joshua and Ilana. They were a great support to us. I don't think we could have made it through all this without them. And, well, I just wanted to tell you that while you were away, I, that is to say, the girls and I— "

At that moment Scott Rosen returned, flanked by two plainclothes detectives who wanted the address of the house where Tom and Decker had been taken hostage and complete descriptions of anyone they saw. Elizabeth's revelation would have to wait.

It was two hours before the police were satisfied they had all the information Tom and Decker could give them. Scott Rosen followed the police back to the station to tell them how to do their jobs. Joshua and Ilana took Hope and Louisa to get something to eat, and Tom fell asleep on a couch. Decker and Elizabeth were finally alone.

"I missed you so much," Decker said softly, as he held his wife close.

"I missed you," she replied.

"I never knew how much you meant to me until I didn't have you. I thought of you every hour," he said.

"Constantly," she affirmed.

As the evening waned, the couple went outside and sat under the stars. Elizabeth listened quietly, holding her husband's gaunt body to her as he recited the poetry he had composed for her over the past three years.

Two days later, Decker was told he would be released from the hospital the following morning. It was nearing Rosh Hashanah, the Jewish New Year, and the hospital wanted to reduce their occupancy as much as possible before the High Holy Days. Tom, however, had developed serious problems with his back and kidneys while in captivity and was to remain for continued treatment and additional tests. That night Decker was able to leave the hospital for dinner, so he and Elizabeth shared a romantic candlelit meal in old Jaffa.

They finished their meal, then stayed at the table to talk. They didn't speak of their time apart but rather of good times they had spent together in years past. As Elizabeth spoke, Decker looked across the table admiringly at his wife, watching her every move. Elizabeth noticed the attention with no small amount of enjoyment.

"Decker," she whispered in feigned embarrassment, "you look like you're undressing me with your eyes."

"Oh," he responded with a smile and a gleam, "I'm way past that." He was feeling much better.

"Elizabeth," Decker said, "I know I've said many times that I never really felt there was any one place I could call home; I've lived so many places." He reached across the small table and placed his left hand over hers. With his right hand, he softly ran the back of his fingers along the soft curve of her face.

"Over the last three years I decided that if I ever got home to you, then that's where home would be. When we get back to Maryland, we're going to make that home, whatever that means and whatever that takes."

Tears came to Elizabeth's eyes. Having Decker back had kept her emotions at a fever pitch since he first called her from the UN outpost. It had been a constant struggle not to cry. Now, the intensity of Decker's feelings nudged her gently over the edge, and she wept.

Derwood, Maryland

The Hawthorne family arrived at Dulles Airport outside Washington, DC early in the morning and were surprised to find a limousine waiting to pick them up — courtesy of Hank Asher. For the next three days Decker, Elizabeth, Hope, and Louisa spent time getting to know each other again. They bought jumbo steamed blue crabs at Vinnie's Seafood and went to a small park they knew at one of the C&O canal locks. They stayed around the house and just talked. They cooked steaks on the grill. They went shopping. They drove around town so Decker could get reacquainted. They did whatever they wanted to do.

At about noon on the third day the phone rang and Decker answered it. The voice was familiar, but it was totally unexpected. It was Professor Goodman.

"Decker, we need to talk," Goodman said with what seemed a bit of self-important urgency.

"Uh, sure, Professor," Decker replied. "I want to follow up on that story we talked about, anyway. How about in a month or so?" After three years as a hostage, even the "biggest story since Columbus discovered America" could wait a few more weeks.

"Not soon enough." Goodman's voice gave no indication he was even aware that Decker had been gone.

"Sorry," Decker responded, void of sincerity. "I just got back from three years in a small cell in Lebanon and I thought I'd take it easy for awhile."

"I know all about that," Goodman said. "But you don't have to go anywhere. Martha and I are in Washington. In fact, we're here in Derwood, at the German restaurant two blocks from your house."

"What? What are you doing here?" Decker winced.

"I came for a scientific conference. Martha had never seen Washington and insisted on coming along. Christopher is staying with a friend from school. So can we come over or not?"

Decker quickly talked it over with Elizabeth and they reluctantly agreed to have the Goodmans come over, although Decker insisted that the professor promise it would take no more than an hour. They arrived in just minutes. Elizabeth had never met Martha Goodman and both women felt a little uncomfortable — Mrs. Goodman for imposing, and Elizabeth for being imposed upon. Professor Goodman made it clear that the subject of the conversation was for Decker's ears only, so Elizabeth suggested that Mrs. Goodman go for a walk with her and the girls.

As soon as they left, Goodman began.

"I really am sorry to barge in on you, Decker, but it isn't really for my benefit that I'm here. There are a thousand other reporters who would love to get an exclusive on what I'm about to tell you."

"Of course," Decker allowed. "It's just that I really need to spend time with my family."

"I understand. But what I'm about to tell you will change the world forever."

Decker's once overpowering curiosity had lain dormant for nearly three years. Deep inside he felt it stir again. A little.

"First of all, you remember that the last time we talked, we discussed the methodology I used for creating the viral cancer antibodies, and I told you that it would probably work on other viral strains. Well, that work has continued with some outstanding results. But as important as that is, I realized that all I could ever hope to accomplish with that methodology was to use the C-cells as an agent for producing antibodies. That's little more than running a pill factory. Even if I could cure cancer or AIDS or even something as complicated as Lyme Disease, it was still such a waste of potential. What I really wanted to do was to figure out some way of altering the cells of living people to enhance their own immune system.

"For a long time it just ate at me. How could I ever hope to alter the genetic structure of every cell in the human body? You can make changes to a few cells in a laboratory; with C-cells it's even possible, as we both know, to create a totally immune individual like Christopher. But how do you give that immunity to someone else like you or me? That had me stumped."

Decker listened quietly, nodding when appropriate. Goodman was going to tell his story the way he wanted to tell it.

"Then I had an idea. Decker, do you know how the AIDS virus works?" Decker thought he had a pretty good idea, but before he could answer, Goodman continued. "All around the outside of the AIDS virus are tiny spikes made of glycoproteins. These spikes are imbedded in a fatty envelope that forms the outer shell of the virus. Inside this envelope are RNA strands, each with a quantity of reverse-

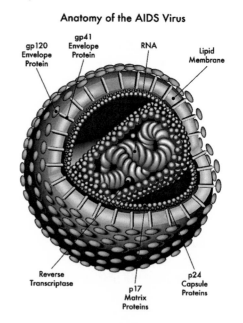

Anatomy of the AIDS Virus

gp120 Envelope Protein

gp41 Envelope Protein

RNA

Lipid Membrane

Reverse Transcriptase

p17 Matrix Proteins

p24 Capsule Proteins

transcriptase enzyme. The spikes bind the AIDS cells to healthy cells of the immune system, called T-cells, by establishing an attractive link with certain receptor molecules that occur naturally on the healthy T-cells. The infection occurs when the virus is absorbed into the interior of the healthy cell where each individual strand of RNA in the virus is converted into a complementary strand of DNA by the reverse-transcriptase enzyme. Enzymes that occur naturally in the cell duplicate the DNA strand, which then enters into the nucleus of the cell. That strand then becomes a permanent part of the heredity of that cell!" Goodman paused for Decker's reaction.

"Okay, so then what?" He had understood most of Goodman's explanation but failed to comprehend the significance.

"Don't you see? The AIDS virus is able to alter the genetic structure of living cells and it does it inside the body!"

Suddenly Decker realized what Goodman was getting at. "You remove the harmful genetic material from the nucleus of the AIDS virus—" he said.

"—and replace it with the specific immunity-providing DNA strands from the C-cells," Goodman said, finishing Decker's sentence. "Except, of course, viral cells don't have a nucleus; they have a simple core." Goodman — ever the professor — couldn't allow Decker's error to pass uncorrected, no matter how insignificant to the main topic. "That way it's not necessary to alter every individual cell of the body. We can accomplish the same result just by altering the T-cells!"

"And that result is . . ." Decker urged.

"Total immunity! Maybe even reversing the aging process! Life expectancies of hundreds of years!" Goodman's voice had grown as excited as he dared risk without sacrificing the appearance of appropriate scientific aloofness.

"So when can you begin to move beyond theory on this?"

"I already have!" Goodman answered. "I've created of an extremely resilient second-generation test strain. Of course, I'm still experimenting to isolate the specific DNA strands in the C-cells that are needed for transplant into the carrier virus.

"But think of it, Decker. It once looked like AIDS could be as bad as the Black Plague. And now, it may — combined with the C-cells — enable virtual immortality!"

By the time Decker and Goodman finished their conversation, Elizabeth, Mrs. Goodman, Hope, and Louisa had returned from their walk and retreated to the patio. They had talked long enough to find that they liked each other's company. After the Goodmans left, Elizabeth told Decker how much she had enjoyed talking with Martha and that Martha had invited her to come visit next time Decker went to Los Angeles.

"I'm glad you two hit it off," Decker said, pleased that his wife was pleased. "She really is a nice person. And as far as you coming along, I'd love that. So what did you talk about?"

"Mostly we talked about you and how wonderful it is to have you back. But, let's see . . . We talked about Professor Goodman. Did you know he's been notified that in December he's going to receive the Nobel Prize for medicine for his cancer research?"

"You're kidding!" Decker said. "He didn't even mention it."

"That's why they were here in Washington. He was invited to address the annual convention of the American Cancer Society."

"I can see I've got a lot of catching up to do."

"And, she told me all about her grandnephew, Christopher. She's very proud of him. He's apparently a very precocious child. Oh, and this is kind of strange: Martha said that two weeks ago she and Professor Goodman were talking about you. He had this important story — I guess whatever he came over to tell you about today — and apparently he was reluctant to give it to another reporter even though at the time you were still being held hostage. But — and this is the strange part — as they were talking about it, Christopher, came over and just sort of matter-of-factly told Professor Goodman he should wait because you'd be free soon. She asked him about it later and he said he wasn't sure how he knew; he just had a feeling."

Chapter 10

Disaster

A light rain began to fall and Decker found himself running, awkwardly making his way through tall grass and trying to avoid the thistles and wild blackberry bushes. Home and safety from the impending storm were just over the next hill. In his urgency, he paid no attention to the odd feeling of being in a small body not yet eight years old.

The storm clouds had gathered quickly and for a while it seemed they might disappear the same way. But as the rain began to fall, the promise of a cloudburst of Noahic proportions seemed to declare itself with the first sudden clap of distant thunder.

As he ran, Decker's nerves twitched with the fear of the somehow inevitable events he knew were about to befall him. It seemed . . . it seemed he had done this all before. There was something in his path — something to fear. But what?

Suddenly the earth disappeared from beneath his feet.

Decker's hands flew up above his head as he grabbed at the moist thick air, trying desperately, instinctively, to slow his descent. Just as suddenly, he felt the earth again as he slammed into a wall of dirt and slipped down a rough incline that threatened to swallow him. The blow knocked the wind out of him, and before he could catch his breath, a sudden sharp pain surged through him as dozens of sharp protrusions scraped against his body, tearing his shirt and pulling it up over his head. His hands, still grasping, caught a tangled mass of small fibers that quickly slipped away but were replaced by one more solid and firm. Stunned, he hung there motionless.

Moments passed as he caught his breath, then began to carefully pull himself upward, hoping his hold wouldn't fail under the strain. Raising himself a few inches, he worked his shirt back down over his head and shoulders. Now able to survey his condition, he found he was holding onto a tree root about an inch in diameter. Near tears, he slowly turned, looked down, and realized his imagination had not exaggerated the danger. Below him the hole continued for about thirty feet and then narrowed and veered off.

He closed his eyes and rested his face against the dirt and rock and thought of the previous summer when he had first heard of such holes. He and his cousin Bobby had been riding two of his uncle's mules in the field north of the milk barn. Bobby brought him to a spot in the field where an old hay wagon had been left sitting long enough for the grass and the purple-flowered thistles to grow up around it. Bobby, who had been riding bareback, lifted his leg and slid off the side of the mule.

"C'mon," he said as he tied the twine of the mule's homemade reins through a rusted iron eye on the wagon. There was a sense of adventure in his voice and Decker was quick to follow.

"Be careful, now," Bobby cautioned as he began to inch his way slowly toward the edge of a hole in the ground on the other side of the wagon. Decker followed Bobby's lead and was soon standing on the precipice looking down.

"Man, that's deep," Decker said. "What is it?"

"A sink hole," Bobby answered.

"A what?"

"A sink hole. It goes on forever," Bobby said authoritatively.

"Aw, that's crazy," Decker responded. "I can see the bottom."

"That's not the bottom, it's just where it turns off in another direction." Bobby gave a slight tug to Decker's shirt and the pair moved to the other side of the hole.

"See down there," Bobby said as he pointed to what had appeared to be the bottom of the shaft. Decker couldn't tell how far it went, but he could see that the shaft continued off in the other direction. He squatted down to get a better look, but there simply wasn't enough light to see any farther.

"Where'd it come from?" Decker asked.

"Whadda ya mean, where'd it come from? Ya think we dug it or sumthin?" Decker gave Bobby a dirty look and Bobby, deciding this was not the place to pick a fight, continued. "They just show up. One day it's flat ground and then the next day there's a sink hole. That's why they call 'em sink holes, I guess."

Decker tried again to get a better look and then an idea struck him. "Let's get a rope and climb down and explore it!"

"Are you nuts?"

"C'mon! We can get a real long rope. Or even better, we can find some flashlights and get that roll of bailing twine in the barn.

We can tie the twine to one of the mules and ease ourselves down. I've seen 'em do stuff like that on television a bunch of times."

"Man, you are nuts! My dad told me about three guys who went down in a sink hole over in Moore County. They never came back up, and two months later they found their bodies in the Duck River!"

Decker looked at Bobby, trying to figure whether he was making this up. Bobby continued, "I told ya, these things don't have no bottoms!"

Just then they saw Bobby's dad stomping through the tall grass toward them. He was mad. "Bobby!" he called out, "What in the Sam Hill are you doin' out here? You wanna fall in there and get yourself killed? You get away from that hole right now or I'm gonna beat the livin' tar outta both of ya!" The boys ran as quickly as they could to the mules. All the commotion gave Decker the clear impression that Bobby hadn't been kidding about the danger.

The rain fell harder now and the dirt under Decker's face had turned to mud. His hands were numb, locked around the root, his clothes were soaked, his stomach was scraped and bleeding, and he was cold. He tried calling for help but gave up as his voice grew hoarse. He was only a few feet below the surface, but there was no way to pull himself any farther up. He tried to think of this as an adventure; he'd get out somehow and then he could tell the kids at school about it. Maybe he'd get a lot of sympathy from his mom and she'd let him skip school tomorrow — if he were still alive. He imagined the headline of the *Times Gazette* reporting his death. He thought about taking off his belt and somehow using it as a rope to pull himself out. *That would make a great story*, he thought as he saw the headline change. But there was nothing to tie it to. And anyway, he wasn't about to let go with one hand to try to take off his belt.

For an hour or more he hung there on the muddy slope, holding to the root. The rain had almost stopped, but the sky was beginning to grow dark with the night. That's when he heard the voices of his mother and older brother, Nathan. They were calling him and they were getting closer. He called out — not for help, but to warn them.

"Stay back, Mom! There's a sink hole."

But of course she didn't stay back. In a moment he saw her terrified face peering down over the ridge of the hole. She had crawled on her hands and knees to the side and was holding back tears as she looked down at him clinging to the root about three feet below the surface. She struggled to think clearly. She looked at his fingers. They seemed so tiny. The blood had long since drained from them, and they were white and wrinkled from the rain. Lying flat on her stomach, she reached down, stretching, sliding a little farther, a little farther, knowing full well that the ground under her could give way at any second, sending both of them to a muddy grave. In a last attempt to gain the extra inch she needed, she held her breath, flattened herself against the ground, and dug the toes of her shoes into the soft dirt as Nathan held her feet to keep her from sliding in.

"Just hold on, honey. I'll have you out of there in just a minute," she said in her bravest, most reassuring, voice.

Decker watched as her fingers grasped his right wrist. It was already far too numb to feel her grip. When she was sure of her hold, she began to pull him upward. She lifted him several inches, surprised at her own strength, while Decker did his best to try to climb with his feet against the muddy slope. "Let go of the root now, honey," she said, "I've got you."

But Decker couldn't let go.

The grip that had held him just out of the reach of death's jaw now refused to release its hold. His hands were numb, locked together, fingers intertwined, and he could not make them move. His mother pulled harder.

"I can't let go! Mommy, I can't make my hands let go," he said, only now beginning to cry.

"It's okay, Mommy's got you and she won't let go." She pulled. With all of her strength and love, she pulled. And then suddenly, she stopped.

Decker sat bolt upright in his bed.

It was a dream.

It had really happened, just that way, but that was years ago.

Still, inexplicably, he felt his mother's tight grip on his right arm. He tried to move it, but it hurt and it was heavy. Groggy, he looked and realized what was happening.

"Elizabeth, wake up. Let go of my arm," he said. "Come on, babe. You've been having some kind of weird dream or something." He mused briefly at the irony that *he* would be telling her *she* was having a weird dream. Finally freeing himself, he shook his arm to get the blood flowing again.

But something wasn't right. Elizabeth was a light sleeper.

"Elizabeth!" he called sharply. There was no response. He shook her, but she wouldn't wake up. Suddenly a horrible thought hit him and he grabbed her wrist.

There was no pulse.

He checked for a pulse in her carotid artery. There was none. He listened for a heartbeat, but there was nothing. His own heart pounded in terror. He tried to understand what was happening.

CPR, he thought suddenly. *Her body's still warm. It must have just happened. Got to try CPR.* He pulled the covers from her lifeless body. It had been years since he had taken a class in CPR; he prayed he remembered how. *One hand on top of the other on the middle of the chest. Wait! Is it just above where the ribs come together or just below? Just above!* he thought. He began to apply pressure, but her body sank with the mattress. Quickly, he grabbed her arms and pulled her to the floor.

He tried again. Much better. "Oh, God!" he said out loud. *I forgot to check her mouth.* He looked but it was too dark to see. He probed with his fingers. There was nothing. "God, help me!" he cried.

Quickly he blew two full breaths into her lungs and went back to his position above her, pressing with his palms against the middle of her lower rib cage. "One, two, three, four, five," he counted under his breath, and then blew air into her lungs again. "One, two, three, four, five." He repeated. "Don't die . . . Elizabeth, please don't die," he sobbed. *Got to call an ambulance. Just a few more.* "One, two, three, four, five."

He ran and grabbed the phone from the nightstand by the bed. His hands were shaking and he struggled to dial 911. Pressing the speaker button, he began again. "One, two, three, four, five." The line was busy. He hung up and pressed redial. Busy. *How can it be busy?* "God, help me!" he said again.

Five minutes. "One, two, three, four, five." Again, and again. "Please, babe. Please wake up! God, please, let her wake up!" Ten minutes. But there was still nothing.

Wondering how long he could last in his weakened state, his lungs ached for air and the sweat poured from his body as he continued CPR for another thirty minutes, pausing only to try the phone again. Finally it rang. Over and over it rang. Could he have dialed wrong? Now that it was ringing did he dare hang up? No, no! How could he have dialed 911 wrong? If he hadn't dialed right it wouldn't be ringing. In his state of panic, anything was possible. He hung up and dialed again. It was busy.

Almost an hour had passed when at last he could no longer deny the truth. Elizabeth's body was growing cold. She was dead.

Panting and exhausted, Decker collapsed on the floor beside her and wept. The thought of losing her now, now that he so truly loved her, was more than his heart and sanity could bear. Outside their window the sun was rising just as it did on every other morning. Elizabeth always loved the sunrise. The clock-radio came on, and an announcer's voice started in mid-sentence, but Decker didn't hear it. He heard the noise, but that's all it was. Tears streaked his face, but he didn't wipe his eyes. If all he had to offer his beloved was his tears, he would leave them where they lay.

Soon Hope and Louisa would wake up. How could he tell them what had happened? For their sake he knew he must be strong. Lovingly, he picked up Elizabeth's body and moved her back to the bed. He pulled the covers up, tucking the blanket in gently around her. Only now did the radio announcer's words begin to pierce the grief that encircled him.

"Reports continue to come in from all around the world," the announcer's voice cracked painfully. "Thousands, hundreds of thousands, maybe more, are reported dead in what is undoubtedly the worst single disaster in human history. The deaths seem to have occurred almost simultaneously in all parts of the world. So far, no one has any idea why this has happened."

The words were distant at first, seemingly unrelated to his own grief. But, what was he saying?

Thousands dead? How could that happen? Radiation? Plague? Poison gas? Was this what killed Elizabeth? But why would it kill only some and not others?

As if in answer, the announcer continued. "There is no apparent pattern to the deaths: black, white, Asian, all nationalities; men, women, children . . ."

"Children?" Decker repeated out loud. "NO!!!"

Decker ran from the bedroom. A moment passed and then a scream of anguish ascended the stairs, shaking the tiny particles of dust as they floated in the morning sunlight. But no one heard it. They were all dead. Decker was alone.

Hovering in the twilight of insanity, Decker stumbled up the half flight of stairs from Hope's bedroom to the living room and made his way to a chair.

Instinctively, his mind attempted to escape into the imagined refuge that had been his sanctum during the years of his captivity in Lebanon. But he found there no relief.

Even there he was alone. Even there his family was dead.

Upstairs in his bedroom, the voice of the radio announcer continued. "Everywhere there is terror, everywhere there is heartbreak. Never has the world faced such devastating loss. No war, no plague, no event in history can compare with the scale of this disaster. And no one can be certain it's over. Whatever has claimed the lives of so many, can it truly have struck so quickly and just as quickly be gone?

"In our studio three of my coworkers have died, one as he stood speaking with me little more than an hour ago. There was no warning. As long as I live, the scene of my coworker and friend simply stopping mid-sentence and collapsing to the floor will be etched in my memory. And as I recall that moment when death struck here and around the world, I cannot help but ask myself: Is it over? Will it strike again? Will this sentence, this word, this breath be my last? Will the same happen again to others, to me, as has happened to so many?

"Is this the end of the world?" he asked. "It's not an unreasonable question.

"Is this some deadly plague? Or is it something more insidious? An act of unmatched terrorism? A crowning achievement in the endless parade of man's inhumanity to man?

"Tens of millions, according to some estimates, lay dead around the world. Dozens of commercial airplanes are reported to have crashed into hillsides or fields or cities. There are reports of nuclear power plants teetering on the edge of meltdown as surviving technicians rush to fill in for those who died at their stations. In Brazil and Argentina, where it's mid-morning, carnage covers the roadways. Cars driven by victims of the disaster sped helter-skelter, careening into other vehicles and pedestrians. Some who survived the initial disaster have been forced to leave their dead behind as they evacuate neighborhoods around overturned train cars spilling out streams of chemicals.

"World leaders are appealing for calm. People are being urged to stay in their homes. All forms of mass transportation are shut down. And many countries are responding by placing their military on high alert and restricting flyover rights to their own armed forces.

"No one knows what's happened, but we can't help but ask: Is this an unprecedented act of terror that's been in the works for decades? Or perhaps it's a response to Israel's construction of a new Temple in Jerusalem on the site where the mosque once stood. Clearly, if this disaster is the result of a terrorist action, they've gone beyond the destruction of a few buildings or the murder of the population of a single city, and we are now truly in a world war." The announcer paused, no longer able to hold back tears.

"At this moment all over the east coast of America and Canada, men and women are waking to find their loved ones dead. It's all so hard to comprehend, so difficult to imagine. In time zones to the west, where it's not yet dawn, many are sleeping soundly, unaware of what has befallen our planet. For some it will be hours before they wake to find their loved ones lying dead beside them."

South of Hanoi, Vietnam

Pedaling her heavily laden bicycle steadily along the unnamed road that runs north along the top of a dike on the floodplain of the Red River Delta, Le Thi Dao made good time on her way to the markets of Hanoi, twelve miles to the north. The handmade wicker baskets she carried were stacked tightly, then tied together in two large rings and hung on either side of her bike, giving an appearance, to someone from the West, that she was balancing two enormous bagels. Squinting to see better the strange sight before her, she stopped pedaling and let the bicycle coast. Ahead on the roadside, next to a grazing ox, a small patch of bright blue and red took on a familiar form. Lying on the ground, wearing her New

York Yankees baseball cap, was Vu Le Thanh Hoa, a friend from school. Her dead fingers still clutched the grazing ox's lead rope.

North of Akek Rot, Republic of South Sudan

Ahmed Mufti held his rifle to his chest as he waited quietly but eagerly for the signal. Just fourteen years old, this would be his first time to participate in an actual raiding party.

Eager for adventure and to prove himself a man, Ahmed had come south from his home in Matarak, Sudan with his father and uncle and the other men to raid the Dinka and Nuba villages of South Sudan for booty and slaves. So far, though, his father had made him stay behind during the actual raids. Officially, the government of Sudan in Khartoum opposed the practice of raiding and taking slaves from their southern neighbor, which until 2011 had been part of Sudan, but in reality, raids against the predominantly Christian population in the south were still encouraged as part of the policy of Islamization. And why should Khartoum condemn a practice that Mohammed himself had so often employed against non-Muslims throughout Arabia in order to enrich his followers?

Then came word from the party's scouts, who had come upon a group of about two hundred slaves held by a competing party near a huge mahogany tree. Stolen from their owners in Sudan and returned to South Sudan — not for rescue, but merely as merchandise — these captives would be sold back to their families and tribes or else to some humanitarian group intending to free them. The slaves were escorted by no more than ten armed men — few enough that Ahmed's father agreed to allow the boy to come along. Now as he waited for the signal to converge on the camp, he stayed low to the ground, filling the time with calculations of the number of Sudanese pounds that would be his share from the sale of two hundred slaves.

Finally the signal came, but it wasn't the one he expected. Knowing only to follow the lead of the other men, Ahmed moved slowly forward. In a moment, he came to where his uncle and three others from the party had stopped to look down at the bodies of two dead SPLA[24] soldiers. He had heard no gunshots or sounds of fighting and there was no blood. Before he could ask, another call came from the direction of the slave encampment.

With adrenaline rushing through his veins, Ahmed ran to catch up with the others, who were now charging the camp. At the clearing they all stopped short. The competing party was there, but there was no sign of battle. Unsure of what he should do, Ahmed stood between his father and uncle. He didn't understand what he saw, but he could see on the faces of the others that neither did they. Beneath the shade of the huge mahogany tree were two hundred slaves, just as the scouts had said, but nearly all of them were dead.

Lavaur, France

Albert Faure tugged at the reins, bringing his horse to a halt as he reached for his cell phone. "Faure," he answered crisply. The Andalusian stallion shook its abundant white mane and took advantage of the pause to graze on the clover at its feet.

"Something has happened," the caller said. It was Faure's secretary from his office at the Conseil Régional, the congress of the Midi-Pyrenees region of France. Faure was the region's youngest member of the Conseil and, according to many, one of the most ambitious.

Gerard Poupardin didn't know how to explain what had happened. "Do not keep me waiting, Gerard!" Faure demanded. "What is it?"

"Sir, it's difficult to . . . A little more than ninety minutes ago, millions of people all over the world suddenly died without any warning or known cause."

Faure tried to understand, but of course could not. There was the desire to believe he had simply misunderstood. "France?" he asked finally, not knowing where else to begin his questioning.

"There's really very little information available so far. I've heard an estimate of perhaps a quarter million dead, but I don't know how they can estimate such a thing."

Faure gasped.

"It does seem," Poupardin continued tenuously, "that France and much of Western Europe may have lost far fewer than some parts of the world. Estimates coming from the United Kingdom are more than a million."

"The United States?"

"It's still early morning there, sir. Based on what we know from their east coast, they seem to have been struck much worse than we."

"Is this some kind of biological warfare? Muslim terrorists?" Faure asked. It was an obvious question, but of course Poupardin couldn't answer it.

"Our borders and the borders of many other countries have been ordered sealed and the military reserves are being called to active service," Poupardin reported.

"Is it safe for me to return to the city?" Faure asked.

"I don't know, sir. No one is sure of anything. Nothing makes sense."

Faure thought for a moment.

"There is one other thing, sir." Poupardin paused. "The Conseil president is among those reported dead."

Faure thought on this bit of additional information and quickly considered how it might be used to his political advantage. Stroking his horse's neck, he scanned the Pyrenees Mountains, which mark France's southern border with Spain. "I'm coming in to the office," he said finally, and hung up.

Kerala, India

Dr. Jossy Sharma sat on the hood of his Mercedes, his laptop resting on his propped-up knees, as he typed notes for an article he was writing for the *Indian Journal of Ophthalmology*. He liked to come here to the Thattekkadu Bird Sanctuary to concentrate. Nestled among a forest of evergreens and home to indigenous and migratory birds, the sanctuary formed a quiet asylum from his busy office at St. Joseph's Hospital in Kothamangalam, twelve miles away. After several peaceful hours, Sharma felt satisfied with his progress on the article and decided to head home for supper.

As he got in the car, he noticed an urgent text message from the hospital. He was needed immediately. He cringed as he saw the message was now three hours old, but when he attempted to call, he was unable to reach anyone. Driving out of the sanctuary toward Kothamangalam, he had gone less than a mile when he came upon a two-car accident. Stopping to help, he was met by a bizarre scene. In addition to the two adult male drivers, the cars' passengers included three adult women and five children. Though everyone in both cars was wearing a seatbelt and the airbags had apparently functioned properly, all were dead. The damage to the vehicles was extensive, but the passenger compartments were basically intact. These people, he told himself, should have survived easily. Then he noticed something else. Though there were multiple lacerations on the victims, there was very little blood. It was as though when the accident occurred, they were already dead.

Again he tried to call the hospital, but with the same result. He stopped at two more accident scenes before finding anyone alive. A middle-aged woman, who had survived the crash, had pulled the lifeless body of her husband from the car and was sitting beside him on the side of the road. She had no serious injuries.

Continuing past six more accidents, Dr. Sharma sped to the top of a hill just outside the city. On the road ahead were more wrecked vehicles than he could count. Abandoning his car when the roads became impassible because of the wreckage, he walked the rest of the way. Passing bodies in the street, he arrived at the hospital only to find that thirty of the forty-two doctors were among the dead.

Four days later

Derwood, Maryland

Hank Asher locked his fingers together, forming a step for his young journalist intern to place her foot. Sheryl Stanford took the task in stride, climbing through the kitchen window they had just pried open. As she made her way to open the front door, she spotted Decker's pale, motionless form slumped in a chair in the living room. Hank Asher entered the house to the now familiar stench of rotting bodies, and at first assumed that Decker had been among the unlucky ones who had died four days earlier in the "Disaster," as it had come to be known.[25]

"He's alive. Sort of," Sheryl told her boss, as she tried to get Decker to drink some water. Decker stared blankly but swallowed eagerly as she put the cup to his mouth.

Asher surveyed the situation and decided she had things well in hand. "You stay here with Mr. Hawthorne. I'll check the house to see if anyone else is alive."

"You don't need to convince me," she answered. The smell of the house left no doubt what he would find.

Hank Asher hadn't known Elizabeth or the Hawthorne children, but his heart ached for his friend. When he returned from the bedrooms a few moments later he directed Sheryl to go around the rest of the house and open all the windows. "I'll see if I can find a shovel," he said.

Asher made no effort to try to revive Decker. Even if he *could* rouse him, it seemed the most humane thing was to allow his colleague to "sleep" through the awful tasks that needed to be done.

Sheryl opened the windows, then went back to the living room. In part this was to sit with Decker, but mostly it was to allow her to turn on the news. Without an answer for the cause of the Disaster and a solid assurance it would not be repeated, the anxiety was nearly debilitating. The only people who seemed to be unaffected were looters and opportunists who burglarized the homes and businesses of Disaster victims. The single reason Sheryl was out was that Hank Asher had come to her house to get her. Most businesses remained closed, but as Hank told her in no uncertain terms, that didn't include the news business. In a way, she respected his attitude of getting on with life; she just wished he hadn't involved her. Most of the *NewsWorld* staff assigned to the Washington office had survived the Disaster, but anyone who hadn't reported in, Hank called. Decker was the only one he couldn't either reach or confirm dead, and so he had come to see for himself.

Every conceivable explanation for the Disaster and many inconceivable ones as well had been put forward. With very few exceptions outside the Muslim population, the first word out of the mouths of most was "terrorists," and to date no reasonable explanation had been found to dissuade those who held that theory. The common wisdom was that it was some new weaponized strain of virus.

Gas masks of every kind, respirators, and even disposable surgical masks were bought up or were stolen from stores that remained closed. Army surplus stores sold out of masks, and Internet stores took hundreds of thousands of orders they couldn't possibly fill, and even if they had the inventory, it would be weeks or months before delivery capability was restored. In some stores there was fierce fighting among customers for paper masks, even though reason dictated that they couldn't possibly filter out the agent of death.

Each new explanation brought panic to someone. Just as many were afraid of what might be in the air, others were afraid to drink the water; still others feared genetically enhanced foods. Most weren't sure what to fear and so feared everything equally.

Whatever the cause, if it was in the air or water or elsewhere in the environment, it must have been there for weeks or months or even years, a ticking time bomb waiting to go off. Ships at sea and even submarines submerged for weeks reported deaths.

In the back yard, Hank Asher found a garden shovel and began digging a single large hole for the burial of Elizabeth, Hope, and Louisa Hawthorne. It wasn't the grave one would have expected before the Disaster, but it was better than the mass graves at the edges of the city. Here at least Decker might someday place gravestones. Looking over the yard, trying to make an educated guess as to where best to dig to avoid any utility lines, Asher went to work. It was slow going and as he dug, he sensed he was being watched. A pre-teen boy had been observing him from the next yard.

"You buryin' sumbody?" the boy called when Asher spotted him. Uninvited, he jumped the fence and came to where Asher was working. His clothes were new but dirty, as though he hadn't changed or washed in several days.

"Yeah," Asher replied.

"I knew 'em," the boy said. "I used to ride bikes with Louisa. I don't guess she'll be needin' hers anymore." The boy paused for a second in thought and then continued. "Too bad it's a girl's bike."

Asher continued digging.

"You want some help?"

Asher's back was starting to hurt and he had already worked up a sweat. The boy's offer was extremely welcome.

"I'll help you dig for twenty dollars," the boy added.

Asher was momentarily disgusted by the boy's profiteering. Instead of offering to help out of friendship for Louisa, he looked at her death as a way to make some money. Still, Asher decided, it was better to forget about motives and simply get some help. "There's another shovel and some work gloves that might fit you in the shed over there," he said.

The boy found the additional shovel and gloves while Asher went to work with a mattock.

"They all dead?" the boy asked, while Asher broke up the ground.

"Everybody but Mr. Hawthorne."

"I remember him from when I was a kid," the boy said. "But then he was kidnapped by the Arabs. He only got free about a week ago."

Asher continued digging without responding and then stopped and looked up at the boy. "Are you going to dig or just hold up that shovel?"

The boy acted as though he appreciated the reminder and went to work enlarging the hole.

"My dad says it was probably Arab terrorists," the boy said after a few minutes of uninspired digging.

"Yeah, well, that seems to be what most people think," Asher replied.

"Yeah, I heard on the news that only a few thousand Arabs died."

"That's old information," Asher informed him. "The figures I've seen put the number much higher: fifty thousand in Saudi Arabia, Iraq, and Turkey; two hundred thousand in Jordan; half a million in Iran and Pakistan, and five million in Egypt."

The boy was temporarily caught off guard by Asher's recitation of figures, but he quickly recovered. "That's probably just lies to keep us from knowing it was them."

Asher continued digging while the boy continued talking. Every other sentence or so the boy would throw out a shovel full of dirt, just to keep his hand in.

Inside the house, Sheryl Stanford was watching Fox News.

"In a press conference this morning from Washington," the news anchor said, "Secretary of Health and Human Services, Spencer Collins, held a press conference regarding what measures are being taken to deal with this crisis and answered questions from reporters. Here's some of what he had to say."

The picture switched to the secretary of HHS reading a prepared statement. "We want to assure the public that no stone is being left unturned in the search for the cause of this tragedy, determining whether there is further risk, and, if so, what can be done to protect against that risk. Everything, no matter how small or unlikely, is being examined. Emergency funding has been authorized by the president and Congress and we will spend whatever it takes to accomplish this mission. We are working around the clock and every imaginable kind of environmental test is being conducted: atmospheric, water, soil, chemical, biological, nuclear. Because this is a worldwide event, we are also looking closely at cosmic data collected from before the Disaster, such as solar activity.

"The Centers for Disease Control in Atlanta and the U.S. Army Medical Research Institute of Infectious Diseases at Fort Detrick, Maryland, have taken the standard protocols used in the investigation of naturally occurring infectious diseases and biological threat agents and have adapted them to the unique circumstances of this event. In coordination with HHS, they are conducting interviews with relatives of victims. Together with their counterpart agencies in other countries around the world and with the World Health Organization, they are looking for similarities in the victims' activities: where they went, what they ate, what they drank, their personal habits, anything they might have received in the mail. As I said, no stone is being left unturned. At the same time, they are looking for similarities in the activities of *survivors* in a search for anything that may have counteracted the threat agent. This is a huge task and we have enlisted the assistance of thousands of researchers from universities and private institutions around the country.

"We are also asking individuals who lost relatives or close friends to assist in this effort by logging onto our website at HHS.gov and answering a comprehensive set of questions for each person lost and also about themselves so we have comparative data from survivors. We expect millions to participate, and we're confident the analysis of all this data will provide us with useful information.

"The National Institutes of Health are conducting DNA studies of large numbers of both victims and survivors, looking for distinguishing genetic markers in the two groups. Notices have been sent to local hospitals and health care professionals requesting collection of DNA samples from victims and their close surviving blood relatives. Again, this is an area where citizen participation is imperative if we are going to succeed.

"The Centers for Disease Control are coordinating the data gathering from autopsies. To date, we have data from the autopsies of more than a thousand victims and more reports are coming in by the minute. These procedures have been conducted by medical examiners and pathologists from around the world. We have some data from autopsies that were conducted within an hour of the Disaster by astute MEs who recognized the importance of their findings to uncovering the cause of this tragedy."

Secretary Collins finished his statement and then took questions from reporters. The first two questions sought some assurance from the secretary on behalf of viewers that the Disaster would not be repeated. Though he attempted to be encouraging, he could offer no assurances.

The third reporter asked a more direct question, but the secretary's answer was neither more helpful nor reassuring: "Based on the autopsies," the reporter queried, "what can you tell us about the actual cause of death of the victims?"

Secretary Collins adjusted his glasses. He knew his answer would only raise more questions that he couldn't answer. "Normally," he began, considering his words carefully, "whatever the cause of death, we would expect that during the autopsy, we'd find indications of how the agent of death had acted. It may, for example, have caused the failure of normal functions of the heart, lungs, liver, kidney, brain, blood . . . something. Whatever we are dealing with here," Collins said, "appears to be entirely asymptomatic. Or, rather, having only one symptom: death. Nearly all of the common markers we would expect to find in an autopsy of someone who went through the normal death process are missing in these victims. The evidence strongly indicates that death occurred extremely quickly with a simultaneous and almost instantaneous shutdown of all essential organs. This has made it impossible, so far, to say exactly how the agent worked or even why the victims died."

This statement brought the expected flurry of questions, but in the end, Collins was able to provide no more information.

Finally a reporter pursued a different matter. "In the U.S. the number of deaths in rural areas appears to be higher, on a percentage basis, than the cities. This seems counterintuitive. Is there some explanation?" she asked.

"We are aware of this anomaly," the secretary answered, "and it's being factored into our investigation. There are a number of bacteriological agents that can remain dormant for years in soil, and perhaps the higher percentage of rural deaths would indicate that contact with the soil is involved. We are investigating that possibility. On the other hand, this hypothesis certainly cannot account for the deaths of the two astronauts aboard the space station.

"But let me point out that there are a number of other anomalous patterns that are beginning to emerge as well, some of which are conflicting from country to country or from region to region. We must stress that this analysis is based on very preliminary figures, but clearly there is evidence that the death toll was not evenly distributed worldwide. We hope that once all the information is assembled, it will provide some clues, but right now we are still gathering data."

"What other anomalous patterns have been identified?" the reporter asked in follow up.

"Well, for example, losses in the U.S. are currently estimated at between 15 and 20 percent. Some European countries, on the other hand, lost as few as one or two people for every one thousand of their population. As a result, the logistical impact of the Disaster in these countries is almost negligible and their governments have been able to finish what they believe are nearly complete counts. Greece, for example, lost approximately ten thousand out of a population of more than ten million. Also in this group are Albania, Monaco, Andorra, Luxembourg, Macedonia, and Malta. Other European countries with losses of one percent or less include France, Austria, and Belgium.

"Another example," continued the secretary, "is India, where estimates say as many as twenty-five million died, or about two percent of their population. This is not a high percentage, but what makes India unusual is that as many as 90 percent of the victims lived on India's southwest coast, on the Arabian Sea."

"What information do you have on the death toll in Islamic countries?" asked another reporter, indirectly asking for information that might confirm or deny theories that the deaths were somehow the result of an attack by Islamic terrorists.

"As you may know, it's not always easy to get accurate information from some Islamic countries. Additionally, in many cases, their ability to gather data isn't as advanced or accurate as it is in the Western world. Based on what we've been able to gather from these countries, however, this may be the most surprising information so far."

The secretary paused for a moment and then clarified his statement to correct any misperception. "I don't mean that it's particularly surprising from a medical standpoint, but rather because it poses some serious challenges to theories that the Disaster was caused by Islamic terrorists. It seems that several Islamic countries have lost a larger percentage of their population than did the European countries I just listed. These include Iraq, Jordan, and most notably Egypt, which may have lost as much as six percent of its population. Indonesia, which is predominantly Islamic, also suffered significant losses. With the exception of Egypt, those percentage numbers are still low as compared to some other countries, but it raises doubts that Islamic terrorists would develop a weapon and then kill a greater percentage of their own population than that in many of the countries of Europe. One would also expect the death toll in Israel to be greater if Islamic terrorism were involved."

The picture returned to the news anchor.

"As you just heard, there is evidence that some Muslim countries may have been hit worse by the Disaster than some countries in Western Europe. Nevertheless, vigilante attacks against Muslims in this country continue. For more on that we go to a special Fox report with Greg Culp."

The picture changed to show a reporter standing outside the smoldering remains of a building with a partially destroyed marquee that read "Gilbert Arizona Islamic Academy." The reporter began, "Throughout the non-Islamic world, Muslims fear for their lives, and with good reason. Islamic homes have been burned, businesses have been looted, their inhabitants beaten and even murdered in mob actions. Islamic schools like this one behind me have been destroyed by local citizens. Fortunately, the school was empty and no one was injured. Throughout America, Islamic schools have been closed since the day after the Disaster, when three men entered an Islamic school in Cincinnati and shot sixteen students and four teachers.

"Despite the president's plea for calm and his promise that FBI and law enforcement will hunt down anyone who participates in such acts, thus far police and other authorities have been unable to stop or even contain the violence."

Sheryl Stanford turned down the sound and went to the window to check on Hank Asher.

When they had dug about four feet, Asher decided the hole was deep enough; the standard six feet under was simply more than he could manage. He was about to pay the boy his twenty dollars but paused with the bill in his hand as he looked at the boy and then down at himself. The distribution of dirt and sweat left no doubt that the boy had done less than his share. Hank checked his wallet again and, as a matter of principle, decided to pay the boy fifteen.

"Hey, what about my other five bucks?" the boy demanded.

"It's more than you deserve for the little bit of work you did."

"Man, what a rip-off! I'm gonna go get my dad. He'll make you pay." With that the boy threw down the shovel and stomped off.

Asher rested for a moment before it suddenly occurred to him that he still had to bring out the bodies and fill the hole back in. "That was really stupid!" he said out loud, realizing he had gotten rid of the boy too soon.

Sheryl Stanford tried talking to Decker from time to time, but there was no indication he could hear her. He just stared blankly into space. She found some food in the kitchen and when she put it in his mouth he chewed and swallowed, but still he just stared. As she fed him, she continued to listen to the news in the background.

There was an urgent and growing concern about disease from decaying bodies. Reports from around the world said that thousands of suicides were adding to the death toll. Most took place in the victims' homes, but others were more public: jumping from buildings and bridges, driving off cliffs, and the like. A few chose to murder others before taking their own lives.

People flocked to houses of worship to find answers, but the Disaster had struck everywhere and members of the clergy had died as well. Stock markets and exchanges remained closed and analysts predicted worldwide financial chaos and economic depression. Insurance companies were seeking legal relief in the form of exemption from payment on deaths from the Disaster. Insurers said that without such legal relief, every life insurance company in America would have to declare bankruptcy, and analysts agreed that if the markets reopened before Congress and the president acted, insurance company stocks wouldn't survive the first fifteen seconds of trading. Opponents of these measures and other critics argued that insurance companies were certainly not the only industry at risk. Everyone suffered, and no one could predict what would happen when the markets reopened. The government couldn't bail out everyone.

Hank Asher finished the burial, returned to the house, and collapsed on the couch across the living room from Decker. "Has he said anything?" Asher asked after a moment.

"He just stares," Sheryl answered as she muted the news. "What are you going to do with him?"

"He needs to be cared for," Asher said. "But the hospitals are packed. I don't suppose you'd take him home with you?"

Sheryl looked at Decker and then back at Asher. The desperate look on her face made it clear that she did not like the idea at all, but neither was she comfortable saying no to her boss. As she struggled to respond, Asher let her sweat it out. He knew it was an unusual request, but these were unusual times.

Just then there was a knock at the door.

"I'll get it," Sheryl said, jumping up from her seat, hoping to evade her boss's question. Asher was too exhausted to argue.

A moment later, she came back. "It's a kid," she said. "He says he wants to see Mr. Hawthorne."

"Tell that lousy kid to go away, that he's not going to get one penny more than I've already paid him! No, wait! I'll tell him myself!" Energized by his anger, Asher picked himself up off the couch and headed for the front door. "Look, you, I'm not—" He stopped himself mid-sentence as he realized this was not the boy from the backyard. "Oh. I'm sorry, kid. I thought you were someone else. Look, Mr. Hawthorne isn't feeling well right now. Can you come back later?" he asked, trying to get rid of the boy.

"I need to talk to Mr. Hawthorne," the boy persisted.

"Like I said, kid, Mr. Hawthorne isn't feeling well. Come back tomorrow."

The boy held his ground.

"Okay," Asher said, "look, maybe I can help you. What is it that you need to talk to him about?"

From the living room, Sheryl Stanford called to Asher, "Hey, he moved his eyes a little!"

Asher went to his friend's side and looked, but saw no sign of awareness.

"Mr. Hawthorne, it's me, Christopher Goodman."

Asher turned around and saw that the boy had followed him into the living room.

"Mr. Hawthorne, please tell these people you know me. I've come a long way and I don't have anywhere else to go. Uncle Harry and Aunt Martha both died in a plane crash. I don't have any other family. Uncle Harry told me if anything ever happened to them I should call you. But you didn't answer your phone."

Asher, who knew of Harry Goodman from Decker's articles, put the pieces together. "Your uncle is Professor Goodman from Los Angeles?"

"Yes," Christopher responded. "Did you know him?"

"I know his work. What are you doing in Washington?"

"Uncle Harry told me that if anything ever happened to him and Aunt Martha, I should find Mr. Hawthorne," he repeated. "I don't have any other relatives and Mr. Hawthorne was my uncle's friend."

"How'd you get all the way out here from Los Angeles?"

Christopher paused, apparently hoping to avoid an answer that might get him in trouble. "I drove my uncle's car," he admitted finally.

"You drove from Los Angeles?" Asher said, surprised. "How old are you, kid?"

"Fourteen," Christopher answered. "I didn't have any other way to get here."

Asher shook his head in disbelief. "How'd you manage to avoid getting stopped by the cops?"

"I dunno," Christopher said. "I guess they're pretty busy with other things."

"Yeah. I guess so. Well, look, kid. I'm sorry you drove all the way out here for nothing, but Mr. Hawthorne won't be able to help anybody for quite a while."

Christopher looked at Decker.

"In fact," Asher continued. "I'm going to have to find someone to take care of *him*."

"But, I don't have anywhere else to go. Most of Aunt Martha's friends are dead and Mr. Hawthorne is . . . well," Christopher paused to think. "Can I just stay here for a while? Maybe I could help you take care of him."

"I think that's a great idea!" Sheryl chimed in, still fearing she'd get stuck with the job. "Let him stay."

"Let him stay," another voice repeated hoarsely.

Asher, Sheryl, and Christopher all turned toward the only other person in the room.

"Let him stay," Decker said again.

Chapter 11

The Master's Promise

Three weeks later

Derwood, Maryland

The cool moisture of morning soaked slowly through the seat of Decker's jeans as he sat on the grass beside the grave of his family. Mindlessly he stared at the upturned soil, still numb from his loss. It would be spring before the surrounding grass would begin to encroach upon the settling mound of bare dirt.

Decker had put in an order for three grave stones but was told it would take at least a year and a half to get stones with names on them. Generic stones with "Beloved Wife," "Beloved Father," "Beloved Daughter," etc. and no date of birth could be had in half the time and at about one fourth the price of a personalized stone, delivery included. Someone else was offering eight-week delivery on personalized grave makers made of reinforced plastic with a "marble look." Decker had decided to wait for the real thing.

His wife and daughters were not all Decker had lost. Shortly after Christopher arrived, Decker had learned that his mother and older brother were also dead. His uncle had buried them, together with others, on his farm in Tennessee.

Still, some had it much worse. The dead who had no one to bury them had been laid by the thousands in mass graves. In the city of Washington the poor had tried to bury their dead on the National Mall, between the Capital and the Lincoln Memorial and in other city parks, but were turned away by U.S. Park Police and National Guard. Some expressed their frustration and protest by leaving the dead in the front yards of city officials or on curbs with the garbage.

Among those who died were many celebrities of one sort or another: politicians, religious leaders, heads of state, a few actors and actresses. The U.S. lost twelve senators, sixty-odd congressmen, three Cabinet members, and the vice president. It seemed that everyone had lost someone: wives, husbands, children, parents.

As the sun rose above the fence slats on Decker's right, and the individual blades of grass released their moist coats of dew into the morning air, Decker heard the sliding glass door open but didn't raise his eyes from the ground to look. Christopher Goodman approached, stopping a few feet short and after a moment, seemed to realize he would have to speak first. "Breakfast is ready," he said brightly, adding that he had fixed Decker's favorite — waffles with plenty of bacon and scalding hot syrup.

Decker looked up, smiled appreciatively, and extended his hand toward Christopher. "Give me a hand up," he said. Christopher never asked Decker about the hours he spent sitting by the grave in the backyard. He just seemed to understand and allowed Decker the privacy of his thoughts.

"What about your family?" Decker asked, opening the subject as if in mid-conversation.

Christopher shrugged. "When they didn't come home or call," he said uncomfortably after a moment, "I checked and found out their plane crashed when the Disaster struck. The map online showed the approximate location." He shrugged again, this time in a defeated expression. "I tried to find it on my way here, but it's in the mountains, miles from any roads." Christopher seemed distraught by the memory.

For three weeks now Christopher had provided Decker with supportive companionship, never once saying a word about his own loss. Perhaps, Decker thought, it was time to start thinking of someone besides himself. Without thinking it through, he asked, "Would you like for me to go with you to find them? We could take them home to Los Angeles and bury them there, or we could bring them here and bury them in the backyard near Elizabeth, Hope, and Louisa."

Christopher seemed appreciative but uneasy at the suggestion. "No, it's, um . . . too far," he answered.

"That's all right. I can help you drive," Decker told the precocious fourteen-year-old, trying to make a joke and not understanding Christopher's reluctance.

"Mr. Hawthorne," Christopher said directly, "their bodies have been there for nearly a month. I don't think . . ."

Decker was shocked at his own stupidity. Exposed to the elements and animals and scattered across numerous acres of rugged terrain along with perhaps a hundred other bodies, it would be an impossible, unbearable task. How could he have missed that? "I'm sorry, Christopher. I wasn't thinking."

"It's okay, Mr. Hawthorne," the boy said, and from the understanding look on his face, Decker could tell it really was. Christopher had apparently accepted the harsh truth with determined resolve to go on. "Come on," Christopher urged at last. "The syrup is getting cold."

Decker was beginning to understand Harry Goodman's love for the boy and his fear of disclosing Christopher's origin. Over the past few weeks, without knowing it, he had come to think of Christopher almost as his own son. Perhaps it was because of the loss of Elizabeth, Hope, and Louisa. Much of the feeling, though, was due to Christopher's totally unselfish attitude, always giving of himself and never asking for anything more in return than room and board. Decker finally and firmly resolved that the story of Christopher's origin was one the world could do without.

* * * * *

At last determined to go on, three days later Decker was spending the afternoon reading through recent issues of *NewsWorld*. It seemed that every article, if it didn't entirely focus on the Disaster, had at least some mention of what had occurred. In the most recent edition, Decker found an editorial by Hank Asher:

> *There comes a time following every great tragedy when someone very authoritatively states that those who have lived through it will never be the same. Perhaps it's a cathartic statement. Perhaps it marks or at least helps to mark the point at which we all agree that it's time to begin to move on, time to get back to the business of life. It's never easy, but it is necessary.*
>
> *I'm not suggesting that we try to forget what happened, or that we forget those who meant so much to us. Most certainly I am not suggesting that we stop looking for an explanation for what happened or a way to prevent its recurrence.*
>
> *In an age in which we've come to expect quick answers, it only adds to the horror that no one can provide anything approaching a plausible explanation for this tragedy. They say funerals are for the*

living, that they give a stamp of finality to the loss of loved ones. But that finality can never really come so long as the mystery of the cause of death remains. Scientists are doing everything in their power to determine the cause of the Disaster and prevent it from happening again, but for most of us there's nothing we can do but wait and hope.

The world has no choice but to go on with life. A psychologist friend told me that in one way, recovering from this disaster will actually be easier than recovering from the individual tragedies that plague our mortal lives. In this disaster, everyone lost someone: a relative, a friend, a neighbor. At the very least they know someone who knew someone who died. In that way this bears some resemblance to soldiers marching into fearsome battle, each drawing strength from the others and from the fact that they are not alone.

As I write this I cannot help but think of each of the relatives, friends, and coworkers I've lost. As I picture their faces and remember events where our lives intersected, I notice that many of them are smiling. It seems that's how I usually saw them in life, or maybe it's just how I choose to remember them. For many, I am gnawed by regret that I didn't treat them more kindly, that I didn't get to know them better, that I didn't give them more of myself while I had the chance.

I know my regrets are shared by many who are reading these words. What wouldn't any of us give for the chance to spend just one more day with those we lost? If we could just go back to one day before the Disaster, how different we would be, how differently we would behave, how much kinder we would treat those we've lost. But there is nothing we can do to bring back that day. There is nothing we can do to bring back those who died.

I wonder about the children. How will their lives be affected? Many of the children of the Great Depression, remembering their parents' reaction to sudden poverty, went through their entire lives in imagined financial insecurity, holding so tightly to every penny that they denied themselves much of what they wanted or even needed. What will children of this generation remember when they look back at how we handled this tragedy? What will they carry with them for having experienced this event?

Regret is natural, but if we allow it to rule our lives, how many more regrets will we pile up? How many more missed opportunities will there be with others whom one day we will wish we had treated with more kindness or gotten to know better or given more of ourselves to? Let us then not flounder in our regrets, but rather let us carry them as reminders to cherish each day we have and to value everyone we meet.

As we lick our wounds in the wake of any new tragedy, we all believe it when we hear the words, "None of us will ever be the same," but inside we know better. Our experience tells us we forget all too quickly. Each time we vow "This time will be different," but we are a resilient lot. We may carve words like "We will never forget" into limestone or granite to remind us, but carving them into the human soul is not so easy. It is made of much more pliable stuff, easily impressed but quick to rebound. And while we may curse that stuff for its conspiracy with time to steal from us the only thing we have left of those who died — our pain — without that resiliency our species would have died out millennia ago.

In a few years our lives may give every appearance of being unchanged by the event we now call the Disaster. But having lived through it, can any of us ever greet another day without the thought that this may be our last? Will any of us ever pass children playing or a flower growing or friends chatting and not look back and thank our lucky stars that we're still alive to witness it?

Perhaps this time it will be different. Perhaps this blow has come with sufficient force to make an impression that will endure. Only time will tell. All we can say for now is: none of us will ever be the same.

This was not the typical biting editorial by Hank Asher that Decker was used to reading. He sat quietly for a few minutes, considering Asher's words. Then the phone rang.

"Mr. Hawthorne's residence," Christopher answered, sounding more like a domestic servant than a fourteen-year-old boy. "Yes, just a moment. I'll get him." Decker got up and headed for the phone as Christopher reported that it was Mr. Asher calling from *NewsWorld.*

"Hank, how are you?" Decker asked warmly.

"I'm fine. How are you?" Asher's voice made it clear he was willing to listen to a detailed response.

"Much better, actually. Really, I'm doing all right," Decker said resolutely.

Asher understood the determination in his voice. Decker was probably a long way from being all right, but he was determined to be so and that in itself was a major step in the right direction. "Good," he said. "How's the boy?"

"Oh, he's great. He's been a big help around here."

"Look, I know we haven't really talked about your plans on getting back to work, but I need a favor. I need you in New York on Friday for an interview with Jon Hansen. You'll be in and out in one day. I'd send someone else, but you're the only one he's agreed to talk to."

"New York? What's this about, Hank? What's the story?"

"Hansen's report on the situation in the Middle East. The UN lost nearly two thousand men assigned to that area in the Disaster. They've tried to replace them with reinforcements but many of the countries that provide the UN with soldiers were hit just as badly. The U.S., Britain, Germany, Switzerland — all have major losses. With the threat of war in the Middle East, there's serious doubt that the UN can maintain the peace, and they may just get caught in the crossfire. We have a tip that Hansen is going to recommend that unless Israel agrees to halt construction of the Temple, the UN should immediately withdraw its remaining thirteen-thousand-man force from Israel's borders. If they do, war is almost certain."

Decker looked over at Christopher. "I'll do it," he said. "But, I'll need two tickets instead of one." Christopher understood and nodded with enthusiasm. "And can you set up a tour of the UN for Christopher?"

"That's a great idea," Asher said. "The kid must be going crazy with cabin fever by now. I'll see if I can make reservations for you in the Delegates Dining Room for lunch. Your appointment with Hansen is set for two o'clock Friday afternoon."

New York

"Where to?" the cabby asked.

"The UN," Decker answered. Christopher got in first. When Decker joined him he noticed a strange look on the boy's face. Something wasn't quite right. It took only an instant for Decker to understand. Sealed in the cab, an awful but familiar smell made its way into their lungs. It wasn't overpowering, but it was definitely there and it wasn't pleasant. Decker thought about getting out and hailing another cab, but it was too late. The driver punched the gas pedal, pulled his cab across two lanes of traffic and was off.

Christopher looked at Decker and silently mouthed, "May I roll down the window?"

Decker held up his hand with his thumb and forefinger spread apart, indicating that about three inches would be acceptable. It was pretty cold outside but that seemed a good compromise with the smell.

After a few minutes, Decker cracked his window as well. It was then that he noticed the driver looking at them in his rearview mirror. He seemed to be studying them. Their eyes met and the cabby quickly reached up, as if he had been checking the mirror's adjustment.

"Ain't been too many tourists 'round here lately," he said after a moment.

Decker chose not to respond, and the driver added, "Well, ya wanna be careful over there — at the UN I mean."

"Why do you say that?" Decker asked.

"Call me paranoid, but I wouldn't go in there widdout a gas mask."

Decker found it almost impossible not to respond with a crack about needing one to ride in the cabby's car. "I don't follow you," he answered instead.

"I don't care what anyone says. The way I see it, it was definitely Muslims that caused the Disaster. Or if not, then it was the Russians, 'cause no way you're gonna tell me all those people just dropped dead for no reason. And, well, I don't know if you ever been to the UN before, but they got foreigners crawlin' all over the place over there. 'Course, that's true everywhere in New York, only especially at the UN."

"If the Muslims or Russians are responsible for the Disaster," Decker responded, "why would they release it on their own people?"

"Muslims kill Muslims every day," the cabby replied. "It's their national pastime, like baseball."

Decker realized there was no sense in trying to reason with the driver, so he settled back in his seat and kept silent. The cabby, however, didn't need an active partner to carry on a conversation.

"'Course, I wanna get the guys that did it — and I don't mean to be cruel or nuthin' — but if ya ask me, I'd tell ya we'z better off widdout so many people in the world. 'Course, there ain't near as many fares on the streets nowadays. Not live ones, anyway. But an entrepreneur like me, well, I figure there's a *gold* linin' to every cloud. So I asked myself, how can a guy like me make some money when the fares're down. An' it didn't take no time till it comes to me. If there ain't as many live ones around, haul the dead ones! So I called up this guy I know who works at a landfill in Jersey. And next thing ya know, I'm in business."

If Decker needed any confirmation of what the smell was, he now had it.

"Yeah, I figured it was a great idea," the cabby said, continuing his discourse. "The wife says it makes the car stink. So, I just stopped at the 7-11 and bought this air freshener." The cabby pointed to a cardboard pine tree dangling from the rearview mirror. "And I ain't had no more problem with it. 'Course, it was a little creepy at first, but I can make upta two hundred dollars a head for haulin' off bodies, dependin' on how bad a shape they're in. 'Course, most of the stiffs from the Disaster have been hauled off by now. Still, I get a call maybe two or three times a day, mostly to haul off suicides — folks that lost everybody in the Disaster and decided ta join 'em. But for a while there, I was rakin' it in. One time I got twelve stiffs in here all at the same time."

The cabby paused just long enough for Decker to get his hopes up that he would remain silent. "And then there's another thing," he said, after catching his breath. "It sure is easier to get apartments 'round here now. 'Course, most of the apartments that ya find still smell like dead folks, but, hey, ya just let it air out a few hours an' it's jus' like home."

The cabby looked over and nodded toward a pawn shop as they passed. "I tell ya another guy that's makin' a buck on the dead besides the grave digger and me: the pawn broker. Ya see this ring," he said, holding his right hand up for them to see. "Pretty nice, huh? I picked this up dirt cheap from a pawn shop last week. But I bet I paid four times what the pawn broker had ta give for it. An' the guy he got it from probably got it for free off some stiff. Some people don't like wearin' dead folk's stuff, but I figure, hey, they don't need it no more."

"Was there a lot of looting?" Christopher asked, apparently unaware that Decker was hoping the driver would just be quiet and drive.

"Oh, yeah, plenty. Let me tell ya, the looters wuz breakin' windows an' rippin' off stores left an' right. A bunch of 'em got shot by shop owners, but then pretty soon the looters started shootin' back. But that only lasted a few days. Then Hizzoner, the mayor, declared open season on anyone on the streets after curfew. So far, I hear the cops have shot more than thirty of 'em."

Decker pointed out the United Nations building to Christopher as they approached.

United Nations Headquarters Building in New York

"Well, here we are," the cabby concluded as he pulled up to the General Assembly building.

Decker paid quickly, and the driver thanked him and warned them again to be careful.

"I hope you know that that cabby didn't know his head from a hole in the ground," Decker told Christopher as the two walked across the North Courtyard to the entrance to the General Assembly building.

"Sure, Mr. Hawthorne, I know. Still, it was an interesting experience."

Decker smiled. "You might make a good reporter," he said.

After going through security, they went to the information and security desk to get visitor's badges for the Delegates Dining Room. Both enjoyed the lunch buffet immensely. There was more variety than either had seen before at one meal and they liked almost everything they tried.

After their meal, as they were in the lobby returning their badges, someone called to Decker. They turned toward the voice and, and over the heads of a group of colorfully clothed people, saw a tall blonde man who smiled and gave a nod of recognition. It was Jon Hansen.

"Mr. Ambassador," Decker said as he approached and extended his hand. "It's good to see you again. But I certainly didn't expect you to come to greet me."

"No problem," Hansen answered with a friendly smile. "To be honest, though I had some business in the building. How have you been? You look much improved over our first meeting."

"Yeah, well, that's not saying very much," Decker joked. "But I have been eating a lot better. Christopher here is a pretty good cook."

Hansen looked curiously at the boy, who was listening intently to their conversation.

"Ambassador Hansen, this is Christopher Goodman," Decker responded in answer to Hansen's glance. "He's been staying with me since the Disaster. His granduncle was Professor Harry Goodman of UCLA."

"It's very nice to meet you, Christopher," Hansen said as he shook the boy's hand. "I've read about your uncle's work in cancer research. He was a brilliant scientist. The world will miss him. Maybe someday you'll continue his work."

"Professor Goodman and I were friends from my college days," Decker continued. "I lost . . ." Decker bit his lower lip to get a grip on his emotions. For a brief moment he had thought he would be able to just say it. Breathing deeply and releasing his bite, he tried again. "I lost my wife and two daughters." He paused and took another breath. "So when Christopher showed up on my doorstep, I invited him to stay. The professor and Mrs. Goodman were his only family."

"I'm terribly sorry about your families," Hansen offered. Decker nodded appreciation.

"Mr. Ambassador," Christopher said politely, waiting for permission before continuing.

"Yes, Christopher," Hansen replied.

"Is the World Health Organization any closer to finding the cause of the Disaster?"

"Well, Christopher," Hansen began, pleased at the boy's interest, "they tell me they've been able to determine several hundred things that it was not. So I guess that's progress. But they still don't know what it was. I have faith in them, though. They'll figure it out soon, I'm sure."

Christopher seemed satisfied with the answer.

"So," Hansen asked the boy, "is this your first trip to the United Nations?"

"Yes, sir. Is your office in this building?"

"Oh, no. I think most people assume that the delegates' offices are here at the UN, but actually each country has its own mission elsewhere in the city. The British Mission is about four blocks from here."

"Christopher is very interested in the UN, so I brought him along," Decker interjected. "He's scheduled for the one-thirty tour."

Hansen looked at his watch. "Well, then. Why don't we walk you over to where the tour starts," he told Christopher, and then addressing Decker, added, "then we can go over to my office."

When Decker and Hansen reached the British Mission on the twenty-eighth floor of One Dag Hammarskjöld Plaza, they were met at the door by an attractive blonde woman in her late twenties who stood at least six feet two inches tall, just two inches shorter than Hansen. Decker was struck not only by her height, but also by her remarkable resemblance to the ambassador. The features were softer, the skin smoother and younger, but there was no mistaking the kinship.

"Mr. Ambassador," she said hurriedly as Hansen and Decker entered through the lobby past the security desk, "Ambassador

Fahd called. He said it was urgent that he speak with you. He left a number, but said if you didn't call soon you may not be able to reach him. I'll place the call," she concluded as she went quickly to her desk and Hansen went to his office.

"Decker, come in and have a seat," Hansen said, not pausing to look back.

Hansen's office was large with sturdy antique furnishings and solid wood paneling. Decker sat in a comfortable leather chair facing Hansen's desk while Hansen sat down and drummed his fingers on the desk in front of the phone.

"It's ringing," came the young woman's heavily accented voice from the outer office.

Hansen picked up the receiver and waited as the phone rang several times. "There's no answer, Jackie," he told his assistant. "Okay. Well, there's nothing we can do then except wait until he calls back and hope nothing happens in the meantime." Hansen turned his attention back to Decker.

"Ambassador Fahd?" Decker quizzed before Hansen could speak. "Isn't he the ambassador from Jordan?"

"Yes, we're old friends. School chums, actually. We've worked together on a number of projects for the UN."

"Like the Middle East project your committee is preparing a report on?"

"Well, yes. But tell me, how can I help you?"

"Well, um," Decker began, unsure of why Hansen would interrupt the conversation on the Middle East project and in the next breath ask how he could help. *That*, after all, was what Decker understood this meeting was about. Could Hansen have forgotten? "I'd like to ask you some questions about the committee's report," Decker responded finally.

"But, Decker, surely you know that that information is strictly confidential."

"Wait a second," Decker said, the confusion showing in his voice. "Didn't you agree to talk with me about the report?"

"Of course not!" Hansen was taken aback at the whole idea, but there was no anger in his voice. He was simply surprised.

"What exactly did my editor tell you I wanted to talk with you about?" Decker probed.

"Mr. Asher . . . your editor?" Hansen asked, seeking verification. Decker nodded painfully, embarrassed by the course this meeting was taking. "He said that you wanted to do some sort of profile piece on me for your magazine."

Decker dropped his forehead into his open hand and expelled a deep breath in frustration and embarrassment. "Mr. Ambassador," he said at last, "I'm afraid you and I have both been misled. Hank Asher told me that I was to interview you about your report — that you had refused to talk to other reporters about it but that you *were* willing to talk with me."

"Now that wouldn't be quite fair, would it?"

"I'm sorry, Mr. Ambassador," Decker said as he felt his face redden further. "I should have thought to question him when he told me you had agreed to give me an exclusive. I guess I let him appeal to my vanity. I — stupidly, I realize now — thought you would . . . Oh, never mind."

Ambassador Hansen's response to this revelation was completely unexpected: He laughed.

"I don't understand," Decker said. "What's so funny?"

"I'd like to meet this Mr. Asher of yours," Hansen said. "He must be quite a good judge of a man's character. I could use a few people like him on my staff."

Decker's expression showed he still didn't understand.

"Oh, but don't you see, Decker? He played us both perfectly. I didn't even think to question his motives when he said you wanted to write a profile story on me. I too was a victim of my own vanity."

Decker forced a smile. He didn't think it was very humorous, but he didn't want to deny the Ambassador his fun. And besides, it was much better to have him laughing than angry. "Well," Decker said after a moment, "I don't see any reason we shouldn't go ahead and do that profile. Maybe we can still get the last laugh on Hank Asher. You'll get the coverage. And he won't be able to say I didn't bring back the story."

"I like the way you think, Decker. You'd make a fine politician."

Decker assumed it was a compliment.

* * * * *

Christopher Goodman stayed close to the guide as she took the UN tour group through two of the three council chambers — first the Economic and Social Council (ECOSOC), and then the Security Council Chamber. From there, they went to the Hall of the General Assembly. As they were leaving the General Assembly, Christopher went to look over the balcony at the visitor's lobby four floors below them. Midway between floors hung a replica of the Russian *Sputnik*, the first artificial satellite.

At that moment a group of men and women approached the rear entrance to the Hall of the General Assembly, led by a man in his early seventies. Each member of the group was politely but intently jockeying for position, staying close enough to hear what the man was saying and hoping to be the next to ask him a question. From their clothing it was obvious they represented many different cultures and nationalities.

"I consider," the man was saying, "Secretary-General U Thant to have been not only my political mentor but my spiritual mentor as well. It was from him that I first learned—" The man stopped suddenly and turned sharply to examine the profile of the boy he had noticed out of the corner of his eye.

"What is it, Mr. Assistant Secretary?" someone asked, but for the moment he seemed unable to respond as he stared at the boy.

Christopher turned and saw that his tour group had moved on and was preparing to board an elevator. In his rush to rejoin the group he didn't even seem to notice the attention of the old man or the others in the entourage as he scrambled directly through their midst, coming within scant inches of the old man and then dashing away to reach his tour group as the elevator's door opened.

"That boy!" the man said finally, as Christopher began to weave his way through a group of Japanese businessmen that stood between him and the elevator. "It's him. I know it's him." Trying to recover while there was still a chance to act, he yelled, "Stop him! Someone stop that boy!" But no one moved except to look around to see what was happening. The former UN assistant secretary-general had no time to explain or to wait for the others to get their bearings. He pushed his attendants aside and ran after the boy himself. He made a remarkable effort for a man his age, but there was no real contest; his momentary hesitation had cost him his chance. Christopher was on the elevator and the doors closed behind him.

There had only been an instant of indecision, a moment's hesitation, but it was enough to make all the difference. Christopher was gone. "No! It's not fair," the man said, without explanation. He took no notice as the others rejoined him. They stared at him and at each other in confusion, hoping to find some hint of meaning to the strange episode.

"No!" he said again. "It wasn't supposed to be like this. It's not fair! I didn't even get to talk to him." His voice was now barely audible. No one had any idea of the significance of what had just taken place or what the old man was saying, and he seemed to have no interest in letting them in on it. Then a thought occurred to him. "Alice," he said. "I must find Alice."

* * * * *

After the tour, Christopher looked for Decker but was met instead by a young aide sent by Ambassador Hansen to retrieve him. When they arrived at Hansen's office, Decker was just preparing to leave. "Well, Christopher," Jon Hansen asked, "how was your tour?"

Christopher was about to answer when a thin bald man with an auburn mustache and a deadly serious expression rushed through the open door into Hansen's office. Every eye in the outer office was on him; every face took on a uniform look of dread. It seemed they all recognized him, and though no one tried to stop him, it was clear there was something to be feared about this man's arrival.

"Jon, they've done it," the man said in a thick German accent. "I just talked to Fahd, and he confirmed that Turkey, Egypt, Syria, and Libya have launched a united attack against Israel."

"Blast!" said Hansen. "When did it happen?"

"Less than fifteen minutes ago. From what we can tell, Egypt, Syria, Turkey, and Libya have all launched a coordinated air strike against Israeli airfields. Rockets are coming in from Gaza and the West Bank. And the Egyptian and Syrian armies are attacking along their borders. The Syrians are also coming through Lebanon, backed up by Hezbollah, which means Iran is a party to this too."[26]

"Blast!" Hansen said again.

"And I think it's a sure bet that Turkey will be moving their Navy south toward Israel," the German concluded.

Decker and Christopher had backed away to keep from interfering, but both listened intently to the conversation, and apparently no one cared. It would all be on the news soon anyway.

As Hansen and the other man talked, they were interrupted by the tall blonde woman. "Father," she said, "Ambassador Rogers is on the phone and says he must speak with you immediately." Her manner was calm and typical of her high upbringing, but Decker could sense the concern in her voice — that, plus the fact that she had called him Father rather than Mr. Ambassador.

Decker had no idea who Ambassador Rogers was, but it seemed both Hansen and the German were very anxious to talk with him. "Hello, Frank," Hansen said. "Ambassador Reichmann is here with me. I understand it's hit the fan over there. What can you tell us about the situation?" Hansen paused to listen but the look on his face said that he wasn't prepared for Rogers' answer.

"Tel Aviv! In the city?" Hansen said into the receiver in dismay. "It's not just the military bases around there?"

Decker's ears perked up and he listened with even greater interest.

Hansen paused again and then put his hand over the phone and spoke to Reichmann. "They're shelling civilian areas of Tel Aviv. Rogers says scores of bombs have already fallen."

Until now, Decker had been satisfied just to listen. Now he had a personal stake in what was happening. He too broke with formality and came right up to the two men. Hansen didn't seem to even notice the breach of protocol, but continued to listen to Ambassador Rogers on the phone.

"Frank, are you all right?" Hansen asked with some concern. "Is the embassy in danger?" Rogers' answer seemed to reassure Hansen about the immediate safety of the embassy staff.

"Okay, Frank," he said after another pause. "Hold on, I'll do it right now. Jackie!" Hansen said, directing his eyes to his daughter. "Get the Syrian ambassador, the Russian ambassador, and the Turkish ambassador on the phone right away, and in that order!"

The momentary break in the phone conversation allowed Hansen's glance to pass to Decker, who took advantage of the opportunity. "Tom Donafin is still in the hospital over there!"

Hansen paused for a fraction of a second, his eyes intently fixed on Decker's. The look on his face was of sincere concern but he didn't answer. He had greater, more immediate responsibilities. He spoke back into the phone. "Frank, I'll apply every ounce of pressure I can on this end, but I don't know what good it'll do. It would help if you can give me a few specifics. Is your email working? Good. Send me details on what parts of the city are being hit and how much damage there is."

Decker realized the comparative triviality of his plea and stepped into the background.

"I have the Syrian ambassador's office on the phone, Mr. Ambassador," Hansen's daughter said, this time remembering to use the proper title. "He'll pick up as soon as you're on the phone."

Hansen was making a note and listening, while looking up at his daughter. "Frank, I've got Ambassador Murabi on the other phone. I'll talk to him first and then make the other calls. If I don't call you back within fifteen minutes, then you call me."

Hansen was just about to hang up when he remembered something and put the phone back to his ear. "Frank," he said loudly into the mouthpiece, hoping to catch Ambassador Rogers before he hung up. There was a brief anxious silence and then he continued. "Frank, one other thing. It's a personal favor. You recall those two Yanks I brought back from Lebanon? Well, one of them is here with me in the office and he says that the other is still in hospital there in Tel Aviv." Hansen listened. Decker listened. "Yes, that's right." Hansen looked at Decker, obviously needing details.

"Tel-Hashomer Hospital," Decker responded.

"Tel Hashomer," Hansen repeated. "His name is Tom Donafin. How much longer is he supposed to be there?" he asked, looking over at Decker.

"He's supposed to get out any day. He had his final surgery last week."

"Frank," Hansen said back into the phone, "apparently he can leave anytime. When you can, have someone check on him, and if he's fit to travel, get him on a plane out of there."

Hansen hung up the phone and acknowledged Decker's look of appreciation. "Rogers is a good man. He'll do what he can." Decker didn't have a chance to reply before Hansen continued. "Right now though," he said as he poised his finger above the blinking light on the phone, "I'm afraid I have to ask you to leave." Decker began to move toward the door. "Leave your number with Jackie and we'll call you if we hear anything about Tom."

* * * * *

Robert Milner, former assistant secretary-general of the United Nations, came through the door of the Lucius Trust with the energy of a man half his age. "I must speak to Alice," he hurriedly told the receptionist. "Where is she?" He didn't wait for an answer, but moved quickly around the young woman's desk toward Alice Bernley's office.

"I'm sorry, Mr. Secretary, Ms. Bernley isn't in," the receptionist said, but Milner's momentum carried him the rest of the way to Bernley's office door.

"Where is she? I must speak with her immediately!" he said, as he moved crisply through a 180-degree turn back toward the receptionist.

"She didn't say. But I expect her back any minute."

Milner's energy seemed to lose direction as he began aimlessly, anxiously to pace the floor of the Trust's front office. The receptionist offered Milner a cup of herbal tea, which he accepted but didn't drink.

Twenty minutes passed before Milner saw the red-haired Alice Bernley returning to her office from across the UN Plaza. She was walking quickly, excitedly, but not fast enough to satisfy Milner, who ran to meet her. As she saw him coming, she quickened her pace. Almost in unison they called out the other's first name.

"Alice!"

"Bob!"

Then in unison: "I've seen him!"

"Where? When?" she asked, hurriedly. She had been running and was trying to catch her breath.

"In the UN, not more than half an hour ago! He passed within inches of me. I could have reached out and touched him! But, quickly, where did *you* see him?"

"Only moments ago, on Second Street, in front of One Dag Hammarskjöld. He was with a man, getting into a cab. I tried to . . ." Alice Bernley dropped the rest of her sentence as she watched the smile on Milner's face grow broad with the excitement of a promise fulfilled. Only then did she come to fully appreciate the significance of this moment. For a minute they just looked at each other.

"We've seen him," she said, finally.

"We have seen him," he confirmed. "Just as Master Djwlij Kajm promised!"

Chapter 12

Why Hast Thou Forsaken Me?

Tel Aviv

Tom Donafin sat on the edge of his bed in Tel Aviv's Tel-Hashomer Hospital, adjusting the strap on the new camera Hank Asher had sent him as a get-well present. Outside Tom's window, a martial performance of major proportion in the night sky was made surreal by the glow of fires from the ground. The sparkle of anti-aircraft artillery painted narrow streaks across the sky as now and then the bright flash of an explosion added brilliant color to the canvas. Tom had captured it all, beginning only moments after the first shots were fired. He had even photographed a dogfight between a squadron of Syrian MiG-25s and Israeli F-15 Eagles.

Tom walked back to the open window and scanned the horizon for action. Like most of the other lights in the city, those in the hospital had been extinguished to avoid drawing the attention of enemy pilots — a condition which, coincidentally, also allowed for better night photography. Behind him Tom heard a knock on his hospital room door and turned quickly, a little startled, whereupon the person at the open door suddenly found himself with a barrel pointed directly at him. Instinctively the man ducked, but even as he did, he realized that the sinister barrel that seemed at first to be some type of small bazooka or shoulder-held anti-tank weapon was in fact, only the telephoto lens of the American's camera.

"I'm so sorry!" Tom said, lowering the camera as he hurried to offer his hand to help his unexpected visitor up from the floor. "Are you all right?"

"Fine," the man muttered in a British accent through his embarrassment while brushing himself off. "Are you Donafin?"

"Yeah, I'm Tom Donafin," Tom responded, offering his hand again, this time in greeting. "Who are you?"

"I'm Połucki from the British Embassy," he said formally. "On behalf of Ambassadors Rogers and Hansen I'm here to offer you the assistance of His Majesty's government in expediting your evacuation from the State of Israel. Please accept my apologies for not notifying you earlier. Communications are not up to snuff of late. At the direction of Ambassador Rogers, I've taken the liberty of inquiring of your doctor regarding your fitness for travel. He entirely agrees that, under the present circumstances, your full recovery would be facilitated by your immediate departure from the area of present hostilities. Besides," he added less formally, "they'll be needing the bed for the wounded."

"Hansen to the rescue again!" Tom said to himself. "Great! Where exactly do you plan to take me?"

"My instructions are to drive you to the British Embassy where you will be provided for until suitable arrangements can be made for your departure on the next U.K., U.S., or UN flight or vessel. If you prefer, I am to deliver you to the U.S. Embassy, where similar arrangements will be made."

In ten minutes they were on their way out the front door. There were no lights in Tel Aviv that night except the fires of burning buildings, which reflected against the smoke-filled sky and shrouded the city with an eerie pulsating glow.

"Połucki," Tom said, as his young British escort slowly drove the Mercedes through the abandoned streets, turning his lights on only when absolutely necessary and only for a few seconds at a time. "What's your first name?"

"Nigel, sir," Połucki replied.

"Połucki is a Polish name, isn't it?" Tom asked.

"Yes, sir. My grandparents escaped to Britain when Germany invaded at the beginning of the Second World War."

At that moment the air around them began to rumble and convulse, finally culminating in the sound of an explosion, followed almost immediately by the screaming whine of a disabled Libyan Mig-25 as it careened in a tight spiral toward the ground. From inside the car it was impossible to determine what the sound was, but from the unearthly noise that shook the ground around them, it sounded like the gates of hell were opening.

The pilot was already dead as the jet slammed headlong into the side of a six-story office building just two blocks from where Połucki had brought the car to a screeching halt. His foot was planted firmly on the brake, and his fingers were locked around the steering wheel, but it did little to steady his shaking hands.

Tom was shaking too, but he grabbed his camera and jumped out of the car to get a shot of the destruction. "Wait here," he directed. Nigel didn't argue — he needed a few minutes to steady his nerves before he would feel ready to drive again. Tom had gone only about thirty yards when again he heard the roar of jet engines. To his left, the horizon was filled with the wingspan of an oncoming Israeli F-35.

Flying just above the roof tops, the plane's engines swallowed huge gulps of air as it passed directly over Tom's head, followed a moment later by a second jet, a Syrian MiG-31, in hot pursuit. The more-maneuverable F-35 banked sharply to the right but, amazingly, the Syrian followed. The Israeli went left, but the Syrian was right behind him. Then, as Tom recorded the images of the duel on his new camera, the Israeli made what Tom thought was a fatal mistake: he started to climb. Recalling the quick Internet research he had done at the hospital, Tom knew the F-35 could never match the MiG-31 in climbing speed. The Syrian narrowed the distance to his target: Wikipedia had been right. As the two planes streaked skyward, the MiG released an AA-6 Acrid air-to-air missile.

The Acrid closed in for the kill and Tom readied his camera to capture the impact. At what seemed the last possible second, the F-35 rolled into a dive. It was a good maneuver, but it had come an instant too late. The heat-seeking missile had caught his scent and turned with him. Downward the Israeli sped, racing for his life against the single-minded Acrid. Soon the pilot would have to pull up, and when he did the missile would overtake him.

Closer and closer he came to the ground, maintaining his course as long as possible in order to build speed. A few seconds more and it would be too late; the F-35 would crash into the earth, followed by the unrelenting missile.

The flyer made a valiant attempt, but it seemed all had been in vain. Tom prepared to record the crash as, finally, the pilot raised the plane's nose. *It's too late*, Tom thought, but to his amazement the pilot raised the machine in a tight arch that missed the tops of buildings by less than twenty yards. The plane shook violently at the demanding effort but the pilot held its course, streaking directly overhead. The missile began to follow but was unable to make the radical course adjustment.

As Tom searched the sky for the trailing missile it suddenly came into full view. It was headed directly toward him. The missile pierced the metal roof of Nigel's Mercedes and exploded in a sun-bright flash, killing Nigel instantly as his body disintegrated into minute particles and joined the wash of other charred projectiles flying in all directions at cyclone speed. Before Tom could even blink, small shards of steel and glass cut painful, bloody paths deep into his flesh, followed an instant later by the car's hood, which knocked him violently to the street.

Derwood, Maryland

Decker sat at the computer in his study, typing up the profile piece on Ambassador Hansen. It was early morning, a few minutes before six. He would post the article on the *NewsWorld* site later in the day, but there was no rush. The real news was the war in the Middle East. Hansen's profile might make an interesting sidebar story to the war but little more. Decker's angle was to look at Hansen as the man who had almost stopped the war. It was a gross exaggeration, but he would tone it down in the body of the story. It was a common ploy: hook the reader with the headline; downplay it in the text; and make the reader think the misinterpretation had been his own.

In Louisa's old room, Decker could hear Christopher's alarm clock ringing. He was starting school on Monday and Decker suggested that he readjust to early mornings. By the time Christopher was dressed, Decker had breakfast on the table.

"Good morning, sleepyhead," Decker said when Christopher came into the kitchen. "I fixed your favorite: waffles with plenty of bacon and scalding hot syrup!"

Christopher gave Decker a knowing smile and rolled his eyes, and Decker laughed at his own joke as he reached for the remote control to turn on the kitchen TV set. It was six-thirty and the news was just starting.

"Our top story," the news anchor said, "is the war in the Middle East. For two reports we go to Peter Fantham in Tel Aviv and James Worschal at the State Department. Peter?"

"Thanks, John. Today is the Sabbath in Israel, a day of rest, but few are resting. Throughout the night and into the late morning, widespread fighting has continued on several fronts, with heavy casualties on both sides. Behind me are the still smoldering remains of a Russian-made MiG-25, one of the most modern planes in the Arab arsenal, shot down last night in a dogfight over Tel Aviv. But sources tell CNN that, while there may have been far more Turkish and Egyptian F-16s and Syrian and Libyan MiGs than Israeli aircraft shot down in last night's fighting, the real story of the first day of this war was not in the air, but on the ground.

"CNN has learned that most of the Israeli Air Force never even got in the air. According to one source, dozens of Israeli fighters and bombers were destroyed and had to be bulldozed off runways to allow undamaged planes to take off. The Israeli military has refused comment and has ignored requests to allow our camera crew onto any of their bases, but unofficial estimates of losses range as high as 60 percent of the entire Israeli Air Force. If these figures are correct, Israel may be in a struggle for its very existence."

The scene switched to another reporter standing in a large hall with flags of various nations behind him. The caption identified the man as James Worschal and the place as the U.S. State Department.

"I've worked with him," Decker interjected pointing to the reporter. "He knows his stuff."

"This is the sixth time Israel has been in an actual war with her Muslim neighbors," James Worschal began. "Each time before, she has emerged the victor against far superior numbers. But this time the odds seem to have changed dramatically.

"In the past, Israel has depended on four strategic advantages: superior intelligence capabilities, more highly trained and motivated soldiers and officers, a world-class air force, and the distrust and disorganization among Muslim allies at the command level. But this morning three of those four strategic advantages seem to have been severely damaged or lost altogether.

"The successful attack not only decimated the machinery of the Israeli Air Force, as Peter just reported from Tel Aviv, it has also shown that the perennial lack of cooperation between Muslim states may have come to an end. Military experts tell CNN that last night's unified attack was nearly flawless. The level of coordination between the Muslim nations was a classic display of synchronized modern warfare.

"Finally, John, the key to the success of last night's attack was surprise. The Muslim allies successfully launched a massive multi-pronged attack in total secrecy. Israel's intelligence agency, the Mossad, has a reputation second to none, but last night they appear to have been asleep on the job."

The scene switched to a split screen of the news desk in Atlanta and the reporter at the State Department. "Jim, what about Israel's "Iron Dome" and their strategic defense that we've heard so much about? Isn't that a factor?"

Decker thought of Joshua Rosen, who had helped design Iron Dome's tracking systems.

"The Iron Dome, Israel's interceptor system to defend against short-range rocket attack, has done a remarkable job so far of protecting the civilian population against rockets launched from Gaza, the West Bank, and Lebanon. It even brought down two surface-to-surface missiles launched from the Mediterranean by a Turkish frigate, but the system is not designed to defend against manned aircraft. As for Israel's strategic defense — as its name implies — that system is designed to defend against a *strategic* attack by incoming missiles ranging from SCUDS to ICBMs. The mere existence of that system probably explains why we've seen no attempt yet from Iran to launch a missile attack. Against small, low-flying aircraft and ground forces, however, their strategic defense is useless."

"What about that Turkish frigate?"

"In one bright point for Israel, after launching those two missiles, the Turkish frigate was immediately hit and sunk by torpedoes from an Israeli sub," Worschal reported. "As a result, the Turkish navy has drawn back, closer to its own ports."

"What's the prognosis there at the State Department?" the anchor asked. "Has the possibility of direct U.S. intervention been discussed? And even if the U.S. does become involved, is there much hope that Israel can recover from this?"

"John, no one is talking openly about direct U.S. intervention, although it is very likely that both the U.S. and Britain will respond with assistance in the form of military equipment and humanitarian aid. To answer the second question, no one is making any bets on the outcome one way or another, but there is some quiet optimism being expressed. Despite the successful first strike, it's important to remember that this isn't the first time Israel has suffered a surprise attack. The first time was in the Yom Kippur War — a war the Israelis came back to win and win big. The other point of optimism is still Israel's air force. Despite the heavy losses, it's possible that the Israelis may be able to make up in quality what they lack in quantity. Two examples have been repeatedly brought up: the first, as I mentioned, is the Yom Kippur War, in which the Israeli Air Force shot down more than two hundred Syrian MiGs without the loss of a single Israeli aircraft. The other example, which is no less impressive, occurred in July 1970. In their only head-to-head meeting with the old Soviet Union, the Israelis shot down six Russian MiG-21s while the Soviets failed to damage even one Israeli aircraft. If the air force can duplicate that kind of record in this war, they may still have a chance of surviving."

"Thanks, Jim. Now, for more on this story we go to Tom Slade in Jerusalem." The scene switched to the Temple Mount.

As the camera panned the scene, Decker noted the changes since he and Tom were there the night the Wailing Wall was destroyed.

"John, Muslims and Jews have never really needed a reason to fight, but on this occasion the reason is clear. This is a holy war, a *jihad*, bringing together Muslim countries that only a few years ago were bitter rivals. Surprisingly, their cause is a piece of land only about the size of two football fields.

"Behind me, construction of the Jewish Temple actually goes on despite the war, on land claimed by both the Jews and Muslims. For nearly twelve hundred years, until it was destroyed by Jewish extremists three years ago, this spot was occupied by the Mosque of Omar, the third most holy shrine in Islam. Before that, on this same spot, stood the ancient Jewish Temple, which was itself destroyed in A.D. 70 by the Roman army.

"Orthodox Jews, who have tried to muster support for rebuilding the Temple since before Israel became a state in 1948, attempted to portray the destruction of the Mosque as a sign from God to rebuild, but for most Israelis, the Temple was a nonissue.

"For nearly three years, since the destruction of the Wailing Wall by Palestinians and the subsequent destruction of the Mosque by Israelis, the land sat cordoned off, guarded and undisturbed behind Israeli police lines. During those years, Israeli politics has moved sharply to the right in response to continuing unrest and suicide bombings. Last year Moshe Greenberg's Ichud party, campaigning on hard-line promises including the symbolic promise of rebuilding the Temple, won a small but solid plurality in the Knesset. Minority religious parties made the reconstruction of the Temple a key issue when they agreed to support the Ichud party in forming a coalition government.

"Today, after years of increasing tensions and violence between Palestinians and Israelis, even many nonreligious Israelis defiantly support the rebuilding of the Temple as a cultural and historic landmark. So, ironically, even as fighting goes on all around it, here on the Temple Mount construction goes on, albeit at a significantly reduced pace."

"Tom, aren't the workmen at risk of being caught in an air strike?" the anchorman asked.

"This may actually be the safest place in Israel, John. Remember that even without the Mosque of Omar, this mount is the third holiest location in Islam. For the present, it's considered highly unlikely that the Muslims will do anything that might damage this site. They won't bomb, but have vowed they will tear down the Temple with their bare hands."

"Thanks, Tom," said the anchor as the scene switched back to the studio. "In New York, the United Nations Security Council will meet this afternoon in emergency session to consider their response. The U.S. and Britain have called on the United Nations to impose immediate economic sanctions against the attacking countries, and suggested that they may seek deployment of the UN's recently commissioned naval forces to blockade the combatants' ports.

"But with the world attempting to recover from losses suffered in the Disaster and still awaiting an official report of its cause, there is a sense that while the words and posturing may be the same as in any other war, realities are very much changed. Most of the world has seen all the death it can stomach for a while and is in no position militarily or economically to intervene."

Decker turned down the volume, "It seems our trip to New York allowed you to get a bird's-eye view of history in the making."

Christopher looked upset. "'Holy war,'" he said recalling the words of one of the reporters. "Once again, man uses religious differences to justify his personal desires. Religion should lift men up, not be used as an excuse to kill and destroy."

Decker's comment about a bird's eye view of history seemed rather petty compared to the thoughtful response from his young ward. He waited to hear what else Christopher might say, but he only sighed and went back to his breakfast. Decker decided to probe. He didn't know what to expect, but here, sitting at his kitchen table was the clone of Jesus of Nazareth — a fact that seemed strangely easy to forget — and he was talking about religion. Decker wanted to keep him on the subject just a little longer. Yet he hesitated — the boy was, after all, only fourteen years old. It wasn't as though Decker would actually be talking to Jesus; Professor Goodman had made it clear that Christopher had no memory of his past life. Still, Decker had to ask.

"Christopher," he began haltingly, "I don't want to pry, so if you don't want to talk about it, just say so. But I'm interested in what you were saying about religion." *Yeah, that was pretty good*, he thought. *Not too pushy; not too probing.* He didn't want to say anything he'd have to explain.

Christopher didn't answer right away. At first Decker thought he was just considering how to answer the question, but the look on the boy's face said it was something altogether different.

"Mr. Hawthorne," Christopher began, looking as serious as Decker had ever seen him, "I've been meaning to talk to you about something, but the time never seemed right." He took a long breath while Decker looked at him in anxious surprise. "I know who I am," he said. "I know that I was cloned from cells Uncle Harry found on the Shroud of Turin."

"What? How?" Decker sputtered.

"I always had a feeling I was different from other kids," Christopher began. "But Aunt Martha told me every kid feels like that sometimes. She could always make me feel better.

"But just before my twelfth birthday, I had a terrifying nightmare that I was being crucified! It was so real. I didn't tell Aunt Martha or Uncle Harry because I thought it was just a nightmare. But over the next few months I had the same dream several more times. I had heard about crucifixion, of course, but it didn't particularly frighten me, especially not enough to cause a recurring nightmare. The dreams were always terrifying while they were happening, but when I'd wake up, it all just seemed crazy, and pretty soon I'd go back to sleep.

"Then about a year ago, I was in Uncle Harry's study. He was working, and I was doing my homework, and I fell asleep, and I had the dream again. When I woke up, Uncle Harry was sitting there with the strangest look on his face. Apparently I was talking in my sleep and he'd recorded what I was saying. He asked what I was dreaming about and I told him. But when he played back the tape, I couldn't understand it. It was my voice, but it wasn't even English."

Decker was too stunned to do anything but listen.

"Uncle Harry called someone in the language department at the university, and asked if he could identify the language. He said it was a mix of Aramaic and Hebrew. And that a couple of things I said were things Jesus said when he was crucified." Christopher shrugged. "That's when Uncle Harry told me the whole story about the Shroud and everything."

Christopher thought for a moment and continued. "It was plenty scary, but I guess it was kinda neat too, especially when he told me his theory that Jesus was from another planet. I guess every kid likes to think he's special. He made me promise not to tell Aunt Martha or anyone else 'cause he was afraid of what people might do. He said that some people would think it was a sin to clone Jesus."

Decker's shock was akin to what he had felt when he first saw the live cells through Professor Goodman's microscope. But he had to know more. "How can you remember the crucifixion?" he managed.

"Uncle Harry wondered about that, too. He had a theory. He said that each cell in the body has the blueprints for the whole body — not just things like race and sex and hair color and eye color and whether you'll be tall or short, but everything that every other cell in the body needs to know to form and function. That's how the single cell of a fertilized egg can reproduce to form something as complex as a human being. It's also what makes cloning possible.

"He thought that maybe the cells include even more information than all that. He said that scientists call some human DNA 'junk DNA' because it's repetitive and they're not really sure what it's all for. He thought maybe the junk DNA is used by cells to record key changes in other cells, including significant memories in the cells of the brain. He said that might also answer some questions about evolution and something he called the collective unconscious of the species, but he didn't really explain that."

Decker recognized the reference to the theories of Sigmund Freud's protégé, Carl Jung.[27]

"Before he and Aunt Martha died," Christopher concluded, "Uncle Harry was experimenting with some white mice to see if a cloned mouse would remember its way through a maze that the original mouse had been trained to go through. I don't think he got very far on that, though."

"Do you remember anything besides the crucifixion? Anything afterwards?" Decker asked.

"No. Uncle Harry said I wouldn't remember anything afterwards because I was cloned from a cell left on the Shroud only seconds after the resurrection. He tried to help my memory by having me read parts of Aunt Martha's Bible." Christopher shook his head. "It was kinda interesting, but it didn't help me remember anything."

Christopher paused, but it seemed there might be something else. Decker waited.

"There was one thing," he added. "It wasn't a memory exactly. More like a feeling. The Bible makes it seem like Jesus knew he was going to be killed, like it was all planned out, but that's not how it was. I know this all sounds kinda strange, but in my dream, before the crucifixion, I just kept thinking that any minute I'd be rescued — I don't know," he shook his head, "by angels maybe. But something went wrong, Mr. Hawthorne." There was obvious pain in Christopher's expression. It was old pain, but it was no less real. "I don't think the crucifixion was supposed to happen. For hours I hung on that cross with spikes through my wrists and feet, trying to understand what went wrong. That's why I said, 'My God, my God, why have you forsaken me?'[28] I don't think I was supposed to die. I think God was supposed to rescue me!"

"I'm so sorry," Decker said, as he stood and put his hand on the boy's shoulder.

"Uncle Harry told me the only other person who knew about me was you. And you were in Lebanon."

At that moment the phone rang.

Decker gave Christopher's back a comforting rub and went to answer the phone. It was Ambassador Hansen. "Decker, I don't know any way to say this to make it any easier on you," Hansen said, "so I'm just going to read you the dispatch I received from Ambassador Rogers.

As per your request, at about 5:00 P.M. Eastern Time, midnight Israel time, a driver was dispatched to Tel Hashomer Hospital to bring Mr. Tom Donafin back to the British Embassy with the intention of expediting his departure from Israel. The driver and Mr. Donafin were expected back within two hours. Three hours later, that is about 3:00 A.M. Israel time, the driver had still not returned to the embassy and could not be reached by mobile phone, nor could his locator be activated.

In keeping with standard operating procedures, a search team was dispatched to cover the route that the driver had indicated on his itinerary. The search team was unsuccessful in finding either the driver or the car, but they did verify that Mr. Donafin had checked out of hospital and left with the driver from the embassy.

The team expanded their search to include some likely alternate routes, and at about 7:30 A.M. Israel time, they located what was left of the car, which was positively identified by the license plate.

"Decker, I'm sorry," Hansen concluded. "It appears that the car took a direct hit from a stray missile or artillery shell and was completely destroyed. There were no survivors."

New York

The wealth of the Bragford family was clearly evident in the solid cherry paneling, rich carpeting, and highly polished brass that presented former UN Assistant Secretary-General Robert Milner and Alice Bernley with perfect mirrored images of themselves and the operator who was piloting the private elevator to the penthouse office of the family's guiding force, David Bragford.

Most of Robert Milner's adult life had been spent in the presence of the wealthy and powerful. Raising large amounts of money from rich patrons for special projects at the UN came with the job of assistant secretary-general, and Milner was quite good at it. The experience had its benefits. He knew what it took to separate the rich from their money — at least small portions of it. He had become adept at getting what he wanted by alternately stroking an ego and stoking a sense of guilt for having so much while others starved.

Still, Milner held a deeply seated distrust of those with great wealth, and certainly there were few on Earth who possessed such wealth as did the Bragfords. Men like David Bragford were altogether different from the garden-variety rich. While it was true the Bragford family had been very extravagant in their support of the UN — indeed, the Bragfords had been instrumental in financing the original organization of the United Nations — Milner had found that such extravagance is never born purely of generosity. When they gave, there was always something they expected in return, and in Milner's experience, at the very least that meant intrusion.

It was, therefore, with some discomfort that he agreed to accompany Alice Bernley to Bragford's office. Bernley was positive, she said, that this was the right thing to do and that Bragford would help them. She had consulted her spirit guide, Tibetan Master Djwlij Kajm, and he had left no doubt that Bragford was to be consulted.

At the conclusion of their ascent to the penthouse, they were met by David Bragford's assistant, who escorted them past two security posts to a mammoth office where David Bragford sat comfortably at his desk, talking on the phone. Beside him, on the impeccably clean white carpet, lay a black Labrador retriever who, unlike their host, seemed to take no immediate notice of their arrival. Bragford quickly finished his conversation and joined them in a sitting area of the office.

"Alice, Mr. Assistant Secretary-General, welcome," Bragford said, affording Milner the honor of his former post. "Can I get you anything? Would you like some coffee?" Bragford had an assistant bring coffee for his guests while he shared niceties with Bernley and Milner about their recent projects. The arrival of the coffee marked the end of small talk and the beginning of discussion of the business at hand.

"So," Bragford said, directing his opening to Milner, "Alice tells me you would like my help with something."

"Yes," Bernley said, taking the lead. "As you know, Master Djwlij Kajm many years ago prophesied that both Bob and I would live to see the true *Krishnamurti*, the Ruler of the New Age. Yesterday we saw him."

One would never have guessed it from the look on his face, but with each word Alice spoke, Robert Milner was dying of embarrassment. Why, he asked himself, had he allowed Alice to do the talking? He should have known this would happen; Alice wasn't one to control her emotions. This was not the correct approach for the uninitiated. Sure, it was all true. They *had* seen him, but Milner knew very well that David Bragford didn't believe one word about Bernley's spirit guide. Bragford, after all, had never been present at a demonstration of Master Djwlij Kajm's power.

"That's great," Bragford replied. "When can I meet him?"

Though there was absolutely no evidence of it, Milner was sure Bragford was patronizing them.

"Oh, well, that's the problem," Bernley said. "We don't know where he is. He was at the UN, but then he left with a man, possibly his father."

"His father?" Bragford asked with raised brow. "Just how old is this ... uh ..." Bragford was trying hard not to say anything that would make his skepticism too obvious, but he could not for the life of him remember what Bernley had called this person.

Alice spared him the difficulty of finishing his sentence. "He's just a boy," she said. "I'd guess he was about, oh, what would you say, Bob?" But 'Bob' wasn't saying. It didn't matter. Alice answered her own question. "Fourteen or fifteen, I'd say."

"Fourteen or fifteen?" echoed Bragford.

"Yes," Bernley said, ignoring Bragford's dubious expression and the now unmistakable skepticism in his voice. "What we need is your help finding out who he is."

To Milner's amazement, Bragford was ready with an answer, eager to hand this off to an unsuspecting lieutenant. "I think I have just the right person to help you. Just a moment," he said as he reached for the phone on the coffee table. "Betty, would you ask Mr. Tarkington to join us in my office?"

Almost immediately, the door opened and a tall, muscular man entered. "Come in, Sam," Bragford said. Bernley and Milner rose to meet him. After the introductions Bragford got right to the point of explaining what was required, while leaving out the stranger aspects of Bernley's and Milner's interest in finding the individuals.

"Do you think you can do it?" Bragford asked.

"I believe so, sir. The security cameras at the UN record everyone entering and exiting the guest lobby. If Ms. Bernley and the assistant secretary-general can identify the man and boy from the tape, then I'll put our people to work finding out who they are. If they went anywhere in the building that required signing a registry, such as the Secretariat Building or the Delegates Dining Room, it'll make our job a lot easier."

"Great," Bragford said, satisfied with the prospects and confident of Tarkington's abilities.

"Great," echoed Bernley. "Now, once we find out who they are, there's one other thing we may need your help with."

Tel Aviv

The darkened streets were nearly silent as the tall, bearded man walked through the rubble scattered across the pockmarked asphalt. His long, purposeful strides and the soft, muffled sounds of the leather soles of his shoes gave no hint of the weight he bore over his shoulder. The long, curled hair of his traditional Hasidic earlock was flattened against his cheek, sandwiched tightly between his face and the load he carried. For more than six miles the darkly dressed man had borne his burden, from the business district of the city down long straight streets to a cluster of apartment buildings near the shore of the Mediterranean.

Finally, the man stopped in front of a ten-story apartment building on Ramat Aviz and went to the front entrance. The glass doors, which had been destroyed in a blast the night before, had been replaced with sheets of plywood. The man knocked, and a moment later the door was cracked open and two eyes peered out at him. As recognition registered in the eyes, the door was quickly shut again and a table moved aside so the door could be fully opened. A rather plain woman in her mid-thirties, dressed in a blood-stained surgical gown, greeted the unexpected guest.

"Welcome, Rabbi," she said, as she led him to an area of the lobby that had been converted to a makeshift clinic. Here and there family members of patients were camped out near their relatives to assist with their care.

"Not here with the others," he said, his words revealing a voice unusually rich and measured. "You must take him to your apartment."

Only now did the woman see the face of the man the rabbi carried over his shoulder. The blood that covered him and soaked his clothes was foreboding enough to his prognosis, but his misshapen skull led her to believe that the patient was as good as dead, and perhaps would be better off if he were.

"Rabbi, I think we're wasting our time with this one," she said.

"You must see to it that we are not," he answered firmly as he turned and walked toward the stairwell. "I have full confidence in your abilities."

"But Rabbi, he's nearly dead if he's not dead already."

"He is not dead," the rabbi said as he opened the door and began to ascend the first flight of stairs, the woman following closely behind. Quickly, she dipped and swerved to get around the rabbi, then placed herself in the middle of the stairs, stopping his advance. The rabbi stared insistently, his eyes telling her to let him pass.

"At least let me check his pulse!" she pleaded.

The rabbi paused as she took the man's wrist and checked his pulse. He watched her eyes, entirely certain of what she would find. To her amazement the pulse was reasonably strong. The rabbi moved past her and continued up the steps.

"Okay," she said, "so he's alive, but you can see the condition of his head. He's probably hopelessly brain damaged."

"There's nothing wrong with his brain. It's an old injury he received when he was a child." The rabbi reached the third floor and opened the stairwell door.

"Okay, okay, so maybe he'll survive." She was becoming frantic to stop him as he made his way ever closer to her apartment with his unwelcome patient. She knew her only hope was to talk him out of his plan. If he insisted, however, she would have to submit; he was, after all, the rabbi. The problem was that as far as she knew, no one had ever talked the rabbi out of anything.

"But why does he have to stay in my apartment?! Why can't he stay downstairs with the others?"

The rabbi, who had now reached her apartment, turned to answer as he waited for her to unlock the door. "He is unclean," he answered in a whisper, though no one else was within earshot. "He is uncircumcised," he added in clarification. "Also, he will need your personal care."

Convinced it was futile to resist, the woman relented and opened the door. "Put him in the extra bedroom," she said as she grabbed some old sheets from the linen closet. "Is he a Gentile?" she asked, as she began spreading the sheets on the bed.

"He believes he is," he answered. "In a week or so, when he is better, I'll see to his circumcision."

"Who is he?" she asked, now reluctantly reconciled to her situation.

"His name is Tom Donafin."

The rabbi waited while the woman ran water into a basin and began to clean Tom's wounds. "He is the one of whom the prophecy spoke, 'He must bring death and die that the end and the beginning may come.'"

The woman stopped her work and looked back at the rabbi, stunned at what she had just been told.

"He is the last in the lineage of James, the brother of the Lord," he continued. "He is the Avenger of Blood."

Chapter 13

The Color of the Horse

Derwood, Maryland

Decker boarded the Metro at the Shady Grove station. It was rush hour and a work day, but he easily found a seat. Several stations later, when the cars continued to be less than fully occupied, he realized the reason: the Disaster. He was aware the DC area had lost about 14 percent of its population — nearly 1.5 million people — but seeing the impact in microcosm on the Metro brought the figure home. The evidence continued to confront him as he exited at DuPont Circle and made his way for the first time in more than three years to the offices of *NewsWorld* magazine.

Decker's *NewsWorld* ID, along with everything else, had been taken from him by his captors, so when he walked into the lobby the unfamiliar receptionist insisted that he sign in and wait for an escort. While he wasn't generally a rude person, he was somewhat territorial, and despite having been gone for so long, to him this was his territory. He had no intention of either signing in *or* waiting for an escort. Fortunately for the receptionist, Sheryl Stanford arrived on the next elevator. "It's all right," Sheryl told the receptionist, "he works here."

For a few minutes Decker just looked around, feeling a growing sense of loss and melancholy. Very few familiar faces greeted him. Over the last three years, most of the people he knew had been transferred to other offices or had retired or taken other jobs; a few were victims of the Disaster.

Hank Asher's door was open. "Decker! Welcome back," Asher called. "You ready to get back in the saddle?"

"I see you reassigned my office," Decker said as he took a seat.

"Funny you should mention that," Asher responded. "I just got word they're putting you in charge of the New York office."

This was news to Decker and it took a few seconds for him to reorient his thoughts. "I don't get it," he said. "I've been gone for three years and now they want to put me in charge of New York?" Decker thought of his house in Derwood — the house he had told Elizabeth they would make their home. He thought about his family's grave in the backyard. This was not what he had imagined for his first day back in the office. "What if I don't want the New York office?"

"Why wouldn't you want it?"

Decker rubbed his chin. "I just . . . I'm just not interested," he shrugged.

Asher suddenly understood. After all, it was he who dug the grave. "Decker if it's about your house, there's no problem. I've been authorized to offer you a very generous raise. You should be able to afford an apartment in New York and still keep your house here."

"Are you crazy?" Decker challenged. "Do you have any idea how much an apartment in New York goes for?"

"There are a lot fewer people in New York since the Disaster," Asher reminded him. "It's a buyer's market."

Decker cringed as he recalled what the cabby had said about 'dead folks' apartments.' "Maybe," he answered, "but I hate apartments."

Asher closed the door and lowered his voice. "Look, Decker, just between you and me, I've been told to offer you whatever it takes."

Decker looked at Asher to be sure he wasn't kidding. "What do you mean, 'Whatever it takes'?"

"Don't get crazy on me now."

Decker thought for a moment. "Why?" he probed.

"Why what?" Asher asked.

"Why are they being so generous? Why do they want *me*?"

"They need a new head for the New York office, and I guess they think you're the man."

"Hank, okay, look, I'm flattered, but there must be more to it. *NewsWorld* is not the type of organization to throw money around. How can they possibly offer to pay me enough to maintain two homes?"

"I don't know, Decker. It sounds out of character to me, too, but I think you'd be crazy to look a gift horse in the mouth. Besides, I think you deserve it."

"What else did they tell you?"

"Ima Jackson called this morning and told me the decision had been made to give you the New York office. I asked her how much

I was supposed to offer and she said, 'Whatever it takes.' When I asked her to be a little more specific, she just repeated herself. She told me not to ask questions, that the decision had come down from way above her head, and that I was to see to it you accepted. I guess somebody on the board of directors must want you there. To tell the truth, I was hoping you might be able to fill me in."

"I have no idea," Decker said shaking his head. "Why would anyone on the board even care who was in charge of the New York office?"

Asher shrugged. It made no sense. The directors never got involved at this level.

"Hank, I appreciate whatever part you played in getting me this offer—"

"I told you; I had nothing to do with this."

Decker slumped back in the chair and blew out a deep breath. "Hank, look," he began. "Things have changed. Not just the world, but me. In the past I would have jumped at this opportunity. But making a lot of money just isn't that important anymore." He looked out Asher's window for a moment, then continued haltingly. "My family's dead. Except for Christopher, I've got no one left. And I've got no reason to be ambitious. I wouldn't tell this to anyone else, but to be perfectly honest, I'm only going back to work as an alternative to blowing my brains out."

* * * * *

That evening over dinner, Decker asked Christopher about his new school. There was still upheaval as the Montgomery County school system adjusted to account for teachers and students who had died in the Disaster. Christopher had been given a battery of tests to see where to place him, because it might be months before his records were received from California.

"How do you think you did?" Decker asked him.

"Okay, I guess. The tests were pretty easy."

Decker had always thought of Christopher as bright; he decided to pursue it a little. "What sort of grades did you get in California?"

"I've always had a 4.0," Christopher answered.

"That's good," Decker nodded approvingly but not really surprised. "Have any of your teachers ever suggested that you should skip a grade?"

"Yes, sir. Every year. But Aunt Martha said I should be with kids my own age. She said it would be bad for my social growth to be put with a bunch of older kids."

"What do you think?"

"I guess she was probably right," Christopher answered. "She said once I got to college I could go as fast as I wanted because I'd be old enough to make my own decisions."

"Your Aunt Martha must have been a remarkable woman. I wish I had gotten to know her better," Decker said. Christopher smiled. They took a few more bites of their food and Decker changed the subject. "How would you feel about us moving to New York?" he asked without explanation.

"New York?" Christopher said with unexpected enthusiasm. "Would we be near the UN?"

"I don't know. I've been offered the job as head of the New York office for *NewsWorld*. It's a couple of miles from the UN, but I don't know where we'd actually live. We'd have to shop around for an apartment."

"I bet I could get a job as a page to one of the delegates," Christopher suggested excitedly. "Did you know they have their own university?"

Decker shook his head. "I had no idea you would be so favorable to the idea."

"Oh, yeah! It'd be great!"

"Well, don't get too excited. I haven't taken the job yet."

* * * * *

The next morning Decker received a call. He recognized the voice immediately as Ambassador Hansen's daughter, Jackie.

"Mr. Hawthorne," she began, "Ambassador Hansen asked me to call you. He was very impressed with your article about him and he wishes to thank you for all the nice things you said."

"Well, please relay my regards back to the ambassador. Tell him I appreciate his graciousness, especially considering the circumstances."

"Thank you, I will," she answered. "Ambassador Hansen would also like to know if you would be at all interested in discussing the possibility of accepting a position as his press secretary and chief speech writer. The position has just come open and the ambassador feels that you would be an excellent choice to fill it."

Decker was surprised. Was this another case of being in the right place at the right time? It made sense to consider another offer before deciding whether to accept the promotion at *NewsWorld.* Then he remembered the expression on Christopher's face when he talked about the UN.

"Sure," he said. "I'd be glad to consider it."

"Good," she responded. "When could you come to New York to discuss it further?"

"I can be there tomorrow afternoon, if that's okay with Ambassador Hansen."

"That would be fine. We'll arrange for your airline ticket and I'll have someone call you back within the hour to confirm the time."

Decker hung up the phone and went to work updating his resume.

In New York, Jackie Hansen sat at her father's desk with the door closed. In a moment she would instruct her assistant to make the arrangements for Decker's flight. Right now she needed privacy to make another call. "This is Jackie Hansen," she said into the receiver. "I need to speak to the director."

"Yes?" she heard after a moment.

"He said yes," Jackie said without explanation. "He'll be here tomorrow for the interview."

"Excellent! You've done very well," Alice Bernley beamed.

Alice Bernley hung up the phone and smiled broadly at Robert Milner. The look on her face left no doubt that their plan had been successful.

"I guess we can tell Bragford to call off the people at *NewsWorld,*" Milner said. "I think this is a better arrangement anyway. We'll be in a much better position to direct the boy's future with Mr. Hawthorne working for Ambassador Hansen than if he had accepted the job at the magazine."

"Assuming Jackie is able to ensure that her father offers him the job," Bernley said, "how can we be sure Mr. Hawthorne will accept the offer?"

"When *NewsWorld* abruptly withdraws its offer of a promotion and a raise, Hawthorne will have to consider it a professional insult. He'll be looking for some way to preserve his honor. Ambassador Hansen's offer will provide him that opportunity," Milner answered.

Chapter 14

Dark Awakening

Tel Aviv

A small electric space heater lifted a warm breeze across Tom Donafin's face as sounds began to fill his ears with the reality that surrounded him. Still more asleep than awake, his mind wandered aimlessly between dream and consciousness. Finally opening his eyes, he recoiled, howling in pain as tiny bits of glass scraped across the inside of his eyelids. Overcome and wincing with the agony that engulfed him, he panted short shallow breaths as he tried to relax his eyes and sort through his memories. The last thing he recalled was the missile that killed Nigel and destroyed the car. He didn't recall being knocked unconscious, nor did he have any idea where he was now. He could tell he was in a bed, which seemed a positive sign.

As the pain eased slightly, he listened for voices or some distinguishable sound but heard none. "Hello," he said finally to anyone who might be nearby. "Hello!" he repeated much louder. In a moment, he heard a door open.

"So, you're awake," a man's voice answered in a not altogether friendly tone.

"Where am I?" Tom asked.

"You're in the apartment of Dr. Rhoda Felsberg in occupied Tel Aviv." The man's voice gave the clear impression that Tom was an unwelcome guest.

"How did I get here?"

"You were brought here nearly a month ago by my sister's rabbi, who found you on the street."

"A month?" Tom gasped. "Have I been unconscious the whole time?"

"Pretty much."

"What did you mean, 'occupied' Tel Aviv?"

"Just that," the man responded, not offering any more information.

"Occupied by whom?" Tom insisted, becoming a little exasperated at the man's apparent unwillingness to provide substantive answers.

"The Russians," the man grumbled.

Tom didn't know whether to take him seriously. He began to wonder if he had awakened in a psychiatric ward and the man he was talking to was a patient.

"You said I was brought here by your sister's rabbi. Is your sister the Dr. Felsberg you mentioned?"

"You got it."

"And she's been taking care of me?"

"Yep."

Tom desperately wanted to know what was going on and what had happened to him, but he wanted to talk to someone who would give him reliable, complete answers. "Well," he pressed, exasperated. "Can I talk to her?"

There was silence.

Tom heard the man dial the telephone.

"Hey, Rhoda," the man said. "He's awake and he wants to talk to you."

"I'll be right there!" Tom heard the woman answer.

A moment later Dr. Rhoda Felsberg arrived, went directly to Tom's side, and began to check his condition. "Is he cognizant?" she asked, a little out of breath from running up the three flights of stairs from her office on the first floor. Like her brother, she had a New Jersey accent.

"Hi, there," Tom said with a half grin in answer to her question.

"Oh," she said, a little surprised. "You're actually talking. How do you feel?"

"When I opened my eyes it felt like somebody was dragging razor blades over them."

"I thought I got all the glass out," Rhoda Felsberg said, followed by an indiscriminate sound that Tom interpreted as a negative assessment of his condition. "When you opened your eyes, did you see anything?"

The full meaning of her question was apparent at once. He tried, but the pain of the moment was all he could remember. "I don't think so," he said haltingly. "Am I . . . blind?"

"We can't say yet," she answered. Her voice had no emotion but seemed somehow reassuring. "I need you to try to relax your eyes and let me open them one at a time so I can look inside. Then we'll go from there."

Tom felt her sit down on the bed beside him. Cringing, he allowed her to lift open one eye and then the other. He hoped desperately to see something. He didn't. He felt Dr. Felsberg's hands on his face as she examined him. They were strong but soft, and despite all else that was going on, he noticed the faint sweet fragrance of her perfume as she leaned down close to him and peered into his eyes with her ophthalmoscope.

"Can you see the light in my hand?"

"I can see a light spot," he said, encouraged.

"Good, that's a start," she replied. "Your pupils are both working properly. But I'm afraid there must still be a few particles of glass." Tom felt her put some eyedrops in his eyes, which brought some relief. "I'm going to bandage your eyes to keep them closed until we can get you to an ophthalmologist."

"Will I be able to see again?" he asked.

"It's too soon to say. You should be glad just to be alive," she advised as she helped him to a sitting position and began to bandage his eyes. "I removed several pieces of glass when you were first brought here. You're actually very fortunate. If the glass had gone any deeper, the vitreous fluid would have escaped and your eyeballs would have collapsed."

Tom had no idea what vitreous fluid was, but the thought of his eyeballs collapsing was quite alarming and at least in this regard, he did indeed consider himself fortunate.

"The scarring on your corneas is quite extensive," she continued. "In addition, both of your retinas have been burned. Was there a bright flash when you were injured?"

"I'm not sure," he said, trying to remember. "Probably."

"The burns on your retinas are our biggest worry. The corneas can be replaced with transplants but there's no way to repair a damaged retina. I may be able to remove the remaining glass myself, but I'd feel better if we had a qualified ophthalmologist take a look at you."

"How soon can that be done?"

"It could take a while." The tone of her voice said a while might be a very long time indeed.

"What's going on here, anyway? Why am I here instead of a hospital?" Tom was trying not to panic, but it wasn't easy.

"Please, Mr. Donafin. You've got to realize a lot has changed since your accident. Israel is an occupied country. If you'll be patient I'll explain everything. But first you need to try to eat something."

Only now did Tom notice he was starving, so he didn't object.

In the kitchen, Rhoda Felsberg and her brother Joel spoke in hushed tones.

"So, now that he's awake, are you finally going to move him in with your other patients?" Joel Felsberg insisted.

"No," Rhoda answered curtly. She really didn't want to have this conversation.

"Why not?"

"Because Rabbi Cohen said he should stay here."

"There's no reason for him to insist that you keep this man in your personal care."

"He's the rabbi," Rhoda answered, as though no further justification were necessary.

"Yeah, well he may look like Hasidim, with his earlocks and all dressed in black, but I've heard that the other Hasidic rabbis won't have anything to do with him." Right now Rhoda was glad Joel wasn't more aware of religious matters; if he had been he would have known that Cohen's standing with the other rabbis was actually far worse than he imagined. It hadn't always been this way. At one time Cohen had been thought by many to be a likely heir to the Lubavitcher Rebbe: Rabbi Menachem Mendel Schneerson, considered to be the most politically powerful rabbi in the world. Now, however, it was not only the Hasidic rabbis who wouldn't have anything to do with him; *none* of the other rabbis, not even the most liberal ones, would even mention his name without spitting to show their disgust.

"Oh, and since when did you start to care what the rabbis think?" Rhoda asked her brother, not letting on.

"The point is, he's a kook," Joel answered.

"Come eat," she said, not wanting to argue the matter.

"Rhoda!" Joel said, trying to get her back on subject as she took the pot of soup and some bowls and headed back to Tom.

"Come eat," she said again more sternly, then added, "We'll talk about it later," though she had no intention of allowing the subject to reemerge.

Rhoda put a spoon into Tom's hand and set his soup on a tray in front of him. Tom found it difficult to eat without being able to see, and his first few bites were a bit messy. Rhoda gave him a napkin, but as he began to wipe his mouth, he felt the scars that covered his face from the explosion. Silently, he traced the disfigurements with his fingers.

"How bad am I?" he asked.

"You had lacerations over much of the front of your body," Rhoda answered. "I had to dig out a lot of glass and other debris. Most of the wounds will disappear eventually. Some minor plastic surgery may be needed later for the scars on your face. We'll just have to wait and see."

"I guess I was never that much to look at anyway," he said, characteristically hiding his pain in humor. He paused. "So, how about that explanation? What am I doing here, and when can I see an ophthalmologist?"

"The night after the war began," Rhoda explained, "you were brought here by Rabbi Saul Cohen, who found you buried under rubble about five or six miles from here. In addition to the lacerations, you had multiple contusions—"

"You were black and blue all over," interrupted Joel.

"—and your nose and skull were fractured," she continued. "You were dehydrated and you had lost a lot of blood. Since then you've been either unconscious or disoriented."

"Okay," Tom whispered, rightly amazed that he was alive.

"Unfortunately, the war didn't go so well," she continued with her promised explanation. "Israel fought hard but the Muslims had the upper hand. The United States and Britain provided emergency supplies and food. I think they could have done a lot more, but their politicians felt they couldn't afford a war, especially after both countries had lost so many people in the Disaster. Then it was discovered that the Russians were supplying arms to the Muslims.

Of course the Russians denied it, but the UN Security Council voted to set up a blockade."

"You're kidding! How on Earth did they get that past the Russian delegate on the Security Council?" Tom asked.

"That's the really strange thing. The Russian delegation didn't show up for the vote," Rhoda answered.

"That's crazy," Tom blurted. "The Russians made that mistake in 1950. That's what allowed the Security Council action against the Soviet allies in Korea. The Russians would never let that happen a second time."

"I don't understand it either," Rhoda said.

"There's no big mystery," Joel snarled sarcastically. "They had the whole thing planned ahead of time."

"What do you mean?" asked Tom.

"Joel, just let me tell the story," Rhoda said. "You can give us your theories later."

"Sure, go ahead. But he'll figure it out pretty quickly for himself if he's got half a brain left."

"Where was I? You made me forget," Rhoda chided her brother.

"The UN voted for a blockade," Joel groaned.

"Okay, so there were a lot of accusations and veiled threats back and forth, but finally the Russians agreed not to provide any more arms to the Muslim nations if the UN agreed not to impose the blockade. A few days later things seemed to be changing in Israel's favor. We had taken back a lot of land that we lost earlier and what was left of our air force was clobbering the Muslim air and ground forces.

"Then the Mossad learned that because the Libyans couldn't get additional conventional weapons, they were planning to launch a chemical attack. To prevent that, the Israeli Air Force launched a preemptive strike against the Libyan storage facilities. Unfortunately, the Libyans anticipated the attack and had moved their stockpiles.

"When it became apparent there was no other way for Israel to stop a chemical attack, Prime Minister Greenberg sent a message to the Libyans saying that if Israel was attacked with chemical weapons, we would immediately respond with a massive nuclear strike."

"So Israel finally admitted it has nukes?" Tom asked.

"The exact wording of the message wasn't released, but he apparently made it very clear that's what he meant," Joel answered.

"Anyway," Rhoda continued, "despite their promises to the UN, the Russians agreed to sell our enemies additional conventional weapons, claiming it was the only way to prevent a chemical/nuclear exchange."

"Yeah," Joel interjected. "It was a perfect excuse for the Russians to do exactly what they wanted in the first place, which is how you can tell it was all a set up."

Tom still didn't understand what Joel was driving at. Rhoda continued. "So the Mossad tracked the Russian ships they thought were going to deliver the arms to Libya, and just before they entered Libyan waters, our air force and subs attacked. They sank fourteen Russian cargo ships and a bunch of escort vessels, but it turned out the whole thing was a decoy. While most of the Israeli Air Force was busy in the Mediterranean and the army was busy on our borders, advance teams of Russian commandos landed north of Tel Aviv, disabled our anti-aircraft artillery, and took over an airstrip. Within minutes Russian troops and equipment began landing."

"Wait a second," Tom sputtered. "You mean Joel was telling the truth about Tel Aviv being occupied by the Russians?"

"Not just the city," Joel answered. "It's the whole country."

There was a long silence as Tom took it all in. "What a world to wake up to!" he said finally.

"Yeah, seems that some of the Russians weren't happy with the way things have worked out since the collapse of the Soviet Union," Joel said. "Some of them still want to rule the world. Of course, they told the UN they were simply responding to our 'unprovoked' attack on their naval vessels and that they were really just a peacekeeping force. They claimed their only intention in occupying Israel was to prevent a chemical/nuclear war. And just to make it seem more legitimate they brought a few troops from Sudan, Somalia, and a few other countries[29] so they could say it was an 'international' peacekeeping force. Only now they refuse to leave."

The next morning Tom awoke to the smell of breakfast cooking and the sound of Rhoda Felsberg's voice calling his name.

"Mr. Donafin, are you awake?" It was hard for her to be sure with his eyes bandaged.

"I'm awake," Tom answered.

"Do you feel like having some breakfast?"

"That sounds great, thank you. But actually the first thing on my mind is finding the bathroom."

"I can bring you a bedpan, or if you feel like you're ready to walk a few steps, I'll guide you there."

Tom was already standing, though his legs felt incredibly unsure beneath him. "I think I'm ready for the real thing," he said.

"Come on then," she said, and put his hand on her arm to lead him through the apartment.

"I'll take it from here," Tom said when he felt tile instead of carpet beneath his bare feet.

"Can you find your way back to your room? I need to go check the breakfast."

"Sure," Tom said. "I'll bet I can even find the kitchen."

After Tom finished, he slowly made his way to the kitchen, where Rhoda had set the table for two.

"A little to the left," she directed as he started to walk into a doorjamb.

Tom found the table and sat down. Rhoda noticed a very strange look on his face. "I . . . um . . ."

"Is something the matter?" she asked.

"I'm not sure," Tom said. "All these injuries I had . . . Did, um . . ." He decided to start again. "When I was in the bathroom I noticed something that didn't seem . . . uh . . . quite the same. I, uh, well . . . I . . ." Tom stammered for another moment and Rhoda volunteered nothing to help. Had he been able, he would have seen the look of embarrassment on her face as she realized what he was talking about. "Never mind," he said finally.

Rhoda was only too glad to let the subject drop. "I have some good news," she said, quickly changing the subject. "I called an ophthalmologist friend and he said he can see you first thing tomorrow."

"That's great!"

"Don't get too excited yet. He said he could examine you and get the rest of the glass out, not that he can get you admitted for surgery."

"But maybe he can at least tell me what my chances are of getting my sight back."

"Yeah, that's what I'm hoping."

"You, know," Tom added, "there's no reason I have to have the surgery done here, is there? I could go back to the States."

"Well, yes, you could," Rhoda said hesitantly. "Ben Gurion Airport is in pretty bad shape, but I understand that the Russians are still letting a few flights out."

"Speaking of the States," Rhoda continued as she served up some scrambled eggs, "Isn't there anyone you need to call to let them know you're alive?"

Her voice said she was fishing for something she didn't want to ask outright. Tom let it pass and replied to her direct question. "I don't have any family," he said. "They all died in a car wreck when I was a kid. That's how I got this mangled-looking skull. I was the only one to survive."

"Sounds like you've had your share of close calls," Rhoda offered.

"Yeah. I guess so."

"Did they do surgery?" she asked out of professional curiosity.

Tom let out an odd chuckle. "Yeah. They waited a while though. They figured I'd die within a few days, and even if I did make it, I'd be a vegetable. I guess I'm lucky it happened so long ago, back in the days before they'd pull your feeding tube to hurry you on your way. Anyway, four days after the accident I woke up and started talking to the nurse."

"You seem to do that a lot," she laughed.

Tom smiled. "I guess so," he allowed. "That convinced them I might make it, so they went in and dug around and pulled out a bunch of broken pieces of skull and a few extra brains I guess I didn't need. They left me with a steel plate that has a habit of setting off metal detectors at airports."

"Anyone else you want to call?" she asked.

"I do have a friend I should call. He probably thinks I'm dead."

"Is that Decker?"

Tom gave her a funny look. "How did you know that?"

"You mumbled his name several times."

"Oh," he replied. "I had some friends named Rosen here in Israel, but they died in the Disaster." Tom was going down a very short list of the people he counted as his friends. Until the Disaster, Joshua and Ilana had visited him every day at the hospital. Their son, Scott, had survived the Disaster, but Tom hardly considered him a close friend. "I really ought to call *NewsWorld*," he said. "That's where I work. But to tell the truth," he grimaced, "I'd rather wait until after we've been to the eye doctor. I'm a photojournalist, or at least I was. I'm not sure there's much call for blind photographers."

"No. I guess not," she said sadly, almost in a whisper.

"How about you?" he asked more brightly.

"Pardon?"

"Your family."

"Oh, well, of course, there's my brother, Joel, you met yesterday. His wife and son died in the Disaster. I really liked her a lot. And Benny was a really great kid. The three of us used to go to worship services together. That's how I know Rabbi Cohen — he's the one who brought you here."

"Yeah, I need to thank him for that," Tom said.

"Joel was a systems analyst for the Israeli government . . . before the Russians relieved him of his responsibilities, of course. You probably noticed he's not the best company these days," she said apologetically. "He's lost everything important to him in the past two months."

Tom nodded. That explained a lot.

She paused for a moment and then wrapped up her family roster. "My parents and younger sister live in the States."

"New Jersey?" Tom asked, based on her accent.

"Yeah," she confirmed.

After breakfast Tom asked if he could use the phone to call Decker.

"Of course," she said. "I should warn you, though, that getting an overseas call out is not an easy task. After the occupation began, I called repeatedly to let my folks know I was okay. I must've dialed a hundred times before I got through. And they've shut down the

Internet, so I couldn't even email. Of course, it's not just the occupation. There was a lot of damage from the war."

Rhoda dialed the number for Tom and handed him the phone. "The button at the top right hangs up and the middle button at the very bottom redials," she said. "If you don't get through, feel free to keep trying."

"It's ringing," Tom said, surprised.

"That won't happen again in a million years," Rhoda assured him.

Tom waited as the phone continued to ring.

"No answer?" Rhoda asked after a minute.

"Not even a voice mail," Tom confirmed.

"What about a cell phone?"

"Yeah, well, we both kinda lost those in Lebanon a few years back," Tom said.

Rhoda's silence sought an explanation.

"It's a long story," Tom replied.

New York

Decker was already in his chair at the conference table when Ambassador Hansen and the other members of his senior staff arrived for a special meeting. The excitement of the new job was still fresh.

"Decker," Hansen said before he sat down, "I need your best work on this."

"I'll have the draft ready by one o'clock, sir," Decker responded. "I've done a search in the archives for any speeches you've given on the makeup of the Security Council and I ran across one where you talked about reorganizing on a regional basis. Of course we don't want to detract from the main issue, but if you like, I think I can work that in as a supporting theme."

Hansen considered the idea. "Yes, that will do nicely. That's always been a hot topic with the countries not on the Council. Peter," Hansen said, turning his attention to his chief legal council, "what's your final prognosis for this effort?"

"For the benefit of the others in the meeting," Peter said, "let me just restate that there's no way on Earth that this measure will ever pass, if for no other reason than simply on the grounds that it violates the UN Charter. There's no provision for removing a permanent member from the Security Council. You might, however, expand on Decker's suggestion and go for a complete reorganization. Another option you might consider would be to attempt something along the lines of what was done in 1971 when the Republic of China was removed because the General Assembly recognized the People's Republic of China as the true representative of the Chinese people."

"Let's not get carried away, Peter," Hansen said. "Remember, this is entirely for effect. We don't actually want to get the bloody thing passed."

"Jack, what about the poll of support from the other members?" Hansen asked his political adviser. "Are we sure that we can at least get this thing to the floor?" Jack Redmond, the Louisiana native who had been with Hansen when Decker and Tom Donafin were rescued in Lebanon, was the only other American on Hansen's staff. When Hansen came to the UN he had wanted someone who understood American politics and this outspoken Cajun was just the man for the job.

"There should be no problem getting it to the floor. They'll listen. But I can't guarantee seconding support," Jack answered.

"That's fine," Hansen said nodding. "As long as we can get it to the floor and ensure proper coverage of my speech, I think we'll be all right."

"Ambassador," Decker interjected, "from a media point of view, I think that would be a mistake. Unless we can get someone to second the motion, there's a good chance the press may focus more on the hopelessness of the motion than on its symbolic intent."

"Good point," Hansen agreed after mulling it over for a second. "You're probably right. If nothing else, perhaps we can get one of the Muslim countries to second the motion. After all, they're not very happy with the Russians right now either. Jack, find me that second."

"Yes, sir," Jack concurred.

"Okay, any other thoughts or objections before we pull this thing together?"

There were none.

"Jackie, do you have anything?" Hansen asked his daughter.

"Your meeting with Russian Ambassador Kruszkegin is set for noon tomorrow in the Delegates Dining Room."

"Okay," Hansen said, "then we're set. Tomorrow at three o'clock, in plenty of time for the evening news in America and the morning news in Asia and Europe, I will make the motion that in response to their invasion and occupation of Israel, the United Nations General Assembly should permanently remove Russia from its position on the Security Council.

"All I have to do now is have lunch with Ambassador Kruszkegin and convince him it's nothing personal."

Tel Aviv

"Are there a lot of Russians on the streets?" Tom asked as Rhoda drove him to the ophthalmologist's office.

"Too many," she answered, but then conceded, "Actually, not as many as you might expect. They patrol the streets — they're very obvious — but the main forces are camped in the wilderness areas. I think they realize that filling the streets with soldiers would just result in more violence. Besides, if they had a bunch of tanks rolling through the city, it wouldn't do much for their claims that they're a peacekeeping force. It's really the best possible arrangement for the Russians, I suppose. They keep their soldiers on a short leash in the unpopulated areas and maintain a show of force here."

"Sort of an 'iron fist in an iron glove' approach," Tom surmised. "Is it the same in the other cities?"

"I assume so. They've shut down messaging and even cell service, so it's hard to be sure."

"So you can't even get an email out? That makes it pretty difficult to form any kind of organized resistance," Tom said.

"Yeah. There are reports of small groups sniping at the Russians in the hills, but I don't think they're very well organized."

"What about the Russians' ultimate goal? Joel seemed to think the whole thing had been planned from the very early stages. Does anybody know what the Russians want with Israel? Have there been any public statements of their long-range intentions?"

"They say they'll leave when the threat of a nuclear/chemical war is removed from the region. But Joel says they already control all of Israel's nuclear weapons. If they planned to dismantle them they would've started by now. Of course if they *do* leave we'll be sitting ducks. The Russians have confiscated and impounded all military equipment as well as the small arms from the people. It's a lousy situation, but right now if the Russians left we'd have no way to protect ourselves except with picks and shovels and kitchen knives.

"It's ironic, I suppose. At best this is going to be a long-term arrangement. At worst the Russians will declare the occupation a success and leave us to be slaughtered by our neighbors. It's actually quite clever — it's a perfect excuse for them to stay indefinitely."

"I wonder when the next plane leaves for the U.S." Tom mused, but Rhoda didn't laugh.

When they arrived at the ophthalmologist's office, Tom took Rhoda's arm and she led him to the door. Inside, the receptionist greeted her like an old friend.

"So this is the special patient you called about. How's he doing?"

"That's what we're here to find out. How long before Dr. Weinstat can see us?" Rhoda asked as she surveyed the nearly full waiting room.

"He said to handle this as an emergency since the patient may still have some particles in his eyes. It should be only a few minutes."

Tom continued to hold Rhoda's arm as they sat down to wait. The chairs were closely placed and it seemed natural to continue the contact. It was a moment before he even realized he was still holding on. His first thought was to let go, but he appreciated the human contact and at the same instant it occurred to him that Rhoda didn't seem to object. Even through the soft fabric of her blouse, the warmth of her skin seemed to penetrate the cold darkness that surrounded him.

The two sat silently. The receptionist's comment about him being the "special" patient had not escaped his attention. He didn't want to assign it too much meaning, but he thought briefly about asking Rhoda to explain the reference. *No*, he thought. If he spoke he would disturb the moment and she might feel compelled by propriety to lightly pull away her arm, and then he would be compelled by the same propriety to release it. Better to leave things as they were.

Unexpectedly, she spoke. "Dr. Weinstat is a good doctor."

"Good," Tom answered, inanely.

It was only small talk. Apparently she was as aware of the silence as Tom was. What was significant was that they were carrying on a conversation, however unimaginative, and she gave no hint she wanted him to let go of her.

In the examination room, it took Dr. Weinstat only one quick look in each eye to make his diagnosis. "I'm sorry, Mr. Donafin. The damage to your corneas is very severe. The scarring from the glass and the corneal burns have formed a nearly opaque cover over about 90 percent of your crystalline lens, and the rest isn't much better. As bad as it is, I'm surprised you still have any light perception at all. Ordinarily we might consider corneal transplants, but in this case, with the ancillary burn damage to the retinas, I think we'd only be causing additional suffering with no real hope of improvement in your sight."

In those few short words, stated with stark clinical coldness, the doctor had pronounced him permanently blind. Tom was lost.

"If you'll lean back, I'll put some fluorescein in your eyes so we can locate the glass that's still bothering you," Dr. Weinstat said. When he finished, he put an antibiotic ointment in Tom's eyes and reapplied pressure bandages to keep the lids from moving. "Leave that on and come back tomorrow so we can see how you're doing. Dr. Felsberg," he continued, now addressing Rhoda, "will you be bringing Mr. Donafin back in tomorrow?"

Rhoda nodded, and then stated her intention verbally for Tom's benefit. "Yes," she answered softly.

"If you'll let Betty know on your way out, she'll try to set up a time convenient with your schedule."

"Thank you."

"Oh, and ask her to give you some pamphlets about learning to live with blindness."

Tom knew that it was entirely normal for doctors to carry on conversations as if their patients were not in the room, but right now what he knew made little difference. What he felt, there in the blackness that had just become his home, was that he was being talked *about* and not *to*. He was an inanimate object. It was just the beginning. He had observed how blind people are obliged to wait for the conversation of others; forced to wait for someone else to speak to them first. The day before, he had joked about blind photographers, but now the reality of the end of his career and of his life hit him full force. When he had made it out of Lebanon alive, he had thought he could survive anything. Now he wasn't so sure.

In the car Tom was silent as Rhoda got in the other side. "How are you doing?" she asked sympathetically, as she put her hand on his.

"Not very well," he answered biting his lip. "And what's worse, I don't think the whole thing has really hit me yet. I keep thinking that I'll just get these bandages off and I'll be able to see again."

"Well," she began as she caressed his hand to comfort him, but she couldn't think of anything else to say.

Tom turned his hand to hold hers; he needed all the support he could get right now. "I have no idea what to do from here," he said. "I can't work. I have some savings and three years of back pay from *NewsWorld.* That'll last me for a while, but then what?" He felt like saying something cliché like, "I'd be better off dead," but the warmth of Rhoda's hand made him reserve judgment.

"Tom, I know you're feeling angry right now, and cheated, but there are things in life we simply have to accept because nothing's going to change it." She was speaking from experience. And of course, Tom knew it too. He could have written a book on the subject

They sat for another moment in silence holding each other's hand. "Tom," Rhoda said finally, "there's someone I want you to meet."

Tom thought he knew who she was talking about. "Your rabbi?" he asked.

"You'll really like him," she said. "He asked me to bring you by when you were back on your feet."

"Yeah, I guess it's about time I thanked him for digging me out and bringing me to you." Reluctantly, Tom let Rhoda's hand slip free so she could drive.

Chapter 15

Plowshares into Swords

Tel Aviv

Scott Rosen sat in a small café eating a bowl of soup, waiting for his friend Joel Felsberg. Soon Joel entered, removed his coat, and sat down without speaking.

"You look upset," Scott ventured, in what seemed to Joel to be a rather irritating tone.

"I hate these arrogant Russians — always stopping you on the street and wanting to see your papers." Joel was exaggerating; most people went days without being stopped. "They're never going to leave, you know."

"Yeah, I know," Scott answered with uncharacteristic resignation as he sipped his soup. "But not everything is so gloomy," he added with equally uncharacteristic good cheer. "I heard the resistance hijacked a supply truck, stole all the supplies, and then loaded it with dynamite and sent it into a Russian camp by remote control. They say it killed nearly a thousand Russians."

Joel sighed and shook his head in disgust, but ordered his lunch before responding. "I've heard that story twenty times in the last three weeks and it gets bigger and more ridiculous with every telling," Joel responded.

"You don't believe it?"

"Yeah, I believe it. But I believe it the way I heard it the first time: The resistance hijacked a truck and drove it into a Russian camp, where it ran into a water tower, accomplishing nothing!"

"At least there *is* a resistance," Scott said.

"Yeah, and they're outgunned and completely disorganized. If Ben Gurion had used their tactics we'd still be a British protectorate! No matter how you paint it, Scott," Joel continued after stirring his coffee, "we're still occupied. I don't care how many water towers we run into or supply trucks we hijack. We were a free, independent state. We're still alive, but Israel is dead!"

"What do you think the resistance should do differently?" Scott asked, as if Joel's opinion made a difference.

"I don't know." Joel shook his head in resignation. "Nothing I guess. That's the whole problem — there's nothing we can do. Even if we got rid of the Russians, as soon as they're gone we'd be attacked by the Muslims, and we'd have nothing to fight them with."

"Yes, but—"

"Stop it, Scott! Is that why you asked me to meet you? So I could wallow in my anger and frustration?!"

Joel and Scott were zealous in their love for their country; either could easily be brought to a fever pitch when it came to Israel. But strangely, on this occasion, only Joel's blood pressure had risen. An unusual calm accompanied Scott's speech, but Joel didn't notice. Neither had he noticed that since his arrival no one had entered or left the café, nor that the café owner had turned the sign on the door to read "Closed." Likewise, the two men standing watch outside the café had escaped Joel's notice entirely.

"We must drive the Russians from Israel and bloody their noses so badly they'll never come back!" Scott said, suddenly animated.

"Big talk! Big talk!" Joel protested angrily.

Scott studied his soup. "If only we had used our nukes on the Russians instead of just waving them around as a threat to the Libyans."

"You're a fool!" Joel said. "By the time we knew we were being invaded, the Russians were all over the place. The only way we could have nuked them was to launch on our own soil."

"I guess that's true," he said. Scott's voice seemed resigned to the hopelessness of the situation, but he continued. "Too bad we can't get control of the nukes now. With the Russians all concentrated in the hills, we could wipe out ninety percent of them with just a few well-placed missiles and the resistance could take out the other ten percent in the cities."

"You really are a fool," Joel said. "What about Moscow? You think they're just gonna sit back and let that happen without responding? What's to stop them from striking back against our cities?"

This was the question that Scott had been waiting for. Suddenly his mood grew much more serious. The gravity of what he was about to say was clear even to Joel. "Our strategic defense," he whispered finally.

Joel stared coldly at Scott, studying his expression. Twice he opened his mouth to speak, ready to accuse Scott again of being a fool, but he held back. It appeared that Scott was serious and when it came to strategic defense, Scott Rosen deserved to be heard. Next to his late father, Joshua Rosen, Scott knew more about Israeli strategic defense than anyone. Finally Joel responded, "You're talking impossibilities. Even if a plan like that *could* work, there's no way in the world our puny, disorganized resistance could get control of the Strategic Defense Control Facility."

"We don't need the control facility," Scott said confidently.

Suddenly Joel became aware of his surroundings. When he'd thought he and Scott were just griping, he hadn't cared who heard them. There was nothing unusual about two Israeli men complaining about the Russians. Everyone in Israel was complaining. Indeed, it might have been considered unusual for them to be talking about anything else. But now they had crossed the line; they were no longer just complaining. The wrong person listening to their conversation might easily mistake this for a conspiracy. He looked around quickly to make sure no one had overheard them.

Scott didn't take the time to mention he had nothing to worry about; each of the seven people in the café had been handpicked for the occasion.

"You mean a remote?" Joel asked finally, under his breath.

Scott signaled an affirmative with his eyes.

Joel had heard talk about a remote, an off-site test facility for the Strategic Defense Control Facility (SDCF), but he had written it off as speculation by people who didn't know any better. If the Off-Site Test Facility (OSTF) was real, it would have been evident in the communications configuration needed for such an operation. True, the communications links could have been intentionally mislabeled to conceal its existence, but Joel had worked at the SDCF for more than five years and had run numerous configuration scenarios on the facility's computers. If the OSTF existed, it would have turned up in the simulations.

Joel was intimately familiar with the concept of an OSTF. Early in his career, before leaving the U.S., he had been a software analyst at the NORAD Off-Site Test Facility in downtown Colorado Springs. When he went to work at the Israeli SDCF, he tried for two years to convince his superiors of the need to develop the same type of system for Israel, to no avail. At one point he considered resigning to protest their refusal to even talk about it, but his wife convinced him to be patient and wait until those in charge were more sympathetic to the idea. Actually, that was one of the most irritating parts: The head of the Israeli SDCF was Dr. Arnold Brown, one of the men who had played a crucial role in developing the OSTF concept for NORAD. It never made any sense to Joel that Dr. Brown would refuse to consider providing the same capabilities for Israel.

Joel's initial response to Scott's suggestion that there was an OSTF was that Scott was simply believing more rumors like the one about the hijacked supply truck. Still, there were some things that Scott, with his compartmentalized clearances, might have had access to that Joel was totally unaware of. And the look on Scott's face said he was serious.

"Is this a game?" Joel said as he leaned across the table. "Are you putting me on?" Scott's eyes answered the question. "I ran configuration scenarios on the facility's computers a thousand times. If there was an OSTF, why didn't it turn up in the simulations?"

"It was there. Its functions were masked to hide its true purpose, but it was there."

Joel's eyes asked, "Where?"

"SF-14," Scott answered.

There was no way of knowing whether Scott was telling the truth. Sensor Facility 14, as far as Joel had known, was a nonoperational and entirely redundant infrared tracking station for terminal-phase acquisition and discrimination of ballistic reentry vehicles. Perhaps by coincidence — and then again, perhaps not — SF-14 was one of only two remote facilities Joel had never actually visited. Now that he thought about it, he couldn't recall ever seeing anyone's name on the duty roster for a site check of SF-14. And this would explain Dr. Brown's lack of interest in considering an

OSTF. After all, why talk about building something that was already fully operational?

If Scott Rosen knew what he was talking about, then Joel wanted to know. But if this was just more wishful thinking, then he wanted to be done with it, and the sooner the better. "Okay," he said, abruptly, "take me there." To Joel's surprise Scott didn't come back with some flimsy excuse but instead got to his feet, put on his coat, and started to leave the café with Joel in tow. "What about the check?" Joel asked.

"It's on the house," answered the café owner.

Scott drove to the eastern business section of Tel Aviv and parked in the basement lot of a tall but otherwise nondescript office building that appeared to have only minor damage from the recent war. Joel followed as Scott walked toward the elevators, pausing to look up at a security camera near the ceiling. In a moment a red light on the camera blinked and Scott pushed the call button for the elevator. As the elevator door closed behind them, Scott flipped the emergency "Stop" switch, and, on the numbered buttons of the elevator, punched in a seven-digit code. Despite already being in the basement, the elevator lurched downward, taking them, Joel guessed, several floors farther beneath the building. The elevator door opened to a room about twelve feet square, where two armed guards waited. Badges were out of the question under the circumstances, so they were operating strictly on a recognition basis. Joel would soon learn this was not a difficult task; very few people were involved in this operation. As Scott introduced him to the guards who were obviously studying every aspect of his appearance, Joel noticed his photograph lying on the desk beside an array of security monitors, one of which was focused on the elevator in the garage where they had entered.

Scott opened the cipher lock of an armored door that was the only other exit from the room. Before them lay a small sea of computers and defense tracking equipment on a raised floor, filling a room about 8,500 square feet. An array of symmetric multiprocessors made up the heart of the operation, with integrated routers/ATM switches feeding real-time input via broadband fiber links. Joel had seen this hardware configuration before, at the Strategic Defense Control Facility in the mountains near Mizpe

Ramon in southern Israel. There was less room here than in the mountain, but at first glance this seemed to be an exact duplicate of the core of the SDCF.

Scattered around the facility were a handful of men and women busy at Sun workstations. A few slowed their pace just long enough to look up and acknowledge Scott's and Joel's presence with a nod or smile before going back to their work. While Joel looked around in disbelief, a short well-built man entered from another room and approached. Scott abruptly ended the brief tour to greet the man.

"Good afternoon, Colonel," Scott said, formally. "Allow me to introduce Mr. Joel Felsberg. Joel, this is Lieutenant Colonel White."

"Welcome to the team," White said. "Glad you could join us."

"Uh . . . thank you, sir," Joel said, unaware that he had.

"You're coming in at a crucial time. Scott's told me all about you and I've seen your record. I'm sure we can count on you to help us make this thing happen.

"Scott," he continued, "introduce Joel to the rest of the team and get him briefed on what his role is. We'll talk later." With that the colonel left.

"Uh, yeah, that's a good idea, Scott. Get me briefed on what my role is," Joel repeated. And then, more to the point, "What on Earth is going on down here?!"

Scott smiled. "Welcome to SF-14."

"The reason you're here," Scott explained, "is that two nights ago Dr. Claude Remey, our software guru, very stupidly got in the way of his neighbors' domestic quarrel. As a result, he's now lying unconscious in a hospital with a stab wound three quarters of an inch from his heart. You've been brought on to finish the project he was working on."

Joel knew Dr. Remey. They had worked together on a couple of projects but had never gotten along well. Still, Joel was sorry to hear of his injury.

"What you see here is not simply a test facility. It's a fully operations-capable backup to the SDCF.

"The initial plan for this facility, in a situation where the SDCF was lost, included three scenarios. First, should the opportunity present itself, this facility could be used to launch on the invader's flank, thus cutting off its supply lines and weakening the forward forces. Second, should there be an attempt by an invading force to use our own nuclear capabilities against us, this facility could frustrate that attempt by overriding the controls at the SDCF. And third, should there be any attempt to remove a warhead from a silo, we have the capability to neutralize the device. Had either the second or the third scenario occurred, the established procedure would be to initiate the destruction of each threatening, or threatened, missile by remotely setting off small explosives in the silos that would disable both the silo and the warhead — without, of course, detonating the nuclear device.

"What actually happened with the Russian invasion was something that had not been considered. But as I alluded in the café, the Russians have also presented us with a totally unexpected opportunity. By concentrating their forces away from populated areas—" Scott paused to point out the Russian troop locations marked on a large wall display, "—they have literally made themselves sitting ducks to the capabilities of this facility.

"The first phase of our plan, then, is to neutralize the SDCF and launch six neutron-tipped, short-range Gideon missiles, one against each of the Russians' positions. There are three very important reasons we've chosen the Gideons. The most obvious is that since we'll be launching on targets within our own borders, it's absolutely imperative that we limit the area of destruction. We'll come back to that in a minute.

"The second reason is that the Gideon-class warhead produces the most rapidly dissipating radiation pattern of any of our warheads. Our forces will be able to reenter the initial kill radius within six to eight hours after impact. Ground Zero will be entirely habitable in three weeks.

"Third, if the launch is successful and our strategic defense successfully defends Israel against a Russian retaliatory strike — that's phase two of the plan — we'll very quickly face a second threat from both Muslim and Russian conventional forces. We hope to limit the immediate response of the Muslims by, one, creating a communications blackout, thus maintaining the highest possible level of confusion for our enemies; and two, by planning the strike during the Hajj." Scott was referring to the annual pilgrimage of Muslims to Mecca in Saudi Arabia. During the Hajj, Muslims are forbidden by the Quran to harm any living being, including their enemies — though it's a sin that is easily overlooked when it suits their purpose.

Scott pulled up a number of satellite photographs on the wall monitor. "As you can see, our satellite reconnaissance of the Russian encampments reveals extraordinarily large caches of weaponry, both Russian-made and captured Israeli weapons."

Joel was surprised by what the photos showed. Dozens of huge temporary warehouses had been constructed, with thousands of tanks, helicopters, and armored personnel carriers parked nearby in neat rows. It looked like a massive car lot. "They don't need that kind of armament simply to keep Israel under thumb," Joel reasoned. "They're planning on using Israel as a base to go after the oil fields and the Suez Canal!"

"That's what it looks like," Scott agreed.

"But if we have these satellite photos, then surely so does the U.S. Why haven't they done anything to stop it?"

"They're pursuing the matter through diplomatic channels. If they have plans for a military response, they haven't let *us* know about it. Apparently their assumptions of the Russians' intent don't match our own.

"As you know," Scott continued, getting back to the subject at hand, "the neutron bomb was developed to destroy personnel, not materiel. It kills primarily by an immediate burst of radiation, not by heat or the sheer power of the blast, as in the case of other nuclear weapons. The third reason, then, for selecting the Gideon is to eliminate the Russian personnel while preserving their weaponry. The Russian stockpiles will provide us with the weapons we need to protect ourselves. To further reduce the damage to materiel, we're actually targeting a point two hundred meters outside of the perimeter of the Russian camps.

"Now let's get back to the first reason I mentioned for selecting the Gideon. The initial kill radius for the Gideon-class warhead is only one kilometer, with a secondary radius extending another three kilometers. In most cases those limits will allow us to hit the Russians and entirely avoid initial or secondary kill of our own population. However, there are two places where because of adjacent villages and *kibbutzim*, that won't be possible. In those cases, and in the case of nearby farmers at the other sites, evacuation teams will be given approximately six hours to effect evacuation of all civilian residents before the launch. The plan is for this to occur under cover of darkness, and to avoid tipping our hand, the evacuation teams won't be given word to begin until after we've secured control of operations from the SDCF."

Joel listened, dumbfounded by the planning that had gone into this and with a growing alarm that he had suddenly been brought into an action that might put the lives of thousands of his countrymen in his hands.

"Neutralizing the SDCF," Scott continued, "and transferring operations to this facility is the easy part, relatively speaking; that's what this facility was set up to do. The hard part is to make the Russians believe they're still fully in control long enough for us to evacuate our people and launch the Gideons. That's where you come in. We need you to give us those six hours. Your job is to create the illusion, through a software dump to the SDCF computers, that their systems are still operational.

"After we transfer control, it'll take approximately twenty minutes for us to download the targeting data into the missiles. If the Russians realize what's happened, they'll attempt to regain control and disperse their troops into the mountains. Should that happen, we'll have no choice but to launch immediately, killing more than a thousand Israeli civilians along with the evacuation team members."

Joel mulled over what he had been told. It was a lot to digest so quickly. "What about the Russians in the cities?" he asked.

"Immediately after the launch, teams of commandos will take over all radio and television stations from the Russians. Where they're unsuccessful, other teams will destroy the stations' broadcast equipment. It's critical to our success that the Israeli people be rallied to attack the Russians in the cities, but it's equally important that we keep the rest of the world, especially the Muslims, confused about exactly what's going on. If we make things too clear for our own citizens, it'll be equally clear to the Muslims, who — Hajj or not — will seize the opportunity to strike while we're still disorganized and before we can take control of the Russian weapons caches. Rather than broadcasting reports that would be picked up by the Muslims, the radio and television will play a continuous loop of a single message, the words of the prophet Joel, from Joel 3:10."

Scott paused. He may have been a scientist but, like his father, he was a zealot first, though for a different religious cause. He was hoping his friend might at least have studied enough scripture to be familiar with the writings of the prophet whose name he bore. But, if Joel was familiar with the verse he gave no indication. Scott gave a sigh of noticeable disappointment and then continued, "'Beat your plowshares into swords and your pruning hooks into spears.'"

"That's kind of obscure, don't you think?" Joel asked, unaware the idea had been Scott's.

Scott started to argue but held back. "I suppose so," he admitted. "But that's the signal that's been passed to the resistance. Hopefully, others will join in when they see the fighting start in the streets."

Three weeks later

New York

The phone rang three times before Ambassador Hansen could rouse himself from sleep to answer it. "Hello," he said, as he checked his clock.

"Mr. Ambassador," said Decker, "I'm sorry to disturb you, but I've just heard that about thirty minutes ago, at 5:30 A.M. local time, there were multiple nuclear explosions in Israel."

The sleep suddenly rushed from Hansen's brain as his eyes opened wide.

"Reports are sketchy so far. It's not clear who's responsible, and there've been no official statements from the Russians."

"Is there any chance there's been a mistake?"

"No, sir. The detonations were detected by U.S., U.K., and Chinese satellites. To make things worse, the explosions were followed by a 9.2 magnitude earthquake[30] along the Dead Sea Rift where the African and Arabian tectonic plates meet."

"Coincidence?" Hansen wondered aloud.

"That's for the geologists," Decker responded.

"Okay, hold on a second while I switch on the telly." A moment later Decker heard the sound of Hansen's television.

"Okay, I'm back," Hansen said, but he and Decker stayed silent as each listened to the report just being read.

"Fox News has just learned that the United States has scrambled Strategic Command bombers. The State Department insists that this is only a precautionary measure and that STRATCOM has been ordered to remain in U.S. air space pending further orders."

"What the devil is going on?" Hansen asked.

"I don't know, sir," Decker answered, stating the obvious.

"Do you have the Russian ambassador's phone number?"

"Right here," Decker said and the relayed Ambassador Kruszkegin's number to Hansen.

"Okay," Hansen said. "I'll call Kruszkegin. You call Jackie, Peter, and Jack and have everyone get to the office ASAP."

The phone rang only once at Ambassador Kruszkegin's residence before it was answered by an official-sounding "Yes?"

"This is Ambassador Jon Hansen. I'd like to speak with Ambassador Kruszkegin immediately on a matter of utmost importance."

"I'm sorry, Ambassador Hansen," the voice answered. "Ambassador Kruszkegin is in a meeting right now and cannot be disturbed."

"I'll take it," Hansen heard Kruszkegin say in the background.

Ambassador Kruszkegin stood by the phone wearing a finely woven black and gold silk dressing gown, his warm Polish slippers protecting his feet from the cold marble floor. "Good evening, Jon," he began. Jon Hansen liked Kruszkegin as a person and respected him as an adversary. For his part, Kruszkegin was fond of referring to Hansen as "a man who has failed to notice that Britain no longer rules the world." Kruszkegin had found that, when possible, it was more productive to cooperate with Hansen than not to.

Anticipating Hansen's question, he continued, "I honestly do not know what is happening in Israel. I've just spoken with the foreign minister in Moscow and he swears we have not launched an attack. I believe they are just as confused as we are."

Hansen was surprised that Kruszkegin had taken his call; the direct answer was even more unexpected. Hansen knew the

Russian well enough to have a pretty good idea when he was lying. Right now he was telling the truth — at least as far as he knew it.

"Thank you, Yuri," Hansen said. Kruszkegin's straightforward answer left little else to be said.

Ambassador Hansen's senior staff watched the news reports at the British Mission as they awaited the ambassador's arrival.

"Can anyone tell me what's going on?" Hansen asked as he walked in the door and handed Jackie his coat just before 2:00 A.M. New York time.

"The Russians claim they had nothing to do with it," began Jack Redmond. "They say the attack was against *their* troops in Israel's mountains."[31]

This was a new twist on the story. "How the devil could that happen?" Hansen asked, incredulously.

Jack shook his head.

In the brief silence, Hansen's attention turned to the reporter on the television. "There is general confusion but speculation at the State Department," the reporter was saying, "is that the attack on Israel could be the result of some internal power struggle inside the Russian government. The battle for control of policy in Moscow has been heated, to say the least. Hard-liners like Foreign Minister Cherov and Defense Minister Khromchenkov seem hell-bent to reclaim Russia's role as a super power, while others like President Perelyakin favor a more measured approach. The Russian invasion of Israel still has many analysts unsure of who's in charge."

Redmond shrugged his broad shoulders as Hansen looked at him for his comment. "It's possible," he said. "But it doesn't really answer the big questions. We know that no cities were hit; apparently the missiles fell in the wilderness areas of the country. That would seem to support Russia's assertion that it was their troops that were hit, but I can't imagine any kind of political situation so bad that one group of Russians would bomb another."

"Okay, let's assume for a moment that the Russians are telling the truth: They're not responsible for the bombing," Hansen said. "Which country with the capability to launch a nuclear attack would actually do it?"

No one had an answer. "All we can do is wait for release of the satellite data to identify the origin of the launch," Redmond concluded.

"Mr. Ambassador," Decker said, "whoever launched the attack, the Israelis have apparently taken advantage of the combined confusion of the explosions and the earthquake. There are reports of fighting between Russians and Israelis in every major city, and Israeli resistance fighters apparently have taken over all of the television and radio stations not destroyed by the quake."

Hansen ran his hand through his hair, thought for a second, and then shook his head. "Except for the quake, I'd wonder if this whole thing was the work of the Israelis!"

"Can we even be sure about the quake?" Jack Redmond mused, only half in jest.

Chapter 16

The Hand of God

Moscow

Eleven hundred miles and nearly due north of Tel Aviv, the Russian Security Council was meeting to discuss the events in Israel. It was now 12:05 P.M. in Moscow, 4:05 A.M. in New York. At eighty-six years old, Defense Minister Vladimir Leon Josef Khromchenkov was the oldest of the thirteen men assembled in the Kremlin's war-room. Khromchenkov remembered with great nostalgia the glory days of the Soviet Union. He had come to the Kremlin during the days of Gorbachev as a proxy of the hard-liners who opposed Gorbachev's reforms and were afraid he might "give away the store," which he did anyway.

Boris Yeltzin and Vladimir Putin had both attempted to weaken Khromchenkov's political power and to remove him from the Security Council, but without success. Khromchenkov knew the inner workings of everything and the hidden sins of everyone; he used these deftly to his advantage. Had he wanted it, he might well have become president himself, but Khromchenkov preferred manipulating to being manipulated. It was said that he believed it was his destiny not to die until the Soviet empire had been restored. And though he gave the credit to others, it was he who had engineered the invasion of Israel as a key step toward bringing about that destiny.

"Comrades," Khromchenkov began in old Soviet style — a practice which irritated some of those around him but warmed the hearts of others — "our intelligence reports have just confirmed that this morning's strike against our peacekeeping forces in Israel was conceived and initiated by Israeli insurgents. We have very recently regained communications with General Serov, who is in charge of the Strategic Defense Control Facility at Mizpe Ramon. He reports that the Israelis apparently took control of the nuclear forces from a remote facility, from which they launched this morning's attack. At present the insurgents are fighting our troops stationed in the cities, and a force of Israelis has set up camp outside the control facility. General Serov has sealed the blast doors so his forces are in no danger from the insurgents outside. Presently, he reports, he is working to isolate the breach in operations in order to regain control. One other point," Khromchenkov added, as if it were only an afterthought, though in reality it was the most significant thing he would say, "in addition to having control of their launch facilities, the Israelis have also taken control of their strategic defense."

Foreign Minister Cherov recognized the importance of Khromchenkov's final point. If the Israelis had control of the strategic defense, then it greatly limited Russia's options for response.

"Our damage estimates indicate that the warheads used were Gideon-class five-megaton neutron devices targeted for just outside the perimeter of each of our six temporary installations. We believe the loss of personnel in the camps is near total."

"What about the materiel?" asked the minister of finance, concerned more about the stockpiles of weaponry than the thousands of lost lives.

"At this moment we have no assessment of damage to our weaponry, but it is likely the equipment has survived the attack."

"What do you suggest?" President Perelyakin asked the defense minister.

"We must assume," Khromchenkov replied, "that the use of low yield neutron bombs was intended to kill our soldiers while allowing the Israelis to seize our weapons for their defense. While we can hope that General Serov will regain control of the nuclear capabilities and strategic defense, we must plan a response in the event those attempts are unsuccessful. Therefore, in addition to immediately replacing our forces, I recommend we prepare both a nuclear and a conventional response. If we regain control of the strategic defense, then our response should be in kind. I recommend a launch of six low-yield neutron bombs on Israeli targets to match the unprovoked attack on our troops. If, however, we are not able to regain control of the strategic defense, then within twenty-four hours, before Israel can avail itself of our equipment, we must launch an air strike against those same six targets. The second option is not as colorful, but it will make the point."

"Mr. Defense Minister," interjected Interior Minister Stefan Ulinov, "if we can regain control of the Israeli's nuclear forces, then I recommend that the launch come from their own silos."

"Excellent!" agreed President Perelyakin, and everyone approved.

"One other point," Ulinov continued, "if Israel's strategic defense is anywhere near as effective as our intelligence reports indicate, then Defense Minister Khromchenkov is absolutely correct. We must not launch a nuclear response unless we are sure the warheads will reach their targets. We cannot afford to provide the world with a demonstration of what a well-developed missile defense can do. It would be," Ulinov said, measuring his words for effect, "a catastrophic mistake if the net result of this entire event was to encourage the West to finally deploy their own full-scale strategic defense." Ulinov paused to allow the members of the Security Council a moment to consider what he felt was the great wisdom of his words and then looked over at Khromchenkov to surrender the floor to him.

"Ultimately," Khromchenkov concluded, "if we are unable to retake the nuclear capabilities *or* the strategic defense, we will have to expend much greater forces to disable the missile silos with conventional air strikes. Once the Israelis have again been stripped of their nuclear forces, I believe we can count on them to again surrender their strategic defenses."

"Excellent," the president said again. "I commend you, Mr. Defense Minister, for your clear thought and planning of a sensible response to this incident."

When the meeting was over, Khromchenkov hung back to catch Foreign Minister Cherov alone. He felt sure he knew Cherov's feelings on what he was about to ask, but one could never be too careful. "Tell me, Comrade Cherov," he said when he was sure no one could overhear their conversation, "what did you think of my recommendation?"

"I think it was well planned . . . if your intent was to satisfy the wishes of President Perelyakin." Cherov's voice hid nothing; it was obvious he was not fully satisfied.

"Perhaps you would prefer a response that was a bit . . . stronger? One that took greater advantage of the opportunity?"

"I had hopes, yes."

"I did prepare an alternate recommendation. Perhaps you would like to have a look?" Khromchenkov handed a large unmarked envelope to his fellow minister, and then left the room.

New York

By 8:00 A.M. New York time, the world had begun to learn what had actually happened in Israel, and concern at the UN quickly turned to calls for restraint.

Jon Hansen had learned early in his political career that the most effective diplomacy is usually carried out in private; the speaker's dais in the hall of the General Assembly was for show business. Still, there were times, such as when he had called for the reorganization of the Security Council — a move that was entirely for spectacle — when the dais was indispensable. The present occasion would require both.

It was ingenious that the Israelis could engineer such a maneuver, Hansen thought; it was insane that they'd actually do it. And it was impossible for anyone to tell how the Russians would respond. Hansen knew enough about Russian politics to recognize there would be serious discussion of launching some sort of limited nuclear response, but he hoped the moderates would win out. Unfortunately, he could learn nothing from Russian Ambassador Yuri Kruszkegin, who was playing it very close to the vest.

Unknown to Hansen were the cards in the hand of the small group of men and women deep beneath the streets of Tel Aviv. They were the ones who held the deck of history, as well as control of Israel's nuclear forces and strategic defense.

Moscow

Defense Minister Khromchenkov had just walked into the restroom and gone over to one of the urinals when he realized that someone had followed him in. Out of the corner of his eye he recognized Foreign Minister Cherov. Khromchenkov knew at once this was no chance meeting; he could count on the fingers of his free hand the number of times he had seen Cherov in this wing of the building. Still, it wasn't wise to make assumptions. "Good afternoon, Comrade," Khromchenkov said.

Cherov only nodded.

"Have you had a chance to examine my alternate proposal?"

"I have," Cherov replied. "It offers some intriguing possibilities for both the short- and long-term goals of our country." Cherov's voice said he was interested.

"Of course," Khromchenkov allowed, "such a plan would depend greatly on the response from the Americans. I have made some assumptions, and it is all conjecture; I am not an expert in these things." He deferred both in recognition of Cherov's position as Foreign Minister and to position himself to avoid blame if his assumptions on the matter proved incorrect. Cherov understood this. "Perhaps you would have a different assessment," Khromchenkov suggested as he left the urinal to wash his hands.

"No. Your assessment seems correct." Cherov said as he joined him at the sink. "Of course, we shall never know for sure. It would be impossible to overrule the wishes of President Perelyakin on this matter." Cherov's voice said he was eager to hear more, if indeed there was more to hear.

"I suppose you are correct," Khromchenkov said with an insincere sigh, and then added, "On the other hand, were it to be proposed by the right member of the Council, there are doubtless others who would follow."

"The right member?" Cherov pressed, wanting Khromchenkov to confirm what he seemed to be suggesting.

"Yes, someone who could offer the strong leadership required to lead the Russian Federation, should the president find it, er . . . impossible to support the view of the majority."

There was now no doubt what Khromchenkov was suggesting. Cherov was "the right member." President Perelyakin would obviously oppose the plan. That was the easy part. The difficult part — impossible, unless it could be prearranged — was to have the majority of the Council side with Cherov. Perelyakin was not a forgiving man. If the plan failed, it would cost Cherov dearly.

"Can one be sure of the numbers?" Cherov asked cautiously.

"As sure as one may be of anything," Khromchenkov answered, drying his hands. "There are three members who supported Perelyakin in the past who have confided to me that they do not wish to see an opportunity such as this pass unanswered."

Cherov did a quick tally of the numbers. It occurred to him that, despite the accuracy of Khromchenkov's math, everything did not add up. "And have these members gone to President Perelyakin with their plea?" he asked.

"Yes, of course."

"And he refuses to listen?"

"He listens. He just doesn't hear. His world is built on caution."

"A sound foundation," Cherov contended.

"Yes, but one that may let destiny slip past unanswered and ignore an opportunity to restore Russia to its rightful place."

There was still one major flaw in the proposal. "You speak of opportunity," Cherov noted. "But there is no such opportunity unless your General Serov is successful in regaining control of the Israeli strategic defense."

"True enough," Khromchenkov admitted. "If he does not," he shrugged, "then the alternate recommendation will not be made, and there is nothing lost. And yet, if he does succeed . . . we should be ready to act."

Cherov considered Khromchenkov's comment. "I will think on it," he said finally.

Tel Aviv

In the Off-Site Test Facility the members of Colonel White's team took turns sleeping. It might be days or even weeks before they saw the outside again. Joel was munching on a bag of Tapu potato chips in front of a computer console and Scott had just stretched out on a cot to rest.

"What's this?" Joel said under his breath. "Colonel White," he called, requesting the team leader's presence.

Colonel White downed the rest of a cup of coffee and hurried over to where Joel was sitting. "What's up?" he asked.

Joel moved closer to the console, studying the computer monitor. "A bad reading, I hope. The master icon for the defense grid just went red."

Colonel White took one look and didn't like what he saw. "Danny, get over here quick," he yelled to one of the two female members of the team.

Danielle Metzger was the one person, other than White, with the most experience in the OSTF, but unlike the Colonel, her work had all been hands on. She knew the facility inside and out.

"No!" she erupted. The noise woke the three team members who were sleeping.

"Quick," Metzger shouted, taking command of the situation. "Everybody, we've got a problem!"

"Tell me what's going on," White ordered.

"We've lost control," Danielle responded as she ran a series of diagnostics to be sure the readings were correct.

"What happened?" several voices said at once.

Danielle continued working, madly trying to reestablish control. Finally she confirmed that this was not simply a faulty reading. "Colonel, it appears that somehow the Russians have retaken control of all defensive capabilities."

"Can we get them back?" he asked, terrified of what her answer might be.

"I don't know, sir. I—"

"Wait a second," Joel interrupted. "We still have control of our offensive forces. How could we lose one but not the other? Could this just be an aberration in the system?"

Like the others, Scott Rosen was studying the situation, trying to get some idea of what went wrong and what could be done to correct it. It was he who answered Joel's question. "It's not an aberration," he replied. "I can't explain *how* they did it, but I can explain *what* they've done. The fiber optics used for communication between the various sites in the offensive and defensive systems go through both the SDCF and the OSTF. For reasons of logistics, control communications of missile silos go first through this facility and then to the SDCF; defensive control communications go first through the SDCF and then to this facility."

"What idiot decided to do that?!" Joel exclaimed.

"Dr. Brown," Danielle Metzger shot back, defending the late doctor who had been her mentor. "But he couldn't have predicted we'd ever be in a situation like this."

Scott continued his explanation. "Somehow they must have discovered that SF-14 was a counterfeit facility and traced its input/output cables."

"So can we get control back or not?" Colonel White asked, reasserting his authority. There was a long pause.

"I don't think so," Scott answered finally. "I think they may have cut the cables."

In all the confusion and disarray, no one noticed the faint sound of the radio in the background as it monitored the continuous loop of the words of the prophet Joel. Nor did they notice at first when the loop abruptly stopped and was replaced by another voice. It was low, rich, and measured. As the room fell silent for a moment, the distinctive sound registered in Joel Felsberg's ears. At first he ignored it, but then suddenly he recognized it. "That's my sister's rabbi," he said, surprising the others, who were trying to figure a way out of the present predicament. "What's going on up there? Why have they shut off the loop?" he asked as he turned up the volume.

"All the Earth has seen what has been done here," Rabbi Saul Cohen said over the radio. "But you, oh Israel, have not glorified God. Instead you have congratulated yourselves for destroying your enemy. You have glorified yourself and now you have falsely used the words of the prophet Joel to suit your own needs. 'These words must not be used as a rallying cry for my people,' says the Lord. These are the words of the son of Satan,[32] who will rally his evil forces to destroy you in the day of the Lord that is coming. Nevertheless, the Lord your God is a patient and merciful God. Hear now the words of the prophet Ezekiel for the enemy of my people Israel:

> *I will execute judgment upon him with plague and bloodshed; I*
> *will pour down torrents of rain, hailstones and burning sulfur*
> *on him and his troops and on the many nations with*
> *him . . .[33] On the mountains of Israel you will fall, you and all*
> *your troops and the nations with you. I will give you as food to*
> *all kinds of carrion birds and wild animals. You will fall in*
> *the open field, for I have spoken, declares the Sovereign*
> *Lord . . . and they will know that I am the Lord![34]*

"Today, oh Israel, today you shall behold the power and wrath of God! Here, oh Israel, is your true battle cry. 'Behold the hand of God! Behold the hand of God!'"

New York

Decker was suddenly awakened as a scream of pure terror erupted from Christopher's room. He found the boy covered in sweat and trembling. "What's wrong?" Decker exclaimed, his own heart racing to match Christopher's.

Christopher sat up, seemingly unsure of his surroundings. The disorientation was slow to leave him, and Decker shook him gently at the shoulders. After much blinking and looking around, finally there was a look of recognition in his eyes.

"I'm sorry," Christopher said after another moment but still breathing hard. "I'm okay now."

Decker had been a father long enough to recognize when a child was attempting to be brave. Christopher was visibly upset and Decker wasn't about to leave him alone.

"Was it the crucifixion dream again?" Decker asked.

"No, no," Christopher answered. "Nothing like that."

Christopher seemed a little reluctant, but Decker's eyes insisted.

"It's hard to explain," he said apologetically. "It's weird. I've had the dream before, but it feels almost ancient, like I had it . . . long ago." He shook his head. "I'm in a room with huge curtains all around me. The curtains are beautiful, decorated with gold and silver threads. The floor of the room is made of stone and in the middle of the room is an old wooden box, like a crate, sitting on a table. I can't explain why, but in the dream I feel like I need to look inside."

"What's in it?" Decker asked.

"I don't know. It's like there's something there I need to see, but at the same time, somehow I know that whatever it is, it's terrifying."

Decker read the fear in the boy's eyes and was glad he had insisted that Christopher tell him about it. This was not the sort of thing he should have to face on his own.

"I start toward the box, but then I look down and somehow the floor has disappeared. I start to fall, but I grab onto the table that the box is sitting on." Christopher stopped.

"Go on," Decker gently urged.

"Usually that's when I wake up. But this time there was something else: a voice. It was a very deep, rich voice and it was saying, 'Behold the hand of God! Behold the hand of God!'"

Decker had no idea what the dream might mean, but it certainly had his attention.

"And then there was another voice," Christopher paused. "Well, not exactly a voice. It was someone laughing."

"Laughing?"

"Yes, sir. But it wasn't a friendly laugh. It was cold and cruel and terribly inhuman."

Moscow

Lieutenant Yuri Dolginov hurried down the long hall of the Kremlin toward the office of the Defense Minister. Despite the importance of his message, he knew well that he had better take the time to knock before entering. "Sir," he said, when he was permitted to enter, "we have regained control of the Israeli strategic defense."

This was good news, indeed. "Excellent," Khromchenkov said to himself as he waved off the messenger. "Then the time has come to strike." He made a quick call to Foreign Minister Cherov and only then notified President Perelyakin of the change in status in Israel. The president called for an immediate meeting of the Russian Security Council.

When the meeting convened a few minutes later, President Perelyakin immediately turned the floor over to Khromchenkov. He had no idea of the intrigue that was brewing and simply felt it was good politics to allow the defense minister to have the pleasure of informing the Security Council of the good news from Israel.

Khromchenkov read the words of the communiqué from General Serov in the Israeli Strategic Defense Control Facility:

> *Have regained control of Israeli strategic defense. Unable to*
> *achieve same for offensive missile forces. Recommend immediate*
> *action as condition could change without warning.*

The members of the Security Council applauded General Serov's accomplishment. Several of the men in the meeting had already been notified of the situation but were obliged to act as though this was the first time they had heard it.

"Thank you," President Perelyakin told Khromchenkov. "Now, I suggest we comply with the general's recommendation and respond immediately."

"One moment," Foreign Minister Cherov interrupted.

"Yes," responded Perelyakin, who had already risen from his seat. Perelyakin's face showed only the slightest hint of concern as Cherov began. Inside, however, his stomach muscles tightened as if bracing for a blow.

"It occurs to me that this presents a remarkable opportunity to accelerate our plans. At this moment the American and NATO forces are struggling to rebuild. Now, certainly I will acknowledge that similar conditions exist for the Russian Federation. The Disaster has struck both sides with severe losses. But the measure of superiority is not what *is*, but how one uses what *is* to his final advantage."

Perelyakin listened to Cherov's words with his ears, but his eyes studied the faces of those around him. He didn't like what he saw anymore than what he heard.

New York

"I appreciate you meeting me for breakfast, Yuri," Jon Hansen said as he greeted the Russian ambassador.

"Good morning, Jon," Kruszkegin responded. "It's all right. I'm on a diet," he joked, anticipating the distasteful nature of the conversation that was about to follow.

Kruszkegin's eyes were red from having to operate in two different time zones. He had been awakened early that morning to be apprised of the situation in Israel. His nephew, Yuri Dolginov, who worked for the defense minister, had sent him an encrypted message from Moscow that Russia had regained control of the Israeli strategic defense, and Kruszkegin had stayed up expecting official notification from the foreign minister of what action was intended. None came. This wasn't the first time he'd had to depend on his nephew for word of what was going on. The foreign minister, under whose direction all Russian ambassadors functioned, was not comfortable with men like Kruszkegin, whom he considered far too internationally-minded to be very useful to the Russian Federation.

Hansen and Kruszkegin continued to exchange small talk as their breakfast was served, and then Hansen attempted to elicit some information. "You seem worried," Hansen said. He was lying. Kruszkegin's face showed no emotion except possibly enjoyment of his breakfast. Hansen had said it solely to observe Kruszkegin's response.

"Not at all," Kruszkegin assured him.

Hansen tried a different tack. "You don't have any more idea what's going on than I do, do you?" But Kruszkegin only smiled and continued chewing. Hansen tried a few more times, to no avail. Kruszkegin continued contentedly enjoying his food.

"I thought you were on a diet," Hansen said at last in frustration. "Why did you even accept my invitation to breakfast if you weren't going to talk?"

Kruszkegin put down his fork and looked Hansen in the eye. "Because," he began, "one day I'll want you to come to breakfast as my guest and *I* will be the one asking all the questions."

"When that happens," Hansen responded, "I shall endeavor to be as tight-lipped as you."

"I'm sure you will be," Kruszkegin said. "And then I'll notify my government that we met, but that I was unable to learn anything new. Just as you shall today."

Hansen gave a brief chuckle and went back to his nearly untouched breakfast. A few moments later, however, the gravity of the current situation resurfaced and Hansen began to push the food around on his plate.

"You look worried," Kruszkegin said, echoing Hansen's earlier statement.

"I am," Hansen confessed. "Yuri, things have changed. I can't tell what's going on in Russia anymore. The men in power are unpredictable. Men like Putin would never have taken chances like these men have. I just don't know what we can expect from them."

Kruszkegin stopped eating, and unlike before, it was obvious he wasn't thinking about his food. Hansen had struck a nerve. In truth, Kruszkegin was as concerned as Hansen, probably more so. Still, he offered no comment.

* * * * *

When Ambassador Yuri Kruszkegin arrived at the Mission of the Russian Federation on East 67th Street, his personal secretary handed him a message. It was from his nephew at the Ministry of Defense. "Uncle Yuri," it began. This was unusual in itself; in the past his nephew had always addressed his correspondence, "Dear Mr. Ambassador." Kruszkegin didn't pause long over the informality, however; his mind was on the simple message that followed. "Say your prayers," it read.

Kruszkegin went to his office and closed the door. Sitting at his desk he took out a Cuban cigar, cut and lit it, leaned back, and put his feet up. He thought about the brief message from his nephew and looked at it again.

It was a joke. That is, it had been a joke four years earlier when he had helped young Yuri, his namesake, get the position on Khromchenkov's staff. "What shall I say," his nephew had asked him at that time, "to warn you, should we ever decide to launch a major nuclear attack?"

Kruszkegin remembered his response: "Just tell me to say my prayers."

Russia

The steel and reinforced concrete hatch rose from the earth, suspended on its giant hinge and driven heavenward by massive hydraulic pistons, revealing the underground silo and clearing the way for the missile inside. At locations scattered around the Russian Federation, the same foreboding sound of metal against metal was followed by the pneumatic release of mooring clamps and then the sudden massive eruption of orange-black smoke and yellow-white flame, followed by the deafening roar of rocket engines. Scattered bursts of light pierced dark banks of exhaust, obscuring the missiles' slow but unstoppable rise from their tranquil catacombs. At last emerging above the rampart, the missiles crept skyward, quickly picking up speed.

Their targets were not limited to Israel alone. Israel had now become rather insignificant. Khromchenkov's plan for restoring Russia to perpetual prominence was to take control of the eastern

Mediterranean by seizing the ports of Libya, Egypt, Israel, Lebanon, Syria, and Turkey; take the Suez Canal; and control most of the oil throughout the Middle East. Across Russia the military was in readiness for the invasion and occupation to follow.

With this launch it would no longer be necessary to use Israel for a staging ground. It would be accomplished with one bold stroke. Israel needed to be taught a lesson, and so six warheads were aimed at its cities. But the hundreds of other warheads, as many as sixteen MIRVed[35] nuclear devices in each missile, were targeted at every military base and major city in the region. And to deal once and for all with the Muslim problem, two were aimed directly at the mosques of Mecca and Medina. Khromchenkov understood the fatalism of the Islamic religion as well as the Muslims' absolute certainty that Allah would never allow the Kabah in Mecca to be destroyed. Destroy Mecca, he reasoned, and he would destroy the religion.

West of St. Petersburg, a farmer ceased milking his cows as the frozen ground trembled and the thunderous roar of engines reached his ears. Running from his barn in confused wonder, he saw the sun briefly eclipsed by a rising missile, which cast a shadow over him and his enterprise.

Outside the Cathedral of St. Basil in Moscow a wedding party looked skyward toward three rising plumes of exhaust.

On a wooden bridge in Irkutsk, children watching a puppet show were startled as the puppeteer suddenly ceased his craft to stare at the foreboding display in the sky.

In Yekaterinburg, at a ten-kilometer race up the frozen river, spectators and ice skaters alike stopped in silent terror as the sun reflected off the hulls of four missiles speeding heavenward.

Throughout Russia, similar scenes played out.

Eighteen and a half seconds into their course, at a point approximately two miles above the Earth, as people in cities, towns, and farms around the country watched, the inexplicable happened.

At the core of each of the multiple warheads — in an area so infinitesimally small — an immense burst of energy was released. In less than a hundredth of a millionth of a second, the temperature of the warheads rose to more than a hundred million degrees Kelvin — five times hotter than the core of the sun —

creating a fireball that expanded outward at several million miles per hour.

Instantly everything within four miles of the blasts was vaporized: not just the farmer and his cows, but the barn and the tools with which he had worked; not just the wedding party, but the cathedral from which they had come; not just the children and the puppeteer, but the bridge on which they stood; not just the skaters and spectators, but the frozen river on which they had raced. Even the air itself was incinerated. For fifteen miles around each of the exploding warheads, all that was not vaporized burst instantly into flame.

And as the fireballs expanded, they drove before them superheated shockwaves of expanding air. Reflecting off the ground, the secondary shockwaves of the blasts fused with the initial waves and propagated along the ground to create Mach fronts of unbelievable pressure. Buildings, homes, trees, and everything that had not already been destroyed were sheared from the surface of the Earth and carried along at thousands of miles per hour.

The death toll in just the first fifteen seconds was more than thirty million.

The huge fireballs, expanding to as much as six miles in diameter, now rose skyward, pulling everything around them inward and upward. Hundreds of billions of cubic meters of smoke and toxic gases created by the fires, together with all that had been blown outward by the blasts, was now drawn back to the center and carried aloft at five hundred miles per hour into scores of mammoth irradiated mushroom clouds of debris that would rain down deadly fallout for thousands of miles around.

Tel Aviv

The unsecured black phone rang and Lieutenant Colonel Michael White answered according to standard operating procedure, simply stating the last four digits of the phone number. The voice on the phone was that of the Israeli prime minister calling from his recently liberated office in the Knesset. "Congratulations," he said. "Not one missile left Russian airspace. All Israel owes you their life and their freedom."

"Thank you, Mr. Prime Minister," Colonel White stammered. "But it wasn't us. Our line of control was cut hours ago. Our strategic defense is still entirely inoperable."

Chapter 17

Master of the World

Three months later

New York

Former Assistant Secretary-General Robert Milner and Namibian Ambassador Thomas Sabudu paused briefly to be sure everything was in order before stepping onto the elevator. When they reached the British Mission on the twenty-eighth floor they were warmly greeted by Jackie Hansen and shown into Hansen's inner office.

"Good afternoon, Bob. Ambassador Sabudu," Hansen said as he left his desk to join his guests in the sitting area of his office. "How have you been, Bob?" Hansen asked.

"Not bad for an old man," answered Milner.

"For an old man, you certainly haven't slowed down at all. I think I see you around the UN more now than when you actually worked there."

Milner laughed. "Well, now that I don't have to be there, it's a lot more fun."

"So, are you just operating out of your briefcase now?"

"Oh, no," Milner answered. "Alice Bernley let me set up shop in a spare room at the Lucius Trust." Jackie brought in tea and scones and the three men sat down to business.

"So, what can I do for you?" Hansen asked, looking alternately at Sabudu and Milner.

"Jon we're here — Ambassador Sabudu officially and me unofficially — on behalf of certain members of the Group of 77," Milner began, referring to the caucus of Third World countries that had originally consisted of seventy-seven countries but that had since grown to include more than one hundred and fifty nations.

"We have come," said Ambassador Sabudu, "because on two occasions you have addressed the General Assembly on the subject of reorganizing the UN Security Council."

"Yes," Hansen recalled. "But I'm sure you understand that on both of those occasions my intent was to dramatize the seriousness of another issue, not to actually change the Security Council."

"Yes, of course," Sabudu responded.

"Jon, we'd like for you to bring it up again," said Milner, "this time in earnest."

Hansen sat back in his chair.

"Ambassador Hansen," Sabudu began.

"Please, call me Jon."

"All right then, Jon. As you know, many things have changed since the Disaster and in the months since the devastation of Russia. Many of us in the Group of 77 believe it is now time for the UN to change as well."

In truth, the Third World countries had been wanting to change the Security Council since they began to make up the majority of members in the UN. "It is totally unreasonable," Sabudu continued, "that five nations should exercise such dominance over the United Nations as do the five permanent members of the Security Council." Sabudu's voice was spiced with the conviction of his message.

"Let me assure you, Thomas," Hansen said, taking the liberty to call Sabudu by his first name, "even though my country is one of those five you refer to, I personally share that view."

"Jon," said Milner, "Thomas and I have polled most of the members of the Group of 77 and a great many of them — one hundred and seven at this point — have committed their support to such a motion. Another thirty-two are leaning strongly in our direction."

Hansen was a bit surprised at the level of support. "But why have you decided that I should be the one to make the proposal?" he asked.

"Three reasons," explained Milner. "First, as Thomas said, you've made the motion before. Second, you're very well respected by all the members, especially the Third World countries. And third, because we feel it's absolutely imperative that the motion be made by a delegate of one of the permanent members of the Council. Some have told me that because of the devastation of the Russian Federation, they think that some sort of restructuring will probably occur anyway in the next four or five years. They're just not sure they want to be involved in rocking the boat to make it happen now. That's why it's so important that one of the permanent members make the motion. Quite frankly, they want someone to pin it on if the motion fails. If Britain proposes, I believe we can pull all or most of the votes from the Third World countries that are leaning our way. With that, we'll be within a dozen votes of the two-thirds majority needed for passage."

"I don't know, Bob," Hansen interrupted, "I have no idea how my government will feel about such a motion. It was one thing for me to suggest it when it had no chance of passing. It's quite another if it might actually come about. I don't even know how I'd be instructed to vote on such a measure."

"How do you feel about it, personally?" Milner asked.

"As I said, I agree it's unreasonable that five countries should exercise dominance over the UN, but on the other hand, I'm not sure I know of a better way to run things and still accomplish as much as we do." Hansen thought for a moment. "Off the record, if we could come up with a more equitable approach and it wouldn't bog down the system for lack of direction and leadership, I guess I'd be for it."

"Would you be willing to work with us to develop such an approach, perhaps based on some regional plan with additional authority resting in the secretary-general?" asked Sabudu. "And if we *are* able to come up with something you're comfortable with, would you present it to your government for consideration?"

Hansen considered this for a long moment, then nodded. "I'll do what I can. But it's possible that even if we can come up with a workable structure and I can persuade my government to support it, I may not be allowed to actually make the motion if it's felt that by doing so we would anger the other permanent members. You know how these things work. Is there any possibility one of the other permanent members would make the motion?"

"We don't think so," said Milner.

"No. I didn't expect so."

Milner opened his briefcase to retrieve a document. "To get the ball rolling," he said, "I've brought along a proposal on restructuring based on regional entities. We may want to use it as a point of departure in developing a final plan."

Hansen glanced at the document and put it on the table beside him.

"Jon," Milner said, "there's one other item we need to talk about, and I think it may just soften the blow to your government of losing its permanent place on the Council. As you know, in order to ensure impartiality, the secretary-general has always been selected from among the members of the UN who have no ties to any of the permanent members. For years that has served as a major counterweight to the power of the five permanent members. But if the Security Council were reorganized on some other basis, there would be no reason for continuing that requirement. There would be no defensible reason that the secretary-general shouldn't be from, say, Britain or the U.S. or any of the other former permanent members of the Council."

"What Bob has said about your personal sway with the Third World members was not just flattery," Sabudu interjected.

"Jon, the secretary-general has already indicated his intention to retire at the end of this session. If you are the one to make the motion and we can get the votes we need for passage, we believe that you would be the obvious candidate to take his place."

Jon Hansen took a deep breath and leaned back in his chair.

In the outer office Jackie Hansen was working at her desk when she looked up to see Christopher Goodman coming in the door. "Hi, Christopher," she said. "How was school?"

"Okay," he answered. "Is Mr. Hawthorne here?"

"He's out right now, but I expect him back shortly. You can wait in his office."

"No, that's okay," he said. "I just wanted to let him know I'd be a little late this evening. I'm going to the seminar and exhibit the Saudi government is sponsoring. Would you tell him for me?"

"Sure, Christopher," Jackie answered. "You seem to stay pretty busy going to all those exhibits."

"Yeah, it's great. There's a different seminar or exhibit or program to go to every couple of weeks. And some can take days to go through."

"I envy you," she said. "I wish I had the time."

Jackie saw the ambassador's door start to open and put her finger to her lips to indicate they'd have to continue the conversation after Ambassador Hansen's guests left.

Christopher picked up a magazine, but before he could start reading, he heard someone call his name. He looked up to see Assistant Secretary-General Milner standing next to Ambassador Hansen.

"Oh, hello, Secretary Milner," Christopher said.

"You two know each other?" Hansen asked Milner.

"Yes. We've bumped into each other on several occasions at some of the exhibits, but we weren't formally introduced until a few days ago when I spoke at Christopher's high school about my World Curriculum project and the goals of the United Nations. He's quite a good student, his teacher tells me. It wouldn't surprise me at all if Christopher went to work for the UN himself someday," he concluded, and then turned his full attention back to Hansen and Sabudu.

"As soon as you've had a chance to review the draft document and to come up with recommendations on how to improve it, please call and we'll get back together," he told Hansen.

"I'll do that," replied Hansen.

With that the men shook hands and Milner and Sabudu left. Afterward Hansen told Jackie to inform the senior staff that there would be a 4:30 meeting and they'd all be working late.

"Well," Jackie told Christopher, as soon as Ambassador Hansen closed the door to his office, "it looks like you'll have plenty of time at the Saudi exhibit. I'll give Decker the message for you."

"Thanks," said Christopher, but before he reached the door, it opened again. It was Milner.

"Christopher, will you be at the Saudi exhibit this evening?" he asked.

"Yes, sir. I'm going there now."

"Good, I'll see you there. They have a really wonderful presentation on Islam, including some exquisite models of the mosques in Mecca and Medina."

Six weeks later

Tel Aviv

Tom Donafin dabbed his finger across the bristles of his toothbrush to see if he had applied enough toothpaste. Satisfied that he had, he licked his finger and replaced the tube in its assigned spot on the counter by the sink. He had now been blind for about seven months and was learning to live with it. Fortunately, he had always preferred wearing a beard so he didn't have to worry about shaving. And when he'd taken an apartment on the same floor in her building, Rhoda had helped him set up his closet and drawers so that he could pick out matching clothes.

He thought it might still be a little early, but as soon as he was dressed he locked up and walked down the hall toward Rhoda's apartment. Feeling his way with his long white cane, he reached the end of the hall, turned, and counted his steps to her front door. He had done this many times by himself, and there was really no possibility he would go to the wrong door. Still, he had suggested to Rhoda that they carve a heart and their initials into her door so he could always be sure he had the right apartment. Rhoda had thought better of the idea.

Tom knocked and was greeted a moment later with a very warm kiss, which he gladly returned. "You're early," Rhoda said. "Come on in. I was just about to change."

"Should I cover my eyes?" Tom joked.

"It's not your eyes I'm concerned about," she said. "It's the pictures in your mind. You just wait here. I'll be back in a minute." In the past Tom had always avoided romantic involvement, fearing rejection because of his disfigurement. Strangely, now that he couldn't see, it was no longer a problem.

Tom made his way to the couch and sat down. On the coffee table Rhoda kept a book for beginning Braille students. He picked it up, intending to get in a little practice, but noticed a single sheet of paper sitting on top. Running his fingers over the formations of bumps one at a time, he determined the characters on the page. "I love you," it said.

He didn't mention the note to Rhoda when she came from her bedroom.

"All ready," she said.

Tom got up and walked toward the door. Rhoda met him halfway and placed his hand in the now familiar spot on her arm. "Rabbi won't know what to think when we get to Havdalah early," she said.

"That won't be his only surprise tonight," Tom added, and though he couldn't see it, he was confident that there was a smile on Rhoda's face.

After dinner at Rabbi Cohen's house, everyone moved to the living room. Benjamin Cohen, who alone with his father was the only member of the rabbi's family to survive the Disaster, turned off the lights as his father prayed and lit the three wicks of the tall blue-and-white braided candle. The Havdalah, or "separation," marked the end of the Sabbath and the beginning of the work week, the distinction of the holy from the secular. Along with the Cohens and Tom and Rhoda, there were nine others present. Originally there had been many more in Cohen's congregation, but the Disaster had reduced their number by more than a hundred and fifty. Now they could fit easily into Cohen's living room. Of those present, some, like Rhoda, had started attending Cohen's services only a few weeks or months before the Disaster. Others had joined the group afterward.

As the flame grew, Saul Cohen took the candle and held it up. In accordance with tradition, those in the circle responded by standing and holding their hands up toward the light with their fingers cupped. Though he couldn't see the flame, Tom could feel the heat of the large candle and he did as Rhoda had taught him. It meant nothing to him beyond being simply a tradition, but it was important to Rhoda and so he did it.

As they had planned, after the Havdalah, Tom and Rhoda waited for everyone to leave so they could talk with Rabbi Cohen alone.

"Tell me," Cohen asked, "how did my favorite skeptic like tonight's message?"

"Well," Tom said honestly, "I understood what you were saying, but don't you think it's narrow-minded to say that there's only one way for a person to get into the kingdom of God?"

"It would be," Cohen agreed, "were it not for the fact that the one way is entirely unrestricted, completely free, and totally accessible to every person on the planet. God is no farther from any of us than our willingness to answer him. Would it be narrow-minded to say there's only one thing everyone must breathe?"

"But air is available to everyone," Tom countered.

"So is God, Tom. It doesn't matter who you are or where you live. The Bible says that God has made himself known to *everyone*.[36] It's up to each person to decide whether he'll answer God's call. And Tom, one of the great things about it is that once you've answered, you'll find it's absolutely the most natural thing in the world. Even," Cohen laughed at his own unexpected turn of phrase, "more natural than breathing."

The subject was worthy of further discussion, but right now Tom had something else on his mind. As a transitional step, Tom decided to ask the rabbi something he had wondered about for a while. "Rabbi," he said, "there's something I don't understand: if you no longer believe as the other Hasidim believe, why do you still wear the attire and earlocks of Hasidim?"

Rhoda looked away in embarrassment; she would never have asked the question herself, but it was something she had often wondered. She felt sure the rabbi would know she had mentioned it to Tom. After all, how else could Tom know what the rabbi wore?

"It's my heritage," Cohen answered. "Even the Apostle Paul changed his ways only where it was necessary to accomplish his mission. Besides," added Cohen, "there are many years of wear left in these clothes. Why should I buy new?"

Cohen smiled at his own stereotypical humor, but Tom, who could only assume that Cohen was serious, had to bite his lip.

"So, what is it I can do for you?" asked Cohen, assuming correctly that Tom and Rhoda hadn't stayed late just to ask him about his wardrobe.

"Well," said Tom, glad for the opportunity to get to the subject he wanted to talk about. "Rhoda and I would like for you to officiate at our wedding."

Cohen didn't respond.

"Is something the matter, Rabbi?" Rhoda asked.

Cohen hesitated. "I'm sorry. Rhoda, could I speak with you alone for just a moment?"

Cohen began to move away and Rhoda automatically followed before Tom could even think to object. In a moment so brief he couldn't speak, they were gone and Tom heard one of the interior doors of the house close behind them.

"Rhoda," Cohen said, as soon as he was alone with her, "do you remember what I told you when I brought Tom to you?"

"You mean the prophecy?" she asked.

"Yes."

"How could I forget it? I've thought about it every day."

"Then you know you may have several years, but then you'll lose him. The prophecy is clear: 'He must bring death and die that the end and the beginning may come.'"

"I know and I understand," Rhoda answered.

"And you still want to go ahead with the marriage?" Cohen's voice showed concern but gave no hint of disapproval.

"Yes, Rabbi. More than anything."

Cohen gave her a look of caution.

Rhoda quickly corrected herself. "I mean, more than anything, as long as it's within God's will."

Cohen let it pass. "All right, then. Just as long as you're going into this with your eyes wide open."

"I am, Rabbi," she assured him.

"There is, of course, the issue of being yoked to an unbeliever, but with Tom, I have always known it was just a matter of time. We shall have to see to that immediately, and by all means before the wedding takes place."

Rhoda willingly agreed.

"Have you told Tom about the prophecy?" Cohen asked as an afterthought.

"I didn't think I should."

Cohen nodded thoughtfully. "Yes, it's probably best that you don't. Better to let God act in his own time and not put any ideas in Tom's head."

Cohen and Rhoda went back to where Tom was waiting. "Well, Tom," Cohen began, by way of explanation, "your Rhoda assures me that she's going into this with her eyes open."

Tom knew how much stock Rhoda put in Cohen's opinions, but he didn't much care for being talked about when he wasn't around to defend himself, and he wasn't at all sure he liked the scrutiny Cohen placed on their plans. Nonetheless, he decided to hold his tongue.

"Speaking of going into things with your eyes open," Cohen said, "Tom, I have a wedding gift for you. Actually, it's not from me. I was told to give you this when I first found you under the rubble. The exact time was left up to me, and now seems as good as any." Cohen came close to Tom, reached out his hand, and placed it over Tom's eyes. "Not through any power of my own," Cohen said, before Tom could even figure out what was going on, "but in the name and through the power of Messiah Yeshua: Open your eyes and see."

Two weeks later

New York

British Ambassador Jon Hansen was widely applauded as he approached the speaker's dais at the United Nations General Assembly. His speech would be translated simultaneously into Arabic, Chinese, French, Russian, and Spanish, which together with English are the six official languages of the United Nations.

Over the preceding three weeks Decker had spent countless hours working on this speech: writing drafts, condensing, expanding, adding, deleting, polishing, and working with linguists to ensure that the words spoken in English would have the proper impact when translated. What Hansen was about to propose would involve a major restructuring of the United Nations and his words would have to be both clearly understood and thoroughly compelling.

What made it possible now that Hansen's motion might actually pass, when before it had not been taken seriously, were the recent events in Russia. The nuclear holocaust had reduced the Russian Federation to a mere specter. Even the name was threatened as survivors in one region after another emerged from the rubble and declared themselves independent republics — much as had happened when the USSR fell apart decades before. Those were the lucky ones; in some areas there were not enough survivors to even worry about things political.

The world had been a much different place on October 24, 1945, when the United Nations officially came into being. The Second World War had just ended, and the victors who had made up the major powers of the world — the United States, Great Britain, France, the Soviet Union, and China — had established themselves as the "Big Five," giving themselves permanent member status and veto power in the United Nations Security Council. Since that time Britain had divested herself of her colonies and, though influential, remained 'great' only in name. She would trade her power on the Security Council for temporary control of the Secretariat under Hansen and the opportunity to direct the UN's reorganization. "It is better to trade away now what might well be taken tomorrow," Hansen had told the British Parliament. Britain knew that the evolution of the UN was unstoppable. Guiding that evolution was a responsibility for which Britain felt itself uniquely qualified.

France, mired in European socialism while simultaneously inundated in political and social strife as it adjusted to a majority Muslim population, could hardly make a valid claim for its permanent position on the Security Council. Nevertheless, France would not willingly surrender power. Even as Hansen spoke, the French were lobbying other members to vote against the measure.

Because of its size, China alone of the five original Security Council members would be guaranteed a seat on the reorganized Council. Nonetheless, China would oppose the measure because its power would be diluted by half in the proposed ten-member body.

What was left of the Russian Federation, though it would protest loudly, certainly no longer had legitimate claim to permanent status on the Security Council or to veto power over its actions.

Like China, the United States could truly claim a right to permanent status based on its position as a world power. Yet in a very real sense, this proposal might be seen as a logical next step toward the "New World Order" first proposed by former U.S. president George H. W. Bush. And though there was no clear majority to support it, a large and vocal minority of American citizens as well as a majority of those in Congress did. It was hoped the change might even result in reducing the UN's heavy dependence on U.S. funding. America would not stand in the way of reorganization if that was what the majority of members of the United Nations wanted.

Hansen's proposal would eliminate the permanent positions of the Big Five and instead structure a newly defined Security Council based on ten major regions of the world.[37] Details would have to be worked out by all member nations, but it was expected that these ten regions would include North America; South America; Europe and Iceland; Eastern Africa; Western Africa; the Middle East; the Indian subcontinent; Northern Asia; China; and the nations of

Asia's Pacific basin from Japan and Korea through Southeast Asia, down to Indonesia and New Guinea, along with Australia and New Zealand. Each region would have one voting member and one alternate member on the Security Council.

As he stood before the great assembly of nations, about to give the most important speech of his life, Hansen was running on adrenaline. He had spent night and day for the past several weeks lobbying for approval. Now was the moment for show business, but immediately afterward, the lobbying and arm twisting would continue anew. Hansen stepped up to the speaker's lectern and began.

United Nations General Assembly

"My fellow delegates and citizens of the world: I come to you today as the ambassador of an empire now divested of all her colonies. I say that not with regret, but with pride. Pride that over time we have grown to recognize the rights of sovereign peoples to set their own course in the history of the Earth. Pride that my beloved Britain, though she will bear a great cost at its passage, has placed justice ahead of power and has authorized the introduction and the support of this motion.

"Since the foundation of this august body, five countries, Great Britain among them, have held sway over the other nations of the world. Today the history of nations has come to a new path.

"A new path — not a destination, for there is no stopping.

"A new path — not a crossroads, for in truth there *is* no other way that just and reasonable men and women may choose.

"A new path — not a detour, for the path we were on has taken us as far as it will go.

"A new path — not a dead-end, for there can be no going back.

"It is the most tragic of situations — the Disaster and the nuclear devastation of the Russian Federation — that has brought us so abruptly to this point in history. And yet, were it not so we would have reached it still. From the first days of the United Nations, it has always been the visionaries' dream that one day all nations would stand as equals in this body. We have come too far toward that dream to refuse now to advance toward its fulfillment.

"The time has come for all peoples of the world to put off the shackles of the past. The day of the empire is gone, and just as certainly the day of subservience to those born of power must also come to an end. Justice is not found in the rule of those who consider themselves our superiors, but from the common will of peers. The greatness of nations comes not from their armaments, but from their willingness to allow and aid the greatness of others."

Decker listened closely, anticipating the pauses and hoping for applause. Although at the UN the timing of applause can sometimes be embarrassingly delayed by the translation to other languages, Decker was not disappointed. Clearly the motion would do well.

One week later

The successful vote to reorganize the Security Council did not mark the completion of the effort for Decker, but only the beginning of a new phase. Now that the motion had carried, media from around the world were calling, emailing, wanting information about the man who likely would become the new secretary-general. Decker brought in extra staff to support the more routine functions of the effort, but he was wary of delegating too much. As he went over a press release for the third time, he realized that he had no idea what he was reading. He was just too tired. Closing his eyes, he slumped down in the chair and thought back to his days at the *Knoxville Enterprise*. It had been a long time since he had worked this hard.

Unnoticed, Jackie Hansen had entered the room and was now standing directly behind his chair. As he sat with his eyes closed, she reached down and placed her long, slender fingers on his shoulders. Decker jumped, but turning and seeing Jackie's smile, relaxed as she began to massage his tired, knotted muscles. "Oh, that feels good," he said gratefully. "I'll give you just twenty minutes to stop it." It was an old joke, but Jackie laughed anyway.

"Your back is one solid knot," she said sympathetically. "I'll bet you're exhausted."

Decker started to nod, but decided it might interrupt the massage and instead answered, "Uh-huh."

"My father really appreciates all the work you're doing. He told me you were working so hard that sometimes he wasn't sure which of you was trying to get elected."

Decker appreciated the compliment. It was nice to know his work was recognized. He smiled back at Jackie, then closed his eyes again to concentrate on the relaxing feel of her hands. Suddenly she stopped. "You know what you need to really relax?" she asked.

"Yeah. More of that."

"Well, yes. But whenever I get tense, I meditate," she suggested as she started to rub his shoulders again. "I may seem pretty relaxed to you most of the time, but I used to be a jumble of nerves. When I first started to work here I was so concerned about doing a good job. I didn't want people thinking the only reason I had the position was because my father was the ambassador." Jackie selected a knot and began rubbing in circles to work it out. "That's when I met Lorraine from the French Mission. She invited me to a go to a meditation class at the Lucius Trust." Jackie stopped again and looked at her watch. "Oh, my goodness," she said in surprise, "speaking of the Lucius Trust: it's 7:55. If I don't hurry I'm going to be late. I've missed the last three weeks because of work; I really don't want to miss tonight."

"Miss what?" asked Decker.

"My meditation class. It meets every Wednesday. Tonight Alice Bernley, the director of the Trust, is going to show new members how to reach their inner consciousness, the source of creativity. It's like an inner guide."

"Oh," Decker said, making no attempt to pretend he knew or really cared what Jackie was talking about.

"Come with me."

"Uh . . . I don't know, Jackie. I'm not really into this New Age stuff. I'm pretty old fashioned."

"Oh, come on," she insisted, as she took his hand and gave it a tug. "When you leave there tonight you'll be more relaxed than you've been in weeks."

The class had already started when they arrived. Quietly Jackie moved through the crowd of about a hundred and fifty people, pulling Decker along until they reached two empty chairs. Around them people sat silently with eyes closed, some with their legs crossed, all listening intently to the speaker. They seemed totally unaware that others were around them. Even in the subdued light, Decker recognized nearly two dozen of the attendees as UN delegates. The speaker was Alice Bernley, an attractive woman in her late forties with long flowing red hair. "Just sit down, close your eyes, and listen," Jackie whispered.

It was easy enough to relax in the deep, comfortable chairs. Decker listened to the speaker and tried to figure out what he was supposed to be doing. "In the blackness ahead of you," Bernley was saying, "is a small point of light just coming into view. As you move closer to the light, you are beginning to narrow the distance, and the light is growing brighter and warmer." Decker became aware of a soft, barely audible hum, almost like a cat's purr, coming from those around him. As he closed his eyes, to his amazement, he too saw a light. It was very distant, but it was clearly visible. He wondered at the sight, and in his mind it *did* seem as though the light was getting closer, or possibly he was getting closer to it. He was certain it was all just a mental picture painted by the woman, but he was surprised at how open he was to her suggestion. *It must be lack of sleep*, he thought briefly. The woman's delicate voice seemed to softly caress his ears and thoughts. "Approach the light," the woman continued, and Decker did. "Soon you will find that it has led you to a beautiful place: a garden." In his mind Decker followed her words and soon he saw it.

Bernley went on at some length describing every detail of the garden. It was so clear, so real and precisely described that later, as Decker looked back to this event and thought of all the others in the room, his greatest wonder — though logically he knew better — was that so many could be sharing the same vision so clearly and yet each be totally alone in his or her own garden. Even in his memory the place seemed so real that he expected to see others from the room there with him.

"Just beyond the shining pool of water you see someone approaching." Decker looked but saw no one. "It may be a person," Bernley continued, "but for many of you it will be an animal, perhaps a bird or a rabbit, or perhaps a horse, or maybe even a unicorn. What form it takes is unimportant. Don't be afraid, even if it's a lion. It won't hurt you. It's there to help you, to guide you when you have questions."

Still Decker saw no one. "When it has come close enough, greet it, talk to it, ask it anything you'd like to know, and it will answer. You might start by asking its name. As some of you know, my spirit guide is a Tibetan master who goes by the name Djwlij Kajm. For some, your spirit guide may be a bit more shy. You may have to coax it out, not by speaking to it, but by listening. So listen. Listen very closely." Decker listened. He moved closer to the pool, trying to hear. Bernley's voice had fallen silent, apparently to allow those with "shy" spirit guides to listen more closely. Still he saw and heard nothing.

It wasn't that nothing was there. If they had spoken any louder, he surely would have heard.

"Why does no one approach him?" one of the voices whispered.

"The Master forbids it," another answered.

Bernley remained silent for another eight or ten minutes. For a while, Decker continued to try to hear or see the guide, but when she spoke again he opened his eyes and realized that he had fallen asleep. "Now say farewell to your new friend but thank him or her or it and let him know you'll return soon."

Decker watched the others in the group as Bernley brought them back from this expedition of the mind. In a moment they opened their eyes and looked around. Everyone was smiling. Some hugged those around them. A few openly wept. Decker looked over at Jackie Hansen, who seemed to be nearly floating. From a corner of the room someone began to clap and soon the whole room was filled with applause.

"Thank you, thank you," Bernley said graciously, "but you really should be applauding yourselves for having the courage to open your minds to the unknown. Now, whenever you need guidance on something that you just don't know how to handle, all you have to do is go to a quiet place for a few moments, close your eyes, and open your mind. Seek out your guide at every opportunity. Ask it the questions you can't answer. What you are doing is allowing the creative nature within each of us to do what it most wants to do: provide visionary solutions to the problems in your life."

Some of Bernley's assistants brought in refreshments and everyone began to talk together in small groups about what they had experienced. Decker politely thanked Jackie for the invitation and told her he had found the experience interesting, but he really needed to get back to work. She seemed surprised that he was leaving, but didn't try to stop him.

As soon as Decker left, Alice Bernley waved to Jackie, who quickly made her way across the room. Without speaking, Bernley took Jackie's hand and led her to a quiet corner where they wouldn't be overheard. "Was that Decker Hawthorne with you?" Bernley asked, sounding a little concerned.

"Yes," Jackie answered. "I asked him if he'd like to sit in on the class. Did I do the wrong thing?"

"No. Actually, it's my fault. I should have told you. The Tibetan has made it very clear that Mr. Hawthorne is not to be a part of the Trust. The Master has special plans for him."

Two days later

At the Israeli Mission in New York, Jon Hansen was shown into the office of Ambassador Aviel Hartzog, who was at his desk talking on the phone. He neither looked up nor acknowledged Hansen's arrival. It was an obvious snub. As Hansen waited he couldn't help but overhear Hartzog's conversation, which didn't sound very important. This made the snub all the greater. To be talking petty business with some bureaucrat while a guest ambassador waited was inexcusable. What made it even worse was that Hartzog undoubtedly realized Hansen was not only a fellow delegate, but most likely the next secretary-general.

Nearly three minutes later, the Israeli ambassador finally hung up the phone and joined Hansen. He made no apology for the delay and immediately began by calling Hansen by his first name, even though the two had never been formally introduced, the Israeli ambassador having just been assigned to the UN. *What a cheeky monkey*, thought Hansen.

"So, Jon, what have you come to offer us?"

Hansen held his temper like a true Englishman. "Reason, Mr. Ambassador. Reason."

"You have brought me a reason that Israel should cut her own throat?" Hartzog mocked.

"No. I have—"

The Israeli cut him off before Hansen could even begin. "Ambassador," he said, now becoming formal, "my government considers the decision by the General Assembly to reorganize the Security Council along regional lines a noble gesture. It is, unfortunately, one with which we cannot abide. Did it not cross your mind that by restructuring the Security Council on a regional basis and then grouping Israel with the other nations of the Middle East, you would force us into a position where we would constantly be at the mercy of our Muslim neighbors? In case you were not aware, Israel has a Jewish population of five million. We are surrounded by twenty-three Muslim nations with a total population of 250 million. Just what do you think Israel's chances are of having a representative on the Council who is favorable to our position on *anything?*" Hartzog paused and then added, "Most of our Muslim neighbors haven't even officially acknowledged that Israel exists!"

"But leaving the UN is not the answer, Mr. Ambassador," Hansen said, finally getting a word in.

"Unless you can make some guarantees . . . perhaps by increasing the number of seats on the Security Council to eleven and guaranteeing that seat to Israel . . ." Hartzog paused for

Hansen's reaction. He was certain Hansen would never agree to such a proposal. He made it only to point out the hopelessness of the situation.

"You know we can't do that," Hansen responded. "It would destroy the whole restructuring. There's no way we can make that kind of exception for Israel without setting the precedent for others wanting the same." Hansen didn't mention it, but there was another precedent he didn't want to set — that of having a nation leave the UN. It had never been done before.

"Then there seems little choice," Hartzog concluded.

"Mr. Ambassador, if Israel leaves the UN, it will be giving in to the very countries you fear."

Reflexively and assertively, Hartzog's hand shot up to stop Hansen in his tracks. "Mr. Ambassador, if you think this is about fear, then you know nothing about my country . . . or about me!"

"The point," Hansen said, "is that they'd like nothing more than to see Israel out of the United Nations."

Satisfied he had made his point, Hartzog dropped his hand and took on a less defensive posture. He was, however, no less determined in his course. "Unfortunately," he said, "you are correct. But neither can we stay."

The conversation didn't improve and Hansen left without having gained any ground. When he returned to his office he was met by Decker. "How'd it go?" he asked.

"Not well," Hansen answered in understatement. "Israel is just too blasted cheeky about what happened with the Russian Federation."

"But they've acknowledged they had nothing to do with it, so what do they have to be so arrogant about?" Decker really wanted to say "cheeky" too, but he didn't think he could do it without sounding like he was poking fun.

"I don't know," Hansen admitted. "Maybe the stories are true that it was a computer worm they created and they just don't want to admit it. The official position of the Knesset is that the destruction of the Russian missiles was a miracle of God."

"You don't think the Israeli ambassador actually believes that, do you?" asked Decker.

"The point is a great many people in Israeli are convinced that what happened was a *literal* act of God, foretold by their prophet

Ezekiel."[38] Hansen shook his head and sighed. "I can't really blame them for their response to restructuring, though. It doesn't offer them much to look forward to."

Chapter 18

Revelation

Seven years later

New York

Decker shook the rain from his umbrella, unbuttoned his raincoat, and walked past the UN guard toward the main elevators.

"Good morning, Mr. Hawthorne," the guard said. "And happy birthday!"

Decker paused long enough to smile and nod. "Thank you, Charlie," he responded.

How did he remember that? Decker wondered, as he stepped into the elevator and pushed the button for the thirty-eighth floor. The view of the East River and Queens from Decker's office was almost obscured by the rain beating hard against the window. He looked through the notes on his desk to decide what he wanted to do first. Among the neatly disorganized clutter were two photographs: one of Decker with Elizabeth, Hope, and Louisa taken in that brief period between his escape from Lebanon and the Disaster, and a picture of twenty year old Christopher, taken two years before at his graduation from the Masters program at the United Nations University for Peace in Costa Rica.

Other than being Decker's fifty-eighth birthday, it was an ordinary day at the UN, a fact for which he was grateful. As director of public affairs for Secretary-General Jon Hansen, Decker had been personally involved in much of the planning and implementation of the worldwide United Nations Day celebration three days earlier, so the return to normalcy was welcome. The observance of the UN's founding had been a big success, with celebrations in 198 of the 235 member nations. Secretary-General Hansen placed great importance on the event. He wanted it to be bigger and better each year in order to build public support for the UN and its programs. In some countries the UN Day celebration had actually grown more important than the individual nations' own birthday celebrations. There were a few countries where they might have even dispensed with their own national celebrations altogether were it not for the fact that it was an extra day off for the bureaucrats and teachers.

Relatively speaking, the world was at peace, and for the moment, Decker was taking it easy, recovering from the massive effort of coordinating celebrations in more than a dozen time zones.

Twenty minutes later Decker finally let his secretary, Mary Polk, know that he was officially in.

"Mr. Hawthorne," Mary said in surprise, "I didn't see you come in. Have you forgotten about your meeting this morning with the secretary-general?"

"What meeting?" Decker asked.

"You were scheduled for a meeting with the secretary-general fifteen minutes ago. Jackie has already called twice."

"Why didn't you check to see if I was here?" He didn't wait for an answer.

It was only thirty yards to Secretary-General Hansen's office so Decker was at the door in just seconds. "They're waiting for you in the conference room," Jackie said as Decker altered his course toward the adjoining room and opened the door.

"Surprise!" yelled about three dozen voices in unison.

In the center of the crowd stood Secretary-General and Mrs. Hansen. Both were enjoying the startled look on Decker's face. Although it was incumbent on him that he laugh, all he could manage was a pained moan and a disbelieving shake of the head. Finally an appreciative smile broke through. Behind Decker, Mary Polk entered the room to join the party. "You're in big trouble," Decker told his secretary as he caught sight of her.

"Don't blame her," interrupted Hansen. "She was just following orders."

"Don't you people know that office birthday parties are supposed to be in the afternoon?" Decker lectured.

"If we did that we might not have surprised you," Jackie countered.

On the table were several dozen doughnuts stacked tightly together to look like a cake, with about half the number of candles Decker was actually due, waiting to be lit. "You guys are nuts," Decker said.

"What's that?" the secretary-general bristled.

"You guys are nuts, *sir.*"

"Much better," Hansen allowed, smiling.

There was still one more surprise for Decker. In a corner of the room was a guest who had been concealed behind the others. "Christopher! What on Earth are you doing here?"

"You didn't think I'd miss your birthday, did you?" Christopher replied.

"You're supposed to be on a cruise around the world."

"I decided to take half now and half later," Christopher explained. "So I flew back."

"Hey, are you going to blow out the candles or not?" pressed Mary Polk.

Decker obliged and everyone dug into the doughnuts, candle wax, and coffee. As with most office parties, a few people stayed only long enough to make an appearance, others just long enough to get seconds and take a couple of doughnuts back to their desks. Others stayed on and reminisced or gathered in small groups to talk business. Decker positioned himself close to the door and made sure to thank each person for coming. Christopher circulated among the attendees, deftly adding his comments and opinions on the topics of conversation in each cluster he visited. Decker watched, pleased at how well accepted Christopher was and at how well he handled himself.

Among the well-wishers were three Security Council members: Ambassador Lee Yun-Mai of China; Ambassador Friedreich Heinemann of Germany, representing Europe; and Ambassador Yuri Kruszkegin, formerly of the Russian Federation and now of the independent Republic of Khakassia, representing Northern Asia. They had grouped on one side of the room and were discussing a recent vote on trade barriers. Christopher seemed just as comfortable speaking with the ambassadors as he had been with the administrative staff.

As the crowd began to thin, Secretary-General Hansen came over to talk with Decker. "I want to thank you again for the spectacular job you did with this year's United Nations Day celebration," Hansen said as he gave him a pat on the back.

"Thank you for saying so, sir."

"I think you're due for a little time off," Hansen said. "I told Jackie to put you down as being on vacation for the next four or five days. I'm sure your staff can hold the world together in your absence."

The offer was a surprise but, like the party, it was a welcome one. "I believe I'll take you up on that," Decker said willingly. "It would be nice to spend some time with Christopher."

"That's quite a young man you've raised," Hansen said, motioning with his coffee cup in Christopher's direction.

"Yes, sir," Decker agreed with fatherly pride.

"Someone else who thinks so is Bob Milner. He sent me a letter — a very favorable letter — recommending Christopher for a position with ECOSOC," Hansen said, referring to the United Nations Economic and Social Council.

"Yes, sir. He's been quite supportive of Christopher's endeavors. He even flew down to Costa Rica last month for Christopher's graduation from the UN University's Doctoral program." Decker said this more to brag on Christopher than anything else. He was always willing to tell anyone who asked that Christopher had graduated first in his class, simultaneously earning both a PhD in Political Science and a second masters degree in World Agricultural Management. At this moment he was supposed to be on a cruise around the world, taking a well-earned vacation before starting to work at ECOSOC in the position for which Milner had recommended him.

"With friends like Bob Milner, he'll go a long way," Hansen said.

Decker had always assumed that Milner's interest in Christopher was simply the result of recognizing his many good qualities. Whether out of altruistic motives or as a way of building a team of loyal young allies, or both, it was common for those in power to nurture promising members of the next generation. Milner wielded a lot of influence, and Decker was glad for all the doors he had opened to Christopher. Still, he couldn't help sometimes being a little ill at ease with Milner and some of his associates. He would never have told Christopher, but for his personal tastes, Milner was just a little flaky.

"Someone said Secretary Milner wasn't feeling well," Decker mentioned.

"Jackie tells me he checked into the hospital three nights ago for observation because of his heart," Hansen replied.

"Oh," Decker said, both surprised and concerned.

"He's eighty-two now, you know," Hansen said.

"That's not so old," Decker responded, thinking about the addition of a year to his own age.

Hansen laughed. "Christopher can probably tell you better than I about how Bob's doing. I understand he went to see him this morning before coming to the party."

Decker now understood more fully why Christopher had cut his trip short.

When the party broke up, Decker went back to his office to tie up some loose ends and clear his calendar. It was nearly noon before he was ready to leave. "Where do you want to go for lunch?" Christopher asked. "I'm buying."

"In that case, there's a hot dog stand on the corner," Decker joked as he stuffed a few papers into his briefcase.

"I think we can do a little better than that," Christopher answered.

They finally settled on the Palm Too, a nice but reasonably priced restaurant on Second Avenue near the UN. "So," Decker began after they had ordered, "are you ready to start putting that education of yours to work?"

"Ready and eager," Christopher answered.

"ECOSOC was a great choice for you," Decker said. "They'll be expanding in the next few years as part of Secretary-General Hansen's plan for greater centralization of authority." He tapped his finger on the table to make his point. "As the role of the UN grows, ECOSOC is going to be more and more on the leading edge of world policy."

"When you look at all that Hansen has accomplished over the last seven years," Christopher said, "and the spirit of cooperation he inspires among the members, it's hard to imagine how we'll manage when he decides to retire."

"Oh, he's having way too much fun to ever retire," Decker smiled. "But, you're right: So much of his success is based on his personal popularity. Peter Fantham in the *Times* called him the 'George Washington of the United Nations,' and I have to agree."

Decker paused briefly to take a bite of his sandwich. "In our internal tracking polls last month, his worldwide approval rating was 78 percent. Of course, there are some who oppose everything he does — a few religious kooks mostly. They think he's the Antichrist or something, and that world government is somehow inherently evil."

"I suppose you're always going to have a few of those," Christopher replied.

Decker nodded. "Unfortunately, our strength is also our weakness. It's based too heavily on Hansen himself." Decker looked around to be sure no one was listening and then, for good measure, leaned over the table and whispered, "Left to themselves, the Security Council would fight like cats and dogs." This was no big secret, but because of Decker's position, it would be embarrassing if he were overheard making such a statement. "Hansen has been able to use his personal charm and skills to bind the Council together, helping them overlook their differences and getting them to work for the common good. The more I watch him, the more I believe he was born for this moment in world history."

Christopher nodded as he chewed and considered the assessment.

"You know," Decker continued, "I've frequently been amazed at the human ability to adapt to the situation at hand. Earthquakes, wars, terrorist attacks, the nuclear devastation of the Russian Republic, even the Disaster: somehow we always manage to go on. I suppose that's why we've survived as long as we have as a species. But at the same time, we seem to have this crazy notion that the way things are at the moment is the way they'll always remain. In the last few years we've gotten used to living in a world at peace, but there's no guarantee that'll last. Rome fell and so might the United Nations one day.

"My fear is that we won't last nearly so long as Rome. As long as Jon Hansen holds the reins, I think we're okay. But there's no structure for succession. The UN Charter lays out the means for electing a new Secretary-General, but how do you find a leader of Hansen's stature and quality?"

Decker and Christopher continued their meal without speaking for a moment, both recognizing there was no more to say on the subject.

"Well," Decker said finally, "in your last email you said you had some news for me. Something to do with your dreams."

"It's about some classes I took this year. Secretary Milner recommended them."

Decker, who had been doing most of the talking and little of the eating to this point, took advantage of the opportunity while Christopher explained.

"The first class dealt with New Age thought and eastern religions like Buddhism, Taoism, and Shintoism. Secretary Milner was involved in the development of the curriculum."

"I thought Milner was a Catholic," Decker said.

"He is. But the eastern religions don't make any claims to exclusivity. You can be Catholic, Protestant, Jewish, Muslim, Hindu, whatever; it doesn't matter. They believe there are many ways to God."

"I know that stuff has gotten real popular," Decker said. "There's been a large contingent of New Agers at the UN for years. And of course, Jackie is deep into it. Still — and I don't mean to be judgmental — but it all sounds pretty weird to me."

"Some of it seems a little crazy," Christopher agreed, "but I think they may be on the right track about some things. I read a little about New Age thought eight or nine years ago."

Decker mouth was full, but his expression asked for more information.

"You remember that Uncle Harry had me read some things in the Bible to see if it would spur any memories?"

Decker nodded.

"I didn't stop with the parts Uncle Harry wanted me to read. I read the whole thing, from Genesis to Revelation." Christopher shrugged. "Afterward I wanted to see what other religions had to say. So I read the *Quran*, the *Book of Mormon, Dianetics, Science with Key to the Scriptures,* and a dozen other religious books. After growing up around Aunt Martha, who was Baptist, and Uncle Harry, who eschewed all religions, I was a little surprised to find that a lot of what others said made a great deal of sense.

"Anyway, the other class Secretary Milner recommended got into some of the same subjects: stuff like karma, reincarnation, channeling, astral projection."

"I've heard Jackie mention that," Decker said while Christopher took a bite. "Isn't that where you float around outside your body or something?"

"Sort of," Christopher replied. "Nearly all religions teach that people are made up of both body and spirit. Astral projection is a process used during meditation that's supposed to allow you to travel in the form of spirit energy to other places while your body remains in one place."

Decker rolled his eyes.

Christopher's expression said there was more.

"What? You've tried this?" Decker asked, recognizing that Christopher wasn't the type to believe something so bizarre without close scrutiny.

"The first time was eight years ago," Christopher answered.

"You never told me this."

"Like you said, it sounded pretty crazy — especially before I took these classes."

"So where did you go in your astral projection?" Decker probed, still far from convinced.

"At first I just went to places I knew," Christopher said. "But then I started going farther. I was surprised at how easy it was."

Christopher's expression suggested there was still more to this story. "And then," Decker prompted.

"Lebanon," Christopher replied.

Decker put down his fork and studied Christopher's face. Apparently he was serious. He had to ask. "Christopher, the night before the Disaster, your Aunt Martha told Elizabeth that you knew I would be coming home soon. Do you remember telling her that?"

"Yes, sir."

"How did you—?"

"I was there with you in Lebanon. I untied you."

Decker took a startled breath.

"I tried to reach you several times, but even after I found you, you couldn't see me. That's when I decided to try to appear to you in a dream. Do you remember the dream?"

Decker finally found his tongue. "Until this moment I thought that was all it was. I never told anyone about it except Elizabeth . . . and Tom Donafin, right after we escaped. From what your Aunt Martha said, I thought you might have had some premonition or something, but I never imagined . . . Why didn't you ever tell me?"

A look of relief swept over Christopher's face. "I wasn't entirely sure about it myself until this moment. It was so dreamlike that I thought the whole thing might have been my imagination. Why didn't *you* ever mention it?"

Decker shook his head. "It seemed so crazy."

Decker and Christopher just looked at each other for a moment. "I guess I owe you more than I realized," Decker said.

"Not nearly as much as I owe you for taking me in when I had nowhere else to go."

"I probably would have died in Lebanon."

"I suppose we owe each other a lot," Christopher said. "You've been like a father to me."

Decker nodded appreciatively. "And you've been like a son." Decker was starting to get a little choked up, so after a deep breath he took a drink and brought the subject back to its previous course. "So, have you done any more of this astral projection?"

Christopher shook his head. "Maybe I made more of it than I should have, but there was something strangely frightening about it. Every time I did it, it was as if there was something more going on than I realized."

"What do you mean?"

"It was like . . ." Christopher seemed to be struggling for words. "Imagine you're walking through a peaceful field. All around you everything is totally tranquil. And yet, even though you can't see or hear it, you know that somewhere just beyond your view, perhaps over the next rise, there's a battle taking place." He shrugged. "That's about the best way I can explain it, except . . . that somehow I knew that I was the subject of that battle. And every time I traveled by astral projection, even though I still couldn't see or hear it, it felt as if the battle had gotten closer and fiercer. It was as though someone or something was trying to get to me — at me — and someone or something else was trying to prevent it. After the last trip to Lebanon I never did it again."

Decker considered this, but was way out of his field of expertise.

"I asked my professor, but she said she had never heard of anything similar."

Decker shook his head, still having no idea what to make of it all.

"But let me tell you about some other things I've discovered from taking these courses. That's what I actually intended to tell you about."

Decker nodded for him to go on.

"I think I've been able to piece together some more parts of my past. One of the classes taught us to do a type of meditation in which you go into a dreamlike state while you're still fully conscious. That way it's possible to have full control while you're dreaming. Since most of the things I've remembered have occurred in dreams, I tried using this type of meditation to draw out other information."

"What have you discovered?"

"I remember, as a child, working in my father's carpentry shop and how hard the work was, and I remember playing with the other children. One thing that's odd is that I've had several dreams where I was in India."

Decker shook his head. "There's nothing in the Bible about Jesus ever going to India, is there?"

"Not in the Bible, but there's considerable other literature that suggests he did. There's a church called the Church Universal and Triumphant that teaches that Jesus studied under an Indian maharishi." Christopher shrugged. "To tell you the truth, sometimes it's hard to know which memories are based on something that actually happened and which are the product of imagination."

"How far back have you been able to go?" Decker asked. "Do you remember anything about . . . God?" His tone bore a strong hint of reverent caution.

"I have had dreams that involved someone who seemed god-like," Christopher said, "but when I wake up and try to remember, it just won't come back to me."

"Do you remember anything about the place?" Decker probed. "Did it seem like you were in heaven?" The word *heaven* coming from his mouth reminded Decker of the bizarre circumstances of this whole conversation, and he looked around again to be sure no one was listening.

"I don't know," Christopher answered. "All I have is a feeling. It didn't seem at all like the heaven Aunt Martha described. I suppose it could have been the planet Uncle Harry thought I came from. But it's like trying to hold water in your hand. I'll start to remember something, and for a moment it seems so real and solid, but the instant I start to grasp it, it's gone. I remember lights — glowing bodies, sometimes in human form, sometimes with no form at all." Decker's expression begged to hear more. "I don't know," Christopher shrugged, then added with an uncomfortable chuckle. "Angels, maybe. But there was one other thing: a voice. I don't remember what it said; I just remember the voice. Something about it was strangely familiar, but I can't say exactly why or how."

"Can you re—" Decker stopped abruptly as a look of recognition suddenly registered on Christopher's face. "What?"

Christopher's voice became a whisper of astonishment. "I just remembered where I heard the voice! But it wasn't a voice exactly. It was laughter." He paused, apparently analyzing the new data.

"Where?" Decker urged.

"Do you remember the dream I had about the wooden box on the night the missiles blew up over Russia?" Decker nodded. "In the dream there was a voice saying 'Behold the hand of God,' followed by someone laughing. The laughter was the part of the dream that was most frightening."

Decked nodded. "I remember that."

"I can't explain how I know, but the laughter I heard then and the voice I heard in 'heaven' or on the other planet or whatever, are the same. It's the same person or being. I'm sure of it!"

Decker waited while Christopher silently continued his analysis. "I'm sorry," he said, finally. "That's all I can remember."

"Do you have any idea what it means?" Decker asked.

Christopher frowned with frustration and shook his head.

"Well," Decker concluded with raised brows, "having you around sure makes life interesting." He started to take a bite of his meal but was struck by another thought. "Christopher," he began, unsure how to word his question, "these classes and meditation — I don't suppose they've given you any insight into why you're here? Whether there's some purpose or anything? If you have a mission?"

Decker was entirely in earnest, but for the first time in the conversation Christopher began to laugh.

"What's so funny?" Decker asked.

"I guess that somewhere in the back of my mind I had always hoped *you* might someday answer that question for *me*," Christopher responded. "After all, the cloning wasn't my idea."

Nor had it been Decker's idea, but in the absence of Professor Goodman, Decker suddenly felt the weight of a responsibility he had never considered his own.

Christopher broke the brief but uncomfortable pause. "I'm just trying to make the best of a very strange situation," he said. "I might just as well ask you why *you* were born. None of us actually chose to be here. We just are." Christopher paused again. "I guess that's one big difference between me and the original. Apparently *he* had some choice in coming to this planet. I had none." He paused.

"I suppose in some ways my lack of choice actually makes me more human." Christopher said. His voice seemed to carry a note of longing — a longing to be like everyone else.

"No, I'm not entirely human," he continued. "I don't get sick and if I injure myself I heal quickly. But I feel what other people feel. I hurt like other people hurt. I bleed like other people bleed. And I can die, too." Here Christopher paused. "At least I guess I can." And paused again. Decker didn't interrupt. "If I were to die, I'm not sure what would happen. Would I be resurrected like Jesus was? I don't know. What was it that resurrected Jesus? Was it in his nature? My nature? Or was it some special act of God?" Christopher shook his head. "I don't know."

Decker had seen Christopher's humanity time and again: in the pain he carried over the loss of his adoptive aunt and uncle; in the compassion he showed Decker for the loss of Elizabeth, Hope and Louisa; in his desire that his life and profession be directed toward helping those less fortunate; and in the concern he had for the well-being of his friend and mentor, Secretary Milner. And here again was another sign of Christopher's humanity, one that Decker had never seen before: his feeling of being lost and alone in a life and circumstances he had not chosen.

"I don't think I'm here for any reason in particular," Christopher concluded, "except maybe, like everyone else, to be the best me I can be."

Abruptly, Christopher's words shifted to Milner, almost as if he had been pushed in that direction by Decker's fleeting thought of the former assistant secretary-general a moment earlier. "I'm really worried about him," he said.

Decker knew immediately who Christopher meant. He would have preferred to stay on the subject of Christopher's dreams and recollections, but they could return to that later. Right now Christopher was displaying the very humanity that Decker had just been pondering. He was obviously more concerned with Milner's well-being than with his own circumstances.

"He put up a good show at the hospital," Christopher continued, "but I think it's much worse than he let on. I asked the doctors, but they wouldn't say much — only that his surgery went well."

"That's pretty much standard policy," Decker said.

"Sure, I know that," Christopher said. "But I've never seen him like this. I know that he's getting on in years, but he's always been so strong. I just wasn't prepared to see him so weak and pale."

"We can drop by the hospital on the way home," Decker suggested, but immediately realized he was making an assumption. "You are planning to stay at the apartment?"

"Sure, if that's okay with you."

"Of course it's okay. Your room is just the way you left it. I haven't even taken out the trash."

Christopher smiled.

* * * * *

At the hospital Decker and Christopher headed for Milner's room. They were in the elevator when a sudden look of dread swept over Christopher's face. "What is it?" Decker asked.

"It's that feeling — the one I told you about where a battle is raging. Maybe it's because I was telling you about it, but I just had it again." The conversation ended abruptly as the elevator reached their floor and the door opened, revealing a stream of people moving as quickly as their feet or wheelchairs would carry them. There was no apparent panic. They weren't running away. Rather they seemed to be going toward something.

"Have you seen him?" one nurse asked another as people walked, rolled, or shuffled past.

"Only a peek," the other answered. "There's too many people around the door to get a good look."

As they walked down the hall with the flow of people, Decker and Christopher couldn't help but notice the excitement. "I wonder what's up," Christopher said.

"Looks like somebody's giving away free money," Decker suggested.

When they rounded the corner, it became clear that the excitement was centered around a room at the end of the hall. Outside the door stood about forty people, most in hospital clothes and slippers, but some in the garb of orderlies or nurses, each trying to get closer to the door.

"That's Secretary Milner's room," Christopher said. They immediately picked up their pace, intending to press headlong through the crowd, but were quickly engulfed in the melee.

Just as they arrived, a very stoutly built nurse led four orderlies toward the crowd. Soon Decker and Christopher were pushed away along with the rest of the throng. They made for an empty alcove as the mass moved by them, driven on like cattle.

"What is going on?" asked Decker in disbelief. But the only one who heard him was Christopher, who seemed as bewildered as Decker.

"Do you think something has happened to Secretary Milner?" Christopher asked.

"Nah," responded Decker reassuringly, though still puzzled. "Didn't you see those people? They weren't acting like they were headed for a funeral. In fact, from the looks on some of their faces, I'd think it was more likely that Milner had a baby."

Christopher smiled. Soon the final stragglers passed, followed closely by the stout nurse and her armor-bearers. From there it was only a matter of getting past the guard at the door, an easy task for someone of Decker's experience and credentials. As the door to Milner's room swung open they saw two doctors huddled around the bed, leaning over as if working on their patient. On closer examination it became clear that the bed was unoccupied except for some medical charts the doctors were examining.

"Where is Secretary Milner?" Christopher asked anxiously.

For a moment the doctors ignored them, and then one turned and called for the guard to escort the intruders out of the room.

"It's okay," the second doctor said as he recognized Christopher from his visit earlier in the day.

"Where is Secretary Milner?" Christopher repeated insistently.

"He's in the lavatory," the second doctor answered.

"What was all the commotion about? Is he all right?" Christopher asked, a little less urgently.

"See for yourself," said a voice from their left. There, standing in the open bathroom door in his hospital gown was a very healthy-looking former Assistant Secretary-General Milner. His eyes were clear and bright, his complexion restored to its ruddy glow, his stance tall and erect, with shoulders and chest broad and firm.

Decker shook his head, bewildered. Christopher simply stared.

"How do I look?" Milner asked proudly.

"You, uh . . . look great," Christopher answered. "What happened?"

Milner cast his eyes toward the doctors, though it seemed he did so less for an answer and more to gloat over their lack of an explanation.

"We're not sure," one of the doctors admitted. "He seems to be in perfect health. He's no spring chicken, but if I didn't know better I'd swear he was twenty years younger than when he checked in."

"They're not sure," Milner said, gleefully repeating the doctor's first remark. "Actually, they haven't the foggiest idea."

"He's right," one of them confessed.

"Why don't you fellas just go on back to your offices and study those charts while I talk to my visitors," Milner urged as he motioned his physicians toward the door.

The doctors didn't resist, but warned Milner not to overexert himself.

"Of course not," Milner responded, unconvincingly.

When they were gone, Milner checked the ties on his hospital gown, dropped to the floor and began doing pushups. "Count 'em for me, Christopher," he said as he began. Christopher objected but then counted anyway as Milner, refusing to let the feat go unmeasured, started to count for himself. As he reached twenty-three Christopher insisted he cease, which he promptly did after completing two more.

Decker was too amazed and too busy laughing at this strange scene to speak, but Christopher asked again, "What's going on? What happened?"

"What do you mean, 'What happened?'" Milner responded, as he adjusted his gown. "It's obvious: I'm well and I feel ready to take on the world!"

"But how?" Christopher pressed.

"It's obvious," Milner repeated, unharried by Christopher's insistence. "It all started after I got the transfusion of the blood you donated."

Decker abruptly stopped laughing, momentarily stunned, not only by the fact that Christopher's blood had this effect, but by Milner's matter-of-fact response. Did Milner know about Christopher? How could he? He wondered whether he should pursue this and risk giving away Christopher's secret. "What are you saying?" he asked, unable to control his own curiosity.

"Mr. Hawthorne," Milner said, formally, "I have known of Christopher since the first moment I saw him. And to some small extent I also know his destiny — though I am forbidden to reveal it, even to him. I cannot claim I knew *this* would happen," he said, referring to his improved condition, "but neither does it surprise me in the least!"

Chapter 19

The Prince of Rome

Eight years later

South of Frankfurt, Germany

The train from Heidelberg to Frankfurt sped quietly along the track through the German summer evening. A few hundred meters to the left, the foothills of the Odenwald Mountains burst forth from the flat plains of the Rhine Valley to form the western wall of what in millennia past had been a massive sea. Every eight or ten kilometers along the crest of the mountains, castles stood in various states of repair, some in ruins, others still inhabited. Along the mountain's base, the picturesque towns and villages of the Bergstrasse were punctuated by the seemingly requisite steeples and onion domes of the state-supported Catholic and Lutheran churches. Farther away in the west, but within clear sight of the train, the steeples of the small village of Biblis Lorsch were overshadowed by the massive cooling towers of Germany's largest nuclear power plant.

Behind the powerful electric engine that pulled the dingy yellow and blue train were three private cars that had been commissioned for the secretary-general of the United Nations, his party, and the ever-present members of the press. Two hours earlier, at the castle of Heidelberg, Secretary-General Jon Hansen had given a speech to a group of international business leaders on the benefits of the recent United Nations decision to remove the remaining barriers to trade among nations. To the casual listener the speech would not have been particularly stirring, but Hansen was preaching to the choir — an audience of men and women from all over the world who had been at the forefront of the effort to eliminate international trade barriers.

Most notable among the rich and powerful in attendance was billionaire David Bragford, who had introduced the secretary-general to the assembly. It was commonly believed that five years earlier Bragford had been the driving force behind the elimination of most of the European trade barriers. It was only a matter of time before he sought their total elimination worldwide.

Jon Hansen was now in the fourth year of his third term as secretary-general, a position that had continually grown in importance since his first oath of office. Now, as more and more power was consolidated both under Hansen and the restructured Security Council, the pace of that consolidation was increasing. The time had passed some years earlier when politicians and news commentators addressed themselves to the subject of *whether* there would be a unified world government. Now they pondered such topics as how that government might best be administered. There were still significant hurdles to be cleared before its final realization. No one of major consequence was calling for the complete dissolution of independent nations — not publicly, anyway — yet the direction was undeniable.

It was not as though one day mankind awoke to find a world where national interests were of no importance and all power resided in a global dictatorship headquartered in New York. Rather, the centralized management of international matters by the UN — under the guidance of Hansen and the Security Council — had facilitated remarkable advances by allowing compromise and cooperation among nations that would have been unimaginable a few decades earlier. The regionalized structure of the Security Council and the even-handed leadership of Jon Hansen had brought balance to the treatment of all nations and had succeeded in bringing about a general peace that was accompanied by soaring prosperity throughout most of the world. As Hansen pointed out quite regularly, now that international matters were handled internationally, the governments of the individual countries were free to focus on their provincial interests.

There were, of course, exceptions to the general prosperity, for no amount of good government could alleviate natural disasters. One such exception was the Indian subcontinent and especially northern India and Pakistan, which were in a rapidly worsening state of famine due to a combination of drought and wheat rust.

In the secretary-general's private compartment, Jon Hansen and Decker Hawthorne were conferring on the upcoming annual State of the World Address.

"I've received drafts of the annual reports from all of the members of the Security Council and from each of the agencies of the Secretariat with the exception of the Food and Agriculture Organization," Decker told Hansen. "This is the latest draft of your address, containing everything except for the information from FAO." Decker handed Hansen an eighty-four page document, which Hansen proceeded to flip through, scanning the contents.

"As you can see," Decker continued, "we've already prepared most of the text dealing with world hunger and agricultural production and we just need to fill in the figures once we have the FAO report. Then we'll liven it up a bit with some personal insights from your upcoming trip to Pakistan."

"Have you addressed each of my eight points on distribution of agricultural resources?" Hansen asked.

"Yes, sir. That begins on page sixteen."

Hansen flipped to the page and began reading. While it wasn't possible to legislate away things such as famine, Hansen felt it was imperative that the United Nations do everything in its power to reduce the suffering by providing massive food shipments to the affected countries. The problem with this was that someone had to pay for the food and it was *this* problem that Hansen's eight points on the distribution of agricultural resources was intended to address.

"Yes, this looks good," Hansen said after a brief review. "You're flying to Rome from Frankfurt?" he asked Decker.

Decker nodded. "Jack Redmond and I are meeting with Christopher at FAO headquarters in Rome to iron out the final projections and recommendations for the agricultural quotas from each region for distribution to the poorer nations. We'll meet you on Wednesday in Pakistan."

"Good. I think it's important we get Jack's input," Hansen agreed, referring to his long-time chief political adviser. "We need to have a solidly defensible position for the distribution quotas when I introduce the measure to the General Assembly next month." Decker nodded. "This program won't be easy to implement," Hansen said. "Those who have an abundance are not exactly standing in line to give it away. The problem with the New World Order is that it's still populated by the same 'old' people," he said, repeating one of his favorite phrases. "Anything you, Jack, and

Christopher can come up with to make it more politically palatable will be helpful."

"I think Jack and Christopher have a few ideas that might help," Decker said. Decker was careful to make any comment about Christopher an understatement. His pride was obvious even to a casual observer, but no one doubted that Christopher's rapid rise as a member of the UN Secretariat was entirely deserved. His success over the past three years as director-general of the UN's Food and Agriculture Organization (FAO), headquartered in Rome, made him the heir apparent to Louis Colleta, the executive director of the Economic and Social Council (ECOSOC) in New York, who had announced he would retire the following spring. Indeed, most of Hansen's eight-point plan had been developed by Christopher in his role as director-general of FAO.

Until the reorganization of the Security Council, ECOSOC had been the umbrella agency for more than half of the UN's dozens of organizations, including FAO. After the reorganization, all the UN organizations were divided into more or less logical groupings and placed under ten agencies, each chaired by one of the Security Council alternates. What remained under the name ECOSOC was far less than it had been when it was one of the five principal organs of the United Nations, but it was still a major agency. And although each alternate member of the Security Council served as the chairman and titular head of one of the ten agencies, actual operations were the responsibility of the agency's executive director, who was usually a career professional, like Christopher, trained in the respective field.

"We should be ready to brief you on our recommendations on the flight back," Decker said.

"I need you to stay in Pakistan with Christopher when I return to New York," Hansen said. "Jack will have to brief me on the plane."

This was not what Decker had in mind; Jack Redmond was a good man, but Decker had planned to direct the briefing himself. "Yes, sir," he answered without argument.

"Good, good," Hansen responded, as he went back to his review of the draft document. "What are your readings from Ambassador Faure?" he asked without looking up.

"I don't think we can count on his support for the plan, if that's what you mean."

"That man is going to drive me to drink," Hansen commented dryly as he took a swallow from a glass of German beer. "It seems no matter what I try to do, he's always there to oppose me."

Decker was well aware of Hansen's feelings about the French ambassador. Albert Faure had always been a thorn in the flesh for Hansen, and it was getting worse. About a year earlier, Faure had managed to get himself elected as the alternate member of the Security Council from Europe. The position carried little actual power. Under the new structure, Security Council alternates couldn't introduce, second, or even vote on Security Council motions. Those privileges were limited to the ten primary members. Perhaps the single greatest power held by the alternates, though it was seldom used, was the right to address the Security Council at any time on behalf of the agency they chaired, if they felt the circumstances warranted — even if it meant interrupting other proceedings. Faure's agency was the World Peace Organization, composed of the various UN peacekeeping forces stationed around the world. In the past, the position had been one of considerable prestige and power, but since there had been no major wars for nearly fifteen years, it proved to be of little consequence to a man as ambitious as Faure. Unfortunately for Hansen, this left Faure with plenty of time to pursue other goals, including lobbying members against Hansen's policies. If Faure succeeded in putting together a coalition of farming nations to oppose the agricultural distribution measures, he could make real trouble. Faure's goal, as Jack Redmond surmised, was to irritate Jon Hansen, to make his job less enjoyable, and thereby to give the Secretary-General more reason to retire.

"There should be some way to handle this fellow other than just ignoring him while he goes on sniping at me," Hansen said.

"Perhaps you could convince the French president to replace him with someone more agreeable. That worked a few years back with the ambassador from Mexico," Decker offered.

"And with the ambassador from Mali," Hansen added.

"Oh? I didn't know that we were involved in that."

"Jack handled it."

Decker made a mental note for what it might be worth in the future.

"The problem," Hansen continued, "is that Faure is far too popular among the French people to be so easily deposed." Then shaking his head, he added, "I will never understand the French."

"What about Ambassador Heinemann?" Decker asked, referring to the German ambassador who represented Europe as primary on the Security Council and who was loyal to Hansen. As Europe's primary, Heinemann carried considerable clout with the nations in his region, including France.

"I'm sure Ambassador Heinemann is well aware of my feelings about Faure," Hansen said. "But I suppose I could take advantage of our trip to Pakistan this weekend to approach him directly on the matter." As the representative from one of the major food-producing regions, Heinemann was one of the three Security Council members accompanying Hansen on his visit to Pakistan.

"Maybe Jack can suggest something Ambassador Heinemann could use to convince Faure to see things your way," Decker suggested.

"Find a weak spot and then apply a little pressure."

"Yes, sir. And Jack is the best person I know to find out what and where those weak spots are."

Secretary-General Hansen liked the idea. "Take that up with Jack when you see him in Rome."

Rome

Decker's plane from Frankfurt arrived the next morning at the Leonardo da Vinci Airport in Fiumicino, just southwest of Rome. Having been warned about pickpockets and luggage thieves in and around Rome, Decker held tightly to his briefcase and carry-on luggage as he scanned the crowd for any sign of Christopher, who was to meet him there.

From behind a group of businessmen Decker saw a hand waving, and then Christopher emerged and hurried toward him. "Welcome to Rome," Christopher said as he gave Decker a hug. "How was your trip?"

"Fine. Fine."

"Do you have luggage?"

"Just this," Decker answered, lifting his briefcase and carry-on.

"Great. Then we can get started on your tour of Rome right away. You've never been to Rome, have you?"

"No. The closest I came was when I was in Turin and Milan on the Shroud research team."

"You're really going to like it."

"I have no doubt."

As they moved through the crowds to the exit, Decker noticed that several people seemed to be pointing at them, and as they waited on the curb for the limo, several cars nearly collided when a very attractive young woman suddenly stopped her car to stare. Christopher ignored the woman's curious gape, but Decker couldn't help but remark. "I think she thought she knew you," he told Christopher as they got in the limo.

"Shall we start with the Colosseum?" Christopher asked, taking no notice of Decker's comment. "I'm afraid all the museums are closed on Monday except the Vatican, but there's still more than enough to see to fill the rest of the day."

"Roma, non basta una vita!" Decker answered in Italian, meaning "For Rome, one life is not enough."

"I didn't know you knew Italian," Christopher remarked.

"You just heard every word I know," Decker confessed. Then, answering his earlier question, Decker added, "There is something I'd like to see that may not be on the usual list of must-see places."

"What's that?" asked Christopher.

"The Arch of Titus."

"Oh, sure. It's at the Forum, near the Colosseum. We can start there if you like."

"Great," Decker said. "Actually, I think you'll find it quite interesting."

The Triumphal Arch of Titus rose imposingly against the backdrop of the Colosseum, barely scarred by the twenty centuries that had passed since it was constructed to commemorate the successful campaign against Jerusalem by Titus. Decker scanned the carved images in the arch and quickly found what he was looking for. "Here it is," he said. Christopher looked at the carving over Decker's shoulder. The scene depicted the spoils of war being taken from the conquered city of Jerusalem.

Arch of Titus and Coliseum in Rome

"I don't know if I ever mentioned Joshua Rosen to you," Decker began. Christopher gave no indication that he recognized the name. "He was a scientist I knew years ago. We met on the Turin expedition." Christopher's ears perked up. "Later he moved to Israel. Anyway, when Tom Donafin and I were there, just before we were taken hostage, Joshua gave us a tour of some of the sites in Jerusalem, one of which was the Wailing Wall. That's what they used to call the western wall of the old Jewish temple before the Palestinians blew it up." Christopher nodded. "While we were there, Joshua told us about the Ark of the Covenant and gave his theory on what had happened to it. I'll have to tell you about it sometime. But the point of the story is that he told us about the Arch of Titus and this carving. Titus was the commander of the Roman forces that pillaged and destroyed Jerusalem in A.D. 70."

"Yes, I know. I prophesied that before the crucifixion," interjected Christopher.

"You never told me you remembered that!"

"No. Sorry," he explained. "I don't. I read about it in the Bible."

"Oh," said Decker a little disappointed. "Anyway, as you can see, the carving is intricately detailed. Despite its age, you can clearly make out the items being taken from Jerusalem."

Christopher looked more closely. "It's amazingly well preserved."

"But don't you see?" Decker asked. "The Ark of the Covenant is not among the treasures."

"I'm sorry, Decker. I don't get your point."

Decker suddenly realized there was a lot he hadn't explained. "I'm sorry. I guess I need to give you some more details, but the reason for my interest has to do with the Shroud of Turin. Joshua Rosen had a fascinating theory involving the Ark that would explain why the original Carbon 14 dating of the Shroud showed it to be only about a thousand years old." Decker proceeded to tell Christopher the whole story as it had been told to him and Tom Donafin by Joshua Rosen.

Detail of Arch of Titus

"So you think the Shroud was in the Ark all those years?" Christopher asked.

"It would certainly answer some questions," Decker replied.

As they talked and looked at the carvings on the Arch, they were unaware that two young boys had approached them from behind. *"Mi scusi, signor Goodman, possiamo avere il tuo autografo?"* the older of the two boys asked.

Decker had no idea what they wanted and was surprised when Christopher took a pen out of his jacket pocket and began to sign his name on some scraps of paper the boys handed him.

"Autographs?" he asked, making no attempt to hide his amusement.

Christopher shrugged and nodded in answer to Decker's question. He spoke for a moment with the boys in perfect Italian, smiling broadly and shaking their hands as if they were important dignitaries, before dismissing them. The boys walked a few steps, each showing the other the autograph he had received. Then, waving their scraps of paper in the air like trophies, they broke into a run toward a lady whom Decker took to be their mother, shouting, "*Il Principe di Roma!*"

For a moment Decker just looked at Christopher, who seemed a little embarrassed by the whole thing. "So that's what all the attention was about at the airport. You're a local celebrity."

Christopher shrugged.

"Don't be embarrassed. I think it's great. You must be doing quite a job here."

"It's not really anything I've done. I've just gotten a lot of credit for some of the UN programs we've implemented. Popular programs make for a popular administration."

The next morning Decker and Christopher arrived early at the headquarters of the UN Food and Agriculture Organization. Jack Redmond's arrival time would be dependent on Rome's morning traffic. FAO headquarters occupied an immense building complex covering more than four square blocks and towering well above the surrounding architecture. Located on Viale delle Terme di Caracalla, the FAO employed more than thirty-five hundred professional and administrative personnel with a biannual budget of $57 billion.

At Christopher's office they were greeted by an attractive young woman. "*Buongiorno, Signor Direttore,*" she said.

"Good morning, Maria," Christopher answered in English. "This is my very good friend Mr. Decker Hawthorne, Director of UN Public Affairs. Decker, this is Maria Sabetini."

"Mr. Hawthorne, it is a pleasure to meet you. Director Goodman speaks of you frequently."

"The pleasure is all mine," Decker replied. "Are you any relation to President Sabetini?" he asked, recognizing that she bore the same last name as Italy's president.

"He is my father," she answered.

"Then it's even more of a pleasure." Decker tried not to seem too surprised, but the question about her name had just been small talk; he never expected the answer he got.

(FAO) Headquarters. Rome, Italy

"Mr. Redmond will be arriving a little later," Christopher told Maria. "When he gets here, please show him in."

After Christopher closed the door behind them Decker blurted out, "Your secretary is the Italian president's daughter?"

Christopher shook his head, trying not to make too much of it. "She's not a secretary. She's an administrative assistant," he said. "She wanted a job, and I needed an assistant."

"Yeah, but the president's daughter?"

"It was Secretary Milner's idea." Decker's expression requested an explanation. "He was here on some business shortly after I became director-general of FAO. He and the president are old friends. I just happened to mention to him in passing that I needed to find a good administrative assistant."

"I don't suppose it's hurt your relationship with the Italian government any," Decker said.

"No," Christopher admitted. "Things have been very cordial."

Christopher's office was spacious and luxuriously decorated and furnished. On the walls were pictures of Christopher with several members of the United Nations Security Council; numerous Italian government officials including the Italian prime minister, the Italian ambassador to the UN, and the Italian president; and with leaders of the Roman Catholic Church, including three cardinals. Most prominent in the room were two pictures displayed side by side, one of Christopher with Secretary-General Jon Hansen, and the other of Christopher with Robert Milner and the Pope. "You haven't said anything about this in your emails," Decker commented shaking his head as he scanned the photos. "You've been busy."

"A lot of it has been Secretary Milner's doing," Christopher said. "He's been here three or four times a year since I became director-general." Milner, now ninety, seemingly hadn't aged a day since the transfusion of Christopher's blood eight years before. If anything, he seemed younger. "I had no idea he had so much business in Italy."

"Neither did I," Decker feigned. Decker was certain that Milner's frequent trips were not a coincidence. He was obviously doing everything he could to advance Christopher's position with those in power in Italy. It was not that Decker objected. Still, there was a mystery here. He didn't have long to think about it, though. His eye was drawn to another picture of Christopher with a very distinguished man in front of the Coliseum. "When was David Bragford here?" Decker asked.

"Last summer. He was here with Secretary Milner for a meeting of world bankers." At that moment Maria announced Jack Redmond's arrival.

"All hail the Prince of Rome," Redmond said, addressing Christopher and bowing in mock obeisance as he came in.

Decker had no idea what had prompted Jack's greeting but assumed it to be a joke; the look of mild annoyance on Christopher's face indicated there was more to it than that. "Okay, I'll bite," Decker said. "What's this 'Prince of Rome' stuff?"

"Haven't you seen last week's issue of *Panorama?*" Jack asked, referring to a major Italian news magazine.

"No," Decker answered, looking back and forth from Jack to Christopher and hoping for an explanation.

"Here," Jack said, as he opened his briefcase and handed the magazine to Decker. On the cover was a very complimentary picture of Christopher with the words *"Christopher Goodman, Il Trentenne Principe di Roma"* boldly displayed underneath.

Decker examined the photo for a moment and then asked for a translation of the caption. Christopher just sat silently, looking a little embarrassed, as Jack answered. "It says, 'Christopher Goodman, the Thirty-Year-Old Prince of Rome.'" [39]

Decker was proud enough to burst. He couldn't read a word, but he quickly flipped through the magazine to find the accompanying article. "Will somebody please tell me what this is all about?" he asked impatiently.

"It seems our boy Christopher has made quite a name for himself around these parts." Jack's voice was laden with an exaggerated Cajun accent — something he did whenever it served his humor.

"It's nothing," Christopher protested. "The editor of the magazine came up with that to insult the *priministro della repubblica*, the prime minister," he added in translation. "They've had a running battle for months. Apparently the people at *Panorama* thought it would serve their purposes to build me up while tearing down the priministro. The article right after the one about me calls the priministro a useless, ineffective bore."

Decker flipped to the article about the prime minister and found a most unflattering picture of the man. He wondered if the photo had been altered to make him look so bad.

"Methinks the prince doth protest too much," Jack said with a grin, intentionally misquoting Hamlet.[40]

"I just think the whole thing is a little silly," Christopher said. "I called the prime minister as soon as I saw the article and let him know I had no idea they were going to use the story as they did. Fortunately, we've had the opportunity to establish a very affable relationship over the past several years. He took the whole thing very well. Now, can we please get some work done?"

"Okay, okay," Jack said. "I'll behave."

"Wait a second," interrupted Decker. "I want a copy of this *and* an English translation."

"You guys make it awfully hard to be modest," Christopher protested, then sighing added, "There's an English translation online."

"Listen," said Jack Redmond, donning his political advisor's hat, "you can be very proud of that article. It's not often a UN official other than Hansen gets that type of recognition in the press. I mean, after all — and not to belittle your job — but you *are* just a bureaucrat. Normally that means you do your job behind the scenes and no one ever notices, except possibly other bureaucrats. From what I saw in that magazine you've done an outstanding job, not only as a bureaucrat, but as a representative of the United Nations to the people of Italy. You keep playing your cards right and there'll be no stopping you."

Christopher accepted the compliment graciously. Decker was too busy smiling to add anything.

"Oh, and speaking of the people of Italy," Jack continued, "the article says you're an Italian citizen. Whose idea was that?"

Decker was sure he knew the answer. "Secretary Milner's," Christopher answered. "He recommended it when I first took over FAO. He thought it would be popular with the Italian people. With the liberalization of citizenship requirements over the past ten years, it only required a ninety-day residency before I could apply. I've been an Italian citizen for nearly five years now. It's really just a symbolic thing."

Jack Redmond nodded approvingly. "Like I said, there'll be no stopping you."

"Can we please get started on this?" Christopher pleaded.

"Not quite so fast. There's one other thing in the article Decker might find interesting." Christopher sat down, folded his hands, exhaled deeply, and looked at the ceiling. He knew where this was going and it was useless to try to stop Jack when he was on a roll. "According to the article, you and the Italian President's daughter are quite an item. Rumors are that marriage may be in your future."

"What?" Decker said, his breath escaping in a huge smile. "You and Maria?"

"No!" Christopher answered quickly. "They're talking about his oldest daughter, Tina."

"Wait a second," Jack blurted, "who's Maria?"

"Nobody!" Christopher shouted before Decker could answer and thereby give Jack even more to speculate about. "Look, there's nothing to that business. Tina and I are just friends. I needed a date for a few political functions, and so we went together. That's all there is to it."

It took a while longer, but the subject finally got around to agricultural quotas. The meeting went on well into the evening and had to be continued on the flight to Pakistan, where they were to meet with Secretary-General Hansen and his party.

Chapter 20

Through a Glass Darkly

Sahiwai, Pakistan

A dark figure moved quietly along the dry river bed, checking each low-lying area for any sign of water. Without it, death would soon overtake him as it had the others. Ahead at a distance, a tree, still green despite the brown that surrounded it, gave shade to the end of his search: a small puddle, inches deep. It was there; he knew it. He could smell it. Gathering strength he didn't know he had, he ran to the small pool and drank until his stomach ached and his legs collapsed beneath him. He would stay here until the water was gone or hunger drove him on. It was possible that the pool might draw some small animal, but he couldn't wait for food to come to him. After a short rest, he would have to scout out the area and hope for the best.

It was shortly after dawn, but the sun already beat down on the dry plain as he emerged from the river bed and peered cautiously through the dead, dry thicket. A motionless form lay about thirty yards away. The week without food and the days without water had dulled his senses or he surely would have noticed it earlier, so close to him. He paused only a moment to examine the area for danger; he was too hungry to expend much care. As he approached the figure, the absence of life became apparent. Two smaller ones lay nearby.

Suddenly, in the distance, he heard a rumbling that sounded like thunder or a stampede of large animals. It was a long way off, but it was coming toward him with remarkable speed. Fear grew as the sound drew down upon him far more swiftly than he could imagine possible. Taking hold of a leg of his dead prey, he tried to drag the carcass to the river bed, but his strength was not up to the task. With insane determination born of unbearable hunger he decided to make his stand despite the stampede. Soon the sound was almost on him and it became clear that it was coming, not from a herd of any sort he knew, but from a single huge bird like none he had ever seen.

Overhead, the secretary-general's helicopter slowly approached the famine relief camp, as those on board got a close look at the surrounding conditions. The drought had been devastating. For twenty miles the helicopter had followed a dry river bed. Just below, about two miles from the relief camp near a small pool, a lone emaciated wild dog looked up at them as it stood over the body of a young woman who had died of starvation or thirst before reaching the camp. Nearby lay the bodies of two small children.

The stark evidence of famine and drought that the secretary-general's party now saw firsthand in Pakistan was mirrored by similar devastation in northern India, where wheat rust had severely reduced the annual harvest. In southern India, tropical storms during the monsoon season had driven seawater into many of the already flooded areas to form brackish water, making the land salty and unarable. The latter was a not-uncommon occurrence in India, and all that could be done was to grow what little they could and wait for subsequent monsoons to leach the salt from the land over the next few years.

The helicopter landed in an open area outside the camp, creating a huge dust cloud that blew into the faces of those waiting. Along with the twenty or so cameramen and reporters, the relief camp's director, Dr. Fred Bloomer, waited for the blades to slow before approaching to welcome the secretary-general and his party.

"I'm anxious to get started," Hansen said as he shook Bloomer's hand.

"I fear you'll find conditions worse than you imagined, Mr. Secretary-General," Dr. Bloomer said. "We've had nearly a thousand new arrivals in the last four days. We're just not set up to handle this many people. We've had to severely reduce rations."

The official purpose of this visit was fact finding, but what Hansen really hoped to accomplish was to build support for the distribution of agricultural resources. He had specific reasons for inviting each of those who accompanied him on this trip. Ambassador Khalid Haider from Pakistan was there because it was his country. The Indian ambassador had been invited because of similar problems in his country and because of the concern that the refugees from Pakistan might begin to spill over into India.

The members from North America and Europe had been asked to come because it was their regions that Hansen's plan would ask to give the most for the food distribution effort. Ambassador Howell of Canada, who represented North America on the Security Council, had been ill for several months and was expected to resign soon. In his place was Ambassador Walter Bishop from the United States, the alternate from North America, who hoped to replace the Canadian ambassador as primary. Aware of this likelihood, Hansen wanted to take the opportunity to get to know the American better and win his support for the plan. Ambassador Heinemann from Germany, who represented Europe on the Security Council, really didn't need to be convinced about the need for food redistribution, but the people of his region did. At Decker's recommendation, Hansen had invited Heinemann to ensure coverage of the trip by the European press. It was an effective way of making sure the people of Europe learned of the urgency and magnitude of the need.

The team started with a tour of the camp and what was left of the surrounding villages. In the afternoon Christopher briefed the ambassadors on the findings from an FAO study of projections for future years. Later, in what was mainly a photo opportunity, the team members worked in the serving line for the evening meal. They spent the night at the camp under nearly the same conditions as the camp's inhabitants.

The next morning the secretary-general and the ambassadors planned to return to Lahore, Pakistan, near the Indian border, while Decker and Christopher remained at the camp to represent Hansen to a second team from the UN who would be arriving in the late afternoon.

Tel Aviv

Rabbi Saul Cohen finished his morning prayers and rose to his feet to answer the knock at the door of his study. Benjamin Cohen — the rabbi's seventeen-year-old son and only living relative since the Disaster took his wife and four older children — stood outside, nervously shifting from side to side. He knew not to disturb his father's prayer time without good cause, and he did not relish comparing his own evaluation of what constituted a 'good cause' with that of his father. Nevertheless, he relished even less the possibility of angering the man who waited in the sitting room.

The man — *guest* hardly seemed like the right word — had arrived without appointment. Benjamin had opened the front door to let him in but then backed away, sensing instinctively that there was something very unusual about this man, and perhaps about the visit as well. As the man closed the door behind him, it seemed to Benjamin that the sitting room grew strangely crowded, and he was only too glad to leave to retrieve his father. He was halfway down the hall before he realized he hadn't asked the man his name. Like it or not, he would have to go back.

Peering around the corner of the doorway, Benjamin's eyes met those of the visitor. He wanted to look away, but he saw something there that held him. He could see clearly now what so unsettled him about this man. Benjamin had been trained to discern wisdom in a man's face. He had been taught that wisdom came with age, but the wisdom in this man's eyes was unnatural for a man no older than this. It was unnatural for a man of any age.

He asked the man his name.

The answer only added to Benjamin's disquiet, but he felt it inadvisable to probe further.

Ordinarily Saul Cohen's morning prayers lasted at least an hour, but for some reason this morning he stopped after only thirty minutes. When he heard the knock on his study door at that very moment, it seemed to him a confirmation. He didn't know what news Benjamin brought, but he was sure it was important or the boy wouldn't have interrupted him. Cohen opened the door.

"What is it?" he asked, with no sign of the consternation Benjamin had expected.

"There's a man here to see you, Father."

Cohen waited for more information, but Benjamin was not forthcoming. "So what is this man's name?" Cohen asked finally.

"He didn't say," Benjamin responded in a muffled voice.

"Well, did you ask him?"

"Yes, Father."

"And, what did he say?"

Benjamin wasn't sure how this was going to sound. It seemed very authoritative when the man in the sitting room said it, but coming from his own lips, Benjamin thought it might sound a little dumb. Still, he had to say something: his father was waiting. "He said to tell you that he is 'he who has heard the voices of the seven thunders.'"[41]

Cohen didn't respond but his face registered recognition. Finally he managed a nod and Benjamin went back to the sitting room to retrieve the man.

Saul Cohen closed the door. The idea was preposterous and yet . . . Mechanically, he began to straighten his desk. A few seconds later, footsteps approached and he watched as the doorknob began to rotate. Suddenly it seemed as though he had forgotten how to breathe. Benjamin pushed the door open, and Cohen, remembering his manners, managed to move around from behind his desk to meet the man. If this man was, indeed, who he claimed to be, then Cohen had no desire to insult him with bad etiquette. For a moment, the man stood in the doorway just looking at Cohen as if savoring the moment, and then finally he entered.

Cohen didn't know how it could be possible for this man to be who he said, but in his vocation he had learned that nothing was impossible. He had known since the Disaster that someday a prophet would come. But could this man really be who he claimed? It was almost more than Cohen could accept.

"Hello, Rabbi," the man said cordially, extending his hand. He was not at all what Cohen expected. He didn't appear to be a day over sixty. Most disconcerting of all was the way he was dressed — in a modern, dark-gray business suit with a red tie. Somehow, as silly as it seemed, Cohen had expected the man to be wearing sandals and a long robe, tied at the waist with a rope. Yet, despite his appearance and the impossibility of his claim, there was something about the man that made Cohen believe he was exactly who he said.

"I'm the one you've been waiting for," the man said, still extending his hand. "But believe me, I've been waiting for you for a lot longer." Cohen was silent, still unsure of what to say. "And you are Saul Cohen," the man continued, "of the lineage of Jonadab, son of Recab, about whom Jeremiah prophesied."[42]

Cohen's mouth dropped open. "That secret has not passed outside of my family for twelve hundred years," he said.

"It's the only explanation for why you weren't taken in the . . . um, *Disaster*," the man explained. "And when you have completed your work, your son, Benjamin, will take your place in the Lord's service, as was promised through Jeremiah."

Cohen deeply pondered his words. How else could the man know this unless. . .

"Why don't we sit down," the man suggested. "We have a lot to talk about." Cohen complied silently. "As our meeting indicates, the time is at hand for the end of this age." Without pausing to allow Cohen to consider the full impact of this statement, the man continued. "I've observed you for a number of years and I am now certain that you are the other witness. The fact that you recognize me confirms that belief."

"You were not sure before?" Cohen asked, surprised that anything could be hidden to such a man.

"I wasn't told who the other would be. I now see that I was led to you, but confirmation was left to the discernment and wisdom God has granted me. I had no special revelation on the matter."

This discovery caught Cohen off guard. "But . . . I don't understand. How could you not know?"

"As the Apostle Paul wrote, 'For now we see through a glass, darkly; but then face to face: now I know in part; but then shall I know even as also I am known.'[43] I can assure you that as long as you and I remain on this side of life, that will never change — not even," the man concluded with a twinkle of humor in his eyes, "if you were to live to be two thousand years old."

"Rabbi," Cohen said, not knowing how else to address this man whom he considered to be hundreds of times his spiritual senior.

"Please," the man interrupted, "call me John."

This had gone on long enough. Cohen had to be sure he understood what was happening. "You are John?"

The man nodded.

"Yochanan bar Zebadee?" Cohen said, using the Hebrew form of the man's full name.

"I am," he answered.

"The apostle of the Lord? You were there, at the foot of the cross?"[44]

"I was there," John answered with a sigh and an expression that showed he still felt the pain of that event two thousand years earlier.

"But how? Have you returned from the dead?"

The man smiled and heaved a sigh. "In many ways I would have preferred that," he said. "But, no, I've been here, alive on this decaying world, waiting for this moment, for two thousand years."

Cohen didn't repeat his question, but his eyes still asked "How?"

"Do you recall what our Lord told Peter about me on the shore of the Sea of Tiberias?"

Cohen knew the words but he had never thought their meaning to be literal. After his resurrection, Jesus told the Apostle Peter how he, Peter, would die. Peter then asked what would happen to John. "If I want him to remain alive until I return, what is that to you?" Jesus replied.[45]

"But you also wrote that what Jesus said didn't mean you'd *never* die, just that you might not die until after his return."[46] As soon as the words left his mouth, Cohen understood. He didn't need an answer; like John, he was fully aware of the fate that soon awaited them both — and *that* fate matched Jesus' words perfectly.

"The Lord told my brother James and me that, like him, we would both die a martyr's death.[47] James was the first of the Lord's apostles to die[48] . . . and I shall be the last. I suppose that in *this* way at least, my mother's request to Jesus will be granted: James and I *will* sit at the Lord's right and left hands in his kingdom. He, the first, and I, the last of Christ's apostles to die."

Cohen still struggled.

"In the Book of Revelation," the man continued, "I said that an angel gave me a scroll and I was told to eat it. I wrote:

> *I took the little scroll from the angel's hand and ate it. It tasted sweet as honey in my mouth, but when I had eaten it, my stomach turned sour. Then I was told, "You must prophesy again about many peoples, nations, languages, and kings."*[49]

Cohen nodded recognition.

"The words of the scroll were sweet," John explained, "because in that moment I came to know I would live longer even than Methuselah.[50] But the scroll became sour in my stomach as I understood I would have to wait longer than any other man to see the Lord's return. Then I was told the reason my life must continue: I have remained on this Earth to prophesy *again*, this time with you, about many peoples, nations, languages, and kings."

Cohen did his best to understand. In this man's presence, he couldn't help but believe. And yet, it was almost too much to accept. Yielding slightly to the thought, he pondered aloud, "I suppose it should have been expected after you survived being immersed in boiling oil.[51] And it does explain the prophesies of Yeshua concerning the end of the age, when he told the disciples, 'Some who are standing here will not taste death before they see the kingdom of God come with power.'[52] If you are John, then indeed that generation has not passed away. Still, what of Polycarp?" Cohen asked, referring to the late first- and early second-century bishop of Smyrna who, according to his student Irenaeus, had said John died during the reign of the Roman emperor Trajan.[53]

"Have you not read Harnack?" the man responded, referring to the German theologian who had propounded that Polycarp was referring not to John the apostle but to another man, a church elder, also named John.[54]

It occurred to Cohen that this might also explain one of the mysteries of the Bible that had always puzzled him. "And is this the reason for the apparent later additions to the original text of your gospel?"[55] he asked.

The man nodded. "I regret the confusion that has caused. From time to time I'd tell someone about something Jesus did or said that I had left out of my Gospel and they'd urge me to include it. It never even occurred to me that, by adding a few things I had left out of the earlier versions, I would cause so much confusion later on. It's no sin for a man to edit his own book.

"Saul, I understand your reason for questioning, and yet I know that at the same time, the Spirit gives witness to you that I am who I claim to be."

"But where have you been?" Cohen asked. "How could you have kept your identity concealed?"

"It's easier than you might imagine," John answered. "For centuries it was possible to travel only a few days' journey and take on a new identity. I must admit, however, I've not always been as successful as I would like. There was a period of a few hundred years that no matter where I went — from China, to India, to Ethiopia — the stories would follow me."

A thought occurred to Cohen. "Prester John?" he asked, referring to the mysterious figure mentioned in dozens of legends and by a few more reliable sources such as Marco Polo, over a span of several hundred years and in widespread locations.[56]

John frowned and nodded. "Though how I ever got tied in with the legends of King Arthur, I can only guess. Perhaps it was the result of speculation that I had the Holy Grail. Since then, I've been a lot more careful. I've had to move frequently — never more than ten or fifteen years in one place. And I've always tried to find work in the Lord's service that wouldn't draw attention. I've pastored a hundred tiny churches in every corner of the world. But is it so surprising," he insisted, "that I could have gone unnoticed in a world of hundreds of millions? After all, God himself became a man and lived on the Earth and went unnoticed by the world for thirty years until the time was right for him to begin his ministry. Now the time is right for me, and for you as well, my friend."[57]

Sahiwai, Pakistan

Decker tried to maintain an encouraging smile as he walked among huddled groups of people squatting on the ground eating their rations. It was just after six o'clock and the day's second meal — one could hardly call it dinner — was being served. It had been nearly two hours since Secretary-General Hansen's helicopter left, four hours late, with the rest of the UN contingent. Decker and Christopher remained to await the second team of ambassadors who were coming to the camp to survey the conditions. Christopher had gone to his tent to take a nap shortly after Hansen's departure.

"Christopher, wake up; it's time for supper," Decker called as he approached the team's small stand of greenish-gray tents. "Come on, Christopher, rise and shine," he said a little louder, but there was no answer. "Christopher, are you in there?"

Decker stuck his head between the tent flaps and past the mosquito netting. Inside, Christopher sat unmoving on the floor of the tent. Sweat dripped from his face, a pained stare filled every feature.

"Are you all right?" Decker asked, though it was obvious he wasn't.

"Something is terribly wrong," Christopher said finally.

Decker ducked inside the tent and closed the flaps behind him. "What is it?" he asked.

"Death and life," Christopher replied slowly, painfully.

"Whose life and death?" Decker asked in the more traditional order in which those words are used.

"The death of one who sought to avoid death's grip; the life of another who sought to embrace death's release."

"Who has died?" Decker asked, wanting to cover one item at a time and seeing the second reference as both less pressing and more obscure.

"Jon Hansen," Christopher replied.

Decker never got around to asking about the second reference.

Chapter 21

When Leaders Fall

New York

It was three hours before search parties reached the secretary-general's helicopter, forty-five miles off course and crumpled like tissue paper among a stand of trees southwest of Gujränwalä, Pakistan. There were no survivors. It was the second time a secretary-general of the United Nations had been lost in an air accident, the first being Secretary-General Dag Hammarskjöld in 1961, whose plane crashed in Northern Rhodesia (Zambia), killing all on board. The earlier crash, though tragic, had hardly carried the impact on the world and its peoples as did the deaths of Jon Hansen and three members of the Security Council. In 1961 the position of secretary-general, like the United Nations itself, had little if any influence on the daily lives of most people in the world. Now, it seemed, the world revolved around the United Nations, and its secretary-general was its center.

The General Assembly adjourned for two weeks to honor the man who had led them for nearly fifteen years through some of the most remarkable times in recorded history. The members of Jon Hansen's staff struggled to get through each moment while attempting to carry out their duties. Few attempted to hide their tears as they spoke of him. As much as anyone, Decker Hawthorne grieved the loss of his boss and friend, but for Decker there was no time to commiserate with his colleagues. At this moment the world waited for him. As director of public affairs, he had to put aside his own mourning in order to coordinate the funeral and numerous memorial events. Hundreds of dignitaries wanted — or expected — to be included in the many memorial ceremonies, each believing that Decker should take their call personally. In many cases he did. Staying busy was probably the best thing for Decker, and he knew it.

But the lust for power never ceases, and it was during this period of mourning that Decker saw the first indications of the odious dealings that were afoot to replace Hansen. The once-united members of the Security Council each called upon Decker, requesting special favors with regard to the funeral or the ceremonies surrounding it. Ambassador Howell of Canada wanted to be the final speaker to eulogize Hansen at the funeral, the ambassador from Chad wanted to be seated near the center of the dais from which the speeches would be made, and the ambassador from Venezuela wanted to escort Hansen's widow. The request that angered Decker most was made by French Ambassador Albert Faure, who, though he had never said a kind word about Hansen while he was alive, now wanted to be a pallbearer for the secretary-general. Worse, he also insisted he be given the right lead position among the bearers. Though he wouldn't say why, Decker understood the reason: In that position, Faure hoped to be able to be most frequently seen by the cameras.

As one of his more pleasant duties, Decker sent a limo to pick up Christopher at Kennedy Airport, but couldn't spare anyone to greet him. Christopher, like hundreds of other diplomats and hundreds of thousands of mourners, was coming to New York for the funeral, filling the already crowded streets to capacity. In the sixteen years since the Disaster and the devastation of the Russian Federation, the population of the world had grown very quickly. Overall, world population was still a billion fewer than before the Disaster and the war, but one wouldn't have guessed it to look at New York on this occasion.

As Decker emerged from his office after a long meeting, he called one of the senior secretaries to be sure the limo had left to get Christopher.

"No, sir," the secretary answered, quickly adding, "Alice Bernley called during your meeting and said she and former Assistant Secretary-General Milner would meet Director-General Goodman."

At Kennedy airport, Robert Milner and Alice Bernley waited — Alice impatiently — for Christopher's flight. When Christopher arrived, he seemed genuinely pleased to see his mentor waiting for him at the gate, and the two embraced in a warm, extended hug. "How are you, Mr. Secretary?" he asked.

"Just great, Christopher," Milner answered.

"And Ms. Bernley. It's so nice to see you again."

"How have you been?" Bernley managed in a somewhat calm tone of voice that did little to disguise her true emotional state. "It's been nearly a year since I saw you last in Rome."

"Yes, it's been a very busy year. But what are you two doing here? I didn't expect a greeting party."

"It didn't seem right that you should have no one to greet you but a driver," answered Bernley, unconvincingly.

Christopher smiled. "I'm so glad to see you both. Thank you for making the effort."

"Besides," added Milner, now getting to the real reason for the airport reception, "there are some things we need to discuss before your arrival at the UN."

Christopher looked curious. Alice was nearly intoxicated with excitement.

"We'll discuss it in the car, where we can talk more freely," Milner said. Then looking at Alice, he cocked his head a little to the left and insisted with his eyes that Alice control her emotions.

Once in the car, Alice Bernley reached for the switch that closed the tinted glass barrier between them and the driver. With their privacy ensured, Milner got to the matter at hand. "Christopher, it is the double curse of wars and politics that when a great leader falls, those who most mourn his loss must, at that very moment, also be most vigilant to defend against the encroachment of those who have lost the least: those who see in our adversity an opportunity for their own gain. So it is, even at *this* moment of loss."

"It's started so soon?" Christopher asked.

"It has," Milner said. "There is more power up for grabs at this moment than at any single moment in world history. The first order of business for the UN will be for Europe and India to elect new members of the Security Council to replace the ambassadors who died with Hansen in the crash. In India there are two strong contenders, including the current alternate, Rajiv Advani, and the Indian prime minister, Nikhil Gandhi. Gandhi, who, as you know, was educated in the United States, is clearly more reasonable and would be easier to work with than Advani. But if Gandhi wins, which appears quite likely, Advani plans to return to India to run for prime minister. I don't know how familiar you are with Indian politics, but polls indicate that without Nikhil Gandhi to head it, the Congress Party's coalition won't be able to hold power. If the polls are right, Advani's Bharatiya Janata Party could win enough of a plurality of the 545 seats in the Indian parliament to easily form a solid coalition with a few of the minority parties. Bharatiya Janata is a Hindu revivalist party that has as one of its goals to revoke all rights of the Muslim minority.

"So while we would welcome Nikhil Gandhi's election as a member of the Security Council, if it results in the election of Rajiv Advani as India's prime minister, it will have come at a very expensive price. There can be no doubt that the hostilities between Hindus and Muslims in India will sharply increase under Advani, and the border tensions with Pakistan will grow even worse.

"In Europe the most likely candidates are Ambassador Valasquez of Spain and, of course, Ambassador Faure of France. It's my guess that Faure has his eyes on something much bigger."

"Secretary-general?" Christopher asked. It was a rhetorical question; there *was* only one position more powerful than that of primary member of the Security Council.

"Exactly," Milner answered.

"That's quite a jump from being an alternate member of the Security Council." Christopher said. "And he can't possibly think the Council is going to vote for a second consecutive secretary-general from Europe."

"I didn't say it was likely he could win, just that that's what he's after . . . along with half a dozen other people, I should add."

Alice Bernley remained quiet, but it seemed to her that the conversation was getting off track.

Milner continued, "Before the new secretary-general is elected, there will be an election to replace the alternate from North America. And if either of the alternates from India or Europe are elected to become primary members, then there will be an election to replace them as well.

"Christopher," Milner said, growing even more serious, "Ambassador Faure has asked me to support his candidacy to replace the late Ambassador Heinemann as primary from Europe."

"You refused, of course."

"I told him I would."

"What? But why?" Christopher blurted. "Isn't Faure the very person you were talking about when you said we needed to defend against those who least mourned Hansen's loss?"

"Certainly one of them," Milner concurred. "But there is more to this than you may realize. As unfortunate as it may seem, Ambassador Faure will succeed in his bid to replace Ambassador Heinemann; there is no way for us to prevent it."

"But why?"

"Two reasons. First, as I said, the only other candidate capable of getting enough votes is Ambassador Valasquez of Spain. No one else has nearly enough support. Frankly, Valasquez is a fool to run against Faure. His closet is so full of skeletons that it's a miracle none has fallen out before this. As soon as Faure's people get around to investigating Valasquez's background, they're bound to start uncovering something embarrassing. If they're smart, they'll wait until the last minute and then get Valasquez to pull out in exchange for not releasing the information to the press. At that late date, no one else will be able to mount a serious candidacy. The second reason is that, as you know, Alice has certain abilities, certain insights into the future, that come to her through her spirit guide, Master Djwlij Kajm."

Alice Bernley took this as her cue. "I am absolutely certain Ambassador Faure will be elected as the primary from Europe," she said. "However, we must view this not as a loss, but as a short-term setback. And as an opportunity."

Milner continued, "Since we know Faure will be elected with or without my support, it's best that I offer it in exchange for something we want. That's where you come in, Christopher."

Christopher seemed a little unsure of the whole situation, but he was always quick to recover. "Whatever I can do to help, just let me know."

"Good," said Milner. "I was sure you'd have that attitude. Now, instead of going directly to the UN, you'll go first to the Italian Mission."

"As an Italian citizen, assigned to the UN, I would do that anyway, as a courtesy to Ambassador Niccoli."

"Good. When you arrive at the Italian Mission you'll be informed that three hours ago Ambassador Niccoli resigned his position as the Italian ambassador to the United Nations in order to pursue other interests."

"What? What other interests?" interrupted Christopher.

"A very well-paid position as a director of the Banque of Rome. A bank in which, not coincidentally, David Bragford owns a twenty-two percent interest. But as I was saying," Milner continued, "at the Italian Mission you'll be given a sealed packet and a message to immediately call the Italian president. When you reach President Sabetini, he will direct you to open the packet. Inside you'll find documents to be presented to the UN Credentials Committee naming *you* as the new Italian ambassador to the United Nations."

Christopher looked at Milner and then at Bernley. Bernley smiled broadly, but for a moment no one spoke. Finally Christopher held his hands out in front of him, gesturing for them to stop. "Hold it a second," he said. "Repeat that last part?"

"You heard me right, Christopher. You are going to be named the new Italian ambassador to the United Nations, assuming, of course, you're willing."

"But this is crazy. I've only been an Italian citizen for five years."

"And for much of those five years," Milner answered, "I have devoted myself to preparing you and the people of Italy for this moment. That's why I urged you to become an Italian citizen in the first place."

"But how could you have known?"

"We didn't know the specifics," Bernley answered. "Obviously, if we had known that Secretary-General Hansen was going to die, we would have tried to prevent it. But what I know and don't know about the future isn't something I get to pick and choose."

"It didn't take Alice's clairvoyance," Milner interjected, "to know that one day Hansen would step down. And when he did, we knew we would have to be prepared to preserve the advances he had made."

"I'm sorry," Christopher said, "but I still don't understand. Why would President Sabetini name me as the new ambassador? And why would the *priministro* agree?"

"There are several reasons," Milner explained. "No doubt they like you and trust you. They believe you care about Italy and the Italian people. As for the president, my guess is he's hoping you will someday become his son-in-law."

"His son-in-law?! Why do people keep saying that? Tina and I are just friends," Christopher said emphatically.

"That's fine, Christopher. I'm just listing a few possible reasons. But, doubtless, the biggest reason the president would name you as ambassador and that the prime minister would back his decision, is that Italy wants a voice on the Security Council."

"Hold it," Christopher said. "I think I've missed something. How does my becoming the Italian ambassador give Italy a voice on the Council?"

"That's why I have agreed to support Ambassador Faure's election as Europe's primary," Milner answered. "Presently, thirteen European nations have committed their support to him. For my part, I am to provide him with the five additional votes he'll need. In exchange, Ambassador Faure will support my candidate to replace him as alternate member. You, Christopher, will be my candidate.[58] And that will give Italy its representation on the Security Council."

Christopher took a deep breath and shook his head in wonderment. "But how can you promise the votes of five countries?"

"One of those votes will come from Italy; that is, from you," Milner answered.

"And the other four?"

"Christopher, Alice and I are not without some influence among the members of the UN. I've quite a large number of chits I may call in. And Alice, well, let's just say that there are many people in the United Nations who greatly value her opinions."

They rode in silence for the next few minutes, but as they pulled up to Two United Nations Plaza where the Italian Mission is located, across the street from the UN, Secretary Milner sought to reassure Christopher. "Christopher, I don't know what you're feeling right now, but let me assure you, you should not for a moment feel like this position was bought. Instead, *you* have been sold to the Italian president as the best person for the position and for Italy's long-term interests."

"Thank you, Mr. Secretary. I'm glad you put it that way. I just keep expecting to wake up and find out this whole conversation has been a dream, or maybe for someone to yell, 'Surprise!' and tell me this is all a practical joke."

Milner knew Christopher well enough to know that no response was necessary, but Alice answered, "It's no joke, Christopher."

As Christopher got out of the car, he had one more thought, "I'm supposed to meet Decker in his office."

"Do you want me to let him know you'll be late?" Milner volunteered.

"No. I'll call him. I'm just wondering how I'm going to explain all this."

Chapter 22

Simple Arithmetic

Three weeks later

New York

Ambassador Lee Yun-Mai of China called to order the session of the United Nations Security Council and welcomed the new members and alternates. The position of Security Council president rotated among the ten primary members on a monthly basis, and though it wasn't a particularly cherished position, in the absence of a secretary-general it provided the only point of focus for the press.

United Nations Security Council Chamber

Ambassador Lee was one of the most experienced members of the Council. Now in her seventies and with more than thirty years of diplomatic service, she had served during all but three of the years during which Hansen had been secretary-general. As much as anyone, she hoped to limit the spectacle of the event that was about to unfold, but the election of the first secretary-general since Jon Hansen would not be without its drama. Under the circumstances, it was unrealistic to hope for total abstinence from grand-standing by the members.

Newly appointed Italian Ambassador Christopher Goodman sat quietly at the C-shaped table in the place assigned to the European alternate member. There was little for him to do but watch; as an alternate he had no power to nominate, second, or even vote on the election of the new secretary-general. On most matters, alternates could speak when the floor was open for debate, but for the election of the secretary-general there would be no debate, only nominations, seconds, and votes.

If Christopher had needed any distraction, there were many other pressing matters to think about. Secretary Milner's projections about India had been right on target; Nikhil Gandhi, the former Indian prime minister, had won the seat as primary from India, and as expected, Rajiv Advani was now seeking to replace Gandhi as India's prime minister. Even more pressing was the famine in Pakistan and Northern India. With Hansen's death, the relief work had come to a virtual standstill. Christopher's replacement at FAO, along with ECOSOC's Executive Director Louis Colleta, were doing all they could with the resources available, but the matter was now stalled, awaiting debate by the Security Council. Even if it did finally come to the floor for a vote, without the driving force of Hansen, there was little hope that the food-producing regions would contribute sufficient relief.

Christopher was in no position to help. As the alternate from Europe, he now replaced Faure as chairman of the World Peace Organization (WPO), the UN's military force. While Christopher's education and experience would have better suited him to work as the alternate in charge of ECOSOC, that position had been held for the last two years by the ambassador from Australia. Under current world conditions, ECOSOC offered far greater political visibility, hence the Australian ambassador had no interest in giving it up, and so Christopher could do nothing.

With Pakistani refugee camps growing ever more crowded, those strong enough were attempting to cross the border into India. Many were intercepted and returned to Pakistan by the United Nations Military Observer Group in India and Pakistan (UNMOGIP), which had monitored the border between the two countries since 1949. But with sixteen hundred miles of border, half of which are traversable (the other half lying in the Great Indian Desert), the number of refugees pouring into India was greater than the UN forces could handle.

The Indian government, while expressing sympathy for the plight of the refugees, had responded to the attempted migration by sending its military to protect its borders against "invasion." India had its own problems with famine and had no interest in allowing any additional mouths at its meager table.[59] So far the Indian military had shown restraint, choosing simply to escort refugees back across the border with a stern warning. There had been reports of beatings, but these were the exceptions. Whether the policy of restraint would continue under Rajiv Advani remained to be seen. Despite efforts to stop the migration, UNMOGIP estimated that hundreds of refugees eluded capture each day. There was no telling how long the Indian government would allow this to go on before stepping in militarily.

At the Pakistani/Indian border, more than just countries and cultures met. It was also the demarcation between the UN regions of India and the Middle East, and between Muslims and Hindus. Adding a third element to the amalgam was China, which shares a border with both India and Pakistan. For decades, even with the easing of tensions that had occurred under Jon Hansen, the Indian government had provided covert support to the Tibetan Buddhist followers of the Dalai Lama, who sought the separation of Tibet from China. China, meanwhile, maintained a very strong relationship with Pakistan. Finally, all three countries had large stocks of nuclear weapons.

Were all this not enough to distract Christopher from the Security Council proceedings, there was another matter as well. Christopher's predecessor at WPO, Albert Faure, had left numerous unfinished matters. Among them was a UN treaty with Israel to formally extend expired diplomatic agreements, ensure the exchange and safe delivery of diplomatic packets, and provide diplomatic immunity for visiting officials. The treaty had very little to do with military issues, but after being shuffled around the other agencies for two and a half years because no one could convince the Israelis it was in their interest to sign it, someone had decided it should go to WPO because one of the provisions was a mutual agreement of nonaggression.

Borders of India, Pakistan and China

Now, appropriately or not, the treaty lay at Christopher's doorstep, and his success in negotiating with the Israelis was seen as the first measure of this untried ambassador's abilities. It was ironic that such a treaty was even necessary, but Israel — which in 1948 had become a nation as a result of a vote by the UN — had later resigned its membership because of the reorganization of the Security Council and was now the only country in the world that refused membership in that body.

As far as the Israelis were concerned, the old agreements with the UN could stand just the way they were. They saw no reason to renegotiate and were reluctant to open themselves up to new demands. The Israeli resignation from the United Nations had originally been viewed by her Muslim neighbors as an opportunity to further isolate Israel from the rest of the world. They had sought a complete and immediate halt of all trade with Israel, but that attempt was doomed from the start. Ultimately, a nonbinding resolution and statement of principles was adopted by the General Assembly that prohibited sales of advanced weapons to Israel, but the resolution had exactly the opposite effect than was hoped for by Israel's opponents. For seven years after their war with the Muslim states and then with the Russian Federation, Israel's defensive arsenal had consisted of their own recaptured weaponry plus the huge weapons caches taken from the Russian invaders.[60] Since that time, while most countries' military budgets were being cut back, Israel had maintained a constantly increasing defense budget. The upshot was that while her Muslim neighbors grumbled loudly, there was no real possibility they'd attack Israel again anytime in the foreseeable future. Israel could afford to be a little smug.

Albert Faure, who had never expended much effort on his responsibilities as chairman of WPO, hadn't even tried to get the new treaty with Israel signed. There was evidence that he had let slide or mismanaged a number of other duties as well. The one thing he did seem to do well was to appoint his friends to positions in WPO's administration.

With the formalities behind them, Ambassador Lee opened the floor to nominations for secretary-general. One of the perhaps less democratic holdovers from the days before the reorganization was the manner in which the secretary-general was elected, which required unanimous approval of a candidate by the Security Council, followed by a full vote of the General Assembly. And no one expected a consensus this early in the process.

First to be recognized by the chair was Ambassador Yuri Kruszkegin of the Republic of Khakassia, representing Northern Asia. Following the devastation of the Russian Federation, Ambassador Kruszkegin had left the UN to help form the new government of his home province of Khakassia, but had returned five years later. His election to represent Northern Asia on the Security Council had been unanimous by the members of that region. Kruszkegin rose and nominated Ambassador Tanaka of

Japan, representing the Pacific Basin. Japan had been very supportive of the countries of Northern Asia in their efforts to rebuild after the war with Israel. Even before the UN voted to eliminate trade barriers, Japan dropped many of the trade impediments between itself and the nations of Northern Asia. These steps had been very important to the reconstruction of that region, and Kruszkegin was repaying the debt. The nomination was seconded by Ambassador Albert Faure of France, representing Europe. Faure's reasons for seconding the nomination were far from clear, but it was assumed he wanted something in return.

The chair opened the floor for additional nominations and recognized the ambassador from Ecuador representing South America, who nominated Jackson Clark, the ambassador from the United States. The nomination was seconded by American-educated Ambassador Nikhil Gandhi of India. Most observers had expected the American to be nominated, but weren't sure how it would play out. Ambassador Clark had only recently resigned as the U.S. president in order to replace Walter Bishop, who had died in the crash along with Hansen. The nomination made it clear just what Clark had in mind when he resigned the presidency: He wanted to be secretary-general. The primary member from North America, Canadian Ambassador Howell — still in poor health but delaying his resignation — was expected to provide a third vote for his southern neighbor.

Again the floor was opened for nominations, and the chair recognized Ambassador Ngordon of Chad, representing West Africa, who nominated Ambassador Fahd of Saudi Arabia. The nomination was seconded by the ambassador from Tanzania, representing East Africa. The basis for this final coalition was easily recognizable as one of common religion and proximity.

The vote was as split as it possibly could be. Since no one could be nominated without the support of at least two regions, and no region could nominate or second anyone from their own region, the maximum number of nominations possible was three. Only China had abstained; all other votes were committed. For now there was nothing to do but to go on to other business.

Jerusalem

Scott Rosen was lost in thought as he walked across the crowded outer courtyard that surrounded the newly completed Jewish Temple. As it had been in ancient days, this large rectangular courtyard, called the Court of the Gentiles, was as close to the holy places of the Temple as non-Jews were allowed to come. The mood here had much more an air of carnival than of worship or reverence. Nowhere was this more inescapable than in the column-lined covered portico encircling the perimeter of the Court of the Gentiles. Here, housed in rows of booths and stalls, temple money changers dickered rates of exchange with worshipers to convert various currencies into one acceptable for temple offerings — no currency bearing the image of a deity or person was allowed. Nearby traders offered pigeons, doves, lambs, rams, and bulls for purchase as sacrifices.

Scott paid no attention to the cacophony. His mind kept going back to a conversation the day before. It had started out as a perfect day. The weather was beautiful, the traffic was light. A meeting he wanted to avoid and for which he hadn't prepared was indefinitely postponed. The extra time allowed him to tackle some interesting and important work and within two hours he had come up with a way to solve a major problem that had seemed unsolvable to everyone else. An overdue rent check for the house that had belonged to his parents arrived in the morning mail. Sol, the proprietor at the kosher deli he frequented, had added an extra scoop of tuna to his sandwich and had given him the biggest dill pickle Scott had ever seen. That's when the day began to sour.

As often happened, Sol came over to talk with Scott while he ate and Scott invited him to sit down. It had started innocently enough: They talked about politics and rising prices and discussed religious issues and the latest gossip from around the Temple — all topics they had covered before and upon which they almost always agreed. Then Sol mentioned he had been reading his Bible in the ninth chapter of the book of Daniel.

"The prophecy at the end of the chapter," Saul explained, "says that King Messiah was supposed to come before the second Temple was destroyed. That happened in 70 C.E.,[61] so he must have already come!"

Scott shook his head. "Obviously you're misreading, Sol. If King Messiah had come, we would surely have known!"

Scott was unquestionably the greater scholar on such matters, so this should have been the end of it. But Sol didn't yield. "According to Daniel's prophecy, King Messiah was to come 483 years after the decree to rebuild the city of Jerusalem,[62] which had been destroyed by the Babylonians. Based on Ezra chapter 7:6-7,[63] the date of that decree can be determined as 457 B.C.E..[64] And when you take into account that there was no year zero," Sol reasoned, "that means King Messiah came in the year 27 C.E.!" Sol pulled up the calculator function on his phone to show Scott the math, but Scott grabbed his wrist to stop him.

"Sol," he warned, "what you are doing is very serious. It's forbidden by the Talmud."

"What?" Sol asked in surprise.

"Calculating the time of King Messiah's coming based on the ninth chapter of Daniel is forbidden," Scott answered authoritatively.

Sol gave him a look of disbelief. "But—"

"It's true," Scott declared. "In the Talmud, Rabbi Jonathan put a curse on anyone who calculates the time of the Messiah based on Daniel's prophecies."[65]

Sol rubbed his chin and mulled this over for a moment, while Scott, confident he had settled the question, took another bite of his sandwich. Taking unfair advantage of Scott's preoccupation with chewing, Sol rejoined the exchange. "But that can't be right. Why would the Talmud not want us to know when Daniel said King Messiah would come?"

Scott's face contorted as he forced down his food. "You can't just pull out a calculator and figure out what a prophecy means!"

"That's exactly what Daniel did to interpret the prophecy of Jeremiah.[66] And that's in the ninth chapter of Daniel, too — the same chapter as the prophecy of when King Messiah would come. Of course Daniel didn't have a calculator, but it's still simple arithmetic."

Sol was refusing to yield to his superior religious training and knowledge, and Scott's patience was waning. "Look, Sol, you're dealing with things you don't understand!"

But Sol wasn't ready to quit. "Don't you see, Scott? If the Messiah came in 27 C.E., then we didn't recognize him. Don't you get it? 27 C.E.! There's only one person who fits the description!"

Scott couldn't believe his ears. Sol was actually suggesting — no, declaring — that King Messiah was in fact Jesus! "Stop it!" he demanded. "I don't know what's gotten into you, but this is wrong, and I won't listen to it. If you fear *HaShem*, you'll be at the Temple tomorrow with your sin offering, begging forgiveness." Ever dutiful, Scott used the orthodox method of referring to God as *HaShem*, meaning "the name," rather than *Yahweh* or even *God*, in order to avoid any possibility of blasphemy.

Sol didn't say any more, but it was clear he felt no guilt that would warrant a sin offering.

Outside the Temple on the broad steps leading down to the street, Scott was distracted from his recollections by someone calling his name. The voice had come from the direction of a large group of tourists, recognizable by their paper yarmulkes, so he assumed the call had been for some other Scott.

"Scott!" he heard again, but this time he spotted its source coming toward him at a brisk pace.

"Joel!" he called back to his friend and professional colleague of many years. Joel Felsberg had been a part of the team with Scott fifteen years before, during the Russian invasion. "What brings you here?"

Unlike Scott Rosen, Joel Felsberg had never spent much time on matters of religion. The only times he came to the Temple were with relatives or friends who were visiting from the United States. "Scott," he said again, out of breath and ignoring Scott's question. "I've found him! I mean he's found me!"

"Slow down, Joel," Scott said. "Who have you found? What are you talking about?"

Joel, who was of average build and just under five feet seven inches tall, leaned close to the much larger Scott Rosen and whispered, "The Messiah."

Scott Rosen looked around quickly to see if anyone else had heard, then grabbed Joel's arm. The smaller Felsberg, who was easily eighty pounds lighter than Rosen, had no choice but to capitulate to Rosen's will as he pulled him quickly down the

Temple Mount, maneuvering through another crowd of tourists. "I've found him," Joel said again as he tried desperately to keep up.

"Be quiet!" Scott demanded as he drug Joel along.

When they reached the parking lot some hundred and fifty yards away, they at last stopped next to Scott's van. Looking around to be sure no one was within earshot, Scott finally spoke, "Are you crazy?! That's nothing to joke about. And of all places — right on the steps of the Temple! Maybe *you* don't take your religion or your heritage seriously but some of us do. If anyone had heard you—"

"No, Scott. I'm not joking. I've seen the Messiah. I've seen him," Joel interrupted.

"Shut up, Joel! You didn't see anybody, so just shut up!"

"But—"

Grabbing Joel's shirt and shaking his fist in his face, Scott said again, "Shut up!"

Joel at last fell silent, but the maelstrom was still in Scott's eyes and his fist was still in Joel's face. After a moment, Scott relented, dropped his fist, and began to release his grip. "Is the whole world going mad?" he asked. "First Sol and now you!"

"But—" Joel said again. Scott took hold of Joel's shirt with both hands now, lifting him onto his tiptoes, and bringing his face up to his own until they were eye to eye.

"If you say one more word," he said through clinched teeth, "I swear by the Temple of HaShem that I'll—" Scott caught himself, but just barely. Swearing by the Temple was serious business; next to swearing by God himself, there was no more powerful and binding oath. It was not to be made in anger or haste. He released his grip and pushed Joel away. "Just get away from me until you've come to your senses," he growled, as Joel stumbled back, slamming into the side of a parked car.

Joel picked himself up and looked into Scott's eyes with a sincerity that even Scott couldn't doubt. "I really have seen him," Joel insisted.

There was nothing else to do. Scott couldn't bring himself to actually hit his old friend. They had been through too much together. They had fought side by side to save Israel those fifteen years ago, there in that bunker beneath the streets of Tel Aviv. They had been heroes together. There was nothing left for Scott to do but ask the obvious question. "Where?! Where have you seen him?" he demanded, finally resigning himself to having this conversation.

"In a dream."

Scott stared, dumbfounded.

Joel knew how weak his answer sounded, but it was the only one he had, and to his mind, it was the answer God had given him to say. "And he's coming to establish his kingdom," he added finally.

Scott's anger quickly changed to concern. He had been wrong to be so brutal. Joel was obviously confused, ill perhaps — unable to separate dream from reality. "Joel," he said firmly but sympathetically. "It was just a dream."

"But, it was more than that," Joel insisted.

"I'm sure it seemed very real. But it *was* just a dream," Scott responded quickly, giving no quarter to Joel's delusion.

"No, Scott. Don't you see? I've been wrong all these years. And so have you."

The conversation was taking an unexpected and even more galling turn. "What do you mean?" Scott asked, anticipating an answer that would make him more angry than ever.

"We've both been wrong all this time. My sister, Rhoda, and her rabbi have been right all along. Don't you see, Scott? Yeshua really is the Messiah!" And then just to be sure Scott fully understood what he had said, Joel used the English version of the name, "Jesus is the Messiah!"

Scott Rosen's eyes filled with rage. This was too much. Grabbing Joel by the shoulders, he shook him violently for several seconds and then threw him to the ground, causing Joel's left wrist to snap audibly as he tried to break his fall against the asphalt. The pain he had caused and the bloody abrasions were obvious, but he wasn't done as he snarled, "You and that traitor rabbi, you're both *meshummadim!*" — the Hebrew word for traitors.

"I don't know you!" Scott screamed. "I never knew you! You're dead! You never existed! If you ever speak to me again, I'll kill you!"

Chapter 23

Offering

New York

Alice Bernley and Robert Milner strolled slowly past the huge wall of ivy along Raoul Wallenberg Walk, their pace giving no hint of the excitement they felt as they talked of the events of the past few weeks.

"It's all coming together; I can feel it," Alice said, exuberantly. "Even if I weren't here to see it for myself, I would still feel it. I think," she said, after a moment, "I could be on the moon and I'd still know."

Milner smiled. He didn't doubt her supposition for a moment. He could feel it too.

"I've gotten calls and e-mails from people all over the world, groups I've never even heard of," she continued. "They don't understand it, but they can sense we're on the very brink of the New Age. They want to know what they should do."

"And what do you tell them?"

"I tell them to organize, add to their number, spread the word that the arrival of the New Age is near. And to wait."

Milner nodded. "Some of it concerns me, though," he said reflectively. "There are those who would like to rush its advent. We cannot allow that."

"No one else knows about Christopher?" she asked for reassurance.

"No. I don't think so. But many suspect that you and I know something. If our friends on the Security Council knew, they'd try to make him secretary-general right now."

"We can't allow that," she said.

"Of course not. The time simply isn't right. He's not ready."

Ahead of them on the walk stood a tall thin man with graying hair, wearing a tailor-cut European suit. He was flanked by two very large muscular men, both easily twice his weight. The eyes of the larger men were hidden by sunglasses, but the thin man stared directly at them. Had Milner and Bernley not been so involved in their conversation, they would have noticed the men long before. Their combined swath blocked nearly the entire walk. They didn't seem menacing, but they did appear determined.

"Secretary Milner?" the thin man asked.

"Yes."

"Ms. Alice Bernley?"

"Yes."

"I have a letter for you," the man said as he handed an envelope to Bernley. The man had spoken only a few words, but Milner, who had traveled to every corner of the world, recognized his accent at once. Most would have guessed French, but there was more. It was rougher, more guttural than a true French accent. There were also traces of German. The man was obviously a native of Alsace-Lorraine, the region of France, which from 1870 to 1945 traded hands between the French and Germans five times. Milner wasn't sure, but he could think of only one item of business that would bring a man of Alsace-Lorraine to this meeting in the park.

Bernley opened the envelope and began to read the letter inside. "Bob, look!" she said, holding up the letter for him to see as she continued to read.

Milner read. It was as he had suspected, but it was important not to appear too eager. Impressions could be critical. "Please convey our appreciation," Milner said as soon as he was sure of the letter's content, but without reading it in its entirety. He knew Alice could be very excitable and he wanted to be the first to speak.

"You will take delivery of the package, then?" the thin man asked.

"Yes," Milner answered calmly.

"Yes, of course we will," Bernley said, in a much more animated tone. "We would be delighted to . . ." From the corner of her eye, she caught the look on Robert Milner's face, and let her sentence trail off. It was the look he gave when he thought she was getting too ardent. Not that he wasn't just as excited as she; it just wasn't always prudent to show it.

"Where would you like it delivered?"

Milner thought quickly and answered with the most obvious place: "The Lucius Trust at the UN Plaz—" He stopped himself. It didn't make sense to ship it across the Atlantic only to ship it back for its final delivery. "No," he said. "Have it delivered to my attention at the Italian Embassy in Tel Aviv."

"We will need some assistance getting it through customs," the man said.

"Of course," Milner answered.

"You can expect delivery in one week, if that is acceptable to you."

"That would be fine," said Milner.

The man reached into his pocket and retrieved a ring with four keys. "You will need these," he said without further explanation. "Ms. Bernley. Secretary Milner." He nodded in farewell, and without another word, the three men walked away. Milner now looked at the letter more closely.

> *We believe that a certain item, in our possession for a number of years, may prove useful to your current enterprise. At your request, we would be most gratified to surrender the item to you to use at your discretion.*

The letter went on to give specifics on the delivery of the item and to note that there were certain precautions to be observed in its transport and handling, of which the writer was sure they would be aware.

Bernley had been right: It *was* all coming together. "I knew they would contact us," said Milner. "It was just a matter of time."

Tiviarius, Israel

"So, what is it you wanted to talk about?" Rabbi Eleazar ben David asked Scott Rosen as he sat down in his favorite chair. The rabbi's study was a little darker than Scott liked; one of the bulbs was out and there was no natural lighting because the room's only window, like every other wall, was hidden by tightly packed bookshelves. It was quite an impressive collection of books, representing each of the five languages the rabbi spoke fluently.

"I'm concerned about Joel," Scott began.

"I haven't seen Joel since the last time the three of us went to the Jerusalem Symphony. How is he? Is there anything wrong?"

"That's why I'm here," Scott said a little uncomfortably. "He came up to the Temple yesterday to find me. He was running and waving his arms," Scott exaggerated, "and yelling 'I've found him! I've found him!' I told him to calm down and asked what he was talking about, and he said," Scott cringed, "that he had seen the Messiah."

The rabbi raised an eyebrow, but his reaction seemed more to convey introspection than trepidation. It wasn't the response Scott expected.

"Rabbi?" he said, seeking confirmation that he had understood.

"The Messiah?" he asked after a moment.

"Yes!"

"Did he say *where* he had seen him?"

"In a dream. But he's convinced it was more than that. He thinks it was some kind of vision."

"Hmm," the rabbi said with the same thoughtful expression. He paused for several seconds, pursed his lips, and then asked, "Can we be sure it wasn't a vision?"

"Yes. Absolutely!"

"How?" asked the rabbi.

"I hate to even say it," Scott said shaking his head emphatically. Rabbi ben David waited. "Apparently, whatever he saw in his dream has convinced him that Jesus, or 'Yeshua' as he called him, was the Messiah."

This time the rabbi raised both eyebrows and grasped his bearded chin. Clearly he was surprised, but still there was no indication that he was appalled as Scott had expected. Instead, again he seemed lost in thought. Obviously, he had something else on his mind. Another man might have asked him about his distraction, but not Scott. He had never been one to openly show concern about other people's feelings. He was much happier with a room full of computers than with a room full of people. The fact that he was here, expressing concern for Joel Felsberg gave witness to how close the two men were.

"Well, what should I do?" Scott asked finally, waving his hands both to make his point and hoping to draw the rabbi's attention back to the subject.

"About what?"

"About Joel!" Scott said, still waving his hands, this time out of frustration.

"I don't think there's anything you can do. If it was just a dream, he'll get over it. Just try to be patient with him."

"What do you mean *if* it was just a dream? Didn't you hear me? " Scott asked in disbelief. "He thinks Jesus is the Messiah!"

The rabbi scooted forward in his seat and leaned toward Scott. "It's interesting that he should have this dream at this particular time," he said. "My studies have recently brought me to a rather interesting passage. Let me read it to you." The rabbi took his reading glasses and a book from the coffee table beside his chair and opened to a place he had bookmarked. Then he began:

> *He had no form or beauty, that we should look at him:*
> *No charm, that we should find him pleasing.*
> *He was despised, shunned by men,*
> *A man of suffering, familiar with disease.*
> *As one who hid his face from us,*
> *He was despised, we held him of no account.*
>
> *Yet it was our sickness that he was bearing,*
> *Our suffering that he endured.*
> *We accounted him plagued,*
> *Smitten and afflicted by God;*
> *But he was wounded because of our sins,*
> *Crushed because of our iniquities.*
> *He bore the chastisement that made us whole,*
> *And by his bruises we were healed.*
> *We all went astray like sheep,*
> *Each going his own way;*
> *And the Lord visited upon him*
> *The guilt of all of us.*[67]

"Rabbi," Scott interrupted, "why are you reading this? 'Wounded because of our sins, crushed because of our iniquities.' That's—"

"Just listen," the rabbi insisted. Scott didn't understand why a rabbi would be reading this, but he had more respect than to challenge him just yet. The rabbi continued:

He was maltreated, yet he was submissive,
He did not open his mouth;
Like a sheep being led to slaughter,
Like a ewe, dumb before those who shear her,
He did not open his mouth.

By oppressive judgment he was taken away,
Who could describe his abode?
For he was cut off from the land of the living
Through the sin of My people, who deserved the punishment.
And his grave was set among the wicked,
And with the rich, in his death —
Though he had done no injustice
And had spoken no falsehood.

But the Lord chose to crush him by disease,
That, if he made himself an offering for guilt,
He might see offspring and have long life,
And that through him the Lord's purpose might prosper.
Out of his anguish he shall see it;
He shall enjoy it to the full through his devotion.

My righteous servant makes the many righteous,
It is their punishment that he bears;
Assuredly, I will give him the many as his portion,
He shall receive the multitude as his spoil.
For he exposed himself to death
And was numbered among the sinners,
Whereas he bore the guilt of the many
And made intercession for sinners.[68]

Scott wasn't sure whether the rabbi was finished, but he had no desire to hear anymore. "Why have you read this to me?" he asked.

"What do you think?" the rabbi posed in return, ignoring Scott's question for the moment.

"I think the Christian writers do a poor job of imitating the style of the prophets."

The rabbi smiled broadly. It wasn't exactly the answer he had expected, but it made the point. "Why do you assume that these are Christian Scriptures?"

Scott still wasn't sure what the rabbi was up to but the question-and-answer style reminded him of his days in Hebrew school. *The rabbi must be using this to make some point about Joel's delusion*, he thought. "Well," Scott answered, as if he were back in a classroom, "there are two reasons. First of all, the writer is obviously writing about Jesus: all that business about being wounded because of our sins and crushed because of our iniquities. That's a Christian belief — that Jesus was a substitutionary sacrifice for the sins of mankind. It's obvious this is one of their Scriptures trying to convince the reader that Jesus was the Messiah."

"Is that what it's saying?" the rabbi asked before Scott could get to his second point.

"Of course. It's obvious. It could be nothing else."

"And the second reason?"

"Second," said Scott, "is that I have never heard nor read that passage before. If it was from the prophets, I would have heard it read in synagogue."

Rabbi ben David handed the still-opened book to Scott. Sitting back again in his chair, he crossed his hands on his stomach and exhaled audibly through his thick gray beard. Scott found the passage quickly; it was well marked. Then he looked at the top of the page. It read "Isaiah."

He studied this for a moment and then as understanding dawned on him, he shook his head in disgust. "Were the Christians not satisfied to add their writings to the back of our Bible with their so-called 'New' Testament?" he charged. "Have they now begun inserting their lies into the very text of the Tanakh? Where did you purchase this? We must put a stop to it immediately, before others are deceived!"

"As you can see," the rabbi said, flipping to the title page, "this is translated according to Masoretic text and was published by the Jewish Publication Society of America. What I read you is in your Bible, too, Scott. You can go home and look."

"That's impossible. My Bible was given to me by my grandfather. The Christians couldn't have—"

"Those *are* the words of the prophet Isaiah, Scott."

Scott squinted in bewilderment. "But then why have I never heard this before?"

"You have never heard it because that passage is never, never read in the synagogue. It doesn't appear in a single rabbinic anthology of synagogue readings for the Sabbath."

"But who can the prophet be talking about?"

The scrutiny of the rabbi's stare turned Scott's question back to him.

"But it can't be. The prophet must be speaking in allegory."

"Perhaps," Rabbi ben David allowed. "In rabbinic school, when I was young and believed everything I was told, they covered this passage briefly and they taught us that Isaiah was speaking allegorically of the nation of Israel. Surely," he agreed, "we have suffered as a people. But if the 'he' the prophecy speaks of is Israel, who then is the 'we'? Clearly there are two parties spoken of. And if the 'he' is Israel, then whose sins — whose iniquities — have we borne? Who was healed by our wounds?

"'*He* was cut off from the land of the living through the sins of *My* people,'" the rabbi continued, reciting a piece of the passage. "Is it not Israel who are God's people? And if Israel is God's people, and 'he' was cut off from the land of the living through our sins, who is 'he'?" Rabbi ben David frowned, breathed deeply, and concluded: "So we are back to the same question: To whom does the prophet refer?"

"But what about the part about dying from disease? Jesus was crucified," said Scott.

Rabbi ben David pointed to an editor's note at the bottom of the page[69] from which he had just read. "The meaning of the original Hebrew is uncertain," he read. "The editors admit that 'disease' was just a guess." The rabbi shrugged. "But even with that, who can miss what the prophet is saying?"

Scott didn't answer.

The rabbi sighed. "So there is the reason for my distraction," he said, "and the reason I find Joel's dream, or at least the timing of it, so curious. You see, it was because of a dream that I recently read that portion of Isaiah. It was not so colorful a dream as the one Joel described. I'm not even sure I was asleep. I just kept hearing a voice calling my name and telling me to read the fifty-third chapter of Isaiah. I was as astounded as you when I read it. I could not understand how I could have so long ignored what you have just said is so obvious; allegory simply cannot explain the striking similarity. If ever a prophecy were exactly fulfilled, then this—" The rabbi stopped himself from saying more. "So now I find myself in a dilemma. As you have said, it seems obvious of whom the prophet is speaking, and yet I cannot allow myself to admit it. But," he said, and then paused, "neither can I bring myself to deny it."

Ten days later

Jerusalem

The black limousine of the Italian ambassador to Israel, Paulo D'Agostino, pulled past the security barriers and stopped outside the front entrance of the Israeli Knesset. Accompanying D'Agostino were Christopher Goodman, Robert Milner, and Milner's guest, Alice Bernley. Close behind the limo, security personnel from the Italian embassy followed in an armored truck carrying a large wooden crate that had recently been delivered to the embassy from the Alsace-Lorraine region of France.

Israeli Knesset, Jerusalem

Inside the Knesset building, in the office of the prime minister, Israel's High Priest Chaim Levin and two Levite attendants had just arrived and were exchanging pleasantries with the prime minister and the minister of foreign affairs while they awaited the arrival of their guests.

"Thank you very much for coming, Rabbi," the prime minister told the high priest.

"I am always willing to be of service to Israel," the New York-born high priest answered. "But tell me, have they still not said why it was so important that I attend this meeting? And why of all days, it had to be today?"

"No, Rabbi. The purpose of the meeting is to allow the new Italian ambassador to the United Nations an opportunity to present arguments for renegotiating our treaty with the UN — nothing that should concern you *and*, I might add, nothing that really concerns me. The old treaty has lapsed and, while I admit it has a few flaws, I am reluctant to agree to any new negotiations. I would have refused this meeting altogether but for the fact that it was requested by former Assistant Secretary-General Robert Milner, a man of some influence with ties to American bankers. As for why he asked that you be invited and why it had to be on this day, I don't know. He said only that they'll be bringing something with them that you'll want to see."

The meeting was soon underway and Christopher began to address those assembled. He would be brief and to the point; all the arguments he would make about the treaty had been made before. But that was not the real reason for this meeting. Still, it was necessary that he offer a clear explanation of the treaty's purpose and the reasons the UN believed that a new treaty — not just an extension of the old one — was required. The duration of the proposed treaty would be seven years,[70] and would allow the parties, upon their mutual agreement, to extend its effect for three additional periods of seven years each. There was nothing particularly remarkable about the treaty; it was just typical matters of state. The only thing of even passing interest was a provision for a mutual agreement of nonaggression. Even this was included primarily as a diplomatic formality. Israel certainly had no intention of attacking anyone. After so many years as a nation under constant threat of war, while it still had problems with terrorism, it had established itself militarily as a nation with which none of its neighbors would even consider engaging in warfare.

Christopher's presentation lasted less than fifteen minutes. He offered to answer any questions, but none were asked. Apparently the prime minister wanted to get through this as quickly as possible.

"Ambassador Goodman," the prime minister said as soon as it was clear there were no questions, "I am sometimes praised for speaking candidly and other times criticized for being too blunt. Either way, it's the way I am. I hope you won't take offense. What you've said, though eloquent and well reasoned, has all been said before. And what was lacking before is lacking still, which is to say an apple will always lack the qualities that would make it an orange. You offer us an apple and make guarantees that we'll like it as much as an orange. We, on the other hand, are happy with the orange we have. We don't seek guarantees that we'll come away from the conference table satisfied with the agreements contained in a new treaty; we're satisfied with things as they are. We find no compelling cause to alter that position."

"I appreciate your position," Christopher answered, "and your frank response. I hope that you also appreciate frankness." Christopher now spoke quickly, allowing no opportunity for interruption. He was about to get to the real reason for this meeting. "What separates us on this issue is not the need for formal extension of agreements in the old treaty. I'm sure we both recognize the importance of the formalization of agreements for the protection of all concerned. Neither is there disagreement on the issues involved. Diplomatic immunity, transport of diplomatic packages without interference, and mutually held agreements of nonaggression are hardly controversial issues. What separates us, Mr. Prime Minister, is trust.

"In ancient times," Christopher continued, "such diplomatic logjams were broken by an exchange of gifts. I would not be so naïve," he said raising his hands, "as to believe that your assent could be bought in such a manner, and yet I recognize and honor the precedent." Christopher, who was already standing, walked briskly to the room's entrance and opened the large double doors in a bit of grand display, which was certain to be excused when it was learned what he had brought.

In the hallway outside, four unarmed Italian security guards stood watch around a wooden crate about the size of a small freezer that sat about three feet above the ground on a very sturdy-looking metal table with wheels. Christopher signaled to the one in charge, and the four men rolled the crate into the room and then left, closing the double doors behind them.

The crate was built of cedar and was itself a work of art, more a display case than a simple crate. The four sides were hinged at the bottom to allow the sides to fold down to display the contents. At the top middle of each side was a locking mechanism that held the sides securely shut. From his pocket Christopher took a set of four keys. "I do not ask for anything in return," he said, "for, with the giving of this gift I gain as well. *What* I gain is hope. Hope that the level of trust between us may grow and that we may, through that trust, come to achieve those things that of necessity governments must accomplish in order to conduct themselves in a manner consistent with the rule of law."

Christopher's appeal could be viewed in either of two ways: as an eloquent plea for something no reasonable person would refuse to grant, or as a bunch of flowery tripe. Either way, it gave Christopher a chance to state again what he was after. For if anything he had said thus far *was* tripe, it was that he was not asking anything in return for this gift. And if his last words were counted as tripe as well, it made no difference; what they were about to see was of such importance to the people of Israel that nothing the prime minister might possibly concede in a new treaty could compare to what they were about to gain.

Christopher took the keys and moved quickly to each of the four locks, opening them in the order directed in the letter that had been delivered to Alice Bernley and Robert Milner. As he opened the last lock, he moved back and it became clear just how special this crate really was. On a three-second delay after opening the fourth lock, eight pistons simultaneously slid through hydraulic cylinders, allowing the four sides of the crate to drop slowly open. The top was supported by the frame against which the four sides had been sealed. Except for Christopher, who was already standing, and Alice Bernley, who knew what was inside and so stood to get a better look, everyone else in the room was seated and it wasn't until the sides were halfway open that anyone caught a glimpse of the contents. As they did, all rose to their feet.

For a moment no one spoke as all stared in awe. And then there was a sound, almost a shriek from the back of the room. The younger of the high priest's two Levite attendants raised his hands as if to shield himself and ran from the room screaming something in Hebrew.

The reaction of the Levite made the prime minister catch himself. For a moment he had almost believed the artifact inside to be real. Now he was sure he knew better. "It is a very nice reproduction, Mr. Ambassador," the prime minister said to Christopher as he sat back down. He spoke loudly, casting his voice in the direction of his foreign minister and the high priest with the intent of bringing them back to reality. "I'm sure one of our *museums* will be very glad to accept it."

The prime minister's words had the effect he hoped for. The foreign minister, the high priest, and finally the high priest's remaining attendant all came to realize this must be a reproduction. There was certainly no possibility it was the real Ark of the Covenant. It couldn't be. The Ark had not been seen for thousands of years. Still, it seemed a singularly impressive reproduction. The craftsmanship and care that had gone into its creation were astonishing.

"I assure you, Mr. Prime Minister, it is indeed the Ark of the Covenant." The speaker was Alice Bernley. Her voice was confident and her words matter-of-fact. It was the first time she had spoken since the introductions. She knew her presence at the meeting was inappropriate; she represented no government, she was simply an observer, and now she was no longer an unobtrusive one. She didn't wait for an answer. She didn't really care what the prime minister thought. Her only interest was in seeing the Ark, and she moved closer to get a better look.

"Alice is correct, Mr. Prime Minister," Milner said.

The prime minister forced a laugh. "Mr. Milner, I don't doubt your sincerity and I appreciate whatever effort you went to in order to procure this for us, but this simply cannot be the true Ark of the Covenant."

Christopher had let the conversation go on without him long enough. "Mr. Prime Minister, I am well aware of the significance of this day in your nation's history. It is *Tisha B'Av*, a day of fasting, the very day on which history records that both your first and second Temples were destroyed. It was no accident that I chose today for this meeting. I chose it to offer your people a sign and symbol of hope for the future — that on this day of all days there is hope for all the people of the Earth, if only we will cooperate and work together. What you see here, Mr. Prime Minister," Christopher concluded, pointing with his open hand to the Ark, *'is the Ark of the Covenant. It's *not* a reproduction. It's *not* an imitation. It is real!"*

"Mr. Ambassador!" the prime minister said, raising his voice, "Do you take us for fools?"

"We can prove it's authentic," Christopher answered emphatically, but without raising his voice.

"How?" demanded the prime minister.

"By its contents."

The prime minister fell silent. The suggestion surprised him. Of course: they could look inside. The validation process would be so simple. So simple, in fact, that maybe there was something to the Italian ambassador's claim after all. "Okay," he said. "Then by all means, open it." Almost as soon as he said it, he realized his error. If this were the real Ark, opening it could be disastrous.

"Oh no, Mr. Prime Minister," Christopher said. "That's not exactly what I meant. The Ark must be handled with great care. It would not be wise for just anyone to open it. According to the Scriptures, many have died for mishandling the Ark."[71]

The Prime Minister knew all this, but the Italian had promised to prove the Ark's authenticity. He must have a plan to do so. "Then how shall we see inside?" he asked.

"I would urge that only the high priest should open it."

The prime minister looked at the high priest, who pondered the thought a moment and then nodded pensively, indicating that at least in general, Christopher was right.

"It does pose some problems," the high priest began in response to the question on the prime minister's face. He moved closer to the prime minister, Christopher, and Milner; leaving Bernley to examine the Ark unnoticed. It was all the same to her; she had no interest in what was being said. "If it truly is the Ark," the high priest continued, "then it should be opened only in the Temple. And yet if it's *not* the Ark, then it would be an abomination to place it in the Holy of Holies to be opened, especially since we're not sure what's inside. Perhaps it could be brought only as far as the porch of the Temple but not—"

Suddenly a blood-curdling cry filled the room. Behind them Alice Bernley's lifeless body collapsed, her head hitting the carpeted floor with a muffled thud.

"Alice!" Milner gasped as he ran to her.

"What happened?" shouted the prime minister.

The remaining attendant of the high priest looked as if he were in shock. "She touched the Ark," he quailed.

The Italian ambassador to Israel, Paulo D'Agostino, who had stayed quiet until this point, ran to the door and shouted for someone to call a doctor.

Robert Milner, finding no pulse, desperately began CPR. A state doctor assigned to the Knesset was there within seconds. He began emergency procedures even as Bernley was being put on a stretcher. Minutes later she was officially pronounced dead.

As her body was taken from the room, followed by a weeping Robert Milner, High Priest Chaim Levin quoted from the Bible: "The Lord's anger burned against Uzzah, and he struck him down because he had put his hand on the ark."[72]

The prime minister looked from the high priest to the Ark and then to the others in the room. The Levite flipped madly through his *Siddur*, the traditional prayer book containing prayers for almost every imaginable occasion. He could find nothing for this moment. Christopher went to the Ark and carefully closed up the sides of the wooden crate to prevent anyone else from suffering Bernley's fate.

Finally, the prime minister spoke. "The high priest will examine your Ark, Ambassador Goodman. And if it is, in fact, the Ark of the Lord, you will have the gratitude of the people of Israel. And we shall consider your treaty."

Chapter 24

The Elect

New York

Over dinner in Decker's apartment Christopher brought Decker up to date on his trip to Israel. "I know it's no one's fault," he said, "but it almost feels like the treaty was bought at the cost of Alice's life."

"It must have been terrible for Secretary Milner," Decker said.

Christopher nodded. "He stayed behind in Israel to take care of the arrangements for her funeral." He sighed and then returned to the subject of the treaty. "There are still some points to be ironed out after they verify the Ark's authenticity, but I'm hoping it can be signed in mid-September and go into effect by the end of the month to coincide with Rosh Hashana, the Jewish New Year."[73]

Decker didn't understand the significance, but neither did he question it.

"Has there been any movement in selecting a new secretary-general?" Christopher asked.

"The candidates and coalitions keep changing," Decker replied. "Fahd dropped out, which left Clark and Tanaka. Then they replaced Tanaka with Kruszkegin in order to pick up the votes of East and West Africa. It's a very strange dance to watch. Whoever is ultimately chosen needs the approval of every other member, so no one wants to risk stepping on anyone else's toes as they climb over each other, hoping to get to the top."

Christopher shook his head. "I'm glad I don't have to get involved in that."

"You may not say that when you hear the next part," Decker warned. "Ambassador Lee decided she couldn't support either candidate. That threw everything up in the air. The members supporting Kruszkegin made another switch."

"Please don't tell me they chose Albert Faure," Christopher groaned.

"Yep," Decker confirmed. "India decided to abstain rather than pick between Faure and Clark. So, it appears Faure now has six votes to Clark's three."

The phone rang. Decker answered and heard a familiar voice. It was Jackie Hansen. After her father's death, Christopher had hired Jackie as his chief of staff.

"Hi, Jackie," Decker said. "How are you?"

"Oh, I'm okay," she sighed. "Although Alice's death is terrible."

"Yeah. I was just talking to Christopher about that."

"May I speak to him?"

Decker handed Christopher the phone.

The reason for the call was an unexpected request for an appointment early the next morning. Two of the top generals from the World Peace Organization, Lieutenant General Robert McCoid, commanding general of the United Nations Military Observer Group in India and Pakistan (UNMOGIP), and Major General Alexander Duggan, recently assigned to WPO military headquarters in Brussels, Belgium, had arrived in New York without advance notice and had asked to meet with Christopher as early as possible. Such a request was quite unusual and for that very reason Christopher quickly agreed.

* * * * *

The two men were hardly noticed the next morning when they arrived to meet with Christopher, which was the way they wanted it. Jackie Hansen had come in early to give the office the illusion of activity at the early hour; the rest of the staff wouldn't arrive for some time, and it didn't seem right to have the generals greeted by an empty office. As a rule generals can be very serious people, but these two had something particularly sobering on their minds. They would have preferred to get right to the heart of the matter, but an issue of this magnitude had to be approached with great care.

'En Kerem, Israel

Scott Rosen sat alone at his kitchen table eating dinner. Outside, as the evening drew near, he could hear the voice of a neighbor calling her children in from their play. For a moment he thought back to his own childhood and the times he had spent playing with the children in his neighborhood. Often his grandfather, who had lived with them, would come out and throw a softball with him, or they would take a walk together through a nearby park and talk about what Scott was learning in Hebrew school or about the weather. Sometimes his grandfather would tell Scott about his grandmother. Scott had never known his grandmother and he could listen for hours to his grandfather talk about her.

The steam from Scott's chicken soup — his mother's recipe — rose before him and brought him back to the present, but as he looked around, he became aware he was not where he thought he was. This was his parents' house — the one they had owned in the United States when he was a boy. The table was set for five. Near his father's place sat a large brass plate with sprigs of parsley, a small dollop of horseradish, a larger dollop of an apple mixture called *charoseth*, the shank bone of a lamb, and a roasted egg. Next to it was another plate stacked with matzah. The table was obviously set for *pesach* — the Passover. Four of the five places were set for Scott, his parents, and his grandfather. The extra place, in accordance with tradition, was set for the prophet Elijah — should he choose to return from heaven and grace their table with his presence.

Scott blinked and gave his head a quick shake, and when that failed to have any effect on his circumstances, he tried rubbing his eyes.

"Scott, come in here and help your mother," said a woman's voice from the kitchen. It was his mother, Ilana Rosen. As he heard the voice, it was as though the memory of his adult life had been but a dream. He tried to recall what he had been thinking, but the memory was fading too fast. All he could latch onto were a few, small, disassociated parts: something about him going to Israel . . . about a war with Russia . . . but the rest of that memory was gone . . . something about his parents dying in some disaster, and . . . Scott shook his head again and brushed the thoughts away as the meaningless vestiges of a daydream and ran in to help his mother in the kitchen.

"Your father and grandfather will be home soon," Scott's mother said when he came into the kitchen. "We need to hurry with the preparations for Passover." Outside, the sun was setting, marking the beginning of the Passover *Shabbat,* or Sabbath. Ilana Rosen worked at the cork in the bottle of red wine. "Here," she said as she handed the bottle to Scott, "see what you can do with it." Scott gripped the bottle firmly and gave it a tug. The already-loosened cork came out easily. "Wonderful!" Ilana exclaimed as she clapped her hands once. "Now take it to the table but be careful not to spill any when you fill the glasses.

Scott poured the wine into the glasses for his parents and grandfather, gave himself half a glass, and then very carefully poured Elijah's cup. This was a very special wine glass, made of hand-cut leaded crystal — though this had always seemed strange to Scott because the glass was clear and he could see no lead in it. Still, it was a very special glass, taken out only for the Passover. For just an instant Scott seemed to have a memory of having broken this glass as he took it from the cupboard when he was fifteen. But that was silly; he was only eleven.

Behind him, Scott heard the front door open and turned to see his father and grandfather. Immediately, he stopped what he was doing, ran to his grandfather, and hugged him with all his might. How wonderful, he thought, to hug his grandfather again. As this thought occurred to him, he remembered a part of his daydream: His grandfather had died. Scott shuddered. But that was all a dream. Still, he took tremendous pleasure in feeling his grandfather's arms around him.

Soon the Passover meal, or *Seder,* began and progressed through each step as directed by the Haggadah, which serves as a sort of a Passover guide book with descriptions, recitations, and the words to songs sung at points during the meal. First was the *brechat haner,* or kindling of candles. Then came the *kiddush,* the first cup, which is the cup of blessing; the *urchatz,* which is the first of two ceremonial washings of hands; and the *karpas,* when parsley is dipped in saltwater to represent the tears Israel shed while slaves in Egypt and the saltwater of the Red Sea. Next was the *yachutz,* when the father takes the middle of three matzahs from a white cloth pouch called the *echad* (meaning unity, or one), breaks the matzah in half, places one half back in the echad and the other half in a separate linen covering. Later, as directed by the Haggadah, the father hides the broken piece of matzah, called the *Afikomen* (a

Greek word meaning "I have come") somewhere at the table. The youngest member of the family then must search until he finds it. When he does, he takes the Afikomen to his father to be redeemed for a gift or money. This had always been Scott's favorite part of the Seder. But he would have to wait until later in the dinner for that.

After the breaking of the middle piece of matzah came the *maggid*, the retelling of the story of Moses and the Passover, and then the *ma-nishtanah*, or four questions. Scott, as the youngest member of the family, would in his best Hebrew recite four questions about the Passover, each of which was answered in turn by his father. Then came the recitation of the ten plagues that had befallen the Egyptians. This part had always been funny to Scott because the Haggadah directs that, as each plague is named, those at the table are to stick a finger in their wine and sprinkle a drop on their plate.

Everything was the same as it had been every other year until the family sang one of the traditional Passover songs called 'Dayenu.' The song is a happy, upbeat piece sung in Hebrew, which names some of the things God did for the people of Israel. After each verse is the chorus, which consists entirely of repeating the one word, *dayenu*, which means, "We would have been satisfied." In English the words to the song would be:

> *If He had merely rescued us from Egypt,*
> *but had not punished the Egyptians,*
> *Dayenu (we would have been satisfied)*
>
> *If He had merely punished the Egyptians,*
> *but had not destroyed their gods,*
> *Dayenu*
>
> *If He had merely destroyed their gods,*
> *but had not slain their first born,*
> *Dayenu*

And so the song continues, each time stating that if God had only done what was mentioned in the previous verses and not done the next additional things, the singers — representing all of Israel — would have been satisfied.

As they sang the last verse, which speaks of the Temple, Scott's grandfather suddenly stopped singing and shouted, "No!"

Scott looked at him, confused.

"It's not true," his grandfather said. "Dayenu is a lie! We only fool ourselves."

"We only fool ourselves!" agreed Scott's parents, nodding.

This wasn't in the Haggadah. Something was wrong. And then without a sound, immediately there was another presence at the table. A man reached across in front of Scott and took the Afikomen, which had not yet been hidden, from beside Scott's father's plate. The man was sitting at the place set for Elijah. Scott recognized him at once as Rabbi Saul Cohen. But this made no sense at all. Scott didn't know anyone named Saul Cohen, except . . . except in that strange dream. How could he be here in Scott's home, sitting in the place of Elijah and drinking from Elijah's cup — the special cup that Scott's parents kept only for the Seder and from which no one was allowed to drink?

"Let us fool ourselves no longer," Cohen said.

It was nearly midnight when Scott found himself once again an adult and in his home in a suburb outside of Jerusalem. His soup was now hours cold and the only light was from a digital clock and a streetlight outside. He was exhausted. For a few moments he just sat there. If he had any thoughts that the events of the past few hours in his childhood home had all been a dream, they were quickly dispelled. Near him at the table, in the position that had been Elijah's place in his dream or vision, where he had seen Cohen, was a three-quarters-empty glass of wine. It was Elijah's cup, the one that had irreparably shattered when he took it from the cupboard when he was fifteen. Even in the subdued light he recognized it. Scott sat back into his chair and noticed the plate beneath his bowl sitting askew on the table before him. There was something under it. He raised the plate and found beneath it the Afikomen, hidden for him to find and redeem.

New York

French Ambassador Albert Faure's secretary showed Christopher Goodman into the office where Faure and his chief of staff awaited his arrival. "Good morning, Mr. Ambassador," Faure said, addressing Christopher. "Please come in."

"Thank you, Mr. Ambassador," Christopher responded. "I appreciate your seeing me on such short notice. I know how busy you must be."

"You said it was urgent."

"It is."

"You know my chief of staff, Mr. Poupardin?" Faure said as he went to sit at his desk.

"Yes, we've met," answered Christopher extending his hand.

Faure motioned toward two available chairs, and Christopher sat down. Poupardin remained standing. "Your message said this has to do with the World Peace Organization."

"Yes. As you know, the situation in Pakistan has become critical. Voluntary relief supplies simply aren't sufficient. And much of what is sent isn't reaching those who need it most. Hundreds are dying every day and thousands of others are nearing starvation. Cholera is claiming thousands more. Unless the UN responds quickly with sufficient quantities of food and medicine and the personnel to administer their distribution, millions could die."

As Christopher spoke, Faure and Poupardin exchanged a puzzled look. The look remained on Faure's face as he began to speak. "Let me assure you, Mr. Ambassador, that I am as concerned as you with the problems in that region. In fact, I met with the new ambassador from Pakistan on the matter just two weeks ago, along with Ambassador Gandhi. It is my sincere hope that more will be done, and soon. But," Faure continued as he wrinkled his brow still further in puzzlement, "isn't this an issue for ECOSOC and the Food and Agriculture Organization? I thought you wanted to see me about the WPO."

"The matter of supplying food to the region is, indeed, a matter for the FAO," Christopher acknowledged, "but the unrest that results from the food shortages is an issue that concerns the World Peace Organization." Faure let Christopher continue without responding. "As the previous chairman of the WPO, you are no doubt aware of the problems that have plagued WPO's supply lines over the last two years: $360 million worth of weapons and equipment lost in warehouse thefts; $14 million lost and two people killed in hijacked shipments; and another $841 million worth of equipment simply listed as unaccounted for."

Faure and Poupardin looked at each other in surprise. Faure had no idea losses had been that high. He didn't want to let on just how little he had kept track of such matters when he was chairman of WPO, but he had to ask. "Just a question of clarification," he began. "What percentages of those losses occurred during the time I was chairman; and how much has been reported in the last three and a half weeks, since you've been in charge?"

"Those figures reflect the losses as of six weeks *before* I took over as chairman of WPO," Christopher clarified.

"Oh," Faure responded. "I had no idea they were so high." Better to openly admit ignorance than acknowledge negligence, Faure decided. Christopher's expression showed neither surprise nor condemnation at Faure's admission.

"So, how does the situation in Pakistan fit into this?" Faure asked, wanting to move from the issue of his failures as quickly as possible.

"In the last twenty-four hours I have been presented with what I believe to be incontrovertible evidence that the director of the WPO, General Brooks, is personally responsible for at least 95 percent of the weapons and equipment missing from WPO."[74]

Faure and his chief of staff looked at each other again. It was beginning to appear as if they had some nonverbal means of communication and that neither would speak without first checking with his counterpart. "But why would General Brooks be stealing his own weapons?" Faure's chief of staff asked.

Christopher ignored the naiveté of the question. "According to those who made me aware of the situation, he has been selling the weapons to insurgent groups, sometimes for cash and other times in exchange for drugs that are in turn sold for cash."

"That's a very serious charge," said Poupardin, this time without stopping to check with Faure. "I assume you have evidence to back it up."

"I wouldn't make such a charge unless I could prove it," Christopher assured them.

Faure and Poupardin mulled this over for a moment, still without words. "Well," said Faure finally, "I suppose you'll be initiating an investigation."

"Time is of the essence, but I don't believe it's possible to carry out a full and complete investigation so long as General Brooks remains in command. That's why I came to you. I intend to ask the Security Council for approval to immediately place General Brooks on suspension, putting Lieutenant General McCoid in temporary command and granting me full authority over the agency until the matter is resolved. Before I do so, I thought that, as I have so recently taken over from you as chairman of WPO, professional courtesy required that I first inform you of my intentions and that I make you aware of the reasons for my actions."

It was obvious from the body language of both Faure and Poupardin that Christopher's plans didn't go well at all with their own. Faure thought fast. "I appreciate that," he said, his demeanor suddenly becoming far more congenial. "Actually, it's a good thing you came to me first. I'm afraid this might be the worst possible time for you to broach this subject with the Security Council."

"I don't believe putting it off is an option," answered Christopher. "The situation on the Indian-Pakistani border requires immediate action."

"Truly, I understand your concern, but . . . Well, let me bring you up to date on a few things." Faure got up and walked around his desk and sat in the chair next to Christopher. In his most altruistic tone, he explained. "As you know, the selection of a new secretary-general has been going on for several weeks now. And I'm sure it's no surprise to you that right now the choice seems to be between myself and Ambassador Clark of the United States. At the last vote, six regions voted for me, three voted for Ambassador Clark, and India abstained. The next vote is scheduled for Monday, four days from now. Nobody else knows it yet, but I've gotten a firm commitment of support from Ambassador Fahd and we're very close to reaching agreement with India. That will leave Ambassador Clark with only two votes: North and South America. With that kind of majority Clark will be forced to concede.

"Now, you're a reasonable man," Faure continued, carefully choosing his words. "You obviously realize that if you're right about what General Brooks has been doing with WPO resources, I had nothing to do with it. But some people, for their own purposes, might try to blame me for Brooks' actions." Faure's was at least a sin of omission; he had almost entirely ignored his responsibilities when he was chairman of the WPO and had handpicked Brooks, an old ally, when the previous commanding general retired.

"If this comes out right now," Faure continued, "Ambassador Clark is sure to try to use it to ruin my candidacy for secretary-general." Christopher was about to interrupt, but Faure held up his hand to stop him. "I understand," he said, "the urgency of getting to the bottom of this, but there must be some other way for you to conduct your investigation without bringing the matter to the Security Council just yet."

"Mr. Ambassador," Christopher responded, "anything less than a direct route will cost time and lives. Even if the Security Council grants my request immediately, it will take six to eight weeks to make the needed changes in personnel and to ensure that adequate equipment and supplies reach our troops."

"Now the last thing I want to do is to prevent you from doing what you feel you must," Faure assured him. "That's not the way I operate. And, besides, if I *should* be chosen as secretary-general, well, then — and of course no one can be sure — but you could very possibly replace me as primary on the Security Council." Faure wanted to point that out, just in case the possibility had escaped Christopher's attention. "The last thing I want is to cast a shadow on our future relationship. However," Faure paused, "with so much riding on this, for both of us and for the whole world, I simply suggest you explore every possible option before you do anything . . . imprudent."

Christopher's response was terse, but his voice showed no anger. "I *have*, Mr. Ambassador. And there is no option that will not cost lives."

Faure's frustration was growing harder for him to conceal. "Can it not wait at least four days?" he urged.

"I do not believe so."

Faure nodded understanding, then rose and returned to his desk chair. Looking at his chief of staff, he shook his head sadly.

"I think he's in league with the American ambassador," Poupardin interjected. "He may be an Italian citizen now, but he was born in America." Then Poupardin addressed Christopher directly. "Why else would you be so inflexible?"

"Gerard!" Faure said sternly, calling his chief of staff to heel.

"Please, forgive me, Ambassador Goodman," Poupardin sputtered with a well-practiced show of remorse.

"I, too, ask your forgiveness for Gerard's injudicious response," Faure said, but after pausing only briefly, continued, "But you must realize that many in Europe may see this the same way." Faure was getting desperate. Poupardin had intentionally made the charge so that Faure could first call him down and then make essentially the same charge while seeming entirely proper about it because the subject had already been broached. It was an effective "tag-team" ploy, and this wasn't the first time they had used it.

Then inspiration struck. "Consider this," Faure said. "Within a week I could be secretary-general and you could be the new primary member representing Europe. While General Brooks' actions are reprehensible — if indeed he is guilty as you charge — his removal will have little immediate impact on the problem. You said yourself, it will take six to eight weeks to make all the changes you want to make. And, in truth, even if you make all of these changes, it will have only limited impact on the delivery of food to the starving — and that, after all, is what each of us really want. If you will delay your action until after the vote on Monday, you have my word that I will apply the full influence and power of the position of secretary-general both to make the changes you feel are necessary for WPO and to ensure that adequate distribution of food reaches those who need it."

Christopher seemed to be considering Faure's suggestion. It had merit.

"Under those circumstances," Faure continued, "the changes you are seeking could be significantly expedited and instead of costing lives, lives could be saved."

After a moment, Christopher nodded agreement.

"Excellent!" Faure said.

"But," Christopher added, "in exchange, I want your assurance that regardless of the outcome of the vote on Monday, you will help get my request approved by the Security Council."

"Of course," Faure promised.

Poupardin apologized again for his comment and Christopher was soon on his way.

Poupardin and Faure breathed a sigh of relief.

"That man could be dangerous," Poupardin warned. "What would you have done if he had refused to wait?"

"Gerard, it is my destiny to be secretary-general. I would have done whatever was necessary."

Poupardin smiled to himself and walked around behind Faure's chair, and began to massage his shoulders.

"It seems the price of Robert Milner's support for my election to the Security Council may be higher than we first anticipated," Faure said. "We will have to keep a very close eye on that young man."

"Shall I call General Brooks?" Poupardin asked.

Faure took a deep breath and held it as he thought. "I suppose so," he said. "Tell him he had better get his house in order, and quickly if he wants to keep his job. But don't take too long with Brooks. We've got other things to worry about. We have to get a commitment from Ambassador Gandhi and try to soften up South America's support for Ambassador Clark. I think we have to assume that Ambassador Goodman won't wait, should another vote be required."

Four days later

Conditions on the Indian-Pakistani border did not improve over the next four days. Relief shipments were too few and too slow and the number of refugees attempting to cross the border continued to swell. To stem the tide, the Indian government increased their border guard sixfold. Reports spread of abusive treatment, torture, and even summary executions of refugees. The government of Pakistan responded by significantly increasing the number of its own troops.

In New York it was the day the Security Council would again try to choose a new secretary-general. It was also the end of the period Christopher promised to wait before requesting emergency authority over the WPO. In a corner of the anteroom outside the Security Council chamber, prior to the meeting, Christopher Goodman stood talking with Ambassador Gandhi about the situation in Pakistan. He had met with the Pakistani ambassador the previous evening, along with Saudi Ambassador Fahd, who was the primary from the Middle East.

Inside the chamber, Albert Faure and Gerard Poupardin went over a few last-minute preparations. At the outset, four days had seemed like plenty of time to get India's vote in line. As it turned out, Ambassador Gandhi insisted on a number of specific guarantees before he agreed to support Faure.

"I wish I felt better about Gandhi's vote," commented Poupardin. "I'm not sure we can trust him."

"I wouldn't worry about the Indian," Faure responded confidently. "He knows he'll never get anyone else to offer the guarantees I've made."

"I just saw him talking to Ambassador Goodman outside the chamber on my way in."

"Did you hear what they were talking about?"

"No, I didn't want to be too obvious."

"It's probably nothing." Faure concluded, waving it off.

"Probably, but Goodman was also seen last night with Ambassador Fahd."

A disquieted look flashed across Faure's face. "Why was I not told of this before?" he asked.

"I only just learned of it myself."

Faure considered this. "Go out there and see if you can hear what they're talking about. If you have to, try to join in. If they seem uncomfortable with you being there or if they change the subject, get back in here and let me know right away."

Poupardin got up to leave, but it was too late — the Indian ambassador and Christopher were just entering the room to take their places for the meeting. Ambassador Lee Yun-Mai of China called the meeting to order and soon the issue of the selection of the new secretary-general was brought to the floor. As expected, the nominees were Ambassador Jackson Clark of the United States and Ambassador Albert Faure of France. The vote was taken in the customary manner by a show of hands. Ambassador Lee called first for those supporting the nomination of Ambassador Clark. Immediately the Canadian Ambassador, representing the North American region, and the Ecuadorian Ambassador, representing the South American region raised their hands. It was just as Faure had planned; he could almost taste the victory he longed for. Then, slowly, without allowing his eyes to meet the stunned gape of Faure, the Saudi slipped his hand upward. From the corner of his eye, Faure's attention was drawn by his chief of staff, Gerard Poupardin. Even across the room the single word on his lips was as clear as a shout: "Goodman."

Faure muttered an epithet under his breath.

From Faure's left, the door to the Security Council chamber opened and a tall blonde woman in her early forties rushed in. Undistracted, Ambassador Lee noted the count of hands: Three regions supported the ambassador from the United States. Without pause she called for those supporting Ambassador Faure. What Faure saw only intensified his despondence. Including his own, only five hands were raised: Ambassadors Kruszkegin of Northern Asia and Lee of China had chosen to abstain. Unlike Ambassador Fahd, Kruszkegin looked directly at Faure while Lee counted. Filled with rage, Faure turned to face Christopher, but he wasn't there.

Quickly he scanned the room, to no avail. He looked back at Poupardin, who pointed to a corner of the great hall. There Christopher stood talking with Jackie Hansen, who had arrived during the vote with an urgent message. Faure's rage went unnoticed or at least unacknowledged by Christopher, who was listening to Jackie while quickly scanning the contents of the message she carried. Even as he read the dispatch, he turned resolutely toward Ambassador Lee.

Contrary to Faure's assumption, the actual reason for the shift in votes was that Ambassadors Fahd, Kruszkegin, and Lee had learned of the promises Faure had made in order to secure the vote of the Indian ambassador. Each felt it was contrary to their interest to have a secretary-general who was under such obligations. Lee and Kruszkegin's response was to abstain; Fahd chose instead to support the American for whom he had voted earlier. None of this would ever be known by Faure, and what was about to unfold would make him absolutely certain that the whole situation had been Christopher's doing.

Christopher finished reading the note and proceeded directly across the room to Ambassador Lee. Handing her the dispatch, he whispered something and she began reading. As she did,

Christopher went back to his seat and stood in order to be formally recognized. All eyes watched as she read. When she finished, she struck her gavel and declared that no consensus had yet been reached, and the selection of a new secretary-general would be postponed for two weeks. She then turned her eyes toward Christopher and said, "The chair recognizes the ambassador from Italy."

"Madam President," Christopher began, "as you have just read in the dispatch, within the last hour a contingent of approximately twenty-seven thousand Indian infantry have crossed their mutual border with Pakistan in apparent response to continued border crossings by Pakistani refugees. The soldiers appear to be headed toward the three UN relief camps. In response to the incursion, United Nations forces under the direction of Lieutenant General Robert McCoid have engaged the Indian forces."[75]

The room erupted. Members of the media tried to move to get a better shot of Christopher as he spoke; several staff personnel hurried from the room. Both the ambassador representing the Middle East and the ambassador from India attempted to be recognized by the chair. But Ambassador Lee refused, and Christopher continued.

"No report of casualties is yet available, but Indian troops in the area outnumber UN forces by six to one. General McCoid has ordered reinforcements into the area, but their arrival isn't expected for several hours and the General warns that such movement will weaken UN strength at other points along the border."

Christopher completed his report and then, exercising his right as an alternate member, proceeded to make his request to remove General Brooks and take over emergency authority of the WPO. It probably wouldn't have made any difference if he had made the request four days earlier. Still, these new events would make it much more complex and difficult to correct the problems.

Near Capernaum, Israel

Scott Rosen wasn't sure how he knew, but there was no doubt in his mind he was supposed to be here. On a grassy hill on the northern shore of the sea of Galilee, he sat and waited, though not at all sure of what he was waiting for. He had been there for nearly an hour, and now the sun was beginning to set. Though this area was known for its constant breeze, the air around him was dead calm; no ripple formed on the water; no leaf blew in the trees; no blade of grass wafted on the ground. It had been like this all day — both here and everywhere.[76]

The terrain around him formed a natural amphitheater with acoustic qualities that allowed a person on the hillside to clearly hear someone speaking near the shore. According to the local tour guides, Jesus had once taught his followers here.

When Scott arrived, there had been tourists on the slopes around him, but as evening set in, he was briefly left nearly alone. Now, over the last ten minutes, a steady flow of people, all men, had begun to fill the hillside. These were not tourists; there were no cameras, no binoculars, no yapping tour guides. In fact, though their number grew into the hundreds, and then thousands, no one spoke at all. Each man simply found a place and sat down.

Quickly, the trickle became a flood; now thousands arrived every minute. And still not an utterance was heard. Scott saw several people he knew. The first was Rabbi Eleazar ben David, to whom he had spoken a few days before. A few minutes later, he saw Joel — his hand and wrist in a cast. Scott cringed at the evidence of their last meeting, but when their eyes met, Joel smiled broadly. Scott smiled anxiously in return, and Joel sat down nearby.

In less than an hour there were more than a hundred thousand, and still no one spoke.[77] Soon there were no new arrivals and the crowd's attention turned toward some movement at the bottom of the hill. Two men stood up and one of them began to speak. His voice was deep and rich and measured. Scott was too far away to make out the man's features in the twilight surroundings, but the man could be heard clearly by all. Scott recognized the voice at once. It was Saul Cohen.

Standing at Cohen's side, the other man remained silent as he looked up at the crowd and thought back to that pivotal summer day when he and his brother and father had fished these very waters two thousand years before.

Chapter 25

Old Enemy, Old Friend

Sixteen months later

Northern Israel

The frigid, rain-starved ground cracked beneath the old man's weight as he marched with a steady, purposeful pace toward the west. Even his gaunt appearance and wind-dried skin didn't reveal the man's true age, which was thirty years beyond what anyone might have guessed. As he crested the top of a small hill, he could see, still some miles distant, the silhouette of the gold-domed Bahá'í temple above the terraced city of Haifa, which marked the end of his trek. After fourteen days in the Galilean wilderness, he looked forward to a few days of regular meals, human contact, and a much-needed bath. The empty pack on his back had been stuffed with dried fruit and nuts when he started. His canteens, now empty, had added considerable weight to his initial load two weeks earlier.

Bahá'í temple and gardens, Haifa, Israel

Normally, after a brief stay at the temple, he would be off again for another sojourn in the wilderness, but this time there were other tasks that required his attention. For more than a year, since the cremation of his close friend and confidante Alice Bernley, Robert Milner, the former assistant secretary-general of the United Nations, had lived the life of a monk, going off into the wilderness of Israel for up to three weeks at a time before returning to the civilization of the Bahá'í temple. His only companion was Tibetan Master Djwlij Kajm, Alice Bernley's former spirit guide. During Bernley's cremation Djwlij Kajm had come to Milner and spoken to him in Bernley's voice. Previously Milner had known the Tibetan only through Alice, his channel to the physical world. Now Milner knew him in a much more intimate way. Over the last sixteen months, Master Djwlij Kajm had taught and trained Milner for the work to be done. Finally, on this most recent journey, Milner had completed his spiritual apprenticeship and had received into himself a guiding spirit who united with his own.

The mission that called Robert Milner out of the desert would take him in a few days to the city of Jerusalem, where he would await the arrival of Christopher Goodman and Decker Hawthorne.

New York

"We cannot afford to compound our mistake by letting this go on any longer!" French Ambassador Albert Faure declared as he brought his fist down on the table before him. Nearby, Faure's chief of staff, Gerard Poupardin silently surveyed the reactions of the other Security Council members. From his perspective, the address seemed to be going well.

"It has been sixteen months since this body voted to give emergency authority to the ambassador from Italy to direct the operations of the World Peace Organization. We were assured by the ambassador at the time that he had substantial evidence to corroborate his charges of corruption by the WPO's commanding general. No doubt the decision to grant Ambassador Goodman the authority he sought came in part as a result of the incursion of Indian forces into Pakistan and in part because of our shared concern for the plight of the Pakistani refugees. And yet now, sixteen months later, we have still been given no concrete evidence of any complicity in, nor culpability for, any wrongdoing by General Brooks. Indeed, while the losses of military equipment have been reduced dramatically, there is every reason to believe that this has been solely due to new security measures, which General Brooks was in the process of implementing even as Ambassador Goodman stood before this body requesting emergency authority to place General Brooks on administrative leave, and then took direct control of the WPO into his own, far less experienced hands.

"And is it possible that a more pernicious hour could have been chosen by the Italian ambassador for making his charges, than at the very moment the incursion into Pakistan had begun? Charges whose only result was to undermine the structure of authority, incite derision, and weaken the *esprit de corps* of our forces when the leadership and guidance of General Brooks was most critically needed?

"And so, what began with the incursion of a few thousand troops has grown into what must be considered a full-fledged war between two peace-loving regions; a war that now threatens the borders of a third region, China. And ironically, though the drought that initially led to the war has now lessened, still the war goes on, prolonging the famine by diverting resources and energy into fighting instead of into planting crops."

For twenty-five minutes this went on. Faure held nothing back. His intent was to ascribe to Christopher as much responsibility for the war as he possibly could. All of his charges hinged on Christopher's inability to produce conclusive evidence proving General Brooks was responsible for the losses of equipment and supplies incurred by the WPO. In the four days Faure had bought for him, Brooks had done an excellent job of covering his tracks. As for Faure's charges that Christopher was responsible for the continued hostilities in the region, history suggested this was a dubious conclusion. Since 1947, when Pakistan was carved out of what had been northern India, the two countries had been at war four times and at the brink of war on a dozen other occasions. That a war, once started, would continue and expand was no more surprising than that a brush fire, once lit, would continue until it has consumed everything around it. And if there was a threat to China, it was a well-deserved one, for China's arms merchants had very quickly accepted the offers of hard currency from the Pakistani government. Even Faure's charge that Christopher had taken control of the WPO into his own hands had only a trace of truth. Although Christopher was consulted regularly on the WPO's efforts, from the outset he had placed Lieutenant General Robert McCoid in charge of operations.

Still, Faure was making his point convincingly. And it was an address for which much preparation had been made. In the weeks prior, General Brooks' supporters and later Brooks himself had heavily lobbied members of the Security Council and other influential UN members. Faure's goal was clearly not just to force a vote to restore General Brooks to power, but to so humiliate Christopher that he wouldn't be able to maintain his position as Europe's alternate to the Security Council. Key to the plan's success was that those who had engineered Christopher's election were apparently no longer a factor: Alice Bernley was dead and Robert Milner hadn't been seen since her funeral.

But removing Christopher was just one part of Faure's plan.

In the months following his unsuccessful bid to become secretary-general, every other imaginable candidate had been considered, but none could muster the unanimous support of the Council. Faure had seen to that. As the possibility of a consensus lessened, the rotating position of Security Council president had come to be treated as "Acting Secretary-General." Faure intended to keep it that way until he could make a renewed bid for the office himself, but it would have to come soon. If the status quo remained much longer, the Security Council might decide to make it a permanent arrangement. In the meantime, Faure was doing favors wherever he could, trying to appear as fair and as diplomatic as possible. Except, of course, to those like Christopher who got in his way.

In a slightly different category was Nikhil Gandhi. He was not inflexible, but his price was high. Faure would have preferred dealing with Gandhi's chief rival, Rajiv Advani, with whom he had gotten along well when they were both alternate members. Advani was now India's prime minister, but Faure had no doubt that he would prefer being India's primary, should anything *unfortunate* happen to Nikhil Gandhi.

Kruszkegin and Lee presented a bigger problem. Both had served many years with Secretary-General Jon Hansen, and both had grown to distrust Faure. The two spoke frequently, and both had come to the conclusion that Faure must never become secretary-general. If Faure was patient, he could hope that Lee would soon retire. Kruszkegin, however, would be around for at least five or six more years. And Faure was not that patient.

* * * * *

When the vote came, it was a humiliating loss for Christopher. In the end only Lee, Kruszkegin, and Ruiz of South America voted to sustain Christopher's emergency powers over the WPO. And in what was a too-obvious face-saving offer, Christopher was allowed to remain in his position as chairman and titular head of WPO, but General Brooks was restored to his position as commander of the actual forces.

Decker watched the vote from his office, then hurried across the street to the Italian Mission to be there when Christopher arrived.

"Did you see it?" Christopher asked as he stormed into his office. He was angry and distraught — two emotions he almost never displayed.

"I saw," Decker replied.

"The worst part is, it's my own fault!"

"Don't be so hard on yourself," Decker consoled. "Faure has been at this game a lot longer than you."

"He played me for a fool! How stupid could I have been to have told him I was going to launch an investigation of General Brooks? I must have been out of my mind!" Christopher steamed and paced and shook his head as he spoke.

"It may not have been the *smartest* thing," Decker allowed, "but your intention was to do the *right* thing. You simply gave Faure the benefit of the doubt."

"I gave him a lot more than that!" Christopher fumed. "I gave him four days of warning: four full days for General Brooks to destroy the evidence! I've made a total fool of myself and I've lost the respect of my peers! It's no wonder Gandhi and Fahd voted against me, but Tanaka and Howell?" he said, referring to the ambassadors from Japan and Canada. "Are they blind? Don't they see what Faure is? He would bring the whole world down around him if when it's all over he could stand at the top of the heap and declare himself king!"

Christopher finally sat down at this desk and began rocking slightly back and forth with the play in his chair as he thought. There was a long silence. Decker had no words to console him. Christopher's eyes still burned as he stood up again and stared out the window at the freezing rain falling on the street-blackened remains of an earlier snow. After another moment, he took a deep breath and sighed and his shoulders slumped in apparent acceptance of defeat. "I've got to get away for a while," he said at last.

Finally, Decker saw an opening. "Why don't you take a few days and stay at the house in Maryland?" he suggested. "I'll go with you." It had been nearly six months since Decker had visited his house in Derwood. He wanted to make sure that it, and more importantly the grave of Elizabeth, Hope, and Louisa, had been well cared for by the agency he had hired to look after the property.

"Thanks, Decker, but I want to get as far away from the UN as possible," Christopher replied quickly. "I'd go to Rome, but the reporters would be on me about this vote before I even hit the ground. And frankly, I can't face President Sabetini right now."

As Christopher continued to stare out the window, it occurred to Decker that there must be more to this than he was saying. As humiliating as the loss in the Security Council was, Christopher's distress seemed beyond proportion. "Is there something more you're not telling me?" Decker pressed after a moment.

Christopher looked at him, and Decker now recognized something he'd missed before: the anger was still there, but it was accompanied by a sense of foreboding and dread.

"I have this feeling," Christopher answered at last, "that something is about to go tragically wrong; that this war is just the beginning; that Faure and Brooks are going to be responsible for an unimaginable tragedy." He closed his eyes in a pained expression and took a deep breath. "And not only am I helpless to stop it," he continued, "but I may have actually facilitated it." He paused, but Decker had nothing to offer. For a very long moment, he stared out the window, then shaking his head, he concluded, "If it's as bad as I fear, I can't help but wonder if in the final analysis . . . my life was all a mistake."

"No!" Decker blurted, shocked at the emotional toll this was having on Christopher, and looking for the right words to respond.

"Am I wrong to want to get away?" Christopher asked, finally. "To leave it all behind?"

"Of course not!" Decker assured him, eager to move on from the question of whether his life had been a mistake. "Just say where, and we are outta here!"

Christopher heaved a heavy sigh without looking back from the window. "This is going to sound crazy," he said, shaking his head, "and I can't explain why, but for some reason I feel I need to go to Israel."

Chapter 26

The Reason for It All

Tel Aviv

The cold, arid, morning air of Tel Aviv quickly absorbed their moist breath as Decker and Christopher left the terminal at David Ben Gurion Airport and hailed a cab. With his attention on the taxi, Decker didn't notice the two uniformed police officers who ran out the door of the terminal behind them; nor did he pay any attention to the young man who stood off to their right talking to an older couple. Suddenly, though, it became impossible not to notice. The young man, seeing the police, quickly broke and ran along the edge of the sidewalk between Decker and the taxi. He got no farther. One of the policemen, anticipating his route of escape, grabbed the man and wrestled him to the ground right at the feet of Decker and Christopher. That's when Decker noticed the strange blood-red marks on the young man's forehead. For a moment Decker thought the man must be bleeding; as he looked more closely he realized it was writing, almost like finger painting, in Hebrew characters.

There was little time to think about it as the Palestinian taxi driver jumped smartly from his car, took their luggage, and threw it into the trunk. He didn't seem to even notice the police or their struggling captive.

"What's that all about?" Decker said, still watching the action as he and Christopher settled into the cab.

"You mean the man the police were arresting?" volunteered the driver as he pulled away from the curb.

Decker had just been thinking out loud and really didn't expect an answer. "Did you see what happened?" he asked. "I think he was just talking to those people."

"He's KDP," the driver replied. The reference meant nothing to Decker. "They're a cult. That's what they do: the talk to people — but it's *what* they talk about that's the problem. They know things about people — things people don't want them to know."

"You mean like identity theft?" Decker queried.

"No," the driver replied and then considered the question further. "Not that I know of anyway. . . . I think they're psychic," he continued, as he turned onto the highway. "They're not supposed to be around the airport or any of the tourist spots: It's bad for business. But that doesn't stop them."

The driver continued. "One day when I was fixing a flat tire — I had burned my hand the day before so I was having some trouble with the wrench — this guy came up, and without asking, just started helping me. When I looked up I saw he was KDP."

"He helped you change the tire?"

"Yeah. Sometimes they start out by doing you a favor, and they never take any money. After we finished with the tire, he told me how I had burned my hand — and he was right. He said that the reason I burned it was so he'd be able to help me, and then I'd listen to what he had to say. I don't know how he knew about my hand, but then he started telling me other things."

"Like what?" asked Decker.

"Well," the driver paused, clearly uncomfortable that he had talked himself into this corner. "Personal things. Things that people would rather not talk about."

"Oh," Decker said, not wanting to pry. "You said that *sometimes* they start out by doing you a favor. What about the rest of the time?"

"Well, my neighbor's wife decided to follow a KDP around, hoping to hear what he was saying to other people. But he turned around and called her by name and said she was a gossip and a liar and she had stolen from her employer." The driver laughed as he thought of it. "He went on and on. It was very funny. She ran away, but he followed her — along with a growing crowd. The farther she ran," he laughed again, "the more people that heard. It was like he was reading a list of everything she had ever done wrong. Finally, she begged him to stop, and he told her she should repent of her sins and believe in Yeshua, and that God would forgive her."

Decker chuckled and shook his head in amusement.

"Did you see the writing on his forehead?" the driver asked.

"Yeah," Decker replied. "It looked like Hebrew letters written in blood."

"They say it's from sacrificial lambs at the Temple. Whatever it is, it won't wash off. The police have tried. It's like a tattoo, I guess. They claim it was put on them by angels."

Decker smiled. "What are the letters?" he asked.

"It says Yahweh and Yeshua," the driver answered. "That's the Hebrew names for God and Jesus."[78]

"So they're a Christian cult," Decker posited.

"They claim they're Jewish *and* Christian," the driver explained.

"What will the police do to him?" Decker asked.

"Hold him a few days, rough him up, then let him go. They can't hold him long. If they arrested all the KDP, there'd be no room in their jails for us Palestinians."

"How many are there?"

"They say there's exactly one hundred and forty-four thousand, but I don't think anyone has actually counted. It was all very mysterious. One day nobody had even heard of the KDP, and the next day they were all over the place. It was about the same time as the drought started. Some people think they caused it."

By now Decker was leaning forward over the back of the front seat to facilitate the conversation. "Why are they called KDP?" he asked. "What does that mean?"

"That's the English. In Hebrew it's *Koof Dalet Pay*. The English is shorter, so most people just say KDP. It's their number: one hundred and forty-four thousand. In Hebrew the same characters are used for letters and numbers," explained the driver. "*Aleph, bet, gimel*: are like a, b, c, but they're also one, two, three. *Yud, kaph, lamed*: ten, twenty, thirty. *Qoph, reish, shin*: one hundred, two hundred, three hundred. So you can add the numbers of the letters in a word. Say you added the letters in the Hebrew word for . . . *bread*," he said pointing at a sign on a bakery; "that would equal, um . . ." he ran the math in his head, "seventy-eight," he concluded. "You can add up the letters in any word. Some of the Orthodox use it as a way to make decisions, like most people use horoscopes." He shrugged. "The Jews call it *gematria*. For example, I've heard that some rabbis say that to memorize something you should repeat it one hundred and one times, because when you subtract the value of the Hebrew word for *remember* from the value of the word *forget* the remainder is one hundred and one. A lot of

Jews think eighteen is lucky because the letters used to write *chai* or 'life' equal eighteen.

"Anyway, sometimes a number will actually be a word. Like, uh . . ." The driver tried to find an example as he looked at signs. "Okay," he said after a moment, "the characters used to write the number fourteen spell out the Hebrew word for *hand.* It turns out that the characters used to write the number one hundred and forty-four thousand are the same as the words *Koum Damah Patar* — KDP for short."

"What do the words mean in English?" Decker asked.

"Arise, shed tears, and be free," the driver answered. "Just nonsense, I guess. It's just an easy name for them."

Decker nodded as he considered.

"There's another strange thing about them," the driver added after a moment. "They claim that one of their leaders is the Christian apostle John."

Decker remembered seeing a short article online about someone in Israel claiming to be John. He was about to ask the driver to explain, when Christopher, who until this point had remained silent and distracted, suddenly asked "What?!" His voice seemed full of both surprise and dread.

"Crazy, huh?" the driver replied.

Christopher didn't pursue it, but sat back in his seat, greatly distressed. He squinted slightly and his eyes moved slowly but erratically, as though there was a very unpleasant scene running through his memory over and over again.

"Are you all right?" Decker whispered. Christopher didn't answer. For the next several minutes they rode in silence, but Decker could see there was a battle raging in Christopher's mind.

"I've just remembered something," Christopher answered finally. Decker wanted to ask, but this wasn't the place; it would have to wait until they reached the hotel.

A half hour later, the driver pulled up to the front door of the Ramada Renaissance Hotel — the same hotel where Decker and Tom Donafin had stayed twenty years earlier. As they got out of the car, Decker's thoughts were torn between his own memories of this place and wanting to know what Christopher had remembered in the cab. Though the distress had passed from Christopher's eyes, he was still deep in thought.

On the other side of the street, two men watched. On one was the mark of the KDP.

"There they are," the smaller of the two men said.

"I see them," answered the one with the mark.

"Let's do what we came for."

The one with the mark hesitated. "Maybe we should wait until they're separated."

"You're not changing your mind, are you, Scott?" the smaller one asked.

"No . . . I mean . . . I don't know; maybe I am, Joel. It all made so much sense before, but now that we're actually here . . ." Scott Rosen shook his head. "All of a sudden I'm not so sure we should do it."

Decker tipped the bellman who brought the luggage to their adjoining rooms and then closed the door. Finally, he and Christopher could talk openly. "What did you remember in the car?" he asked.

Christopher seemed to be searching for words. "It's about the crucifixion. It's . . ." He paused, and then started again. "Somehow, what the driver said about the Apostle John brought back a memory that . . . I don't know, maybe I've suppressed it. Maybe I don't want to remember."

"It won't help to ignore it," Decker prodded.

Christopher shrugged. "The Bible says it was Judas who betrayed Jesus." He shook his head. "But it wasn't Judas who betrayed me. He had a part in it, but he was deceived. I remember it clearly, but I still don't understand it. It was John. He was one of my closest friends and yet he betrayed me. John planned it, then got Judas to do his dirty work. He convinced Judas it was necessary to turn me over to the *Sanhedrin* — the Jewish officials — in order to fulfill an Old Testament prophecy. He convinced Judas that when the prophecy was fulfilled, I would call down the armies of God to defeat the Roman legions who occupied Israel, then I'd usher in a Jewish kingdom that would be like heaven on Earth."

Decker shook his head in amazement at this revelation.

"I can see it like it was yesterday. As I hung there on the cross, of all of the disciples, John was the only one who came.[79] I thought he had come to ask forgiveness. I called to him to come closer, and to my surprise, he admitted it freely, but without remorse; he almost seemed to boast about it. And poor Judas, overcome by guilt, hung himself.[80]

"John even bragged that forevermore Judas would be known as the betrayer of the Messiah, while he would be remembered as 'John the beloved.'

"I told him that despite his lack of repentance, I forgave him for what he had done to me, but that I couldn't forgive what he had done to Judas." Christopher dropped his head, almost weeping.

"But that was two thousand years ago," Decker argued. "How could John still be alive?"

"I don't know," Christopher answered. "But it's him."

Exhausted, Decker and Christopher decided to rest for a few hours before going out for the afternoon. Decker hadn't seen the Temple since it was completed and Christopher, who was well known in Israel as the man who had returned the Ark, had an open invitation from the high priest for a personal tour. Much of the Temple was forbidden to non-Jews, so they wouldn't be able to see all of it, but they would see more than most.

* * * * *

Decker awoke to find he had overslept by several hours. He knocked at the door between their two rooms, but there was no answer. Looking in, he found that Christopher was gone. On the mirror was a note.

> *Decker, I decided to let you sleep. I'm going to wander around the old city for a while. I need some time to think. Don't wait up if I'm late.*

He called Christopher's phone, but heard the ringing from Christopher's briefcase in the room. With no better options, he decided to wander as well. The old city wasn't that big — maybe he'd run into Christopher before dinner.

* * * * *

Walking down the narrow streets and still narrower alleyways of the city, Decker thought back to the time when he had been here with Tom Donafin. He was looking forward to sightseeing with Elizabeth and the girls when they arrived for Christmas vacation. But that had never happened. Decker sighed. Even after all these years, he thought of them every day and the pain was no less fresh.

By five o'clock the sun was setting and Decker found a small restaurant down an alley where he had dinner. Afterward he headed back to the hotel, but Christopher had still not returned, so he left the door between their rooms open and watched a movie until he fell asleep. When he awoke it was nearly six in the morning; Christopher had been gone all night.

Decker called the front desk, but the night clerk hadn't seen him. He tried the hotel restaurant, but it wasn't yet open. The hotel bar too was closed. He called the Italian embassy but the answer was the same. Short on alternatives, Decker went down to the hotel lobby to wait. Time went by very slowly as he sat there, but Decker felt he should wait until at least eight o'clock before calling the police.

Sensing a presence nearby, he looked up to find a man standing over him. He was significantly thinner than the last time Decker saw him, but he recognized him immediately. "Secretary Milner?" Decker said, surprised to see him there.

"Hello, Decker," Milner answered.

"Have you seen Christopher?" he demanded, rising to his feet.

"Christopher is safe," Milner assured him.

"Thank God! Where is he? I thought he might have been taken hostage by the—" Decker stopped himself.

"By the KDP?" Milner finished his sentence. Decker didn't respond, though he was surprised that Milner understood his concern. "No," Milner continued, "He's safe."

"Well, where is he?" Decker insisted.

Milner reached out and took hold of Decker's shoulder "Look," he said. Decker sensed a power flowing from Milner's hand and suddenly in his mind's eye, he could see Christopher. The scene was as clear to him as the room around them. Christopher was alone, sitting on a large stone in a rugged mountainous area, near the mouth of a cave.

"How?" Decker asked, and then, "Is he all right?"

"He's fine, though by now he's beginning to grow hungry." Milner removed his hand from Decker's shoulder and instantly the vision vanished.

"If you know where he is, take me to him."

"That's not possible," Milner said. "He must be alone. This is his time of preparation."

"Preparation for *what?*" Decker demanded.

"Mr. Hawthorne, the world is about to undergo a time such as it has never known before. A time so dark and bleak that the destruction of the Russian Federation and the Disaster will seem mild by comparison. Unfortunately, there's nothing anyone can do to prevent it. But if we as a species are to emerge and to go on to our ultimate destiny, it will happen only under Christopher's leadership. Without it, the world as we know it will utterly perish. What Christopher goes through now will prepare him for that hour."

Decker was too stunned to respond right away. In the back of his mind he had always wondered if there wasn't some greater purpose to Christopher's birth than simply being the product of Harry Goodman's experiment. After a moment he managed to ask, "What about the KDP?"

"Christopher is safe for now," Milner assured him, "though the KDP would relish an opportunity to interfere."

"Who are they?" Decker asked. "Are they a part of this?"

"They are," Milner confirmed. "As you know, when Alice Bernley was alive she headed the Lucius Trust near the UN. That location wasn't a coincidence. For years the Trust has been a sort of clearinghouse for thousands of what we call New Age groups from all around the world." Decker started to speak, but Milner anticipated his response and continued. "The New Age is not just some fad, some passing fancy. It's the result of a maturing, a ripening of the human species in preparation for the final and most glorious step in its evolution. Humanity is on the very threshold of an evolutionary stride that shall place us as far above our present state as we are now above the ants on the forest floor.

"The KDP were to have been the spearhead of that," Milner explained. "Unfortunately, at the very moment of their inception, their course was subverted by the two men who are now their leaders."

"One of whom is the Apostle John?" Decker asked.

"Yes," Milner confirmed. "And another man named Saul Cohen. You have heard of the strange ability of the KDP to look into a person's past?"

Decked nodded.

"Such an ability is only a faint precursor of what is to come. Soon that ability shall seem as no more than a firefly in the blazing sun. Such powers should be used to look into the hearts of others, to find those places where compassion is so desperately needed, and to offer comfort. Instead, under the leadership of John and Saul Cohen, the KDP uses their gift to dredge up what would be better left forgotten, to savagely claw open old wounds, and to call attention to human frailties. But that is the least of their monstrous inhumanity. Their powers for evil are far greater than any sane mind could imagine. This drought that Israel has suffered these past sixteen months is their work.[81] And they'll do far worse before it's over."

"Can anything be done to stop them?" Decker asked.

"By ourselves we can do nothing. The fate of the world and of humankind rests squarely on the shoulders of the one you have raised as your own son. But the conclusion is by no means foreordained. Let us hope he is equal to the task."

For a moment both men were silent. Decker struggled to contemplate the magnitude of what Milner had just told him. "How long will he have to stay out there?" Decker asked, finally.

"Forty days."

"Forty days!" Decker blurted loud enough for everyone in the lobby to hear.

"There's no other way," Milner answered, exaggerating his whisper to quiet Decker.

"But if he doesn't freeze or die of thirst first, he'll starve!"

"He'll do neither," Milner insisted, "though the preparation will certainly be brutal and unmerciful. Still, he's there by his own choice. No one could force this upon him. He has chosen it for himself. If he wishes, he can withdraw from the preparation at any time."

"Then I'll stay here and wait for him."

"You can do that," Milner allowed. "But there's nothing you can do here. If you return to New York, you may be able to provide essential information that will help Christopher in the decisions he must make when he returns."

Obviously there was no real choice; Decker had to return to the UN. But just as inescapable was his concern about leaving Christopher. He was sure Milner would never let any harm come to him; next to Decker, no one was closer to Christopher, and in some respects Milner was probably closer. Still, this could be a matter of life and death. Milner could see the worry in Decker's eyes and so once more placed his hand on Decker's shoulder. Suddenly, a peace such as he had never known swept over Decker and his anxiety vanished.

"Will you stay here?" Decker asked.

"I cannot go to him, but I will stay as close as I can."

Decker sighed and reluctantly nodded his approval. "I'll leave on the next available flight," he said. "But I'll be back in thirty-eight days — before Christopher returns."

"Good," Milner said. Decker shook Milner's hand firmly and Milner turned to leave but stopped before he had gone two steps. "Decker," he said as he turned back, "be particularly careful of Ambassador Faure."

"Is he a part of this somehow?" Decker asked.

"Not exactly," said Milner. "He's just a very ambitious man who will stop at nothing to become secretary-general. The forces who oppose us seek out such men as willing surrogates to accomplish their goals for them."

Chapter 27

Stopping at Nothing

New York

"Back so soon?" Jackie asked. "I expected you two to be gone for at least a week." Decker showed himself into Christopher's office and signaled for Jackie to follow. "What's up?" she asked after closing the door. "Where's Christopher?"

"He's still in Israel," Decker answered. "He'll be there about a month and a half." Decker was hoping to make this explanation as simple as possible, but it wasn't going to be easy.

"A month and a half!" Jackie exploded. "He can't do that! He's got things to do, meetings to attend, speaking engagements." Decker held up his hands to cut Jackie off, but she had never yielded to that ploy in the past, and she wouldn't now. "I'll just call him!" she said.

"He doesn't have his phone."

Jackie gave a disapproving look. "What's the number at his hotel?" she insisted.

"He's not at a hotel—"

"Fine. What's the number where he's staying?"

"Jackie, it's just not possible to reach him."

"Well, I'll—"

"Jackie, stop! Please, just wait a minute." She crossed her arms and stopped talking. Decker seized the opportunity. "We found Robert Milner."

Reflexively, Jackie relaxed her aggressive posture and dropped back, sitting against the edge of Christopher's desk. "Is he all right?" she asked. "Is he alive?" After going missing for sixteen months, nothing could be taken for granted.

"He's fine. He looks just fine," Decker assured her. The news had the disarming effect he was hoping for. "Christopher is with him." It was a little less than the truth, but a lot easier to explain.

"They must be staying somewhere," Jackie recovered.

"Yes, of course. But there's no phone and there's no way to reach them."

This understandably made no sense to Jackie. "You mean they're camping out or something?" she asked, offering the only suggestion she could think of.

"Well, yes. In a manner of speaking, I guess you could put it that way."

"But it's the middle of winter. They'll freeze!"

Decker had run out of simple explanations. "Look, they'll be fine. You know how I feel about Christopher; he's like my own son, the only family I've had since the Disaster. I wouldn't leave him there unless I was sure he'd be all right." As he finished, he realized his words had been as much to reassure himself as they were to convince Jackie.

"But why didn't he at least call?" she pressed.

"There just wasn't an opportunity. Look, I don't really understand it either. Milner said it all had to do with some New Age stuff."

"Oh," Jackie said, not as though she now understood, but rather as though suddenly she no longer needed to. "Well, then . . . um." Jackie took a breath. "Then I guess I'd better get to work canceling Christopher's appointments."

Decker was dumbfounded by Jackie's sudden change of attitude, but was glad he didn't need to explain any further. Now at least he could concentrate on his own anxiety about leaving Christopher in the first place — not a very comforting accomplishment, he realized.

"Jackie, there's one other thing," Decker added, "something I need your help with. When Milner and Christopher are finished with whatever they're doing in Israel, I'm supposed to meet them there and brief Christopher on everything that's happened at the UN while he's been gone. He's especially interested in any information on Ambassador Faure's activities. I know you've got friends in nearly every office—"

"Not in Faure's," Jackie interrupted.

"What about through the Lucius Trust?" Decker suggested.

"Faure doesn't let anyone from his office associate with the Trust."

"You're kidding! It's against international human rights and labor laws to bar free association."

"He doesn't exactly prohibit it," Jackie explained. "It's more a matter of very careful hiring. Secretary Milner looked into it a few years back and apparently didn't think we could prove anything."

"Too bad," Decker sighed.

"I'll do what I can," Jackie promised.

"Great," he said. "But be careful how you go about it. It could be very damaging if any of this gets back to Faure."

* * * * *

Two days later Jackie came up with a contact, a friend from the Lucius Trust who had a friend who was a low-level staffer in Faure's office. This meant that anything the staffer provided would be limited to what was said openly around the office. The first piece of information to emerge was simply a vague indication that Faure was leaning hard on General Brooks to end the war as swiftly as possible — hardly a major news item. But it did help explain Brooks' action a week later when he issued an ultimatum to Chinese arms merchants to immediately cease sales to the combatants. The move didn't set well with Ambassador Fahd, the Middle East primary. The Chinese arms were not going, in the generic sense, to the 'combatants,' as Brooks described it, but only to Pakistan, a country in Fahd's region. Stopping the sale of Chinese weapons would only benefit India.

Fahd attempted to get the Security Council to condemn Brook's ultimatum but he was supported only by the representatives of East and West Africa. The Security Council was reluctant to interfere with the specific actions of the World Peace Organization. They saw their role as one of setting policy, not regulating tactics. As long as General Brooks' actions stayed within the conventions established in the WPO charter, the Security Council could be expected not to interfere.

China abstained from the vote. Ambassador Lee felt that voting to condemn General Brooks would be seen as tentative approval of the arms sales from her country. China's official position had always been that while it opposed the sale of weapons, it was not willing to interfere with the free trade of its citizens. Ambassador Lee, however, did proceed quickly and forcefully to prohibit Brooks from crossing into Chinese territory to enforce his ultimatum. Any efforts to interdict the flow of military equipment from China would have to be from the Pakistani side of the border. Her motion passed nine to one, with only India opposing the directive.

Coincidentally, it was to be one of Ambassador Lee's final acts as a member of the Security Council. Two days later, while taking her regular early morning walk, Ambassador Lee was struck by a hit-and-run driver in a stolen car. She died on the way to the hospital. Following her death, the Security Council voted to take a two-week recess to allow China to select a replacement. A memorial service was held for Lee in the Hall of the General Assembly before her body was returned to China for burial.

Two weeks later

"Welcome back, Mr. Ambassador."

"Thank you, Gerard," Ambassador Faure responded as he gave Pourpardin his overcoat to hang up.

"How was your flight?"

"Too long. We sat at DeGaulle Airport for more than an hour before we even got off the ground." Faure sat down at his desk and began flipping through a short, neatly stacked pile of papers. "What's the news from General Brooks?" he asked his chief of staff without looking up.

"Things appear to be going well," Poupardin reported. "As you predicted, the interdiction of Chinese arms into Pakistan has resulted in a distinct advantage for the Indian forces. General Brooks estimates that it will probably take another few weeks before we see the full effect, but he thinks we can look forward to a swift resolution of the conflict. More important," Poupardin asserted, "we can expect India to support your bid to become secretary-general. I think Ambassador Gandhi will find it difficult indeed to vote against you, under the circumstances."

"Good. And our relations with Ambassador Fahd? Anything new there?"

"No. You're scheduled to have lunch with him tomorrow, so you should get a clear reading on his thoughts then. So far there has been no indication that he holds you responsible for General

Brooks' actions. I think your support of Ambassador Lee's motion to prohibit UN forces from entering Chinese territory helped delineate you from Brooks in the minds of most of the other members."

Faure didn't respond; he was distracted from the conversation by a document in the stack of papers. Poupardin knew the look and waited silently as Faure examined it. After a moment, Faure began to glance through the rest of the accumulated stack and picked up the conversation where it had left off. "Yes," he said, smiling. "That couldn't have worked better if I had planned it."

"A few more fortuitous circumstances like that and you might have gotten China's support without—"

"Fortune is a very uncertain ally, Gerard," Faure chided. "Besides, we don't have the luxury of waiting for fortune. Mark my words, if a new secretary-general isn't chosen within six months, the Security Council will vote to do away with the position altogether and have the responsibilities permanently rotate among the Council. We must make our own fortune." Poupardin nodded in agreement. "What about Lee's replacement?" Faure asked.

"You're scheduled for dinner with the new Chinese ambassador tomorrow night. I've prepared a briefing for you." Poupardin handed him a packet. "I don't think you'll find anything outrageous there. Our intelligence indicates he's a pragmatist. His main criterion in selecting a new secretary-general is simply that the candidate be willing to give a fair hearing to China's position."

"Excellent," Faure said, as he put the papers back in a pile on his desk. "Then I'd say we made a pretty good trade for Ambassador Lee."

"Yes, sir."

"What about Kruszkegin?"

"The consultants are watching his schedule closely for the right opportunity."

"Be sure you clear it with me before you authorize any specific action. We can't afford any mistakes."

* * * * *

Ambassador Lee's replacement was a much younger man in his early fifties. His stamina for the responsibilities of his new office would soon be tested. As the Security Council reconvened, they tasted the first bitter fruits of General Brooks' ultimatum and the resulting blockade at the Pakistan-China border. Forced to take up fixed positions to enforce the blockade, UN troops had quickly become the targets of sniper fire and guerrilla attacks by Pakistanis. The Pakistani president condemned the attacks, stating that the snipers were independents, not associated with the Pakistani army. He also took the opportunity to reiterate that because the blockade was not in Pakistan's interest, the UN forces were not acting within their charter or in accordance with the original invitation to place troops within its borders. He went on to explain through clenched teeth that because all available Pakistani forces were engaged elsewhere, there was really very little he could do about the guerrilla attacks.

Far worse than all of this, however, were the threats of a rogue Pakistani militia called the Islamic Guard. According to the reports, the Guard, fearing that the war would soon swing in India's favor, had planted nuclear devices in eight major Indian cities. Though it seemed unlikely the Guard could have acquired nuclear weapons, the magnitude of the threat compelled the Security Council to take them seriously. The Guard's demands were straightforward enough. First, all UN and Indian forces must leave Pakistan, and second, for good measure, India must surrender the long-disputed Jammu-Kashmir province to Pakistani control. Indian Prime Minister Rajiv Advani would consider neither demand, and thus far was satisfied to hurl insults and counter-threats.

Chapter 28

The Power Within Him —
The Power Within Us All

The wilderness of Israel

It was just after dawn. Robert Milner acted as navigator while Decker drove the rented jeep through the mountain pass on their way to meet Christopher. In the jeep, Decker had brought food, water, and a first-aid kit. His thoughts alternated between worry about Christopher's condition and anticipation of what Robert Milner had told him forty days earlier. The barren countryside brought back memories of Decker's own wilderness experience eighteen years earlier, when he and Tom Donafin had made their way through Lebanon toward Israel before being rescued by Jon Hansen. He recalled the powerful shift of his emotions in that moment as he lay on the ground, tangled in barbed wire, with three rifles pointed at his head, expecting to be shot, and then suddenly recognizing the UN emblems on the soldiers' helmets and realizing that he and Tom were safe.

In the past, when Decker had recalled that moment, he'd thought of it as just another case of being in the right place at the right time. Now he couldn't help but believe it was much more. Had it not happened, he wouldn't have met Jon Hansen, and he surely would never have become his press secretary. And had Decker not worked for Hansen, who later became secretary-general, then Christopher wouldn't have had the opportunities he did to work in the UN and later to head a major UN agency and then become Italy's ambassador serving on the Security Council. Surely this was more than chance.

It occurred to him that this chain of events hadn't started on that road in Lebanon. There was the destruction of the Wailing Wall, and then he and Tom were taken hostage. And even before that, had he not gone to Turin, he certainly never would have been called by Professor Harry Goodman on that cold November night to come to Los Angeles to see what Goodman had discovered on the Shroud.

As he continued to think through the chain of events that had brought him to this point, he tried to find the single weakest link, the seemingly least important circumstance that, had it not occurred, would have averted any of the later events.

"Some things we must assign to fate," Robert Milner said, breaking the silence. It was as though he had been listening to Decker's thoughts.

"Uh . . . yeah, I guess so," Decker answered.

The days leading up to his return to Israel had been some of the most anxious of Decker's life. At times he could barely concentrate on his work as he counted the days until Christopher's return and anticipated what would follow. Milner had talked about a time so dark and bleak that the destruction of the Russian Federation and the Disaster would seem mild by comparison. Somehow the horror that might otherwise have consumed Decker at such a thought was mitigated by the hope that Milner also foresaw. Certainly, to this point, nothing cataclysmic had occurred, though the unrest in India and Pakistan might well foreshadow such events. Decker realized he would have to accept the bad along with the good. He just didn't want to dwell on it, especially if, as Milner indicated, such events were inevitable.

Ahead on the trail, a shapeless form began to take on definition. Had Decker noticed it before, he would have thought it was a bush or a tree stump or perhaps an animal, but until this moment it had blended so well into the background that it seemed an inseparable part of its surroundings.

"There he is," Milner said.

Decker pressed a little harder on the gas pedal. As they got closer, he began to wonder again in what condition they would find Christopher. In New York, Christopher had told him he was beginning to wonder whether in the final analysis his life had been a mistake. Now, just forty days later, he was — as Milner averred — the man who would lead mankind into "the final and most glorious step in its evolution."

In another moment they could see him clearly. His coat and clothes were dirty and tattered. He looked thin but strong. Over the forty days his hair had grown over his ears and he now had a full beard. When Decker saw his face, he was startled for a moment by the astounding resemblance to the face on the Shroud. One thing, however, was very obviously different. The face on the Shroud was peaceful and accepting in death. On Christopher's face was the look of a man driven to achieve his mission.

Milner was first out of the jeep. He ran to Christopher and embraced him, patting him on the back and causing a small cloud of dust to rise from his clothes. Christopher then went to Decker, who reached out his hand, which Christopher refused, hugging him as well. He smelled awful, but Decker didn't care.

"Are you all right?" Decker asked.

"Yes, yes. I'm fine." Then turning slightly to address both Decker and Milner, he continued. "It's all clear now. It was all part of the plan. I've spoken with my father. He wants me to finish the task."

"You mean . . . God?" Decker asked. "You talked with God?"

Christopher nodded. "He wants me to complete the mission I began two thousand years ago. And I need your help, both of you."

Decker felt as though he was standing on the crest of a great tsunami. Suddenly his life held more meaning than he'd ever imagined possible. He had believed what Milner told him about Christopher's destiny; if he hadn't, he never would have left Christopher alone in the desert. But then it had all been cerebral. Now he was hearing it from Christopher's own lips. This was a turning point, not only in the lives of these three men, but of time itself. Just as the coming of Christ had divided time between B.C. and A.D., this too would be a line of demarcation from which all else would be measured. This undoubtedly *was* the birth of a New Age. Decker only wished Elizabeth were alive to share it with him.

"What can we do?" Decker asked.

"We must return to New York immediately," Christopher answered. "Millions of lives are at stake."

* * * * *

Before leaving New York, Decker had arranged for the loan of a private jet from David Bragford, telling him it was for Milner. As planned, the jet and crew were waiting at Ben Gurion Airport when they arrived. Decker had brought clothes and a shaving kit for Christopher, but though he eagerly took advantage of the shower on Bragford's plane and welcomed the clean clothing, Christopher decided to keep the beard.

Three hours into the flight, one of the crew members came into the cabin, obviously distraught. "What is it?" Decker asked.

"The captain has just picked up a report on the radio," he said. "Apparently, the war in India has just gone nuclear."

"We're too late," Christopher whispered to himself as he let his head fall into his open hands.

The crewman continued, "The Islamic Guard have detonated two nuclear bombs in New Delhi. Millions are feared dead."

For a long moment they sat in stunned silence, then Decker turned to Milner. "This is what you were talking about in Jerusalem, isn't it?"

"Only the beginning," Milner said sadly as he reached over and hit the remote control to turn on the satellite television.

Immediately the screen showed the mushroom cloud of the first atomic bomb set off in New Delhi. The billowing cloud of debris seemed to roll back the sky like an immense scroll of ancient tattered parchment.[82] Two days after the Pakistani Islamic Guard first warned of hidden nuclear weapons, the news network had set up remote cameras outside the targeted cities just in case the Guard carried out its threats. Even from ten miles away, the camera began to shake violently as the earth trembled from the blast's awesome shock wave.[83] Several hundred yards in front of the camera a small two-story building shuddered with the quake and then collapsed. An instant later a bright flash on the screen marked the second explosion.

"That was the scene approximately one hour ago," the network anchor said, his voice registering his horror, "as two atomic blasts, set off by the Pakistani Islamic Guard, rocked the Indian subcontinent. According to sources close to the Islamic Guard, leaders of the Guard were convinced that UN special forces were close to locating the bombs, which would have left little to prevent India from expanding its invasion of Pakistan.

"Within minutes of the explosions, the Pakistani government strongly condemned the action by the Guard who, they repeated, are rogue forces *not* associated with Pakistan's government. But by then India had already retaliated, launching two nuclear-tipped missiles on Pakistan. Apparently prepared for such a response from

India, China immediately launched interceptors, which successfully brought down the Indian missiles before they could reach their targets.

"Prior to that launch, China had attempted to maintain a neutral position in the long-running conflict between its neighbors. That neutrality was frequently called into question, however, because of Chinese arms merchants who served as the main source of weaponry for Pakistan."

As Christopher, Decker, and Milner watched, new information poured in at an incredible rate. In a matter of only a few hours, the entire war was unfolding. In response to China's action, India launched a conventional air attack on the Chinese interceptor bases, while simultaneously launching five additional missiles on Pakistan. Three were intercepted; two reached their targets.

Pakistan then responded to India's attack by launching a volley of its own nuclear weapons and within minutes, the Pakistani Islamic Guard set off the six remaining bombs they had planted in Indian cities.

In a temporary lull, the picture switched to a satellite feed from a camera mounted on top of a remote-control all-terrain rover, which showed the first horrifying scenes from the suburban areas of New Delhi. Fire was everywhere. Rubble filled the streets. The sky was filled with thick black smoke and radioactive fallout, which blocked the setting sun as though it were covered by a loosely woven black cloth.[84] Scattered around the landscape were hundreds of bodies. Immediately in front of the vehicle, the mostly nude body of a young Indian woman lay twisted in the street. All but a few scraps of her clothing had been burned away. On the less charred parts of her body, where some skin remained, the flowered pattern of the sari she had been wearing was seared into her flesh like a tattoo.

Sitting on the street beside her, a girl, three or four years old, looked up at the rover. The bombs had not been so merciful to her as to her mother; she might languish for hours before life released its grip on her. For a moment the camera dwelled there, studying the numerous open blisters that covered her skin.

Christopher turned away. "I could have prevented this," he said. It took a moment for the statement to sink through the horror and register with Decker.

"There's nothing you could have done," Decker assured him.

"But there *is*," Christopher insisted. "I told you Faure was going to do something that would lead to an unimaginable catastrophe, and that I was helpless to stop it." Christopher paused. "But it wasn't true. There was one thing I could have done. And now, because I hesitated, millions have been killed and millions more will die." Christopher shook his head. "Even after the war is over, the fallout and radiation will continue to kill. And unless the UN acts to provide immediate relief, millions more could die of starvation and disease from the rotting corpses."

"Faure may not have *intended* this," Milner interjected, "but his ceaseless quest for power, his criminal neglect of the WPO, and his appointment of corrupt men like General Brooks created the environment where this war could happen. Then in his lust to become secretary-general, he pushed the combatants over the edge.

"It was Faure who put Brooks back in control," Milner continued, "and it was Faure who directed him to issue the ultimatum to the Chinese. He was hoping to end the war quickly in India's favor. In return, he expected to gain Nikhil Gandhi's support for his bid to become secretary-general. When the Islamic Guard complicated things, General Brooks assured Faure that the Guard couldn't possibly have nuclear weapons."

"But Faure knew the risk he was taking," Christopher declared. "If Brooks was right, then by continuing to enforce the ultimatum, he would call the Guard's bluff and bring the war to a quick close. But if the Brooks was wrong, Faure was willing to risk a nuclear exchange because it would so destabilize India that Gandhi would return to rebuild his country, and Rajiv Advani would replace him as primary on the Security Council. Either way, Faure calculated that he'd benefit."

Decker couldn't believe that even Faure would be willing to sacrifice so many lives. "Christopher, are you sure about all this?" he pressed.

He nodded sadly.

"Christopher is correct," Milner affirmed.

"Faure is also responsible for the murder of Ambassador Lee," Christopher added. "And he's planning the assassination of Yuri Kruszkegin."

While this was a shocking charge, it seemed to Decker to point to a flaw in what Christopher and Milner were saying. "But then why didn't Faure just kill Gandhi, instead of risking a nuclear war?" Decker argued.

Milner answered. "The death of Ambassador Lee was believed to be an accident," he said. "If Kruszkegin died, questions would arise, but ultimately most would conclude it was a tragic coincidence. Even those who believed there was a connection would have no reason to accuse Faure. But no one would believe that the death of three primary members was just a fluke. Especially if soon after that, Faure became secretary-general precisely because of the replacement of those three members. Besides, killing Gandhi would still leave Faure the problems in India and Pakistan to deal with."

Decker was still not convinced, but neither had he gotten an answer to his previous question. "Even assuming all of this is true," he began, directing his query to Christopher, "what could you possibly have done to stop it?"

"In the third chapter of Ecclesiastes," Christopher answered, "King Solomon wrote: There is a time for everything: a time to be born and a time to die, a time to plant and a time to reap; a time to heal . . . and a time to kill."[85]

Decker looked back and forth from Christopher to Milner and then back to the screen. As the camera panned the devastation, in the distance, where the smoke and radioactive cloud had not yet entirely shrouded the Earth, the moon rose above the horizon, glowing blood red through the desecrated sky.[86]

* * * * *

It was another two hours before their plane landed in New York. Immediately, they sped to the United Nations, where the Security Council was meeting in closed session. As night fell in the east, the war continued to spread. Nuclear warheads dropped like overripe fruit, appearing as falling stars in the night sky.[87] The destruction spread six hundred miles into China and to the south, nearly as far as Hyderabad, India. Those who survived took shelter underground, in caves, in crags under rocks, or wherever protection from fallout might be found.[88] West and north of

Pakistan, the people of Afghanistan, southeastern Iran, and southern Tajikistan gathered their families and all they could carry on their backs, and beat a hurried path away from the war. In just days the local weather patterns would fill their fields, rivers, and streams with toxic fallout.

Pakistan was now little more than an open grave. India's arsenal was completely spent. What was left of its army survived in small clusters that were cut off from all command and control. Most would die soon from radiation. China was the only participant still in control of its military and it had no interest in going any further with the war.

In the few hours it took to fly from Israel to New York, the war had begun and ended. The suffering and death, however, had just begun. The final estimate of the number killed would exceed four hundred and twenty million. There were no winners.

* * * * *

Christopher reached the door of the Security Council Chamber and burst through, followed closely by Decker and Milner. For a moment the members just stared at the intruders. Everyone knew Decker, but they had not seen Milner in a year and a half, and the change in Christopher was more than the beard; his whole demeanor had changed. When he recognized Christopher, Gerard Poupardin looked over at another staffer and laughed, "Who does he think he is? Jesus Christ?"

Christopher seized the opportunity provided by the startled silence. "Mr. President," Christopher said, addressing the Canadian ambassador who was the acting president of the Council. "Though I have no desire to disrupt the urgent business of this body in its goal of providing relief to the peoples of India, Pakistan, China, and the surrounding countries, there is one among us who is not fit to cast his vote among an assembly of thieves, much less this august body!"

"You're out of order!" Faure shouted as he jumped to his feet. "Mr. President, the alternate from Europe is out of order." The acting president reached for his gavel, but froze at the sheer power of Christopher's glance.

"Ladies and Gentlemen of the Security Council—" Christopher continued.

"You're out of order!" Faure shouted again. Christopher looked at Faure. Suddenly and inexplicably Faure fell back into his chair, silent.

Christopher continued. "Seldom in history can the cause of a war be traced to one man. On this occasion, it can be. One man sitting among you bears nearly the total burden of guilt for this senseless war. That man is the ambassador from France, Albert Faure."

Faure struggled to his feet. "That's a lie!" he shouted.

Christopher quickly stated his charges.

"Lies! All lies!" Faure shouted in reply to each. "Mr. President, this outrage has gone on long enough. Ambassador Goodman has obviously gone completely mad." Faure could feel his strength returning. "I insist that he be restrained and removed from this chamber and that—" Faure once again fell silent as Christopher turned and pointed at him.

"Confess," Christopher said in a quiet but powerful voice.

Faure stared for a long moment in disbelief. The Italian ambassador really had gone mad. Suddenly he began to laugh out loud.

"Confess!" Christopher demanded again.

Abruptly, Faure's laughter ceased. The sudden panic in his eyes couldn't begin to reveal the magnitude of his torment. Without warning it seemed as though the blood in his veins was turning to acid. His whole body was on fire from the inside.

"Confess!" Christopher thundered.

Faure looked in Christopher's eyes and fully understood the source of his sudden anguish. He staggered and caught himself on the table. Blood began to trickle from his mouth as he bit through the tender flesh of his lower lip; his jaw clenched uncontrollably like a vice as he moaned in unbearable agony. Gerard Poupardin ran toward him, and those nearby tried to help him to his seat.

There was no way out.

"Yes! Yes!" he cried suddenly, writhing in excruciating pain but pulling free of the grip of those trying to assist him. "It's all true!" he confirmed. "Everything he has said is true! The war, Ambassador Lee's death; the plan to kill Kruszkegin, all of it!"

Everyone in the room stared in disbelief. No one understood what was happening, least of all Gerard Poupardin. But everyone heard him — Faure had plainly confessed.

In offering his admission, Faure's only wish was that it would somehow bring an end to his torment, and in that he was not disappointed. No sooner had he finished, than he fell to the floor, dead.

Someone ran for a doctor and for about fifteen minutes the chamber was filled with confusion, until finally Faure's lifeless body was taken from the room.

"Mr. President!" came a somber voice from near the spot where Faure had fallen. It was Christopher. "A quarter of the world's population is dead or at risk.[89] There is so much that must be done, and must be done quickly. As indelicate as it may seem: with the death of Ambassador Faure, until the nations of Europe can elect a new primary, as alternate for that region, I am now its acting representative. Please, let us get to the business at hand!"

* * * * *

The coroner's report would find that Albert Faure had died of a massive heart attack, brought on, it seemed, by the tremendous burden of guilt for what he had done. For Decker, no explanation was necessary: Christopher had begun to exercise the unexplored powers within him. He could only hope and pray that these powers would be equal to the challenges the world would soon face as Christopher led mankind through the final stage of its evolution and into the glorious dawn of the New Age of humankind.

Prophecy Cross Reference

To find where a specific Bible passage is depicted or discussed in *The Christ Clone Trilogy*, find the passage in the first two columns of the table below. The columns to the right of the passage indentify the book of the trilogy and the chapter in which the reference is covered, as well as an associated endnote. For example, from the first listing below, reference to Genesis 1:26 is found in book 2 (*Birth of an Age*), chapter 16. There you would look for the text surrounding endnote 81. The endnotes for each book are found in the <u>Study Guide Notes</u> for that book, and include the referenced Bible passage (unless it is a very long passage) as well as any needed explanation. Note that a single passage may be covered in multiple places in the trilogy, and so will appear in multiple rows of the table.

Bible Reference	Chapter & Verse	TCCT Book Number	Chapter	Endnote Number
Genesis				
Genesis	1:26	2	16	81
Genesis	2:9	3	Epilogue	341
Genesis	2:16-17	3	Epilogue	352
Genesis	2:17	2	16	63
Genesis	3:3	3	Epilogue	341
Genesis	3:4-5	2	16	64
Genesis	3:4-5	3	17	159
Genesis	3:7	2	16	65
Genesis	3:15	3	10	117
Genesis	3:17	3	Epilogue	341
Genesis	3:17-19	3	Epilogue	313
Genesis	3:22	3	Epilogue	341
Genesis	3:24	3	Epilogue	341
Genesis	5:25-27	1	20	50
Genesis	6:8–7:7	3	7	68
Genesis	9:4	3	14	131
Genesis	11:1-9	2	17	100
Genesis	11:1-9	3	Prologue	14
Genesis	11:5-7	2	16	67
Genesis	11:6	2	1	15
Genesis	19:15-25	3	7	68

Bible Reference	Chapter & Verse	TCCT Book Number	Chapter	Endnote Number
Genesis	25:29-34	3	19	178
Genesis	25:34	3	17	165
Genesis	37	3	21	202
Genesis	41	3	21	218
Genesis	43–47	3	21	203
Exodus				
Exodus	2:11-14	3	21	204
Exodus	4:21	2	16	68
Exodus	4:22-23	2	16	69
Exodus	4:24	2	16	73
Exodus	4:25	2	16	74
Exodus	6:6-9	3	21	205
Exodus	7:8-13	1	10	25
Exodus	14:11-12	3	21	206
Exodus	15:24	3	21	206
Exodus	16	3	7	59
Exodus	16:2-3	3	21	206
Exodus	16:7-8	3	21	208
Exodus	16:34	1	6	15
Exodus	17:1-4	3	21	206
Exodus	17:4	3	21	207
Exodus	20:3-5	2	16	66
Exodus	20:25	2	17	91
Exodus	20:25	3	Prologue	4
Exodus	25:10	1	6	17
Exodus	32:1-6	3	21	209
Exodus	32:9-10	3	21	213
Exodus	32:22	3	21	214
Exodus	33:3-5	3	21	215
Leviticus				
Leviticus	1:5-17	2	16	75
Leviticus	3	2	16	71
Leviticus	4	2	16	70
Leviticus	5:14-18	2	16	70
Leviticus	6:24-39	2	16	70
Leviticus	7:1-10	2	16	70
Leviticus	7:11-21	2	16	71
Leviticus	7:12-15	2	16	72
Leviticus	11:13-19	3	Epilogue	348

Bible Reference	Chapter & Verse	TCCT Book Number	Chapter	Endnote Number
Leviticus	17:10-16	3	14	131
Leviticus	19:18	3	9	102
Leviticus	22:29	2	16	72
Leviticus	23:42-43	3	11	121
Numbers				
Numbers	11:18-20	3	21	206
Numbers	12	3	21	210
Numbers	14:1-5	3	21	206
Numbers	14:10	3	21	207
Numbers	14:11-12	3	21	213
Numbers	14:40-45	3	21	206
Numbers	16:1-3	3	21	206
Numbers	16:41-45	3	21	206
Numbers	17:10	1	6	15
Numbers	20:2-5	3	21	206
Numbers	20:13	3	21	208
Numbers	21:4-5	3	21	206
Numbers	22:20-22	2	16	77
Numbers	23:19	2	16	78
Numbers	25:1-9	3	21	206
Numbers	33:51-52	2	16	79
Numbers	35:19	3	10	113
Numbers	35:19	3	17	157
Numbers	35:20-27	3	17	157
Joshua	20:3-9	3	17	157
Deuteronomy				
Deuteronomy	1:26-27	3	21	206
Deuteronomy	1:42-43	3	21	206
Deuteronomy	6:5	3	9	101
Deuteronomy	7:1-2	2	16	79
Deuteronomy	7:6	3	21	217
Deuteronomy	8:4	3	15	146
Deuteronomy	9:7	3	21	212
Deuteronomy	9:9-17	3	21	206
Deuteronomy	9:23-24	3	21	206
Deuteronomy	11-12	3	10	113
Deuteronomy	14:2	3	21	217
Deuteronomy	19:6	3	10	113
Deuteronomy	19:6	3	17	157

Bible Reference	Chapter & Verse	TCCT Book Number	Chapter	Endnote Number
Deuteronomy	19:12	3	17	157
Deuteronomy	29:5	3	15	146
Joshua				
Joshua	3–4	3	22	235
Joshua	6	3	16	150
Joshua	20:2-3	3	10	114
Judges				
Judges	11:29-39	2	16	76
1 Samuel				
1 Samuel	6:19	1	23	71
1 Samuel	15:3	2	16	80
2 Samuel				
2 Samuel	6:6-7	1	23	71
2 Samuel	14:11	3	10	115
2 Samuel	14:11	3	17	157
1 Kings				
1 Kings	18:19-40	2	17	94
1 Kings	18:19-40	3	Prologue	7
2 Kings				
2 Kings	2:11	2	1	17
1 Chronicles				
1 Chronicles	13:10	1	23	72
Ezra				
Ezra	1:5-7	1	6	10
Ezra	7	3	8	89
Ezra	7:6-7	1	22	63
Ezra	7:6-7	3	8	89
Nehemiah				
Nehemiah	1:1-4	1	22	63
Nehemiah	2:1	1	22	63
Nehemiah	2:5	1	22	63
Nehemiah	9:21	3	15	146
Job				
Job	14:10-12	3	Epilogue	318
Job	19:25-27	3	Epilogue	318
Psalms				
Psalms	6:5	3	Epilogue	318
Psalms	14:3	3	21	216
Psalms	16:9-10	3	8	96

Bible Reference	Chapter & Verse	TCCT Book Number	Chapter	Endnote Number
Psalms	16:9-10	3	21	201
Psalms	16:18	3	8	93
Psalms	16:18	3	21	200
Psalms	22:7-8	3	8	93
Psalms	22:7-8	3	21	200
Psalms	22:27-31	3	8	98
Psalms	30:3	3	8	96
Psalms	30:3	3	21	201
Psalms	53:3	3	21	216
Psalms	79	3	24	266
Psalms	79:2-3	3	24	263
Psalms	80	3	24	266
Psalms	111:10	3	1	34
Psalms	115:17-18	3	Epilogue	318
Psalms	118	3	24	275
Proverbs				
Proverbs	1:7	3	1	34
Proverbs	9:10	3	1	34
Ecclesiastes				
Ecclesiastes	3:3a	1	28	85
Ecclesiastes	3:3a	2	Prologue	4
Ecclesiastes	7:20	3	21	216
Isaiah				
Isaiah	1:18	3	9	105
Isaiah	2:1-4	3	Epilogue	331
Isaiah	7:14	3	8	83
Isaiah	8:3	3	8	83
Isaiah	9:1-2	3	8	86
Isaiah	9:1-2	3	21	192
Isaiah	9:2-7	3	8	83
Isaiah	9:6	3	21	191
Isaiah	9:6-7	3	8	85
Isaiah	11:1-2	3	8	81
Isaiah	11:6-9	3	Epilogue	347
Isaiah	11:10	3	8	81
Isaiah	11:10-12	3	Epilogue	328
Isaiah	14:13-14	3	17	163
Isaiah	16:4b	3	24	303
Isaiah	16:5	3	Epilogue	343

Bible Reference	Chapter & Verse	TCCT Book Number	Chapter	Endnote Number
Isaiah	21:9	3	3	50
Isaiah	21:9	3	23	256
Isaiah	24:21-22	3	24	304
Isaiah	25:6-8	3	Epilogue	311
Isaiah	25:9	3	24	283
Isaiah	26:21	3	16	147
Isaiah	33:17	3	Epilogue	330
Isaiah	33:20	3	Epilogue	330
Isaiah	34:2-3	3	24	306
Isaiah	34:4	3	24	281
Isaiah	35:5-6	3	8	87
Isaiah	35:5-6	3	21	193
Isaiah	38:18-19	3	Epilogue	318
Isaiah	40:31	3	Epilogue	348
Isaiah	41:17-20	3	11	122
Isaiah	46:9b-10a	3	8	80
Isaiah	49:5-6	3	8	97
Isaiah	49:5-6	3	21	197
Isaiah	53	1	23	67
Isaiah	53	1	23	68
Isaiah	53	1	23	69
Isaiah	53	3	22	236
Isaiah	53:4-6	3	8	95
Isaiah	53:4-6	3	21	195
Isaiah	53:7	3	8	92
Isaiah	53:7	3	21	194
Isaiah	53:8-9	3	8	94
Isaiah	53:8b	3	8	95
Isaiah	53:10-11	3	8	96
Isaiah	53:10-11	3	21	196
Isaiah	57:1-2	3	7	60
Isaiah	63:1-4	3	24	305
Isaiah	64	3	24	274
Isaiah	64:11	3	23	259
Isaiah	65:2-5	3	21	211
Isaiah	65:17	3	Epilogue	327
Isaiah	65:21-23	3	Epilogue	346
Isaiah	65:23	3	Epilogue	348
Isaiah	65:23	3	Epilogue	349

Bible Reference	Chapter & Verse	TCCT Book Number	Chapter	Endnote Number
Isaiah	65:24	3	Epilogue	353
Isaiah	65:25	3	Epilogue	347
Jeremiah				
Jeremiah	3:16	3	Epilogue	334
Jeremiah	17:5-6	2	9	42
Jeremiah	23:5	3	8	82
Jeremiah	23:5	3	21	189
Jeremiah	25:11-12	1	22	66
Jeremiah	31:31	1	6	20
Jeremiah	35:18-19	1	20	42
Jeremiah	51:6	3	22	233
Ezekiel				
Ezekiel	18:21-23	2	2	19
Ezekiel	18:23	3	24	294
Ezekiel	33:11	2	2	19
Ezekiel	33:11	3	24	294
Ezekiel	38:1-6	1	14	29
Ezekiel	38:18-20	1	15	30
Ezekiel	38:22	1	16	33
Ezekiel	38-39	1	11	26
Ezekiel	39:3-5	1	15	31
Ezekiel	39:4-6	1	16	34
Ezekiel	39:9-10	1	22	60
Ezekiel	39:11-20	1	15	31
Ezekiel	39:21	1	17	38
Ezekiel	40–43	2	16	83
Ezekiel	40–43	3	Epilogue	333
Ezekiel	44:17-18	2	16	82
Ezekiel	45:1-3	3	Epilogue	332
Ezekiel	47:7-11	3	Epilogue	354
Ezekiel	47:12	3	Epilogue	339
Ezekiel	47:12	3	Epilogue	340
Ezekiel	47:13–48:29	3	Epilogue	329
Ezekiel	48:8-10	3	Epilogue	332
Ezekiel	48:32	1	24	77
Daniel				
Daniel	7:7	1	17	37
Daniel	7:7-8	2	1	18
Daniel	7:7-8	3	1	22

Bible Reference	Chapter & Verse	TCCT Book Number	Chapter	Endnote Number
Daniel	7:7-8	3	5	54
Daniel	7:10b	3	24	286
Daniel	7:11a	3	24	289
Daniel	7:11	3	24	303
Daniel	7:13-14	3	Epilogue	343
Daniel	7:17	3	1	22
Daniel	7:18	3	Epilogue	328
Daniel	7:19-20	3	1	22
Daniel	7:21-22	3	23	255
Daniel	7:23-24	3	1	22
Daniel	7:25a	2	17	101
Daniel	7:25a	3	Prologue	15
Daniel	7:25a	3	1	23
Daniel	7:25a	3	3	46
Daniel	7:25b	3	1	36
Daniel	7:26	3	24	303
Daniel	7:27	3	Epilogue	328
Daniel	8:15-16	3	24	286
Daniel	9:1-3	1	22	66
Daniel	9:25	1	21	58
Daniel	9:25-26	1	22	62
Daniel	9:25-26	3	8	88
Daniel	9:25-26	3	21	188
Daniel	9:26	1	19	39
Daniel	9:27	1	21	58
Daniel	9:27	1	23	70
Daniel	9:27	1	24	73
Daniel	9:27	2	17	92
Daniel	9:27	3	Prologue	5
Daniel	9:27	3	1	24
Daniel	9:27	3	1	26
Daniel	9:27	3	3	48
Daniel	9:27	3	9	109
Daniel	9:27	3	19	175
Daniel	10:4–11:1	3	17	161
Daniel	10:5-6	3	24	286
Daniel	10:13	3	17	161
Daniel	11:36a	2	17	101
Daniel	11:36a	3	Prologue	15

Bible Reference	Chapter & Verse	TCCT Book Number	Chapter	Endnote Number
Daniel	11:36	3	1	21
Daniel	12:1	3	17	161
Daniel	12:2	3	Epilogue	318
Daniel	12:11	1	21	58
Daniel	12:11	3	1	42
Daniel	12:11-12	3	Epilogue	312
Hosea				
Hosea	2:18	3	Epilogue	347
Hosea	2:19-20	3	Epilogue	311
Hosea	2:23	3	21	219
Hosea	5:15–6:3	3	23	238
Hosea	6:1-2	3	23	247
Joel				
Joel	2	1	21	58
Joel	2	2	14	54
Joel	2:2-9	2	14	56
Joel	2:30	2	5	27
Joel	3	1	16	32
Joel	3:2	3	24	268
Joel	3:3	3	21	230
Joel	3:9-11	3	21	224
Joel	3:12-13	3	24	305
Joel	3:16	3	24	279
Amos				
Amos	5:18-20	1	21	58
Micah				
Micah	2:12	3	7	58
Micah	4:11–5:1	3	19	179
Micah	5:1	3	24	265
Micah	5:2	3	8	84
Micah	5:2	3	21	186
Micah	5:2	3	21	190
Micah	6:6-8	3	9	104
Zephaniah				
Zephaniah	3:8	3	21	224
Zephaniah	3:9	3	24	277
Zechariah				
Zechariah	2:10-12	3	Epilogue	310
Zechariah	5:9	3	24	286

Bible Reference	Chapter & Verse	TCCT Book Number	Chapter	Endnote Number
Zechariah	5:9	3	Epilogue	348
Zechariah	9:9	3	21	198
Zechariah	9:10b	3	Epilogue	343
Zechariah	11:12-13	3	8	91
Zechariah	11:12-13	3	21	199
Zechariah	11:16-17	2	15	58
Zechariah	12	3	19	179
Zechariah	12:8	3	23	258
Zechariah	12:9	3	24	267
Zechariah	12:10	3	9	111
Zechariah	12:10	3	21	221
Zechariah	12:10a	3	19	181
Zechariah	14:2	3	23	257
Zechariah	14:2	3	24	262
Zechariah	14:2	3	24	264
Zechariah	14:4	3	24	267
Zechariah	14:4	3	24	269
Zechariah	14:5	3	24	270
Zechariah	14:6	3	24	271
Zechariah	14:6-7	3	24	278
Zechariah	14:6-7	3	24	307
Zechariah	14:8	3	Epilogue	335
Zechariah	14:9	3	Epilogue	343
Zechariah	14:12	3	24	301
Zechariah	14:13	3	24	298
Zechariah	14:13	3	24	299
Malachi				
Malachi	4:5-6	2	1	16
Malachi	4:5-6	2	17	93
Malachi	4:5-6	2	17	96
Malachi	4:5-6	3	Prologue	6
Malachi	4:5-6	3	Prologue	9
1 Maccabees (apocryphal)	2:4-8	1	6	11
Matthew				
Matthew	1:23	3	8	83
Matthew	4:5-7	2	17	105
Matthew	4:13	1	10	25
Matthew	5:30	3	19	183

Bible Reference	Chapter & Verse	TCCT Book Number	Chapter	Endnote Number
Matthew	6:8	3	Epilogue	353
Matthew	11:12-14	2	1	10
Matthew	13:55-56	3	10	116
Matthew	13:57	3	1	35
Matthew	16:28	1	20	52
Matthew	17:10-13	2	1	10
Matthew	18:14	3	24	294
Matthew	20:20-23	1	20	47
Matthew	22:23-33	3	Epilogue	318
Matthew	22:23-33	3	Epilogue	348
Matthew	22:37	3	9	101
Matthew	22:39	3	9	102
Matthew	22:40	3	9	103
Matthew	23:39	3	24	276
Matthew	24:1-2	1	6	8
Matthew	24:5	2	16	86
Matthew	24:9	3	15	143
Matthew	24:11	2	16	61
Matthew	24:14	3	3	44
Matthew	24:15-16	3	1	38
Matthew	24:22	3	16	149
Matthew	24:23-24	2	17	98
Matthew	24:23-24	3	Prologue	11
Matthew	24:27	3	24	282
Matthew	24:28	3	24	273
Matthew	24:29	3	24	281
Matthew	24:30	3	24	282
Matthew	24:31	3	24	287
Matthew	24:34	1	20	52
Matthew	25:21	3	Epilogue	309
Matthew	25:23	3	Epilogue	309
Matthew	25:31-46	3	Epilogue	323
Matthew	26:15	3	8	91
Matthew	26:50-52	1	6	13
Matthew	27:5	1	26	80
Matthew	27:5	3	8	91
Matthew	27:7	3	8	91
Matthew	27:46	1	12	28
Matthew	27:50-51	1	6	14

Bible Reference	Chapter & Verse	TCCT Book Number	Chapter	Endnote Number
Mark				
Mark	6:4	3	1	35
Mark	6:4-6	3	14	130
Mark	9:1	1	20	52
Mark	9:11-13	2	1	10
Mark	12:18-27	3	Epilogue	318
Mark	12:18-27	3	Epilogue	348
Mark	13:2	1	6	8
Mark	13:6	2	16	86
Mark	13:12	3	18	171
Mark	13:14-16	3	1	38
Mark	13:20	3	16	149
Mark	13:21-22	2	17	98
Mark	13:21-22	3	Prologue	11
Mark	13:25	3	24	281
Mark	13:26	3	24	290
Mark	13:26-27	3	Epilogue	336
Mark	13:27	3	24	287
Mark	13:30	1	20	52
Mark	14:47	1	6	13
Luke				
Luke	2:46-47	2	16	84
Luke	4:9-12	2	17	105
Luke	8:30-33	2	14	57
Luke	9:27	1	20	52
Luke	9:29	3	24	284
Luke	15:11-31	3	Epilogue	318
Luke	15:11-32	3	9	99
Luke	16:14	3	Epilogue	318
Luke	16:19-31	3	Epilogue	318
Luke	20:27-40	3	Epilogue	318
Luke	20:27-40	3	Epilogue	348
Luke	20:34-36	3	Epilogue	316
Luke	20:35-36a	3	Epilogue	348
Luke	21:6	1	6	8
Luke	21:8	2	16	86
Luke	21:21-22	3	1	38
Luke	21:25	2	6	33
Luke	21:26	3	24	281

Bible Reference	Chapter & Verse	TCCT Book Number	Chapter	Endnote Number
Luke	21:27	3	24	290
Luke	22:50-51	1	6	13
Luke	23:42	3	9	106
Luke	23:43	3	9	107
Luke	23:43	3	Epilogue	318
Luke	24:31	3	Epilogue	337
Luke	24:36-37	3	Epilogue	337
John				
John	1:29	2	17	87
John	1:29	3	Prologue	1
John	2:19-20	1	22	63
John	2:19-20	3	8	90
John	3:2	3	21	187
John	3:7	2	17	103
John	3:7	3	Prologue	17
John	4:16-18	3	7	70
John	5:4	1	20	55
John	6:45	1	17	36
John	6:45	3	11	123
John	7:53–8:11	1	20	55
John	11	3	9	108
John	12:28-29	3	1	30
John	18:10	1	6	13
John	19:25-27	1	20	44
John	19:25-27	1	26	79
John	21	1	20	55
John	21:20-22	1	20	45
John	21:23	1	20	46
John	21:25	3	Epilogue	318
Acts				
Acts	1:6	3	Epilogue	327
Acts	1:9	3	Epilogue	336
Acts	1:11	3	24	290
Acts	2:19	2	5	27
Acts	2:29	1	28	84
Acts	2:29	1	28	86
Acts	2:29	2	Prologue	3
Acts	2:29	2	Prologue	5
Acts	2:29	3	Epilogue	318

Bible Reference	Chapter & Verse	TCCT Book Number	Chapter	Endnote Number
Acts	2:34	3	Epilogue	318
Acts	8:39-40	3	Epilogue	337
Acts	12:1-2	1	20	47
Acts	12:1-2	1	20	48
Acts	15:20-21	3	14	131
Acts	15:29	3	14	131
Acts	21:25	3	14	131
Romans				
Romans	1:20-25	1	17	36
Romans	1:20-25	3	11	123
Romans	1:23	3	7	64
Romans	3:10-12	3	21	216
Romans	5:8	3	19	182
Romans	8:29a	3	Epilogue	348
Romans	9:25	3	21	219
Romans	11:25-26	3	23	246
Romans	11:25-27	3	21	220
Romans	14:10-11	3	Epilogue	323
1 Corinthians				
1 Corinthians	3:13-15	3	Epilogue	344
1 Corinthians	4:5	3	Epilogue	344
1 Corinthians	13:9-12	2	1	14
1 Corinthians	13:12	1	20	43
1 Corinthians	15:22-23	3	Epilogue	320
1 Corinthians	15:35-44	3	7	67
1 Corinthians	15:50	3	Epilogue	321
1 Corinthians	15:35-44	1	10	25
1 Corinthians	15:50-53	1	10	25
1 Corinthians	15:50-53	3	7	62
1 Corinthians	15:53	3	7	65
2 Corinthians				
2 Corinthians	5:1-4	1	10	25
2 Corinthians	5:1-4	3	7	66
2 Corinthians	5:8	3	Epilogue	318
2 Corinthians	5:10	3	Epilogue	323
2 Corinthians	5:10	3	Epilogue	344
2 Corinthians	11:14	2	17	104
2 Corinthians	11:14	3	Prologue	18

Bible Reference	Chapter & Verse	TCCT Book Number	Chapter	Endnote Number
Ephesians				
Ephesians	2:8-9	3	19	180
Philippians				
Philippians	1:23	3	Epilogue	318
Colossians				
Colossians	3:23-24	3	Epilogue	344
1 Thessalonians				
1 Thessalonians	4:16-17	3	7	61
2 Thessalonians				
2 Thessalonians	2:1-7	3	7	69
2 Thessalonians	2:4	2	17	97
2 Thessalonians	2:4	3	Prologue	10
2 Thessalonians	2:8	3	24	297
2 Thessalonians	2:9-10	3	13	127
2 Thessalonians	2:1-12	1	10	25
2 Thessalonians	2:7-8	1	10	25
2 Thessalonians	2:9-11	1	10	25
2 Thessalonians	2:9-12	2	17	102
2 Thessalonians	2:9-12	3	Prologue	16
2 Thessalonians	2:10b	3	24	294
2 Thessalonians	2:10b	3	Epilogue	325
1 Timothy				
1 Timothy	4:1-2	2	16	61
2 Timothy				
2 Timothy	4:7-8	3	Epilogue	344
Hebrews				
Hebrews	1:12	3	7	65
Hebrews	9:4	1	6	15
Hebrews	9:27	3	10	112
Hebrews	11	1	10	25
2 Peter				
2 Peter	1:13-14	1	10	25
2 Peter	1:13-14	3	7	66
2 Peter	2:5-9	3	7	68
2 Peter	3:9	3	24	294
2 Peter	3:9	3	Epilogue	324
1 John				
1 John	4:3	3	1	23

Bible Reference	Chapter & Verse	TCCT Book Number	Chapter	Endnote Number
Jude				
Jude	14	3	24	286
Jude	14-15	1	21	58
Jude	14-15	3	24	287
Jude	14-15	3	Epilogue	336
Revelation				
Revelation	1:4	3	10	118
Revelation	1:5b-6	3	Epilogue	310
Revelation	1:7	3	24	290
Revelation	1:8	3	10	118
Revelation	1:13	3	24	292
Revelation	1:14	3	24	296
Revelation	1:15b	3	24	295
Revelation	1:16b	3	Epilogue	308
Revelation	1:17-18	3	24	292
Revelation	2:7	3	Epilogue	341
Revelation	2:26	3	Epilogue	344
Revelation	3:9	3	19	174
Revelation	3:10	3	7	60
Revelation	4:6b-8a	3	24	286
Revelation	4:6b-8a	3	Epilogue	348
Revelation	4:8	3	10	118
Revelation	5:6	2	15	59
Revelation	5:9-10	3	Epilogue	310
Revelation	5:11	3	24	286
Revelation	6:1-2	1	21	58
Revelation	6:3-4	1	22	59
Revelation	6:3-4	1	24	74
Revelation	6:5-6	1	22	59
Revelation	6:7-8	1	24	75
Revelation	6:8	1	28	89
Revelation	6:8	2	Prologue	8
Revelation	6:8	2	1	9
Revelation	6:9-11	1	28	83
Revelation	6:9-11	2	Prologue	2
Revelation	6:12	1	28	83
Revelation	6:12	1	28	84
Revelation	6:12	1	28	86
Revelation	6:12	2	Prologue	2

Bible Reference	Chapter & Verse	TCCT Book Number	Chapter	Endnote Number
Revelation	6:12	2	Prologue	3
Revelation	6:12	2	Prologue	5
Revelation	6:13	1	28	87
Revelation	6:13	2	Prologue	6
Revelation	6:14	1	28	82
Revelation	6:14	1	28	83
Revelation	6:14	2	Prologue	1
Revelation	6:14	2	Prologue	2
Revelation	6:15-17	1	28	88
Revelation	6:15-17	2	Prologue	7
Revelation	7	2	9	45
Revelation	7:1-3	1	24	76
Revelation	7:2-3	2	9	45
Revelation	7:2-4	2	1	11
Revelation	7:3-8	1	24	77
Revelation	8:7	2	5	25
Revelation	8:7	2	5	26
Revelation	8:7	2	5	27
Revelation	8:7	2	5	28
Revelation	8:7-12	2	1	12
Revelation	8:8-9	2	6	29
Revelation	8:8-9	2	6	30
Revelation	8:8-9	2	6	32
Revelation	8:8-9	2	6	34
Revelation	8:8-9	2	6	35
Revelation	8:10-11	2	2	21
Revelation	8:10-11	2	6	29
Revelation	8:10-11	2	7	36
Revelation	8:10-11	2	8	38
Revelation	8:12	2	8	39
Revelation	8:13	2	8	40
Revelation	9:1-6	2	9	43
Revelation	9:1-3	2	9	44
Revelation	9:4	2	9	45
Revelation	9:5	1	21	58
Revelation	9:5	2	12	48
Revelation	9:5-6	2	10	47
Revelation	9:7-10	2	9	46
Revelation	9:10	1	21	58

Bible Reference	Chapter & Verse	TCCT Book Number	Chapter	Endnote Number
Revelation	9:11	2	9	44
Revelation	9:11	3	17	160
Revelation	9:12	2	8	40
Revelation	9:13-14	2	14	51
Revelation	9:13-16	2	12	49
Revelation	9:15	2	14	52
Revelation	9:16	2	14	54
Revelation	9:17-19	2	14	53
Revelation	9:20-21	3	1	19
Revelation	9:20-21	3	1	32
Revelation	10:3b-4	1	20	41
Revelation	10:6-7	3	9	110
Revelation	10:8-11	1	20	49
Revelation	11	1	20	42
Revelation	11	1	20	47
Revelation	11:2	1	21	58
Revelation	11:2b	3	3	45
Revelation	11:3	1	21	58
Revelation	11:3-4	1	20	57
Revelation	11:3-6	2	1	13
Revelation	11:14	2	8	40
Revelation	11:5	2	8	41
Revelation	11:6	1	26	81
Revelation	11:7	2	17	88
Revelation	11:7	3	Prologue	2
Revelation	11:7	3	17	160
Revelation	11:8-9	2	17	90
Revelation	11:8-9	3	Prologue	3
Revelation	11:8-9	3	1	27
Revelation	11:10	3	1	20
Revelation	11:11	3	1	28
Revelation	11:12	3	1	29
Revelation	11:13	3	1	31
Revelation	11:13	3	1	33
Revelation	11:13	3	1	34
Revelation	12:5-6	3	1	39
Revelation	12:6	1	21	58
Revelation	12:6	3	1	42
Revelation	12:6	3	1	36

Bible Reference	Chapter & Verse	TCCT Book Number	Chapter	Endnote Number
Revelation	12:6	3	11	120
Revelation	12:9a	3	1	39
Revelation	12:11	3	15	141
Revelation	12:13-14	3	1	39
Revelation	12:14	1	21	58
Revelation	12:14	3	1	36
Revelation	12:14	3	1	41
Revelation	12:15-16	3	1	40
Revelation	12:17	3	5	56
Revelation	13:1	3	1	22
Revelation	13:1	3	5	54
Revelation	13:3	2	15	59
Revelation	13:3	2	17	99
Revelation	13:3	3	17	158
Revelation	13:3-4	3	Prologue	13
Revelation	13:4b	3	22	234
Revelation	13:5	3	1	21
Revelation	13:5-6	2	17	101
Revelation	13:5-6	3	Prologue	15
Revelation	13:7b	3	1	21
Revelation	13:7	3	5	55
Revelation	13:8	2	17	99
Revelation	13:8	3	Prologue	12
Revelation	13:8	3	5	53
Revelation	13:9-10	3	15	144
Revelation	13:9-10	3	18	170
Revelation	13:12	2	15	59
Revelation	13:12	3	17	158
Revelation	13:13	2	17	95
Revelation	13:13	3	Prologue	8
Revelation	13:13-14a	3	13	127
Revelation	13:14	3	3	47
Revelation	13:15	3	19	176
Revelation	13:15a	3	3	49
Revelation	13:16-17	3	13	125
Revelation	13:16-18	3	4	51
Revelation	13:18	3	1	25
Revelation	14	2	9	45
Revelation	14:1	1	26	78

Bible Reference	Chapter & Verse	TCCT Book Number	Chapter	Endnote Number
Revelation	14:1	2	1	11
Revelation	14:2-3	3	11	119
Revelation	14:6-7	3	3	43
Revelation	14:8	3	3	50
Revelation	14:9-11	3	5	52
Revelation	14:9-11	3	19	177
Revelation	14:9-11	3	Epilogue	322
Revelation	14:12	3	15	142
Revelation	14:13	3	15	141
Revelation	14:14-16	3	17	166
Revelation	14:17-19	3	24	300
Revelation	14:19-20	3	24	305
Revelation	15:1	3	9	110
Revelation	15:2-5	3	18	172
Revelation	16:1-2	3	12	124
Revelation	16:2	3	15	135
Revelation	16:3	3	13	126
Revelation	16:3	3	15	136
Revelation	16:4	3	15	137
Revelation	16:4-6	3	14	128
Revelation	16:8-9	3	15	138
Revelation	16:9	3	15	139
Revelation	16:10-12	3	15	145
Revelation	16:12	3	18	168
Revelation	16:12	3	24	305
Revelation	16:13-14	3	16	151
Revelation	16:13-14	3	18	169
Revelation	16:13-14	3	18	173
Revelation	16:16	3	21	224
Revelation	16:18a	3	23	249
Revelation	16:18	3	23	250
Revelation	16:18-20	3	23	253
Revelation	16:19	3	23	251
Revelation	16:19a	3	23	252
Revelation	16:21a	3	23	254
Revelation	17:2	3	21	229
Revelation	17:3-5	3	17	161
Revelation	17:4b-5	3	21	229
Revelation	17:6	3	21	232

Bible Reference	Chapter & Verse	TCCT Book Number	Chapter	Endnote Number
Revelation	17:8	3	Prologue	13
Revelation	17:8	3	10	118
Revelation	17:8	3	17	162
Revelation	17:8a	3	17	160
Revelation	17:9-11	3	17	161
Revelation	17:12-13	3	5	54
Revelation	17:14	3	24	287
Revelation	17:15	3	21	227
Revelation	17:16-17	3	24	261
Revelation	18:3a	3	21	229
Revelation	18:3b	3	21	228
Revelation	18:4-5	3	22	233
Revelation	18:8	3	23	256
Revelation	18:9-10	3	24	260
Revelation	18:9-10	3	24	261
Revelation	18:11-13	3	21	228
Revelation	18:13c	3	21	230
Revelation	18:21-24	3	Epilogue	326
Revelation	18:23c	3	21	226
Revelation	18:23d	3	21	231
Revelation	18:24	3	21	232
Revelation	19:6-9	3	Epilogue	311
Revelation	19:11	3	24	285
Revelation	19:11	3	Epilogue	336
Revelation	19:11a	3	24	280
Revelation	19:12a	3	24	296
Revelation	19:13	3	24	291
Revelation	19:14	3	24	288
Revelation	19:14	3	Epilogue	336
Revelation	19:15c	3	24	305
Revelation	19:16	3	24	293
Revelation	19:17-18	3	24	273
Revelation	19:19	3	23	248
Revelation	19:20	3	24	303
Revelation	19:21	3	24	302
Revelation	20	3	Epilogue	327
Revelation	20:1-3	3	Epilogue	342
Revelation	20:4	3	15	140
Revelation	20:4	3	17	166

Bible Reference	Chapter & Verse	TCCT Book Number	Chapter	Endnote Number
Revelation	20:4	3	Epilogue	310
Revelation	20:4	3	Epilogue	345
Revelation	14	3	17	166
Revelation	20:5a	3	Epilogue	323
Revelation	20:5b-6	3	Epilogue	310
Revelation	20:7	3	Epilogue	342
Revelation	20:11-15	3	Epilogue	323
Revelation	21	3	Epilogue	327
Revelation	22:1-2	3	Epilogue	338
Revelation	22:1-2	3	Epilogue	341
Revelation	22:5b	3	Epilogue	308
Revelation	22:3a	3	Epilogue	313
Revelation	22:12	3	Epilogue	344
Revelation	22:17	3	Epilogue	314

Study Guide Notes

The Christ Clone Trilogy includes hundreds of twists and turns that address specific biblical prophecies. The following notes, which are linked to the events depicted in the story, provide the Bible passage (unless it is a very long passage) that is being addressed, as well as any needed explanation. Where necessary to distinguish the author's comments from scripture, the author's comment appears in brackets and Calibri font. Also included are notes of general interest including source information and brief explanations on matters of science and history related to the events depicted in the story.

––––––––––

[1] B. J. Culliton, "Mystery of the Shroud of Turin Challenges 20th Century Science," Science, 21 July 1978, 201:235-239.

[2] For the resulting article see K. F. Weaver, "Mystery of the Shroud." *National Geographic*, June 1980, 157:729-753.

[3] Heller, *Report on the Shroud of Turin*, 181-188, 197-200, 215-216.

[4] Ibid., 126, 163.

[5] Francis Crick, *Life Itself* (New York: Simon and Schuster, 1983).

[6] The meaning of the cloning and the Scriptural evidence that suggests the possibility will be presented in *Acts of God*, Chapters 10 and 17.

[7] Josephus, *The Jewish War*, VII, 1. See also *Midrash Rabba*, Lamentations 1:31, where it is reported that Vespasian's General Pangar, when asked why he had not destroyed the Western Wall of the Temple, responded, "I acted so for the honor of your empire ... When people look at the Western Wall, they will exclaim, 'Behold the might of Vespasian from what he did not destroy!'"

[8] Matthew 24:1-2. 1 Jesus left the temple and was walking away when his disciples came up to him to call his attention to its buildings. "Do you see all these things?" he asked. "Truly I tell you,

not one stone here will be left on another; every one will be thrown down."

Mark 13:2. Do you see all these great buildings?" replied Jesus. "Not one stone here will be left on another; every one will be thrown down."

Luke 21:6. "As for what you see here, the time will come when not one stone will be left on another; every one of them will be thrown down."

[9] 1981, Paramount.

[10] Ezra 1:5-7. Then the family heads of Judah and Benjamin, and the priests and Levites—everyone whose heart God had moved—prepared to go up and build the house of the LORD in Jerusalem. All their neighbors assisted them with articles of silver and gold, with goods and livestock, and with valuable gifts, in addition to all the freewill offerings. Moreover, King Cyrus brought out the articles belonging to the temple of the LORD, which Nebuchadnezzar had carried away from Jerusalem and had placed in the temple of his god.

[11] 2 Maccabees 2:4-8. The same document also states that the prophet commanded, with a solemn divine pronouncement, that the meeting tent and the chest containing the covenant should go with him. The documents reported that he went to the mountain that Moses ascended to see the inheritance that God promised. When Jeremiah arrived, he discovered a cave where he deposited the meeting tent, the covenant chest, and the incense altar. He blocked up the opening. Some who had accompanied him went along to mark the way but couldn't find it again. When Jeremiah found out, he rebuked them and said: "The place will remain unknown until God gathers the people together again and shows mercy. Then the Lord will disclose these things. The Lord's glory will appear with the cloud, as they were revealed in the time of Moses and when Solomon prayed that the place might be made holy." (Common English Bible)

[12] Jerome, on Eph. 5:4. (Migne PL 26, cols, 552 C-D), cited by J. K. Elliot in *The Apocryphal New Testament* (Clarendon Press, Oxford University Press, 1993).

[13] Matthew 26:50-52. Jesus replied, "Do what you came for, friend." Then the men stepped forward, seized Jesus and arrested him. With that, one of Jesus' companions reached for his sword, drew it out and struck the servant of the high priest, cutting off his ear. "Put your sword back in its place," Jesus said to him, "for all who draw the sword will die by the sword.

Mark 14:47. Then one of those standing near drew his sword and struck the servant of the high priest, cutting off his ear.

Luke 22:50-51. And one of them struck the servant of the high priest, cutting off his right ear. But Jesus answered, "No more of this!" And he touched the man's ear and healed him.

John 18:10. Then Simon Peter, who had a sword, drew it and struck the high priest's servant, cutting off his right ear. (The servant's name was Malchus.)

[14] Matthew 27:50-51. And when Jesus had cried out again in a loud voice, he gave up his spirit. At that moment the curtain of the temple was torn in two from top to bottom. The earth shook, the rocks split . . .

[15] Exodus 16:34. As the LORD commanded Moses, Aaron put the manna with the tablets of the covenant law, so that it might be preserved.

Numbers 17:10. The LORD said to Moses, "Put back Aaron's staff in front of the ark of the covenant law, to be kept as a sign to the rebellious. This will put an end to their grumbling against me, so that they will not die."

Hebrews 9:4. . . .which had the golden altar of incense and the gold-covered ark of the covenant. This ark contained the gold jar of manna, Aaron's staff that had budded, and the stone tablets of the covenant.

[16] 1956, Paramount.

[17] Exodus 25:10. Have them make an ark of acacia wood—two and a half cubits long, a cubit and a half wide, and a cubit and a half high. [The maximum length of 4'9" is calculated using the formula for a diagonal of a cube, and assumes an 18" cubit.]

[18] 1964, Disney.

[19] BBC.

[20] Jeremiah 31:31. "The days are coming," declares the LORD, "when I will make a new covenant with the people of Israel and with the people of Judah."

[21] See, for example, Dan Bahat, "Jerusalem Down Under: Tunneling Along Herod's Temple Mount Wall," *Biblical Archaeology Review*, Vol. 21, No. 6 (November/December 1995), 30-47.

[22] Daniel Pearl was kidnapped in Karachi, Pakistan, on January 23, 2002, while working on a story.

[23] Nguyen Chi Thien, "I Just Keep Silent When They Torture Me," in *Flowers From Hell* (Southeast Asia Studies, Yale University, 1984), 105. Used by permission.

[24] Sudan People's Liberation Army.

[25] The meaning of the Disaster and the scriptural evidence for it will be presented in Chapter 7 of *Acts of God*.

NOTE: THE FOLLOWING EXPLANATION INCLUDES REFERENCES THAT REVEAL SIGNIFICANT EVENTS LATER IN THE STORY.

Answering the When, How, and Why of the Rapture (known here also as the Disaster)

Of those who believe there will be a Rapture, there are generally three camps: those who believe it will occur before the Tribulation (pre-trib); those who think it will occur during the Tribulation (mid-trib or pre-wrath); and those who place it at the end of the Tribulation (post-trib). There is a great deal of literature available from other sources on this topic, so it is not my intention to argue that point here. There is general agreement among all three camps that the Tribulation will be seven years in length and will begin with the signing of a treaty with Israel by the Antichrist.

In most end-times books that take the pre-trib position, the Rapture happens very shortly before the start of the Tribulation. There is nothing in scripture, however, that associates the signing of the treaty with the Rapture, so we can't make that direct temporal link. There could be a single moment between the two events or there could be many years. To estimate how long there is between the Rapture and the beginning of the Tribulation, I examined how and why the Rapture will occur. We'll look first at the question of HOW.

Most who believe in a pre-trib Rapture also believe it must be largely misunderstood by the rest of the world. If the Rapture were obvious, it is reasoned, the fear of God would cause millions would turn to Christ. If that happens, then the Rapture is self defeating. Why would God take one group of Christians out of the world just to replace them with a fresh batch?

Fifty years ago, typical descriptions of the Rapture included graves opening to allow resurrected bodies to rise, followed by Christians flying bodily through the air for all the world to see. More recent depictions omit mention of the open graves and portray the Rapture of living Christians as a disappearance or dematerialization. It has always been inconceivable to me that the Rapture could involve hundreds of millions of open graves and the flight or disappearance of millions of people, and that the world would somehow not realize what had happened. Such an incredible lack of insight by so many is not believable in a novel, and it's certainly not believable in real life. I haven't forgotten that God sends a powerful delusion in the time of the Antichrist (2 Thessalonians 2:9-11), but even Pharaoh required the evidence offered by his magicians before he would dismiss the miracles performed by God through Moses (Exodus 7:8-13).

There must be a believable explanation in order to deceive those who are left behind, or else the Rapture must occur in some other way. The explanation provided by the Antichrist in one popular end-times series that the disintegration was caused by the "spontaneous atomic reaction caused by lightning reacting with atomic energy floating around in the atmosphere," may be acceptable in fiction where the reader has willingly suspended disbelief, but it would not be believed in the real world.

If we believe the Rapture is going to happen in the real world, then there must be a real-world explanation for how it could occur.

When he describes the Rapture in 1 Corinthians 15:50-53, Paul uses the Greek word "allasso" to describe the transition from corruptible to incorruptible body. Allasso is properly translated to English as "exchanged." It is the same word that is used when one sheds old clothes for new. In 2 Corinthians 5:1-4, Paul describes it as exchanging a tent for a house. Peter describes it similarly in 2 Peter 1:13-14. The tent doesn't become the house. Its materials aren't used to build the house. The tent is entirely discarded in exchange for the house. And in 1 Corinthians 15:35-44, Paul confirmed that the bodies of Christians who are buried are not the bodies that are resurrected at the Rapture.

My position then, as is depicted in Chapter 10 of In His Image and explained in Chapter 7 of Acts of God, is that the old body is exchanged (Greek: allasso) for the new body. The old body is left behind as the spirit/soul of the person is clothed in the new, perfect, and incorruptible body.

To the world it will appear that millions have died. This will be devastating and the world will desperately look for an explanation. But death is a natural occurrence, and if a suitable answer is NOT found, few will look beyond the natural world for an answer. In addition, I suspect that many churches will lose few of their members, so the world will not think twice that this has been the fulfillment of prophecy. Even if no suitable answer is found for the "deaths," with time the world will put it behind them and move on.

Now let's consider the question of WHY God would rapture his church in the first place. If you ask Christians who believe in the Rapture, why God will remove his Church from the world before the Tribulation, the first answer most will give is that God wants to spare his children the torment. Those who argue against the pre Tribulation Rapture theory have many reasons, but one point they rightly raise is to ask why God would do this. They ask for examples of where God has done this in the past. Certainly there are individual incidents where God delivered Christians from trials, but Hebrews 11 reveals that this is not the model. God did not spare Stephen or the Apostles. Nor did he spare the other martyrs of the early Church. Nor has he spared the Church of any other century. It has been said that far more Christians have suffered and died for their faith in the last 100 years than at any other time in history.

Rather than seeing this as an argument against the pre Tribulation Rapture theory, however, I see it as cause to ask: why else would God remove His Church prior to the Tribulation?

To answer that question of WHY, let's consider what would result if the Church was removed. We live at a time where Christianity has fallen from favor by many, but even now, polls reveal that a majority of people in the Western world still call themselves Christian. I'm not ignoring the rest of the world, but I am recognizing the huge influence Western culture has throughout the world. As a political scientist, I look at Western culture and the history of its institutions and I see the imprint of millions of men and women of faith. Hospitals, universities, public schools, many governments, democracy itself, and the rights and value of the individual, all can be traced to biblical teachings and to those who have believed in the God of the Bible. Humanists will argue otherwise, but even humanism could not have risen in an environment that did not cherish the individual, and no other religion on earth places such great worth on the individual as does Christianity. Where do we find humanism born of Islam, or Hinduism, or Buddhism? Show me a humanist in those cultures and I will show you the influence of western culture.

Since Eden, our planet has been in open rebellion against God. And yet where is the evidence of sin's full power? Clearly there is evil. Clearly there is suffering and death. But just as clearly, the God who created us has not abandoned us. All is not as evil as it could be. But what if God removed his influence? What if God removed his Church and largely restrained his Holy Spirit? What if God gave Satan free reign?

Paul tells us in II Thessalonians 2:1-12 that there will be great "falling away" (KJV) or "rebellion" (NIV) in the time of the Antichrist. In verse 7-8, Paul says that there is one who now stands in the way and prevents the rise of the Antichrist, and that only when this one is taken out of the way, can the Antichrist come to full power. I interpret that the one who holds back the Antichrist is the Holy Spirit who is present in the Church. When the Church is gone, unimaginable corruption will set in. Jesus called his followers "the salt of the earth" (Matthew 4:13). If the salt is removed, the world will fall into unparalleled sin. It is in this environment that the Antichrist will ascend to power.

Returning to the question of WHEN the Rapture will occur relative to the beginning of the Tribulation, the question becomes how long it will take for the world to sufficiently corrupt once the church is removed. In TCCT, I have allowed about 16 years, which I think is more than sufficient.

[26] Thus begin the events of the war prophesied in Ezekiel 38 and 39. Opinions vary on identities of the countries listed there.

[27] Carl G. Jung, *The Archetypes and the Collective Unconscious.*

[28] Matthew 27:46. About three in the afternoon Jesus cried out in a loud voice, "*Eli, Eli, lema sabachthani?*" (which means "My God, my God, why have you forsaken me?").

[29] Ezekiel 38:1-6. [Opinions vary on identities of the countries listed there.]

[30] Ezekiel 38:18-20. This is what will happen in that day: When Gog attacks the land of Israel, my hot anger will be aroused, declares the Sovereign LORD. In my zeal and fiery wrath I declare that at that time there shall be a great earthquake in the land of Israel. The fish in the sea, the birds in the sky, the beasts of the field, every creature

that moves along the ground, and all the people on the face of the earth will tremble at my presence. The mountains will be overturned, the cliffs will crumble and every wall will fall to the ground.

[31] Ezekiel 39:3-5. Then I will strike your bow from your left hand and make your arrows drop from your right hand. On the mountains of Israel you will fall, you and all your troops and the nations with you. I will give you as food to all kinds of carrion birds and to the wild animals. You will fall in the open field, for I have spoken, declares the Sovereign LORD.

Ezekiel 39:11-20. On that day I will give Gog a burial place in Israel, in the valley of those who travel east of the Sea. It will block the way of travelers, because Gog and all his hordes will be buried there. So it will be called the Valley of Hamon Gog. "'For seven months the Israelites will be burying them in order to cleanse the land. All the people of the land will bury them, and the day I display my glory will be a memorable day for them, declares the Sovereign LORD. People will be continually employed in cleansing the land. They will spread out across the land and, along with others, they will bury any bodies that are lying on the ground. After the seven months they will carry out a more detailed search. As they go through the land, anyone who sees a human bone will leave a marker beside it until the gravediggers bury it in the Valley of Hamon Gog, near a town called Hamonah. And so they will cleanse the land. Son of man, this is what the Sovereign LORD says: "Call out to every kind of bird and all the wild animals: 'Assemble and come together from all around to the sacrifice I am preparing for you, the great sacrifice on the mountains of Israel. There you will eat flesh and drink blood. You will eat the flesh of mighty men and drink the blood of the princes of the earth as if they were rams and lambs, goats and bulls—all of them fattened animals from Bashan. At the sacrifice I am preparing for you, you will eat fat till you are glutted and drink blood till you are drunk. At my table you will eat your fill of horses and riders, mighty men and soldiers of every kind,' declares the Sovereign LORD.'"

[32] See Joel 3 for context. Event is depicted in *Acts of God*, Chapter 21, and noted there in endnote 224.

[33] Ezekiel 38:22. [Quoted in text.]

[34] Ezekiel 39:4-6. [Quoted in text.]

[35] Multiple Independently targetable Re-entry Vehicle.

[36] Romans 1:20-25. For since the creation of the world God's invisible qualities—his eternal power and divine nature—have been clearly seen, being understood from what has been made, so that people are without excuse.

John 6:45. It is written in the Prophets: 'They will all be taught by God.' Everyone who has heard the Father and learned from him comes to me.

[37] Daniel 7:7 After that, in my vision at night I looked, and there before me was a fourth beast . . . It was different from all the former beasts, and it had ten horns. [The fourth beast is the United Nations. The ten horns are the ten regions that comprise the Security Council. Further exposition on this verse will be provided as the story progresses.]

[38] Ezekiel 39:21. I will display my glory among the nations, and all the nations will see the punishment I inflict and the hand I lay on them. From that day forward the people of Israel will know that I am the LORD their God.

[39] Daniel 9:26 (KJV). And after threescore and two weeks shall Messiah be cut off, but not for himself: and the people of the prince that shall come shall destroy the city and the sanctuary; and the end thereof shall be with a flood, and unto the end of the war desolations are determined. [The city and the sanctuary were destroyed by the Romans in A.D. 70. Thus "the prince that will come" is the prince of Rome.]

[40] Act 3, Scene 2.

[41] Revelation 10:3b-4. When he shouted, the voices of the seven thunders spoke. And when the seven thunders spoke, I was about

to write; but I heard a voice from heaven say, "Seal up what the seven thunders have said and do not write it down."

[42] Jeremiah 35:18-19. Then Jeremiah said to the family of the Recabites, "This is what the LORD Almighty, the God of Israel, says: 'You have obeyed the command of your forefather Jonadab and have followed all his instructions and have done everything he ordered.' Therefore this is what the LORD Almighty, the God of Israel, says: 'Jonadab son of Recab will never fail to have a descendant to serve me.'" [To truly be a servant of God in our current age, one must be a Christian. But if the descendant of Jonadab who is alive at the time of the Rapture is a Christian, we would expect that he would be Raptured with the rest of the Church. But this would leave no descendent of Jonadab on Earth to serve God. Even if the next descendent were to become a believer as a result of the Rapture, there would be a momentary gap, and the promise would fail. The only explanation is that a descendent of Jonadab who is a Christian must not be Raptured, and the only reason that would occur is if that person was to be one of the two witnesses of Revelation 11.]

[43] 1 Corinthians 13:12 (KJV). For now we see only a reflection as in a mirror; then we shall see face to face. Now I know in part; then I shall know fully, even as I am fully known.

[44] John 19:25-27. Near the cross of Jesus stood his mother... When Jesus saw his mother there, and the disciple whom he loved standing nearby, he said to her, "Woman, here is your son," and to the disciple, "Here is your mother." From that time on, this disciple took her into his home. [It is nearly universally agreed that "the disciple whom he loved" refers to the Apostle John.]

[45] John 21:20-22. Peter turned and saw that the disciple whom Jesus loved was following them... When Peter saw him, he asked, "Lord, what about him?" Jesus answered, "If I want him to remain alive until I return, what is that to you? You must follow me."

[46] John 21:23. Because of this, the rumor spread among the believers that this disciple would not die. But Jesus did not say that

he would not die; he only said, "If I want him to remain alive until I return, what is that to you?"

[47] Matthew 20:20-23. Then the mother of Zebedee's sons came to Jesus with her sons and, kneeling down, asked a favor of him. "What is it you want?" he asked. She said, "Grant that one of these two sons of mine may sit at your right and the other at your left in your kingdom." "You don't know what you are asking," Jesus said to them. "Can you drink the cup I am going to drink?" [This is a Jewish expression that means to share someone's fate] "We can," they answered. Jesus said to them, "You will indeed drink from my cup, but to sit at my right or left is not for me to grant. These places belong to those for whom they have been prepared by my Father." [The cup from which Jesus would drink was his death for the Church. Jesus tells James and John that they will drink from his cup, i.e., share his fate. For James, martyrdom came about 14 years later in A.D. 44, and is recorded in Acts 12:1-2. But there is absolutely no evidence or testimony from the early church that John died for his faith. According to tradition, John died of old age, but there is evidence against even this (reference endnote 54 below). In any case, though John suffered for his faith, there is no evidence of him being martyred. Taken together with the numerous other verses offered here in evidence, it seems John's death as a martyr may be at the hands of the Antichrist as one of the two witnesses of Revelation 11.]

[48] Acts 12:1-2. It was about this time that King Herod arrested some who belonged to the church, intending to persecute them. He had James, the brother of John, put to death with the sword.

[49] Revelation 10:8-11. Then the voice that I had heard from heaven spoke to me once more: "Go, take the scroll that lies open in the hand of the angel who is standing on the sea and on the land." So I went to the angel and asked him to give me the little scroll. He said to me, "Take it and eat it. It will turn your stomach sour, but in your mouth it will be as sweet as honey." [Remainder quoted in text.]

[50] Genesis 5:25-27. When Methuselah had lived 187 years, he became the father of Lamech. After he became the father of

Lamech, Methuselah lived 782 years and had other sons and daughters. Altogether, Methuselah lived a total of 969 years, and then he died. [Methuselah's life is the longest recorded in the Bible.]

[51] As Tertullian reported, *De praescriptione hereticorum* 36.

[52] Mark 9:1. And he said to them, "Truly I tell you, some who are standing here will not taste death before they see that the kingdom of God has come with power."

Matthew 16:28. Truly I tell you, some who are standing here will not taste death before they see the Son of Man coming in his kingdom.

Matthew 24:34 and Mark 13:30. Truly I tell you, this generation will certainly not pass away until all these things have happened.

Luke 9:27. Truly I tell you, some who are standing here will not taste death before they see the kingdom of God.

[All of these verses suggest that the prophetic events Jesus described are time-restricted, and must occur within a few decades of Jesus crucifixion. If, however, John were still alive, then that generation has not yet passed away.]

[53] Irenaeus, *Adversus haereses*, 2.22.5.

[54] Adolf von Harnack, *Lehbuchder Dogmengeschichte*, 1885-1889. Please note, I am not endorsing anything about Harnack's theology, but even a broken clock (pre-digital) is right twice a day.

[55] John 5:4 and John 7:53–8:11 do not appear in the earliest manuscripts of John's gospel. The original inclusion of John 21 is questioned based on contextual issues. I am suggesting John could have added these pieces to later versions of his Gospel.

[56] For information on Prester John, see for instance: E. D. Ross, "Prester John and the Empire of Ethiopia," Arthur P. Newton (ed.), *Travel and Travellers of the Middle Ages* (New York: Barnes & Noble, 1968; first published in 1926), 174-194; C. F. Beckingham, "The Quest for Prester John," *Bulletin of The John Rylands University Library*, LXII (1980), 290-310.

[57] Revelation 11:3-4. And I will appoint my two witnesses, and they will prophesy for 1,260 days, clothed in sackcloth. They are "the two olive trees" and the two lampstands, and "they stand before the Lord of the earth."

[58] Revelation 6:1-2. I watched as the Lamb opened the first of the seven seals. Then I heard one of the four living creatures say in a voice like thunder, "Come!" I looked, and there before me was a white horse! Its rider held a bow, and he was given a crown, and he rode out as a conqueror bent on conquest.

Christopher, the first of the four horsemen, begins to acquire power. There are two events included in this passage: 1) the rider of the white horse is given a crown, and 2) he rides out to conquer. Because this is the first seal, we know it occurs first in the sequence, but we are not told when, nor are we told the impact or the duration. However, because the Antichrist must already be in power to sign the treaty that starts the 7 year Tribulation period, the first event (being given a crown) must occur before the Tribulation begins. The second event (riding out to conquer) has no specific description of conquest associated with it, so it probably refers to his overall intention to rule the world, which will play out over the period of the Tribulation.

According to Jude 14-15, prophecies of the "last days" may have begun even prior to the time of Noah. Certainly they go back the prophet Amos in the eighth century B.C. (Amos 5:18-20). Prior to the writing of the book of Revelation, however, there was no framework into which last days prophecy could be placed or interpreted. Daniel provided us with periods of duration: 483 years (Daniel 9:25); 7 years and 3.5 years (Daniel 9:27); 1290 days and 1335 days (Daniel 12:11). But Revelation gives us order and sequence. In Revelation we find seven seals. Within the seventh seal are seven trumpets. Between the sixth and seventh trumpets are three angels of warning. Within the seventh trumpet are seven bowls. Each of these (seals, trumpets, angels, and bowls) are sequential and numbered.

Like Daniel, Revelation also provides some periods of duration: 5 months (Revelation 9:5 and 9:10), 42 months (Revelation 11:2), 1260 days (Revelation 11:3 and 12:6), 3.5 years (Revelation 12:14). We are also given some specific locations where events occur: Heaven, Jerusalem, Babylon, the Euphrates River, Armageddon, the Valley of Jehoshaphat, worldwide, the sun, the moon, and the stars.

Most of the descriptions of prophetic events, however, tell us nothing as to their location, duration or initiation (i.e., starting point) within the 7 year Tribulation period. To find these, we must begin with the fixed points and work outwards. We know, for example, that the sixth trumpet judgment begins at the Euphrates River and that the impact will include the death of one third of the world's population. As will be seen in Chapter 17 of *Birth of an Age*, from this information, and with the help of Joel 2, we can calculate approximately how far the destruction of the sixth trumpet judgment might spread. Other events can be surmised based on description and scope of the event. We can, for example, identify where the first trumpet judgment will occur because we are told the effect it will have on forests and vegetation (Chapter 5, *Birth of an Age*). And because of the prophetic description, we can determine that the second trumpet judgment spreads across the world from one of the deepest points in the Pacific Ocean (Chapter 6, *Birth of an Age*).

The location of some events, however, can be found only by identifying the geographic/political regions that possess the attributes necessary to fulfill a described event, and then eliminating the areas that must be preserved for later events. We must look at each event in the context of all other end-times events and account for cause-and-effect relationships with other events. We must also ensure that the scenario we develop enables or at least allows for all other last days prophecies of both the Old and New Testaments. Initiation and duration of a given event are similarly calculated, by allowing sufficient time for all other events. This is a complex process, but it will become clear as the story plays out that each event is tied to all the others so that the prophecies are fulfilled in a scenario that is internally consistent, scientifically feasible, sociologically and politically reasonable, and is within the realm of possible interpretation of Scripture.

[59] Revelation 6:5-6. When the Lamb opened the third seal, I heard the third living creature say, "Come!" I looked, and there before me was a black horse! Its rider was holding a pair of scales in his hand. Then I heard what sounded like a voice among the four living creatures, saying, "Two pounds of wheat for a day's wages, and six pounds of barley for a day's wages, and do not damage the oil and the wine!" [Note that the second seal of Revelation 6:3-4 (giving power to the rider of the red horse) will be seen in retrospect in Chapter 24. Because the prices given here in verse 6 ("Two pounds of wheat for a day's wages, and six pounds of barley for a day's wages") are exorbitant, the rider of the black horse is generally believed to represent famine. The passage provides no specific location, duration, range, or resulting impact for the famine. To determine these, we must look at it in the whole context of end-times events. The description of the sixth seal is specific enough to necessitate that it be centered in a region that possesses a substantial quantity of nuclear weapons. By eliminating the areas that must be preserved for later events (which will be revealed later) we are left with China, India, and Pakistan, all of which possess large nuclear stockpiles. Figuring backward from there, we can determine the locations of the third and fourth seals by identifying a scenario that will lead from the third trumpet to the fourth and establishing the conditions for the sixth. (The fifth seal is a heavenly event with no specific impact on the Earth.) As note before, this is a complex process, but it will become more clear as the story plays out.]

[60] Ezekiel 39:9-10. Then those who live in the towns of Israel will go out and use the weapons for fuel and burn them up—the small and large shields, the bows and arrows, the war clubs and spears. For seven years they will use them for fuel. They will not need to gather wood from the fields or cut it from the forests, because they will use the weapons for fuel. And they will plunder those who plundered them and loot those who looted them, declares the Sovereign LORD. [For the simple reason that it seems inconceivable that modern weaponry would be suitable for burning as fuel, I have assumed that Ezekiel is speaking figuratively, i.e., that the weapons

intended for use against Israel will instead be used by Israel for defense.]

[61] Current Era, or A.D.

[62] Daniel 9:25-26. Know and understand this: From the time the word goes out to restore and rebuild Jerusalem until the Anointed One, the ruler, comes, there will be seven 'sevens,' and sixty-two 'sevens.' It will be rebuilt with streets and a trench, but in times of trouble. After the sixty-two 'sevens,' the Anointed One will be put to death and will have nothing. The people of the ruler who will come will destroy the city and the sanctuary. The end will come like a flood: War will continue until the end, and desolations have been decreed. [The Anointed One means literally the Messiah. "Sevens" refers to periods of 7 years, thus "seven 'sevens' and sixty-two 'sevens,' equates to 69 periods of 7 years each, or 69x7= 483 years.]

[63] Ezra 7:6-7. …this Ezra came up from Babylon. He was a teacher well versed in the Law of Moses, which the LORD, the God of Israel, had given. The king had granted him everything he asked, for the hand of the LORD his God was on him. Some of the Israelites, including priests, Levites, musicians, gatekeepers and temple servants, also came up to Jerusalem in the seventh year of King Artaxerxes. [Artaxerxes reigned from 465-424 B.C. The seventh year of King Artaxerxes was 457. Adding 483 years to this date (and accounting for the fact that there was no year zero) we arrive at A.D. 27.]

John 2:19-20. Jesus answered them, "Destroy this temple, and I will raise it again in three days." They replied, "It has taken forty-six years to build this temple, and you are going to raise it in three days?" [Note that it was not an single individual who made the comment about 46 years. John says, "They replied." One person might have made a mistake in his math, but not all. Additionally, John does not challenge the math. Thus we can be very certain that this statement was correct. And from this we can conclude that Jesus ministry began and he first preached in the Temple approximately 46 years after Herod had begun its renovation. This would place the event in A.D. 27.]

Note that there are many who calculate the 483 years beginning in 444 B.C. based on Nehemiah 2:1. This approach has three major problems. First, the events of Nehemiah 2 occurred only because (as we see in Nehemiah 1:1-4) he was distressed to discover that "The wall of Jerusalem is broken down, and its gates have been burned with fire." The destruction of Jerusalem by the Babylonians had occurred 141 years earlier in 586 B.C., so learning that the city was destroyed more than a century before is certainly not what caused Nehemiah's distress. Rather, he was distressed to learn that it was <u>still</u> in ruins. Despite Artaxerxes' authorization for Ezra to rebuild Jerusalem 13 years earlier (Ezra 7:6-7, above), it remains undone. Thus, Artaxerxes' authorization in Nehemiah 2:5 for him to go to Jerusalem to rebuild the city is the second time reconstruction has been authorized.

The second problem with calculating the 483 years from 444 B.C. is that because simple math would result in A.D. 40 (a date that has no significance to the coming of the Messiah) it requires the invention of a "prophetic year" consisting of 360 days. Their math works as follows. By multiplying the 483 years by 360 days, they calculate 173,880 days, which they then divide by 365.25 days in an actual year, resulting in 476.06 real years. By adding 476 years to 444 B.C. (and accounting for the fact that there was no year zero) they reach their desired goal of A.D. 33, the supposed year of the crucifixion. The justification given for the 360 day "prophetic year" is the assertion that a Jewish year is 360 days. In reality, the Jewish year varies, being 354, 355, 383, or 384 days, based on a 19 year cycle, consisting of 12 years of 12 lunar months each, and 7 years of 13 lunar months each to account for the actual length of the solar year. In effect, the Jewish calendar inserts a "leap month" just as the modern (Gregorian) calendar inserts 1 day on leap years. Taken over the 19 year period, the average year length is 365.25 days, the same as the Gregorian calendar.

[64] Before Current Era, or B.C.

[65] Sanhedrin, Tractate 976, Nezikin Vol. 3, Rabbi Samuel B. Nahmani speaking in the name of Rabbi Jonathan.

[66] Daniel 9:1-3. In the first year of Darius son of Xerxes (a Mede by descent), who was made ruler over the Babylonian kingdom—in the first year of his reign, I, Daniel, understood from the Scriptures, according to the word of the LORD given to Jeremiah the prophet, that the desolation of Jerusalem would last seventy years. So I turned to the Lord God and pleaded with him in prayer and petition, in fasting, and in sackcloth and ashes. [Daniel was apparently referencing Jeremiah 25:11-12. This whole country will become a desolate wasteland, and these nations will serve the king of Babylon seventy years. "But when the seventy years are fulfilled, I will punish the king of Babylon and his nation, the land of the Babylonians, for their guilt," declares the LORD, "and will make it desolate forever.]

[67] Isaiah 53, *The Prophets Nevi'im*, A new translation of the Holy Scriptures according to the Masoretic text, second section (Philadelphia: The Jewish Publication Society of America, 1978), 477-478.

[68] Ibid.

[69] Ibid., 477.

[70] Daniel 9:27a He will confirm a covenant with many for one 'seven.'

[71] 1 Samuel 6:19. But God struck down some of the inhabitants of Beth Shemesh, putting seventy of them to death because they looked into the ark of the LORD. The people mourned because of the heavy blow the LORD had dealt them. [Most Hebrew manuscripts and the Septuagint put the number at 50,070.]

2 Samuel 6:6-7. When they came to the threshing floor of Nakon, Uzzah reached out and took hold of the ark of God, because the oxen stumbled. The LORD's anger burned against Uzzah because of his irreverent act; therefore God struck him down, and he died there beside the ark of God.

[72] 1 Chronicles 13:10. [Quoted in text.]

[73] Daniel 9:27. He will confirm a covenant with many for one 'seven.' In the middle of the 'seven' he will put an end to sacrifice and offering. And at the temple he will set up an abomination that causes desolation, until the end that is decreed is poured out on him. [The signing of this treaty marks the beginning of the seven-year Tribulation.]

[74] Revelation 6:3-4. When the Lamb opened the second seal, I heard the second living creature say, "Come!" Then another horse came out, a fiery red one. Its rider was given power to take peace from the earth and to make people kill each other. To him was given a large sword. [While the rider of the first (white) horse was given a crown and then rode out to conquer, the rider of the second (fiery red) horse is given power and a sword. Neither the first nor the second seal include descriptions of any specific acts of conquest or war. Rather they are setting the stage for the events to come. Here General Brooks, the second of the four horsemen, is positioned to "take peace from the earth and to make people kill each other," as we will see.]

[75] Revelation 6:7-8. When the Lamb opened the fourth seal, I heard the voice of the fourth living creature say, "Come!" I looked, and there before me was a pale horse! Its rider was named Death, and Hades was following close behind him. They were given power over a fourth of the earth to kill by sword, famine and plague, and by the wild beasts of the earth. [And so war begins, and will ultimately grow to threaten a quarter of the planet.]

[76] Revelation 7:1-3. After this I saw four angels standing at the four corners of the earth, holding back the four winds of the earth to prevent any wind from blowing on the land or on the sea or on any tree. Then I saw another angel coming up from the east, having the seal of the living God. He called out in a loud voice to the four angels who had been given power to harm the land and the sea..."

[77] Revelation 7:3-8. "Do not harm the land or the sea or the trees until we put a seal on the foreheads of the servants of our God." From the tribe of Judah 12,000 were sealed, from the tribe of

Reuben 12,000, from the tribe of Gad 12,000, from the tribe of Asher 12,000, from the tribe of Naphtali 12,000, from the tribe of Manasseh 12,000, from the tribe of Simeon 12,000, from the tribe of Levi 12,000, from the tribe of Issachar 12,000, from the tribe of Zebulun 12,000, from the tribe of Joseph 12,000, from the tribe of Benjamin 12,000. [Note that while the tribe of Dan is not mentioned among the 144,000, according to Ezekiel 48:32, Dan is apportioned territory in the Kingdom. Clearly, that Dan is missing from the 144,000, does not indicate that God has disowned the tribe.]

[78] Revelation 14:1. Then I looked, and there before me was the Lamb, standing on Mount Zion, and with him 144,000 who had <u>his name and his Father's name written on their foreheads</u>.

[79] John 19:25-27. Near the cross of Jesus stood his mother, his mother's sister, Mary the wife of Clopas, and Mary Magdalene. When Jesus saw his mother there, and the disciple whom he loved standing nearby, he said to her, "Woman, here is your son," and to the disciple, "Here is your mother." From that time on, this disciple took her into his home. [It is universally agreed that "the disciple whom he loved" refers to the Apostle John.]

[80] Matthew 27:5. So Judas threw the money into the temple and left. Then he went away and hanged himself.

[81] Revelation 11:6. <u>They have power to shut up the heavens so that it will not rain during the time they are prophesying</u>; and they have power to turn the waters into blood and to strike the earth with every kind of plague as often as they want.

[82] Revelation 6:14. <u>The heavens receded like a scroll being rolled up</u>, and every mountain and island was removed from its place.

[83] Revelation 6:12. I watched as he opened the sixth seal. <u>There was a great earthquake.</u> The sun turned black like sackcloth made of goat hair, the whole moon turned blood red... [Note that the events described under the fifth seal, described in Revelation 6:9-11, do not occur within the view of those on Earth.]

Revelation 6:14. The heavens receded like a scroll being rolled up, <u>and every mountain and island was removed from its place.</u>

[84] Revelation 6:12. I watched as he opened the sixth seal. There was a great earthquake. <u>The sun turned black like sackcloth made of goat hair</u>, the whole moon turned blood red...

Acts 2:29. <u>The sun will be turned to darkness</u> and the moon to blood before the coming of the great and glorious day of the Lord.

[85] A misquotation of Ecclesiastes 3:3a. ...a time to kill and a time to heal...

[86] Acts 2:29. The sun will be turned to darkness <u>and the moon to blood</u> before the coming of the great and glorious day of the Lord.

Revelation 6:12. I watched as he opened the sixth seal. There was a great earthquake. The sun turned black like sackcloth made of goat hair, <u>the whole moon turned blood red</u>...

[87] Revelation 6:13. ...and the stars in the sky fell to earth, as figs drop from a fig tree when shaken by a strong wind.

[88] Revelation 6:15-17. Then the kings of the earth, the princes, the generals, the rich, the mighty, and everyone else, both slave and free, hid in caves and among the rocks of the mountains. They called to the mountains and the rocks, "Fall on us and hide us from the face of him who sits on the throne and from the wrath of the Lamb! For the great day of their wrath has come, and who can withstand it?"

[89] Revelation 6:8. I looked, and there before me was a pale horse! Its rider was named Death, and Hades was following close behind him. They were given power over a fourth of the earth to kill by sword, famine and plague, and by the wild beasts of the earth.

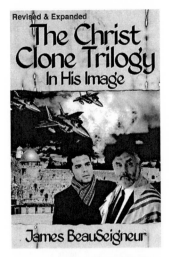

Book One
In His Image

"BeauSeigneur knows how to write, deploying a tough, driving style in perfect cadence."
Booklist **(Starred Review)**

Book Two
Birth of an Age

"Astoundingly intelligent . . . inventive . . . dizzyingly well-described."
Kirkus Reviews
(Starred Review)

Book Three
Acts of God

"Undeniably riveting... daring...wonderfully creepy...Readers will be enthralled by the author's science-fortified vision of the Apocalypse."
Publishers Weekly

SelectiveHouse
Publishers